I0550183

BLOOD DANCE

A Novel

By Rick Poveromo

Copyright © 2014 Rick Poveromo
All rights reserved.
Blue Coral Books

ISBN-13: 9780991641000

ISBN-10: 0991641000

This book is dedicated to my wife Janet who supports me in all my endeavors.
To my son Rich and my daughter Jessica, I am so proud of you both.
And to my mother and father, with much love and respect.

To the memory of John T. McAuley.

AUTHORS NOTE

This book is a work of fiction. Characters, names, places, brands, events and incidents are either creations of the authors imagination or used fictitiously. Any resemblance to actual events, locations or persons, living or dead are purely coincidental and unintentional.

ACKNOWLEDGMENTS

I owe a huge debt of gratitude to my wife Janet who endured endless hours of watching me peck away at my laptop, awaiting the completion of this novel. NEWSFLASH! Dear, I'm finally finished!

I'd like to thank Erin Potter my editor extraordinaire and Christa Holland for the amazing artwork that adorns the cover. Also a special thanks to Eileen, one of my first readers who religiously read every chapter as it was typed. A HUGE thanks to everyone in my writers group who put aside their smoke-blowing machines and painstakingly critiqued my work week after week, especially Peter (who offered a logical opinion), John (my cliché catcher), Colleen (who did some preliminary editing), Arlene, Noemi, Shumi, Bob and Fran. I especially want to thank Marana, whose firsthand accounts of her childhood experiences in South America proved to be a great inspiration to me. Kay and Jane, your words of encouragement kept me moving forward. A big shout out to Fort Lee Bob (formerly Princeton Bob), who reined in my adverbs. A special thank you goes out to Marlon, for translating my English phrases into Spanish.

Thank you John Perna for taking a fantastic photo for my *About the Author* page. I also want to thank the late John McAuley whose insightful critiques and firsthand accounts of the five years that he spent in South America proved to be invaluable. I speak for the entire writers group, when I say John, dear friend, you will be greatly missed.

PREFACE

It is hard to estimate the exact number of lost tribes who live in the Amazonian rainforest. Experts have placed the number between thirty-nine and sixty-four separate indigenous groups. Some anthropologists believe that several of these tribes live along the Peruvian-Ecuadoran border, refusing to make contact with the outside world or even other tribes. They live an isolated stone-aged existence, adhering to their own traditions, customs and beliefs, just as their ancestors have done for thousands of years. We must lend our voices and speak out for the people of the rainforest, respect their way of life and protect their natural habitat, because without a voice in our world, they cannot speak for themselves, for these are the true Invisible People.

PROLOGUE

Hope Holloway rinsed the lather from her raven black hair, using both hands; she pushed the wet silk back onto her shoulders. With three loud squeaks, she twisted the shower knobs, stemming the flow of water. Stepping from the shower onto the bathmat, she wrapped herself in a white cotton towel and breathed in deeply. The mist-filled air cleared her head, if only for a moment, and the soft cloth felt good against her skin, covering most of her slender 5'9" frame.

The large mirror above the vanity covered in condensation, offered no reflection. She wrapped another towel around her head and opened the door, stepping bravely into the cold bedroom. Goose bumps sprouted, like miniature corn kernels across her exposed arms and legs. She pulled the towel tight against her chest and adjusted the thermostat, desperate for an increase of a few precious degrees.

Bad thoughts swirled through her mind; she could feel the vortex growing. She'd tried to banish those thoughts earlier that evening, compartmentalizing them inward, but now they were back. She turned on her iPod, an attempt at distraction.

Adele's *Rolling in the Deep* blared through the tiny speakers of her docking station. Turning up the volume, she sang along with the soulful lyrics, "There's a fire starting in my heart. Reaching a fever pitch and it's bringing me out the dark…." But the lyrics couldn't bring her out of the dark. Instead, they brought her deeper into the rainforest and that dreaded mission trip. She felt trapped, because there was no way out, she had to go and she knew it.

The nightmares began about two weeks ago, right after her nineteenth birthday, just brief snippets at first, quick flashes of jungles and caves and strange painted faces. The dreams seemed to last longer and were getting more intense. They didn't occur every night, but often enough to make her feel apprehensive about falling asleep causing great angst, resulting in many restless nights. More recently, quick flashes of images were coming to her even while awake.

I have to concentrate hard that's all. She thought.

Sometimes she could push back the evil, forcing it into the dark corners. After meditating for several minutes, she cleansed her mind of all thoughts both good and bad–it seemed to work, at least for the moment.

The room already felt warmer. Hope removed both towels, and carefully draped the drier of the two over the seat of the wooden chair that matched her antique white vanity. Sitting down, she gazed into the mirror. Her skin looked dry and blotchy, especially around her knees and elbows. Finding the lotion on her vanity top, she squirted out a palm full of the creamy liquid and generously applied it to her body, covering her already milk-white skin. Again she looked in the mirror and noticed the dark rings under her steel blue-eyes. Those black circles weren't there two weeks ago and it became obvious that lack of sleep had taken its toll.

If only I could forego this trip, Hope thought. But she knew that she couldn't, not if she had any hopes of getting into Princeton.

Damn that D- in English Lit! If it hadn't been for that, she would've maintained her perfect *A* average. Along with her near perfect score on her SAT's, she'd be a shoe-in for a spot in the fall freshman class. But now she felt that she needed more. She needed a letter of recommendation from Dr. Bill Drake, who was not only a professor at Princeton, but also the church council President and the leader of the mission expedition into the rainforest, not to mention, her best friend's father. And even though he was an anthropologist and she wanted to become a botanist, two areas of study that couldn't be farther apart. A well-placed letter of recommendation from a member of the Princeton faculty was her golden ticket into the Ivy League. Besides, doing mission work for the church and studying the rare medicinal plants of the rainforest would showcase her talents; like her desire to help others and her love of botany, making her a well-rounded person in the eyes of the admissions office. So despite her horrific dreams and her more recent daytime flashes, she had to go. Somehow, she had to get through this trip and the rest of her senior year.

Rising from the chair, she found her nightgown in her bottom dresser drawer and slipped it on over her head. It was only 10:30 p.m., but she felt exhausted. Opening the door, she called downstairs, "Goodnight mom."

"Goodnight dear." Her mother, Anna Rose Holloway replied from the family room of their Burlington, New Jersey split-level.

Hope fluffed her pillow, pulled back the sheets and crawled into bed. With her head on the pillow, and tears welling in her eyes, she folded her hands in prayer, "Dear Lord, please keep my demons at bay and allow me to rest peacefully for just this one night. Amen." Breathing in deep, she released a tremendous sigh. Moments later, she fell fast asleep – but not for long.

As the red LED's on her digital clock changed from 2:59 a.m. to 3:00 a.m., a strong static charge arced across her woolen blankets, leaping into her forearm. Jolted awake by the charge, she felt hot with fever. Jumping from bed, she dropped to her knees, pressing both hands hard against her temples, "No!" she screamed, "Leave me alone!" But it was too late; there was no way to stop it.

Her elbow made contact with the metal bed frame, resulting in another torturous jolt. She gasped for air, unable to scream. Her hands trembled. Sweat beaded on her forehead and again she gasped. Her conscious mind left her surroundings. No longer in her bedroom, the image of a torch lit cave closed in around her. The pungent odor of burning animal fat emanated from the torches. With eyes still shut, his image then appeared.

A primitive tribesman stepped from the darkness. Hieroglyphic-like tattoos covered his bare chest and arms. Several red and green feathered jettisoned from his straight, black hair. A bone necklace encircled his neck. Tightly woven reeds fashioned a primitive skirt that covered his privates. His wide brown eyes burned with hatred and his nostrils flared like a bull as he sporadically bared his teeth.

He held a round, slick, object in his bloody, maroon hands. With two more steps, the object became clear. Hope gagged, tasting the sour rising from her throat. She watched him dance wildly, gripping the freshly severed head of a young female as he moved across a raised plateau inside the vast cavern.

Hope stood transfixed, close enough to see clearly the dead girl's features. She looked about the same age as herself, no older than nineteen. She watched the eyes blink and facial muscles twitch as motor functions persisted, controlled by reluctant nerve endings not yet willing to accept death.

Dark blood oozed from the neck. The shaman smeared it across his arms, face, and chest.

The cavern glowed from lava circulating in a deep pool at the bottom of a chasm. Orange light flickered across the shaman's skin, lending him a demonic appearance. The drumbeat intensified and he moved faster, holding the head of his victim in his hand, moving it up and down to the rhythm as he danced, working himself into a frenzy.

Chanting words in a strange language, he stood at the edge of the abyss and raised the dripping head high above his own. The drumbeat stopped and the tribesmen assembled below, raised their spears, and cheered.

Hope gasped as the shaman tossed the head into the fiery pit; she tried to scream, but her throat contracted while the head tumbled end over end, plummeting toward the liquid fire below. The head splashed, incinerating in a flash of orange.

The image disappeared, she opened her eyes and she was back. Her pain began to dissipate, but she was still burning up; her nightgown drenched in sweat. Hyperventilating, she screamed out in the night, running her fingers across several painful welts that had formed on her face and neck – heat blisters erupting through the skin.

Not again, she thought, her blue-eyes widened, shifting back and forth as her mother burst through the door. Flicking on the lights, Anna Rose knelt beside her daughter.

"Help me! Make it stop!" Hope shouted, ringing her hands.

"It's okay. Relax baby, take deep breaths. Just relax. Everything is okay now" Anna Rose wrapped Hope in her arms and rocked her back and forth.

Hope saw fear in the eyes of her mother, whose brave words fooled no one. Several minutes passed before Hope's heart rate slowed and her breathing returned to normal. Her fever began to subside, but the welts remained.

"It was horrible!" she said.

"Just like before?" her mother asked.

"The same but worse, I don't even want to talk about it!"

"You need help! This can't go on. I'll call someone."

Hope's mind raced. She didn't want to see some shrink. She'd been that route before.

"If I have to, I'll talk to someone when I get back," she offered.

"Forget about it, you're not going," her mother said.

"I have to go, I have no choice. Remember Princeton? I've explained all of this to you before."

Tears welled in her mother's eyes and Hope grasped her trembling hands.

"Mom, it's going to be all right. I'm nineteen years old. I'm not a baby anymore. I'll get through this."

"But...?" her mother started.

"But what?"

"What if this has something to do with—you *know?*"

"I knew you were going to bring that up. That hasn't happened for a long time and you know it!"

Premonitions have plagued Hope since she was twelve. That was the year she predicted her father's death months before his doctors diagnosed the deadly colon cancer that quickly metastasized throughout his body. Overcome by grief, she shut down socially and academically causing her to repeat the sixth grade.

Hope's parents instilled in her a basic belief in God, but they weren't all that religious. Three words summed up the Holloways' church attendance—Christmas and Easter.

That all changed after the funeral. Hope's mother enrolled her in Sunday school. Both she and her mom became regular churchgoers, members of Our Lady of Fatima church that met just two blocks from their Burlington New Jersey home. Hope accepted Jesus Christ into her life, praying to Him on a regular basis. It gave her strength, but the visions continued.

She hated being different and cursed her so-called gift. With nowhere to turn, she turned to God, praying to Him, asking Him to banish her *gift* forever. She felt like the Lord had answered her prayers, because there it stayed, never to return—until two weeks ago Tuesday, the day after her nineteenth birthday.

Never before had her nightmares physically manifested themselves into sores. *These were real blisters and welts!*

Hope had heard of stigmata, wounds and sores appearing on the hands and feet of true believers, corresponding with the crucifixion wounds of Jesus Christ, but her welts were different, vile; unholy.

With trembling fingers, mother and daughter folded their hands together in prayer. They prayed to God asking Him, no, begging Him, to release Hope from her ghastly visions. This time their prayers would go unanswered.

⊷╬╬⊶

The windshield wipers kept perfect rhythm, like a metronome ticking off the final coda between mother and daughter. Anna Rose maneuvered the RAV4 into an empty parking spot. After putting the vehicle in park, she shut off the wipers but left the engine running.

"Look at this weather, it's a bad omen. The airport will be closed in another hour, let's turn around and go home," Anna Rose half-muttered to herself.

Miniature ice pellets pinged off the windshield and roof; the retracted wiper blades made Hope acutely aware that their time together was fleeting. The mesmerizing sleet caused her thoughts to drift, and her mother's words failed to register. "I'm sorry, what?"

"I said the airport will be closed by the time you get there. Forget about the trip, I'm taking you home."

"Our flight isn't for another three hours; everything's supposed to pass through by then. They'll clear the runway and deice the plane, we'll be fine."

"You have an answer for everything, don't you? There's just no talking to you."

"We've been through this already. I told you; don't worry, everything's going to be all right, I promise."

"How can you make a promise like that? You don't know. But you're hell bent on going!"

"I'll be fine. Remember, we're going to do God's work and like you've always said, He will provide. He always does."

Hope threw her mom's own words back at her. Words her mother couldn't refute.

Anna Rose shut off the engine, removed her keys, and sighed. "You know I'm going to miss you. I may be overprotective, but after everything that's happened, I can't help but worry."

Hope hugged her mother and said, "I'm going to miss you too Mom, but this is important to me, I need this trip. It takes time to spread the good word, especially to people who've never heard of Jesus. About the other night; I think a change in scenery might do me good."

"I hope so, baby, I hope so. Listen, stay close to Bill Drake. Beverly Johnson told me that he knows a lot about the people in that area."

Hope smiled and poked her mother in the shoulder. "Ready to freeze your butt off?"

"No, but let's grab your stuff anyway."

A fine sleet stung Hope's cheeks as she stepped from the SUV and the wind cut through her slender frame. Her mother helped her unload a green nylon knapsack and a large denim duffle bag from the rear of the vehicle. Shielding their faces with white knitted scarves, using their gloved hands as visors, they marched headlong through the cold, icy curtain toward the church van.

The church parking lot bustled with teenagers and their parents. Christmas, celebrated only eight days earlier, was now a distant memory. Hope's mind was adrift in a sea of uncertainty. Most of the others had arrived and were already sitting in the van. Up ahead through the sleet, Hope watched Tim Kirby and Brenda Bean, the mission group advisors, greet Mary Drake and her father while relieving them of their bulky belongings.

Tim resembled a lumberjack. A red flannel jacket covered his brawny 6'4" frame and his wavy red hair peeked out from under a camouflaged hunters cap.

He's cute, there's no denying it. Hope thought as she approached

Brenda's gray knitted hat covered most of her mousy brown hair. She looked petite standing next to him, but in actuality, the attractive twenty-four- year-old stood taller than most women, taller than Hope, her thin, ballerina-like body now hidden under layers of thick winter clothing.

Mary waved coyly at Hope, flashing a brace-faced smile of what seemed to be nervous excitement. Hope felt detached and conjured up a half-hearted wave in return, unable to share in her friend's enthusiasm. She watched Mary and her father take refuge in the semi-heated van, along with the other weather-beaten teens.

Bad feelings had festered within Hope for days. She thought constantly about her visions and at times fought off episodes of extreme panic. The images frightened her, despite her brave words to the contrary. What was it that she felt? Dread? That's the only way she could describe it, but she kept those feelings to herself, not wanting to further alarm her mother.

⊰⊹⊱

January 29th
(Nine hours after the mission groups return from Ecuador.)

Statement made by Timothy Kirby to Burlington Police Chief Edward Barnes when asked: Why they decided to go to the Ecuadorian Rainforest in the first place?

Originally we had no intention of going. Brenda and I had talked about much tamer destinations like Costa Rica and Belize, but Bill Drake insisted we go to Ecuador. Not only was he Mary's father, but he also sat on church council as president; a persistent man, hard to argue with. His committee approved the funding for the trip, so he had a lot to say about where we went.

I guess you probably already know he was an anthropology professor at the university. More like the nutty professor if you ask me, but a lot of parents felt better with Bill on the trip. As if Brenda and I were some kind of irresponsible jerks. I guess they figured he was smart and educated and also a parent, their surrogate, an extension of themselves so to speak. More than one mother told me that in an emergency she could count on him to make the right decision, as if we were part of the lunatic fringe—sorry, bad choice of words. But somehow the good professor's judgment made them feel safer; pretty ironic now, huh? Brenda and I knew him for the reckless bastard that he was; the master of ulterior motives; that was his real specialty.

Anyhow, one day I passed the church office and overheard him muttering to someone on the phone about a dissertation he had to publish on the Shuar Indians, something about already having done some research and if he didn't finish soon he could forget about tenure. That's why it came as no real surprise when he volunteered to lead the expedition. It was so obvious, he had to research and publish his work for the University; and he was hell-bent on doing it at the church's expense. That's the reason why he really pushed for this trip from the start.

Our co-sponsor, an Ecuadorian priest named Father Ricardo, emailed me about possibly delaying the trip until spring; he'd heard about a few skirmishes along the Peruvian/Ecuadorian border. When I printed the emails and showed them to Bill, he tore them up. He pooh-poohed the warning, claiming that there've been border disputes in that region for decades and they've never amounted to a hill of beans. Hey, he was the expert, the PhD in anthropology. What did I know? Brenda and I just rode shotgun on this stagecoach.

Bill kept insisting there wasn't any real danger. After a while I started to believe him. His daughter was on the trip and I figured he'd never put her in harm's way— was I ever wrong.

CHAPTER ONE

Hope peered out the van's window as it headed south through the Ecuadorian capital. A few trendy restaurants dotted the streets of modern Quito, where pretty women munched on garden salads, flirting with well-dressed men. She presumed that these places doubled as hot nightspots once the sun went down and the salsa music heated up.

Many more women populated the sidewalk cafés, wearing colorful summer dresses. Some sipped on cappuccinos and lattes while others spooned fried bananas and ice cream out of elegant glassware. A shopper's paradise appeared before Hope, an oasis of high-end stores, many with familiar names, scattered among a desert of thrift. She'd now have to forgo all of them. *Damn that weather!* She thought.

The van headed south through the city, passing a park where kids played soccer. The varied shouts and sounds of excitement from the players filtered through the trees over the murmur of oncoming traffic. A second larger park appeared; this one mostly undeveloped with visible hiking paths, bike trails, and a few unsavory looking characters.

The smooth pavement transformed itself into a bumpy cobblestone road. Gone were the restaurants and high-end stores, now replaced by bodegas and three-story eighteenth century Spanish architecture. The narrow streets combined with red and green pastel structures almost gave Old Town Quito a European flair. The streets narrowed further and the driver inched his way past an old man with a pushcart selling fresh fruits and vegetables. Shaking a large zucchini at them as they passed; the man shouted, "Estùpido." Several minutes later, the van came to a stop at the old train station. After unloading the vehicle, Tim paid the fare and the driver started off again reversing his route across the cobblestones.

The group waited on the platform for the locomotive to arrive which seemed to take forever. Hope watched Peter and Luke conversing with Dr. Drake who was holding an orange at arm's length for all to inspect at the far end of the platform. She could only imagine what they were talking about.

Peter was the same age as herself, he stood tall and strong and had an air of confidence about him. He wasn't pretty boy handsome, nor butt ugly. He'd be better looking if only he'd comb his dark brown hair once in a while and stopped wearing his condiments on the front of his shirt. Hope could never quite define their relationship. He was more than a friend, but less than a boyfriend. *Hey, it is what it is,* she often thought, *whatever that meant.*

Luke was Peter's polar opposite, neat and clean by comparison, his black hair always trimmed and neatly parted to his left. The seventeen-year-olds' small physique matched his timid nature, which made him invisible to girls and the target of high school bullies everywhere. Hope stuck up for him more than once in the hallways, shouting down his tormentors. After collecting his books and scattered chess pieces, she'd dust him off and offered words of encouragement.

"Don't listen to them. Those guys will be collecting your garbage in a couple of years. You're bright and intelligent, trust me, none of this will matter after high school," she remembered saying.

Glancing at her watch, Mary said, "This is taking forever."

Mary's voice broke Hope's train of thought.

"I know; we should've just stayed downtown like we were supposed to."

"Tell me about it!"

They weren't spending the day at the hostel as originally planned. Bad weather delayed their flight more than six hours. What was supposed to be an early afternoon flight turned into the red-eye. Everyone slept on the plane including Dr. Drake, so he didn't see the need to "waste a day in Quito."

In addition to the shopping, Hope had wanted to check out the sidewalk cafés with Mary, maybe sip on a latte or two, perhaps even spoon some fried banana into her own mouth. But it was not to be. Hope knew that Mary had looked forward to their shopping excursion just as much as she had, but the good natured seventeen-year-old seemed to take it all in stride.

That's typical of Mary, Hope thought.

She really was the little sister that Hope never had. They had met working a booth together at the church bake sale several years before, and their personalities instantly clicked. Despite their two year age difference, they became best friends, even more so since the death of Mary's mother. *Has it already been three years?* It happened after a fundraising dinner at the university—in a car driven by Bill Drake. Despite taking advantage of the open bar, the breathalyzer proved that he hadn't been legally drunk when he ran off the road and slammed into a tree, blowing a number just below the legal limit. Those were dark days for Mary, but Hope did her best to cheer her up. After several months, things began to improve and Mary began to blossom, transforming both mentally and physically, emerging from her cocoon of deep depression into a vibrant young woman.

Mary stood several inches shorter than Hope and was far more curvaceous where it counted, but she lacked Hope's cheek bones and suffered from a mild case of acne. And Mary had braces, not

Invisaligns, real old fashion metal braces. Hope just couldn't understand it. She knew Dr. Drake was cheap, but how could he do that to a seventeen-year-old. This was cruel and unusual punishment. Dr. Drake might as well have doused her with boy repellant; it would have had the same effect. But wasn't that Bill Drakes intention all along? Hope was sure that it was. The good doctor defined the meaning of the words, *hidden agenda*. Not the way to treat her BFF. Hope took it personally, because Mary reminded her of a younger version of herself. They both had the same steel blue-eyes and the same raven black hair, which made people sometimes ask if they were sisters, despite their different body types and hairstyles. Hope kept her hair just beyond shoulder length, while Mary allowed her silky mane to flow down to the middle of her back.

Instead of exploring Quito, Hope stood with Mary, disappointed on the platform waiting for the Chiva Express to take them to Riobamba. From there they'd travel on to Macas, their final destination.

The approaching single coach train bewildered Hope as she watched it grind to a halt. The *train* was nothing more than a multicolored bus on tracks. Its brilliant colors and haphazard design assaulted her eyes, reminding her more of a retro 1960's bus than any train she'd ever seen. Open-air seats covered the roof, much like on an old English double-decker.

The engineer/driver opened the doors and Hope followed the group on board, each person scrambled for the seat of his or her choosing. Several local merchants and their wares already occupied most of the lower, inside seats. One man stacked two bamboo cages on the floor in front of him. They contained four red, clucking roosters. Escaping this menagerie, Hope followed Peter, Luke, and Mary up the metal stairs to the roof, where they chose their outdoor seats together near the rear. Ryan, Matthew and Jason clanged up the stairs behind her, choosing three seats by themselves over the front of the train.

Dr. Drake, armed with his camera, strategically selected his seat up top near the middle, presumably to get the best shots of the mountains. Brenda and Tim shared the lower compartment with the merchants and a young Austrian couple with whom they'd chatted enthusiastically with on the platform.

Hope watched in awe as the train brought them through the Avenue of the Volcanoes, with its amazing panoramic view. The lush green landscape sharply contrasted the tall, snow-capped mountains. The middle-aged professor's annoying camera clicked constantly, breaking the quiet serenity of the surrounding beauty.

The train stopped at the old Station of Machachi, where Hope ate a quick lunch with her friends and waited her turn to use the facilities before re-boarding. With all aboard, the one car train started moving again, chugging its way up the slopes of the Cotopaxi volcano.

The little engine that could, Hope thought, that's what the train reminded her of. A smile crossed her lips as she remembered her mother reading to her in bed the children's book of the same name. She couldn't have been more than three. On other nights, her father would sit beside her on the edge of her bed and read Dr Seuss. Tears welled in her eyes at the thought of Star Belly Sneetches being the best on the beaches, and her father's deep soothing voice. Some days, she still can't believe that he's gone.

Now it's just me and mom. I hope she's doing okay. The smile left her face, her lips pursed.

Less than twenty-four hours had passed since she'd seen her last, still she was concerned, knowing that her mother was sick with worry, especially after her most recent episode. Hope ran her finger across a bump on her neck and then another one on her forehead; the last remnants of the painful welts, now easily covered by makeup.

I don't want to think about it. She shuddered, removing her finger.

She forced her attention to the mist floating across the mountain, a tall peak hid in the clouds. There was something alluring and mystical about the volcano.

Turning toward Peter, she forced a smile, "If there was ever a place where heaven met earth, this is it."

"I'll say, we're not in Jersey anymore," Peter said, returning the smile.

The train stopped mid-afternoon at the small Indian market. Dr. Drake's face betrayed his weak bladder. Hurrying from the train, he searched for relief.

Tim and Brenda allowed the large group to break up into several smaller ones, making it easier to move through the crowds.

"Be back at the train in one hour," Tim said, tapping his finger against his watch crystal, "I mean it."

Ryan, Matthew, and Jason embraced their newfound freedom, marching off together on some unknown adventure toward the far end of the market. The know-it-all eighteen-year-olds were as obnoxious as they were inseparable, with husky, foul mouthed Ryan being the worst of the bunch. Matthew stood a few inches taller than Ryan, and a summer spent in the weight room had done wonders for his strength and physique. Sandy haired Jason was small but scrappy, an All-County wrestler before separating his shoulder this past November.

Hope watched Peter purchase a bottle of Acai juice from a fruit vendor, downing the cold drink with several large gulps in front of her.

"Thanks for asking, we're not thirsty." Hope mocked.

"Yeah, don't worry about us, drinking is overrated anyway." Mary added.

"Sorry, you girls want one? I could get…"

Hope ignored Peter, turning her back on him; she walked over to another merchant. Mary feigned disgust as well and followed her friend. Something of interest caught Hope's attention, something far more interesting than Peter and his stupid bottle of Acai juice.

Hope picked up the hand-painted wooden cross and inspected it carefully. The beautifully crafted cross would make a nice memento of the trip or maybe even a gift for her mother. She noticed a dime sized sticker stuck to the bottom of the cross, penciled into the middle of the circle was the number five.

"One dollar!" Hope shouted, deciding to barter with the Indian merchant. The man didn't speak English and appeared confused by her words.

Hope switched to Spanish, "Un dolar," she said, holding up one finger.

The merchant shook his head no and held up five fingers.

"Give him two!" Mary shouted.

Hope caught Luke holding in a chuckle out of the corner of her eye, apparently amused by her bartering skills and the man's rapid hand gestures.

"What's so funny?" Hope asked, visibly annoyed.

"Ah, nothing," Luke sheepishly replied, bowing his head to avoid her gaze.

"Yeah, I didn't think so." Hope said.

Again the man held up five fingers.

"The cross is amazing," Hope held up two fingers, "Vale dos!"

The merchant smiled and held up three fingers.

Mary bounced on her toes. "Give him three, give him three, it's worth it!"

Hope reached into her red, quilted leather, Guess bag and found her matching purse. She fished out three singles and handed them to the merchant, who gladly accepted the US currency. His smile widened as he wrapped the cross in tissue paper and handed it to Hope.

The cross, painted in the Spanish style, depicted a crucified Jesus wearing an orange robe, rising up toward an orange sun. Bright, yellow rays beamed down from the heavens and a sky blue background accented His orange robe. Brushed against the cerulean sky were two puffy, white clouds. A pair of floating white doves completed the scene. A leather strand looped to an eye-ring made the thin cross wearable. Discarding the tissue, Hope draped the colorful crucifix over her head and proudly displayed it across her chest.

◆━◈━◆

Brenda and Tim strolled through the market together. A young, pock-faced Spanish man approached them. Several pieces of straw stuck to his hair as if he'd recently slept in a haystack. Reaching into his ripped shirt pocket, he pulled out three small packets of white powder, holding them out in the palm of his greasy brown hand. "*¿Cocaiña senorita?*"

Brenda instinctively stepped forward.

"We don't want that shit; get the hell out of here!" Tim yelled, swiping his hand at the man, shooing him away like a disgusting fly.

The startled man closed his hand and scurried into the crowd.

"Tim, your language!" Brenda panned the area, thankful Dr. Drake and the kids were out of earshot.

"I'm sorry, but that really irks me. Selling drugs like that, right out here in the open. What if he'd pushed that crap on one our kids? Then what? You understand my point?"

"Yeah, I understand." But Brenda didn't *really* understand. Her eyes had grown wide at the sight of the familiar white powder. She remembered how alive it had made her feel back in college, really not all that long ago. That first snort had always given her such a rush, and that wonderful post-nasal drip numbed her entire throat. She would use every last bit of the powder, rubbing the residue into her gums until they, too, were numb. It took every ounce of will-power not to chase after the man and make a *onetime only* purchase, but she remembered her pact with God and knew that she had to stay strong. She remembered how hard it had been to support her habit. First came the pole dancing, followed by the other stuff. She'd never prostituted herself—not for money, not exactly; she wouldn't cross *that* line.

Having looked in the mirror, she'd become frightened by the exhausted girl gazing back at her. Soon thereafter she quit her dancing job, entered rehab, and moved back in with her parents, vowing to become a born-again virgin.

Tim, who now held a blue llama-haired blanket, startled Brenda. The sound of his voice brought her back to the present. "Look at those colors and check out the tight weave."

The vendor held up five fingers.

"Five bucks? I'll take it!" Tim pulled out his wallet, retrieved a crisp picture of Lincoln and handed it to the merchant.

Brenda laughed, "Don't you know that you're supposed to haggle a bit."

"I never haggle, it stresses me out. If I like something and the price seems fair, I buy it."

Tim seemed boyish in that moment, like an innocent child. "Feel this," he said, smiling. He took hold of her hand and rubbed it across the blanket. Brenda tried to remember back to when she too had been that innocent.

⋙╪╫⋘

Hope followed Peter and Mary toward the center of the market. Luke still in Hope's dog house, tagged along behind her with his head hung low, like some pesky little brother. They passed women wearing blue and red dresses, sitting behind long wooden tables covered with Indian crafts of every kind.

Hope and Mary fingered colorful, beaded necklaces while Peter and Luke looked delighted as they watched an elderly man control several marionettes as he performed a makeshift puppet show for his potential customers. The foursome passed several more fruit and vegetable stands. At another table, a woman sold hand-woven blankets. Two young Indian girls, no older than twelve, sold wicker baskets piled high into the air. The girls called out to them,

"Cestas artesanales a un precio justo." Hope quickly translated the phrase in her head, *handmade baskets at a fair price*. She didn't respond, but smiled politely at the girls as she walked deeper into the marketplace.

Something must have caught Peter's eye because he veered off to the right. After jogging a few steps ahead of Luke and the girls, he came to a stop in front of a table presided over by an old Indian man. Hope guessed the man was close to one hundred. His wrinkled skin looked like leather and his white hair sharply contrasted his dark complexion. Clouds of white covered the old man's pupils. Hope then realized he was blind. She looked down at the table to avoid his empty gaze. That's when she saw them and screamed. Mary gasped, clinging to Hope's arm. The girl's sudden reaction humored the old man, whose smile revealed a single yellow tooth. Peter had already picked up the object to inspect it. Luke peered over Mary's shoulder. Hope couldn't believe what he held in his hand—a shrunken human head. There had to be a dozen of them on the table.

The grapefruit-sized head in Peter's hands had taut, leathery brown skin. All of the openings on the face had been sewn shut, except for the nostrils.

Peter chuckled, "Stop freaking out; it's a fake."

"What makes you say that?" Hope asked.

"Dr. Drake told us at the train station we might come across some shrunken heads in the market, but ninety-nine percent of them are fakes. He said that laws were passed in Ecuador in the 1930s that prevented the trading of human heads."

"How can you be so sure these are fakes?" Hope asked.

"He said the real ones are smaller, the size of oranges not grapefruits," Luke said.

Peter held the head at eye level. "Yeah, the heads are hung over a fire, turning the skin darker, almost black. These larger, lighter skin heads are either made from monkey or goat hides."

"You're just guessing. You don't know." Hope said.

"Oh believe me, I know. There are two surefire ways to identify the real ones." Peter said.

Mary sighed, "Really? What? If my father told you, it's probably disgusting."

"Nose hair, the real ones have nose hair."

"Eww," Hope said.

"And the second way?" Mary asked.

Luke pointed at the head. "Your dad said that human ears are hard to fake. It's obvious that these ears are crudely manufactured."

"Okay so now we know it's a fake. Let's go," Hope said.

The old blind man gestured with his hand, speaking in broken English. "Come."

"No, thanks, I think I'll stay here," Luke said.

Peter followed the old Indian into a large tent behind the table. Hope didn't want to tag along, but she didn't want to stay with Luke and the creepy heads either, even if they were fakes, so she followed Peter and the old man. Mary clutched Hope's arm and walked in step with her. The Indian led them to an old wooden cabinet at the back of the tent. Flashing a wicked smile, he hesitated a moment before flinging open the cabinet doors. Hope gasped at the three baseball-sized shrunken heads with tar black, leather skin. Their eyes, mouths, and noses were sewn shut; fine nose hairs protruded through the coarse stitching. The ears were miniature—but perfect.

The old man smiled his yellow-toothed grin once again and announced what she already knew. "Real Tsansta. Me kill!" The old man cackled.

Panic shot through Hope's veins, carrying with it a feeling of imminent death. It threatened to consume her. She had to get out of there, as far away as possible, away from the three black faced victims and the wicked old man who'd proudly confessed to killing them. Bolting through the tent flap, she could hear his dreadful laugh behind her. Hope hit full stride, moving faster, like a frightened gazelle, with Mary, Peter and Luke sprinting just a few steps behind her. Weaving through the crowd, they didn't stop running until they'd reached the train. They were the first ones back. Hope pounded on the mechanical doors until they swung open.

Falling into the seats, they collapsed in a heap. This time all four opted for the inside compartment. Hope felt safer within the confines of the steel enclosure, glad that the startled engineer/driver had let them in, and even more thankful when he sealed the door shut behind them.

Hope's heart pounded as she tried to catch her breath and said, "Oh my God! That was so freaky!"

Mary covered her eyes with her hands. "More like gross and disgusting!"

"Yeah, that guy ain't right," Peter said.

"I told you guys not to follow him," Luke said.

"Why were the eyes, noses, and mouths sewn shut?" Mary asked.

Peter wiped sweat off his brow, "Sewing up the openings in the head locks in the spirit of the dead person, preventing him from seeking revenge on the headhunter."

"This is really grossing me out. Stop, I think that I'm going to be sick," Hope said.

The rest of the group boarded the train about a half hour later; Matthew's clothing reeked of cigarette smoke as he passed. Dr. Drake brought up the rear, smiling; he mustered up a quick wave and a "hello," oblivious to the fear in his daughter's eyes. Cornering Tim, he rambled on about the great pictures he'd taken of the Indians and their wares.

The Austrian couple returned with a quick wave and a smile before taking their same seats. The train began its slow chug around the mountain on its final trek to Riobamba. Hope and her friends sat in silence for the rest of the trip. She watched Dr. Drake's rotund body disappear up the metal steps and listened to Brenda and Tim chatting with the Austrian couple just a few feet away.

No longer interested in the scenery, Hope stared at the floor, glancing up only briefly as the train approached Mt. Chimborazo, the tallest volcano in Ecuador. The magnificence of this natural wonder eclipsed that of the Grand Canyon, but she didn't care about the awe-inspiring view. She felt safer sitting close to Tim. Those awful images stayed in her mind. The three tiny heads, with their black, leathery faces, completely sewn shut. And that man, that horrible old man, with his clouded white eyes and single yellow tooth. Worst of all was his laugh, that hideous, evil laugh.

CHAPTER TWO

After disembarking the Chiva Express in Riobamba, the mission group traveled by van for less than an hour to Macas, arriving in the small jungle town late in the afternoon. They passed a small airport with a terminal that looked more like the nineteenth hole of a golf course than a place to land planes. Only a few puddle jumpers lined the runway.

The town consisted of a hodgepodge of stone and mortar buildings haphazardly constructed without any central purpose or design. Hope peered out the window at the dusty streets; they were anything but quaint, still, it was civilization. A large volcano rose in the near distance behind the city, casting dark shadows across the valley.

The driver wove the vehicle through the cobblestone streets, coming to a stop at their final destination in front of a large cathedral. The new church was the town's saving grace. Completed in the early 1990's, it rose up above the mediocrity to claim its rightful place as the grand mosaic of Macas.

Hope and the others climbed out of the van and started up a series of stone steps that led to the cathedral. Built upon a large plateau, the church rose more than forty feet above the street. The steps rose through the stone walls built upon the slope. A top layer of red volcanic stone accented each wall. After ascending the steps, the group reached the plateau.

The entranceway of the church consisted of several Spanish arches. Hope gazed at a large mural of Christ centered above the middle arch. It depicted Jesus painted against a blue sky background, with rays of light illuminating His head. It looked very similar to the cross hanging from her neck. Red bricks surrounded the mural, offering a nice contrast to the pious painting. A short, white steeple and a large, wooden cross topped the church. As the group walked behind the structure, more of the lush green valley became visible, stretching out toward an impressive mountain range. Hope and Mary retreated inside the church as a hint of cow manure blew in from the valley on the warm breeze.

The church contained the famous painting *The Virgin de Macas*. Hope marveled at the twelve stained glass windows depicting the story of the virgin and the mysterious changes that had occurred to the painting over the centuries. After a thorough exploration of the church and its surroundings, Tim and Brenda rounded up the group. Dr. Drake glanced at his watch and said, "It's time to meet our host."

The group concluded their exploration and retraced their path down the steps toward the dormitories that stood to the right of the church. The long, barrack-like building, painted a bright pastel yellow, provided housing for both the nuns and kitchen staff.

Tim had made prior arrangements with Father Ricardo for the group to occupy the dorms. The young man of the cloth offered a warm greeting to the mission group when they appeared at the front door of his rectory.

"*Hola, mí nombre es Padre Ricardo. Buenos dias.*"

Bill and Tim shook hands with the Franciscan Priest.

"We're from the congregation of Our Lady of Fatima, in Burlington, New Jersey, USA," Bill said.

Father Ricardo switched to English. "Welcome to Macas. I trust that your journey has been a safe and pleasant one?"

"Except for some bad weather in Philly, the trip has gone without a hitch." Tim said.

"Then my prayers to Saint Christopher have been answered. Follow me and I'll show you to your quarters."

"Saint Christopher? Mary whispered.

"The patron Saint of travel," Hope replied in a hushed voice.

Escorting the group across the pavers to the dorms, the priest unlocked the old wooden door with a skeleton key, and led them inside. "This dorm houses the nuns and kitchen staff, but most of the sisters are on sabbatical at a nearby retreat in the foothills just outside of town and a lot of the kitchen staff are on vacation. We have plenty of room until they return, stay the full three weeks if you want."

"A retreat in the foothills? Sounds pleasant," Brenda said.

"I'm going too, but not until next week; I have to say mass on Sunday."

"Well, we appreciate your hospitality. Thanks for having us," Bill said.

Father Ricardo handed Bill the keys, "Oh, you're more than welcome, my son. The second and third floors of the dorm are all yours. I have to attend to another matter, but Brother Hector and Brother Joseph will be in shortly to help with dinner. You must all be famished. I'll be back around eight; maybe we should get together then?"

⸻✦ ✦⸻

The group sat on hardwood benches at a long, wooden table joined by seven Franciscan monks. Brothers Hector and Joseph introduced themselves and the other five monks. They were all dressed in brown robes with white rope belts tied in a large knot around their mid-sections. Leather sandals covered their feet. Most of them spoke in broken English; despite their hard time communicating, they seemed friendly enough to Hope.

Brother Hector cooked, and Brother Joseph served each of them a hearty meal of chicken fajitas, Spanish rice, and black, refried beans.

Father Ricardo returned just as Hope downed her last bite. The group rose from the table and followed their host through a corridor toward the back of the dorm, settling into a general sitting room consisting of a couch and a number of worn leather chairs. Several large candles flickered on strategically placed tables throughout the room, providing the only lighting as early evening approached.

The priest motioned toward the furniture. "Make yourselves comfortable."

Tim, Brenda, and Dr. Drake eased themselves into well-worn leather chairs. Brenda sat prim with her hands in her lap and legs crossed.

Hope, Peter, and Mary occupied the couch, while the others filled the remaining seats. The lit candles couldn't mask the stale smell of burnt incense.

Back in Burlington, Tim had praised Father Ricardo for being the kind of priest who made a difference, always championing the cause of the underdog no matter what the consequences. He fed the hungry and reached out to the weak and poor, especially children.

Father Ricardo's early mission work included spending a significant amount of time with the Shuar Indians. Brenda had shown Hope the letter outlining the priest's zealous ideals about introducing Christ to the indigenous people. In fact, he'd already made some strides in that direction several years ago and wanted the church group from New Jersey to pick up where he'd left off. At least that was the idea.

The priest stood up front waiting for silence before addressing the group. Using his firsthand knowledge, he taught the group the most basic Shuar customs. The lessons included traditional methods of greeting the Indians and sharing a meal. The young priest introduced the group to a basic sign language that might help them communicate better with the people of the rainforest.

"Don't use flash photography, it will scare them," Father Ricardo said. "In fact, don't show them any photographs at all."

"They must've seen pictures before. I understand that some have relatives who live in the modern section," Bill said, fingering the camera attached to his belt.

"Yes, they know what a photograph is. But it's their belief that if you take a picture of them, you'll steal their soul."

"That's bitchin," Ryan said.

Tim shot Ryan a hard, angry glare.

Father Ricardo paused for a moment, refraining from speech until he once again had the group's full attention. His warm smile disappeared from his face.

"Now I'm going to talk to you about something very serious," he said, pausing another moment for effect. "Never leave the safety of the Shuar village. Never wander off into the rainforest. There is true evil out there. Always stay in the village."

Hope's blue-eyes widened; Peter flashed a feigned look of fear. She smirked, finding humor in his mockery. She whispered to Mary, "Father Ricardo does seem a little over dramatic."

Mary spoke in a hushed tone, "What could possibly happen? My father wouldn't have brought us here if it really were dangerous. Would he?"

"These days, everybody's trying to cover their ass, especially the church," Peter whispered. "It's like a disclaimer against the obscure chance some idiot does something stupid. Father Ricardo could then wash his hands of the whole matter and say I told you so."

Tim placed his index finger in front of his lips. "Peter! Shush, listen up!

Father Ricardo continued. "As I mentioned earlier, I'm going to be staying at a Christian retreat on a three week sabbatical. It's only nine miles from Sucua, the Shuar village. If you should run into any difficulties, contact me at once. I'll be there within the hour."

The meeting adjourned. Father Ricardo said goodnight and headed back to the rectory.

Brenda assigned the girls to the third floor, leaving Tim, Bill, and the boys to spread out on the second. All three women entered the long room. There were two rows of six beds on each side, creating a walkway down the middle of the room. Brenda selected a bed on the right side, farthest from the door. Hope chose the one on the same side, closest to the entrance. Mary chose the bed next to Hope. Pulling out clean sheets from their duffle bags, the women began making up their bunks. Hope secured the bottom sheet and collapsed on the mattress. Mary did likewise, lying down on the cool cotton. After making up her bed, Brenda left the room, presumably to meet Tim downstairs. Hope turned to face her friend and said, "Do you want to explore the dorm?"

"Nah, I just want to stretch out and rest for a while."

"Don't you want to snoop around a bit?"

"Yeah, but let's do it in the morning. I'm beat."

"You stay and rest; I'm checking the place out."

Hope walked out of the room and down a flight of stairs to the first floor. She peeked around the corner and saw Brenda and Tim talking in the kitchen. Sneaking out the back door, she stepped into the darkness and found herself in a grand flower garden. Stone pavers divided the garden into four equal parcels. A pale moon provided the only illumination along the walkway, shading the flowers a grayish white. A large stone fountain stood in the center of the garden. Water gurgled up the finial into the top tier, spilling over into the second tier and finally cascading into the round pool below.

The hypnotic sound of spilling water and the sparkle of moonbeams reflecting off the pool mesmerized Hope. As she stood in the garden, her mind drifted into an altered state.

She found herself in the rainforest, standing with Peter and Mary before a beautiful waterfall. The sun shone bright and Hope wore a red and white floral one piece bathing suit, Mary wore a bright turquoise bikini. The girls stretched out on a large, flat rock. Basking in the sunlight, Hope felt the warmth radiate over her body.

Peter, standing shirtless at the water's edge, pulled several flat stones from the pocket of his cut off shorts and skipped them, one by one across the crystal clear pool that formed at the bottom of the waterfall. "Watch, I'll make this sucker hop all the way across!"

"Come on, let's shower under the falls." Mary stood and reached out to Hope, pulling her to her feet. Peter gave up on the stones and followed the girls to the falls.

Hope joined hands with her two friends to steady herself on the slippery rocks as they stepped into the narrow space behind the falls. Together, they shimmied forward to position themselves under the water. Hope loved the feel of the cool water cascading over her skin, pouring over her back and shoulders.

Peter lost his footing and slipped without warning. Flailing his arms wildly, he kept from falling, but his sudden motion threw Hope off balance. She first wobbled, and then slipped off the rock, plunging into the deep pool below. Swimming underwater, the clear pool transformed into liquid darkness.

Disoriented in the black water, she wasn't able to see the bottom or determine which way was up. Making a random decision, she prayed it was the right one and swam hard in that direction, becoming short of breath, her lungs craved oxygen. On the verge of passing out, she broke the surface, gasping for air. Confused and bewildered, she found herself still engulfed in darkness. After catching her breath, she came to the realization that she was in a different spot from where she'd fallen in; her friends and the waterfall were gone.

Hope swam toward her left, guided only by her outstretched arms. She felt her way through the darkness until her fingers touched a slimy rock. Struggling to pull herself from the water, she climbed up onto a solid stone floor. She inched along the surface, feeling her way through the void until her fingers touched a cold rock wall. It appeared that she was in a cave.

Hope stood alone, crying in the dark. Her ears detected a faint sound that grew louder until her ears rung with loud chanting.

A man stepped from the darkness, illuminated by his own aura. The strange shaman from her nightmares stood before her. An array of colorful feathers made up his headdress. Strange tattoos resembling hieroglyphics covered his face and chest. Woven grass reeds covered his groin. The shaman raised his right arm, holding something in his hand.

Concentrating, she tried to find her way back to the garden, back to the fountain, but she couldn't. She looked closer. *What is it? Another shrunken head! Oh my God! It's a small boy—he's just a child!*

The image morphed again, transforming into yet another figure—a shadow of a man moved within a fine, glowing mist; he seemed strange but familiar. Each swirl of the mist brought him closer. His translucent form solidified as he stepped from the mist. Hope stood aghast. Her father stood before her. *Dad you have returned! It's impossible, but there you stand. This can't be happening.* But it felt real and she was powerless to stop it.

His lips moved, but his words were inaudible. Pain shot through her gut, up her spine, and into the stem of her brain. She felt his cancer, the blackness spread through *her* body. He made her feel it, if only to prove that this *was* real. The hurting stopped when he spoke, his whisper, like morphine, relieved her pain but it was still a whisper.

"I can't hear you!" Hope shouted, straining her ears to absorb his words. He stepped closer with a sense of urgency; veins bulged on his neck and forehead. His eyes burned with determination, desperate to make his message clear.

"Leave at once! DANGER! DANGER! DANG…" His words faded along with his image.

Hope's body shook as if she was having a seizure. She came to, finding herself lying on the stone pavers next to the fountain with her body coiled in a fetal position. Only her hands trembled now, but she felt weak and washed out. Still, she remembered her father's ominous message and the tiny sewn-up face of that poor little boy.

She sat up and took several deep breaths, drinking in the mountain air, trying to find the strength to stand. The moon held a new position in the sky, a clear indication that several hours had elapsed since she'd first entered the garden. A chill swept through her body and she felt woozy. She thought, *I'll sit for just a few minutes,* and she did so. Several more minutes elapsed before she took a deep breath and forced herself to stand. Her knees buckled as she rose, but she found her footing. Frightened and exhausted, she found her way to the door, pulling it open with some difficulty. Staggering inside the dorm, she climbed the stairs to the second floor.

The halls were empty, with the exception of Dr. Drake whose noisy flip-flops clacked toward her from the far end of the hall. He wore a satin burgundy smoking jacket, just like the ones you'd see on Hugh Hefner or in those old movies.

Hope's eyes widened and her jaw dropped, she thought she might be delirious. A tied, red satin belt looped around his waist and hung down to his crotch. The skimpy jacket exposed his flabby, white legs. The short garment, depending on the gender of the wearer, could easily double as a miniskirt.

She felt his eyes upon her, his hands were submerged deep in the jacket pockets, and he looked her up and down as he walked, undressing her with every step. He held his lecherous stare, nodding at her as he approached, releasing a primal grunt that sounded something like "hey" or "huh." Hope saw the lust in his eyes and smelled the whiskey on his breath as he passed. She felt him inspecting her backside, causing her to glance over her shoulder. Seemingly surprised, he stammered on his words, pulled his hands from his pockets, and ducked into the bathroom.

She was used to men gawking at her; they always did. It was a fact of life, but this was different; this was the father of her best friend, a man more than twice her age. The thought of his penetrating eyes disgusted her. She reminded herself that it was only his stare that had violated her, but it felt much worse, like a complete breach of trust. In the future she'd be sure to keep her distance from the good Dr. Drake.

Entering the room, she found Mary asleep and Brenda nowhere in sight. Hope's fingers trembled as she got undressed, her clothes drenched in sweat. Bill Drake's creepy antics disturbed her almost as much as her vision in the garden, but the image of the child's shrunken head seared her mind, making her hands shake. With teary eyes, she jumped into bed and hid herself beneath the covers.

⇒⇇ ⇉⇐

Brenda wandered down to the kitchen to fix herself a cup of tea. She startled Tim, who sipped on a freshly brewed cup of coffee.

"Howdy, ma'am, fancy meeting you here," Tim said, tipping an invisible hat.

Brenda filled her kettle and put it on to boil. "We simply must stop meeting like this."

"Can't sleep?" he asked.

"Haven't tried yet. How 'bout you?"

"Me neither."

"Believe me I want to sleep, it's just that…" she started.

"What?"

"I have this uneasy feeling. What if the Shuar Indians aren't as tame as we think?"

"Relax. Bill said that there've been other mission groups here before us and they've never had a problem. In fact, they even had some success converting a small group of them over to Christianity."

23

"I know. I just want to make sure that the kids are safe, it's a big responsibility."

"The kids will be fine, they're smart and talented. I'm hoping that our mission trip brings some measure of success."

"I know, but for some reason I feel like I should warn them to be extra careful around the Indians," she said.

"I see no reason to alarm the kids. We want them to feel comfortable when they interact with the Shuar, not become frozen with fear. Bill's the expert and he says there's nothing to worry about."

"You're right, I guess that I'm just being paranoid and silly," she said.

Tim picked up a small notepad and a blue pen from the counter. "Let's hash over some of the basic details for tomorrow. We need to make the most of our time in the rainforest."

"I guess our first contact with the Indians will be the most important," Brenda said.

Tim wrote the word TRUST in capital letters at the top of the page and said, "We will try to gain their trust by taking things real slow at first. Let's make the cathedral our home base, at least for now. We can make daily pilgrimages to the Indian village. Father Ricardo said we can use the church van until he leaves for his retreat as long as we make small donations to the Poor Box for use of the propane."

"Propane?"

"Yes, apparently Father Ricardo has gone green. I spoke to him about the van after the meeting and he seemed proud of the fact that he'd recently converted the engine, even installed a huge tank at the rear of the property."

"I'm liking him better all the time," Brenda said.

"So, you think it's a good idea to travel back and forth?" Tim said.

"It kinda makes sense. We don't want the Shuar to feel overwhelmed by our presence."

"Father Ricardo said it's only twelve miles to Sucua. We'll rise at dawn so we can get in a full day."

"Sounds like a plan. I'll have the girls ready; you do the same for the boys."

"What do you think? Seven o'clock for our departure time?"

"Make it 7:45, the girls and I need a little more time in the bathroom."

Tim smiled at Brenda, "Did anyone ever tell you what pretty blue-eyes you have?"

"Only the big bad wolf, are you the big bad wolf, Mr. Kirby?"

Tim held Brenda's hand. "I'm just a kind and gentle shepherd here to protect you."

Brenda sighed and pulled back her hand. "Look, Tim, I know you're a nice guy, and I like you, but I think we need to keep our relationship strictly professional. We have to be good role models for the kids."

Tim sighed, "You're right—role models—for the kids."

CHAPTER THREE

Mount Sangay loomed like a sleeping giant in the distance as the van left Macas. Hope watched the active volcano exhale smoke from its snowcapped mouth and felt a little uneasy, knowing they'd just left civilization. She thought about her father and his warnings. *If only I could understand its meaning. He told me to leave, but why?*

Her thoughts turned to Bill Drake and the way the middle-aged professor had salivated over her in the hallway. She wanted to tell Mary about her father, the perverted ass-watcher that he was, but why make the daughter pay for the sins of the father? Why burden her with this nasty knowledge? Hope had a hunch that Mary already knew about her father's unsavory ways; she prayed that her knowledge didn't come firsthand. She'd let the matter drop, at least for now.

Hope couldn't help but wonder why Father Ricardo once again gave the group yet another warning about "the evils" of wandering off into the rainforest as they said their goodbyes. *Why the drama?*

She also overheard the priest give Tim and Brenda a separate warning as he escorted them to the awaiting van. The man of the cloth spoke in a somber tone as they walked.

"Be very careful, my children; always be aware of your surroundings and remember that the sins of a few can lead to the slaughter of the innocent."

The priest's strange message left a puzzled look on the faces of both group leaders. Hope repeated Father Ricardo's warning to her two friends.

"That doesn't sound like any sermon I've ever heard," Mary said.

"Maybe Father Ricardo got into the communal wine," Peter joked.

It didn't take long to travel the twelve miles to Sucua. The town, if one could call it that, broke down into several parts, a blend of the old and new. Some areas already showed signs of modernization, with new schools and houses.

Hope watched through the window as the van passed several children walking along the roadside dressed in jeans and T-shirts, not very different from themselves. Up ahead, several young men whose fashion blended somewhere between modern and traditional walked shirtless in jeans along the roadside with their ears attached to iPods. Others wore colorful, beaded necklaces and feathers, while sporting wristwatches.

They drove deeper into the Indian village until they reached the traditional area where the Shuar broke down into smaller communities or tribes. The van soon left the pavement, bouncing down a long, dirt road surrounded by thick forest on both sides.

Three shirtless Indians crossed the road in front of them. They wore beads and carried spears. Bright feathers crowned their heads and a woven, reed-like material fashioned into a primitive skirt, covered from their waists down to their knees. Tattoos adorned their torsos and faces.

Despite Father Ricardo's warning, Bill Drake leaned toward the window and snapped several pictures in rapid succession. One of the tribesmen gave him a menacing look before disappearing into the forest.

"A small hunting party," Tim shouted out to the group.

They look similar to the shaman in my dream. Could it be a coincidence? Hope thought.

She wondered if there was a common thread of knowledge that she'd somehow stored in her subconscious. Maybe she'd retained the information from the South American exhibit at the Museum of Natural History during last year's field trip.

Peter whispered to Hope and Mary, "We're going to take Shuar warriors and convert them to Christianity; good luck!"

"God works in mysterious ways," Mary replied.

Hope sighed, "Sometimes I think we're disturbing nature. We should leave them to their own culture and traditions."

"I never thought of it like that," Mary said.

The van continued to bump, turn, and twist down the dusty dirt road, until it came to a stop at its final destination, the village of a small, traditional tribe. Hope climbed out of the van with the others to survey her surroundings.

The village consisted of eleven grass huts. Some were enclosed structures, while others were of the open air variety. Most of the huts were just thatched roofs supported by bamboo poles.

Beneath one thatched roof, a group of bare-breasted women strung beads and wove baskets. Matthew's, Jason's, and Ryan's eyes bulged and their mouths hung ajar, adding credence to Hope's suspicion that the big talkers had only seen bare-breasted women between the pages of *Playboy* magazines pilfered from their fathers' dresser drawers.

Peter's eyes shifted from right to left, "It's the land of the lost. We've entered the Stone Age."

"Yeah, but it's cool, I like it," Hope said.

At last count, sixty-two Shuar men, women, and children lived in the village. At another open air hut, several women lifted the headless torso of a small, wild piglet into a large, iron pot. Children ran to and fro unsupervised; most of them wore minimal clothing.

Icy stares greeted Hope and the others as they passed the women. Dr. Drake seemed oblivious to the cool reception, leading the group farther into the village. Finally, he stopped at an open air hut where several older men sat on cut log stumps, smoking clay pipes, speaking Shuar amongst themselves with a hint of Spanish blended in. Bill and Tim greeted the tribal Elders; their response seemed friendly, but less than enthusiastic. Father Ricardo had spent time with them several weeks earlier, securing final permission for the visit.

Teja, one of the most respected Elders, invited the group to eat and drink. Father Ricardo's crash course on Shuar sign language and dining etiquette paid instant dividends. They ate fish and drank a warm, sticky, yellow liquid that looked like corn chowder and had the same consistency.

Hope sipped the drink from her earthen mug. "This is very bitter. What is it?"

Aitiak, a young Shuar woman who had failed at her attempt to modernize several years before, still remembered a little of the English she'd been taught. "*Chicha*," she replied.

"It's an ancient beer brewed by the Shuar women. Don't drink too much or you'll get drunk," Bill said.

That was all that Jason, Matthew, and Ryan needed to hear. They gave each other a smug look before chugging down the warm beer. Somehow, they managed to get a refill and chugged that down as well. After several minutes, Matthew began slurring his words and Ryan insisted on using his *outside voice,* speaking as if he were addressing a gathering of the hard of hearing. Jason withdrew into himself without saying a word. Hope also felt a little tipsy from the strong brew. It wasn't long before Ryan's boisterous voice proved intolerable.

"Simmer down, boys!" Tim finally shouted.

Several Shuar women giggled at Ryan's scolding. After several more rounds of *Chicha*, the mission group and the Shuar felt comfortable in each other's company.

Hope and Mary befriended a nineteen-year-old boy named Kuja, who spoke Shuar, English, and Spanish. He'd learned the foreign languages in school, having lived in the modern section before his father died of stomach cancer. After his father's death, Kuja moved to the traditional village to live with his grandfather.

The church group made daily pilgrimages from Macas to the village. After several days of commuting, Tim asked the Elders if the group could build temporary shelter so they could live full time in the village. Teja agreed, but Carak, the youngest Elder and the most outspoken, voiced his objection. They argued in Spanish. Hope got the gist of the conversation, having taken four years of the language in high school, but Carak talked fast and used local slang, making it nearly impossible to follow. It became clear; he didn't want the mission group in the village.

"It's bad enough they've come to visit, now they have to live here?" Carak said.

"You were here when we agreed to this," Teja said.

"Well, I've changed my mind; they'll poison our children with their outside teaching."

"This is not new; these groups have visited many times before and we still have our traditions and beliefs," Teja said.

"I say no, let them go live in the modern section."

Two Elders sitting together on the left nodded their heads in agreement.

"We told the priest we'd allow this. He's been good to the tribe, bringing us food during the rainy season and medicine for our children. We must keep our promise," Teja said.

"All right," Carak said, "but let it be known, I'm against it!"

The next day, Father Ricardo dropped the group off in the village for the last time and headed off for his retreat with the church van. Hope had an uneasy feeling as she watched the van bounce down the dirt road and disappear from view. *There goes our umbilical cord.*

Teja brought them to an empty clearing near the eleven existing huts. The group spent two entire days building three shelters— one wigwam style hut for the men, a similar but smaller shelter for Hope and Mary, and a tiny grass hut for Brenda who had requested a little more privacy.

Everyone pitched in to help with the exception of Dr. Drake, who chose instead to spend his time interviewing Teja. After enlisting Kuja as a translator, Bill captured the Elder's every word on his mini-recorder with his seemingly endless supply of batteries.

Somehow the group managed to carry on without Bill's help. They framed their structures by tying bamboo poles together. Grass and mud covered the frames. The hot sun baked the mixture, turning it into hard clay. This provided adequate shelter from the elements and any nocturnal animals that might wander into the village.

With the huts complete, Hope and Mary began spending a lot of time with Kuja; that was, when he wasn't translating for the good professor. As the days went by, Hope helped him hone his English, while Kuja introduced the girls to many Shuar customs and traditions.

Peter, snubbed by the girls, began spending more time with the rest of the boys. Some of the Shuar men taught the boys how to hunt with a blowgun. The five boys found this fascinating, even Luke who claimed he couldn't eat anything that had a face on it. The following day, the Indians taught the boys how to carve out a canoe from a fallen tree. This was way too much fun for Peter to pass up, as it was for all of the boys.

Tim and Brenda worked hard together as they began construction on an open-air church. Tim perspired through his shirt as he strained to tie several bamboo poles together. Brenda couldn't help but notice his muscles rippling across his bare arms. She breathed in his musk, finding him irresistible. What had started out in Macas as a casual flirtation had grown into real sexual tension. Tim looked strong and rugged and Brenda caught him checking her out more than once.

Despite her rejection, she knew that he'd soon make another play for her. She hadn't imagined just how soon that would be.

Tim placed the poles down and began hammering a wooden stake into the ground. The hammer veered off the stake, smashing his thumb. "Shit!"

"You okay?"

Tim sucked his thumb for a moment before pulling it from his lips. "I'll live."

Wiping the sweat from his brow, he smiled and stepped toward Brenda. "But thanks for your concern." He grabbed her hand and gazed into her eyes. "Your eyes are like deep blue pools. I could get lost in your eyes; I could go swimming in your eyes."

"Stop it, Tim, the kids will hear you." *Was he for real?*

Brenda scanned their surroundings; they seemed to be alone for the moment. Tim leaned toward Brenda and tried to kiss her.

"Control yourself, Mr. Kirby." She pulled back.

Tim disarmed her with his smile. Those cute dimples and wavy red hair were hard to resist, but she had to stay strong for the sake of her own wellbeing.

Tim squeezed her hand. "Meet me tonight on the footbridge by the stream; we'll have a drink to toast our success."

Brenda hesitated. "Just one drink and no monkey business."

"How 'bout two drinks and all monkey business?" Tim asked with a grin.

Brenda knew she was blushing. "I'd better go check on the girls," she said as she turned and walked away.

That evening, after everyone was asleep, Brenda snuck out of her hut and walked toward the brook. Through the moonlight, she saw the silhouette of a tall man waiting on the footbridge.

"Tim is that you?"

"Yeah, it's me; beautiful night, huh?"

Tim held a bottle of wine and two plastic cups in his hands; a big, earthen jug rested near his feet. Using his Swiss army knife, he opened the wine with the corkscrew.

"You're right, look at the moon; it's so full and beautiful."

"You're beautiful!"

"Tim, behave." Her heart fluttered.

He smiled, gazing into her eyes, creating a moment of uncomfortable silence.

Brenda broke the quiet. "A bottle of wine? Where'd you get that?"

"I picked it up in Macas for just such an occasion."

"Oh, did you now?"

Tim filled the two glasses with a Chilean wine and handed one of them to Brenda.

"Here's to our success." She raised her glass.

"Here's to your beauty." Tim's glass touched hers.

Brenda tilted her head back slightly to take a sip and to avoid his piercing gaze. The wine tasted light and fruity. She met his stare and smiled, feeling the blood rush into her cheeks.

A gentle breeze filtered through the trees, bringing along with it the tropical scents of the forest. Brenda felt a chill and folded her arms across her chest, taking a sip of wine every now and again. Tim slid his arm around her waist; it felt very unnatural to her. They stood on the bridge, gazing at the moon, listening to the sound of crickets and tree frogs chirping all around them. They made several more toasts until they'd finished the bottle.

"Tim, this is nice, but we should probably go back."

"Hey, we still got this jug."

"Jug of what?"

"*Chicha*, that fine ancient brew."

"Ya think?"

"I figured we'd drink the good stuff first. The alcohol will dull our senses, so the beer won't taste so bad."

Brenda laughed, "Okay, bar setter, give me a beer."

Sitting down on the bridge, she removed her sandals, dipping her feet into the cool, flowing water. Tim sat beside her, pulling the tight cork from the jug, pouring them each a glass of the yellow chowder like brew. The moonlight glistened off the water. Tim looked deep into Brenda's eyes and tried to kiss her, but she leaned away from him. He looked hurt—then surprised—when she playfully bit his ear.

She felt his hand slip under her blouse, working his way toward her breast. His fingers easily found their way inside her bra, touching her nipple, his large hand caressing her; his touch felt gentle and caring, and she wasn't used to that. She felt like tainted goods, undeserving of Tim's affection. He tried to kiss her again. This was no good. Those old guilty feelings came rushing back, breaking the moment.

"We should really go," Brenda said, taking a deep breath.

Tim sighed and removed his hand from her shirt. "I'll walk you back to your hut."

Together they walked in the moonlight, holding hands as they strolled; hers palms felt clammy, the clasp of their hands unnatural, fingers meshed together almost arthritically. She wobbled as she walked. Tim tried to steady her as they approached the hut, giving her hand a final squeeze in front of her entrance. "Well, I guess this is goodnight."

She allowed him to lean in for a goodnight kiss, but their lips didn't line up correctly—by her design.

Brenda felt a craving from within, feeling aroused, she wanted sex, nothing more; she would allow herself just that.

Love and affection were for other women, ones who had never traded their bodies for coke. Still, she had needs. "Would you like to come in for a minute?"

"I should probably get going. The rest of the crew will wonder we're I'm at."

His sweet refusal made him even more delicious. Tim was too good for her and she knew it, far better than she deserved. Still, she felt that deep ache. It had been so long since she'd felt a man inside of her. And it would just be sex, nothing more; she promised herself that, a quickie and then he could go.

"Stay for just a few minutes; everybody's probably asleep," said the spider to the fly, at least that's how she felt. Holding his hand, she led him into her lair. Brenda sat on her bed; it consisted of straw and reeds matted down with the sleeping bag rolled over the top. It was primitive but comfortable. She patted the sleeping bag twice. "Come, sit with me."

Tim seemed to hesitate before complying with her request. Again he tried to kiss her, but with the speed of a ninja, she flailed her elbows and pulled her shirt over her head, her bra soon followed. *Here, you can play with my boobs, just don't kiss me.*

He squeezed her breast with his left hand; she quivered as he ran his fingers across her sensitive nipple. Working his hand downward across her tummy, he unsnapped her jeans. She pushed his hand aside, pulling down the blue denim and panties herself with one swift motion.

Tim disrobed and crawled onto the bed near her feet. Using his fingertips, he barely touched the fine hairs on her leg; she'd allow this, but no hugging or kissing. Only wholesome women deserved *those* things.

He crawled on top of her; moments later she felt him inside of her, penetrating deeper; she moaned as her pelvis met his thrusts, he felt good, damn good. Despite the ecstasy she felt within, she wouldn't allow herself that ultimate pleasure; her body wouldn't permit it. His face contorted as he approached his moment of release. With a final grunt, he withdrew from her, dispersing his seed across her belly, collapsing in a heap next to her. Trying to catch his breath, he reached his arms around her, but she'd have none of that. Fending him off with her elbows, she moved away from him on the bed.

The intense guilt came quick, sobering her up like a bucket of cold water. "We shouldn't have done that. I think it would be best if you got dressed and left."

"What? Why?"

"We teach the kids one thing, then we go and do the exact opposite. We're hypocrites!"

"Don't worry about it; they'll never know."

"I know and God knows."

Tim smiled, "You worry too much; besides, we did it missionary style; that makes it okay."

Brenda punched him hard on the arm.

"Hey, that really hurt!"

"I'm serious; I think you'd better leave!"

"Don't beat yourself up over this and more importantly, don't beat me up either," Tim said, still rubbing his arm. "How 'bout I stay with you for a few hours, then go."

"I think not—if we oversleep and Bill or the kids catch us together, we'll have a lot of explaining to do."

"Goodnight, I'll see you in the morning." Tim tried to kiss her, but she turned her face and his lips only found her cheek. Looking defeated, he headed for the door.

"Goodnight."

"Goodnight."

She had gotten rid of him and breathed a sigh of relief. He had no sooner left, when the tears started to flow, running down her cheeks, soaking her bed of straw. She stared up at the thatched roof knowing she'd disappointed herself again, breaking her promise to God. *I'm weak. I'm so fucking weak.* Worse yet, she couldn't stop thinking about the young, disheveled man at the Indian Market and his glorious white powder. She couldn't control her cravings. *I would* do *anything for just one more snort.* Tears turned into sobs, because she knew it was the truth; she *would do anything.* The harsh realization that sex had triggered an insatiable craving for coke disturbed her even more. Despite rehab, her mind and body still felt conditioned like a lab rat. The equation was simple, Have Sex=Get Coke. *I have to stop thinking like that. I have to stop!* She wondered if she could ever have a normal relationship with a man.

In spite of her promises, she knew in her heart nothing had changed. After a while, she cried herself to sleep.

During the middle of the night she started to dream. She found herself back at the cathedral in Macas stepping from the dorm out into the garden. Her eyes needed a moment to adjust to the bright sunlight. Father Ricardo stood by the fountain with his back turned to her.

"Father, help me, for I am weak," Brenda cried out.

The young priest turned to face her. He raised his arm and pointed at her, chastising her in a thunderous voice, "The sins of a few will lead to the slaughter of the innocent!"

"Yes, Father, I did sin, but no one knows of my evil deed. The kids will never know."

"God knows! Satan knows!" Father Ricardo's voice thundered louder. Brenda awoke in a pool of sweat, shaking and scared.

The break of dawn, like her dream, was unforgiving. Brenda got up and walked outside to her makeshift shower. A huge, galvanized watering can hung from a tree branch. Two strings controlled the flow of water, one to tip the can forward, the other to pull it back to its original position. A bamboo partition provided some level of privacy.

Brenda dropped her towel and stepped naked into the shower. She pulled on the string, attempting to wash away her sins from the night before. Scrub as she may, her sins remained, stronger than ever in the light of day.

CHAPTER FOUR

At first, Kuja's English sounded broken and rough; he hadn't spoken it in years, but Hope's informal tutoring soon brought his speech back to its former fluency. The young Shuar practiced the language by teaching the girls about his heritage, tribal legends, and oral history.

Peter and the other boys busied themselves with their canoe project, leaving the girls to Kuja and their own devices.

On this morning, Hope and Mary carried wicker baskets and followed Kuja along the moss-covered banks of the brook. Under a canopy of tall trees, they picked mushrooms. Kuja pointed out which fungi were poisonous and which types were edible. Hope pulled several specimens from the rich, moist soil and placed them into her basket. Mary did likewise, pulling a rather large one from the ground. The smell of fresh dirt blended with the sweeter scents of the forest as they walked deeper into the woods. From the treetops, a small squirrel monkey screeched his displeasure at the human intruders, holding his ground momentarily, before disappearing into the dark green foliage.

A question had been gnawing at Hope for days; there was no right time to ask it. Strolling along the banks, they came upon a patch of purple flowers whose sweet fragrance hung in the air. Kuja picked two bouquets of the purple petals and handed one to each girl. Before she'd even realized it, the words had escaped her lips, "Were your relatives really headhunters?"

Kuja's boyish smile disappeared from his face, replaced by a gleam of pride radiating from his dark brown eyes. "My people are great warriors. We've crushed the once powerful Incas in the mountains and pushed the Spaniards out of the forest back to their stone cities."

Mary placed her basket down. "But did your people really hunt heads?"

"War is sometimes necessary to maintain order and balance in the forest. A Shuar warrior needed to cut off the head of his enemy to begin the ritual of Tsantsa."

"Why? For what purpose?" Hope asked.

"To prevent the soul from reaching the afterlife. If he escaped, he'd seek revenge on our dead relatives. Sewing up the eyes, nose, and mouth protected our ancestor's spirits."

"What was the ritual like?" Hope asked.

"Only those who took heads participated. One warrior beat the drum, while the others covered themselves in the blood of the enemy, dancing with their heads in celebration. They'd reenact the killings for the whole village to see."

"Eww!" both girls shouted in unison.

"I knew you wouldn't understand." Kuja looked agitated.

"I'm sorry, Kuja. The story's fascinating, please continue," Hope said.

"Sometimes the old ways are still the best ways. I've heard many stories about the battles my ancestor's fought. The Elders also told tales about the Invisible People."

"The Invisible People?" Hope asked.

"They often spoke of a small tribe who live in the forest known as the Invisible People."

"Are they really invisible?" Mary's quivering mouth betrayed a smirk.

"They're called the Invisible People because they're never seen. They've lived in the forest for over ten thousand years, refusing to have contact with the outside world."

"Don't you think somebody would've stumbled across a campsite by now?" Hope asked.

"They move like shadows through the forest. Where they are today isn't where they'll be tomorrow," Kuja said.

"If the legend's true, don't ya think that somebody would've come across a dead one in ten thousand years, a grave site, old bones, something?" Mary asked.

"They practice magic and hide in the shadows. The art of not being seen is their way of life—it continues even beyond death."

"Do they believe in good spirits?" Hope asked.

"It's said that they're protected by a dark spirit who lurks in the forest called the *Iwanci*."

"Dark spirit? *Iwanci*?" Hope asked.

"My tribe believes that after death your spirit changes form. You may return as a human or a jaguar, a mouse, even a plant. We believe you'll stay in that new form for the rest of your new life, changing again only after death—but the dark spirit is different."

"How so?" Hope asked.

"It's a shadow spirit, the Iwanci's always changing. It never moves on to the afterlife, it changes form, but is never reborn. It lurks in the forest and preys on the souls of its enemies for all eternity. It seeks revenge for injustices suffered while alive."

"But whoever wronged it must also be dead." Hope said.

"The spirit's vengeance is aimed at the descendants of the wrongdoers."

"No offense, Kuja, but that sounds really out there," Mary said.

"Believe what you want."

"If you say it's true, then I believe you," Hope said.

"Some of our tribesmen have seen the strange race that walks side-by-side with the dark spirit. They've seen such warriors while on hunts deep in the rainforest, but only for a moment. They'd glance up and they'd be gone, leaving them to wonder if they'd really seen them at all."

"It was probably just their minds playing tricks on them," Mary said.

Kuja shook his head. "I've seen one myself."

"Please!" Hope said.

"A few years ago, while walking deep in the forest. My eyes caught movement to my left. For a brief moment, I saw a warrior holding a spear; blue war paint covered his face. I turned to face him and he was gone."

"Are you sure that's what you saw, or did your imagination and those old stories go to your head?" Mary asked.

"I'm sure of what I saw. That's it; I'm not telling you anymore." Kuja's face turned red.

Hope touched his arm. "I'm sorry, please continue. We'll stop goofing, I promise."

Kuja hesitated and then spoke, "My grandfather said they're seen only when they want to be seen. Sometimes they'd vanish for many years. Their shaman is thought to be a powerful master of magic who only answers to the dark spirit."

"But what makes him any more powerful than a shaman in your tribe?" Hope asked.

"It's believed he makes human sacrifices to the Iwanci—he even kills children. They draw their powers from the captured souls of the dead, they too practice Tsantsa."

"How horrible if it's true," Mary said.

The images from Hope's dreams came rushing back and her face grew pale. "Let's go back; I feel queasy," she said, now sorry she'd ever broached the subject with Kuja.

As they started back through the woods, they came upon an old twisted tree different from all the rest. Hope froze on the path, her eyes transfixed by the deformity that sprouted up in front of her. The thick trunk stood as a testament to hundreds of years of growth. Two tall men linking hands couldn't wrap their arms around it.

The hideous tree seemed to invoke an inexplicable sorrow. Its gray leaves appeared dry and lifeless in contrast to the rest of the lush green forest.

Two obscene knots protruded from the trunk at eye level. The odd formation bulged out like a pair of giant testicles. Gray bark flaked off the tree, shedding its thin skin like an old man with a bad case of psoriasis. A few flakes fell to the ground in swirling spirals, while hundreds of paper thin pieces encircled the base of the trunk, jostling in the breeze.

Deep cracks split the gray wood, spider webbing in every direction across the trunk. Red sap seeped from its gaping wounds, filling in the cracks in places, creating a gooey amber scab. Two long branches as thick as a man's torso jettisoned from each side of the trunk more than fifteen feet above the ground. The right limb twisted upward in an ascending spiral, making its contribution to the dull gray canopy.

The left limb sprouted almost straight outward for a dozen or so feet before branching off into many thinner offshoots. Hardened drops of tree sap hung in a gummy perpetual drip, oozing from a distinct crack on the underside of the limb. A solidified puddle of dark amber collected on the ground below the drip. The resin pool seemed to be less than two feet across; its hardened surface resembled black tar. This drastic change in pigmentation baffled Hope. She wondered what logical explanation there could be for this unnatural secretion.

A black Nunbird flew out of the canopy and landed on the left limb of the tree. The ominous bird seemed to mock its pious name by producing several loud squawks. Its red and orange beak sharply contrasted its dark black plumage. The bird's bright green eyes seemed to be looking straight through Hope. Its beak opened slightly, changing into something similar to a smirk, if birds could smirk.

The warm breeze dissipated and the surrounding air became stale, weighing heavy in Hope's lungs, making it difficult to breathe.

Kuja, having heard enough, hurled a rock at the dark bird. The feathered creature stood its ground, as if it sensed that Kuja would miss. The rock made a cracking sound as it careened off the wood just inches below the bird; still, the winged menace didn't budge. It squawked three more times, mocking him; its glaring eyes seemed ablaze with hatred.

Kuja found another stone, this one much rounder than the first. Taking careful aim, he threw the rock. The stone found its mark, winging the wretched creature, but the rock passed through it. The image of the bird wavered for less than a second like ripples on a pond before fading away into nothing. Hope's mouth hung open and palpitations fluttered in her chest.

Mary gasped, "What the heck was that?"

"A dark spirit! The *Iwanci*—it knows you're here!" Kuja said.

"Let's get outta here!" Hope said.

She followed Kuja and Mary down the path that led them back to the brook. Hope felt eyes upon her; she scanned the treetops searching for any sign that something was amiss. Twigs snapped behind her and she jumped at every sound. Her mind raced and her eyes darted back and forth, trying to look everywhere at once. Her trembling hands felt clammy and her legs ached with every step. Her heartbeat returned to normal only after she reached the safety of the Shuar village.

CHAPTER FIVE

S everal days had passed since Hope's scare in the rainforest. She didn't go near the woods, trying her best to put the thoughts of, "The Tree," and that horrible bird-like thing out of her mind, but she couldn't. The images were always there; she thought about them constantly, it had become an obsession. It seemed like the tree reached out to her, beckoning her, calling her into the forest. With each passing day, the feeling got stronger. It pulled at her inner fiber, crying out for her return.

Hope decided that delving into her work would be the best way to eradicate those thoughts. She had to pull herself together because in just two short days, the youth group would be giving a performance for the Shuar children and she knew both Brenda and Tim were depending on her.

It was just a skit, but to Hope it felt like a Broadway production. She'd waited for this opportunity since Christmas. Everyone agreed it seemed like a great way to get their Christian message out to the people of the rainforest.

As Tim put it, "The best way to introduce Christ to the Shuar children would be to visually tell them a biblical story, not bore them with stuffy sermons." And with almost as much fanfare as Mary giving birth in the manger, the idea for the Nativity Skit was born.

Brenda seemed equally enthralled with the idea, saying, "Let's begin at the beginning! This is the perfect place to start teaching about Jesus."

They allowed Peter to direct the Nativity Skit for the church before Christmas and he had done an okay job. This time Hope would be the director. She and Peter were the oldest and Brenda thought it only fair to give Hope equal billing. Bill and Tim agreed, making the decision unanimous.

Because it was the same skit that the youth group had put on for the congregation at Christmas, almost everyone knew their parts. For this reason, Hope felt that a full dress rehearsal wasn't necessary; a few dry readings sitting around the campfire would suffice. If there had been more time, Hope would have preferred to put on The Passion Play, but that would have required a lot more work.

After several successful readings, Hope was confident that each of the cast members knew their part. It was already past 11:00 and Hope felt exhausted and ready for bed.

"Okay, good work, that's enough for tonight," Hope said.

"Do you think we're ready?" Luke asked.

"Keep reading over your lines, remember practice makes perfect."

"My part's a piece of cake; you should've given me something a little more challenging," Ryan said.

"Your role might be small but it's important. Okay, goodnight everybody." Hope and Mary got up and started their short walk back to their hut. Hope was thankful that she'd been able to dismiss Ryan without incident.

"I'm really wiped," Mary said.

Hope was about to respond when an image of a gold cross flashed into her mind. It lasted for just a second but the details were astonishing. The handcrafted gold, inlaid with emeralds and rubies, glittered for just a second before it wavered and transformed into a larger red cross made of cloth, sewn against a black background. It appeared to be an article of clothing; Hope saw the form of a man's chest.

"Hope, Hope! Are you listening to me?" Mary shouted, grabbing hold of Hope's arm.

Mary's touch brought Hope back, making the image disappear.

"I'm sorry, I must've been daydreaming," Hope said.

After entering the hut, Hope lit a kerosene lamp. In her peripheral vision she saw fuzzy shapes scampering into the corner. Both corners appeared to be empty when she approached with the lamp.

"What are ya doing?" Mary asked.

"I thought I saw something running into the corners."

"What kind of thing? Was it a rodent? I hate mice; if it's a mouse I'm outta here!"

"No, it didn't look like that. I just saw quick movement heading for the corner. It happened so quickly, it's hard to describe. They were wavy, like when you stand up fast and see stars, but yet different. Whatever they were they shot into the corner."

"They? Was there more than one?"

"Could've been, I'm not sure."

Mary walked toward the back of the hut and crouched down. "I don't see anything; there's no burrowing and no holes in the walls. The baked mud is flush with the ground; an earth worm would have a hard time squirming underneath."

"I know, it must've been my imagination, but it seemed very real."

"Let's try to get some sleep. If it happens again, just give me a shake."

Mary changed into her pajamas. Hope, because of the humidity, preferred to sleep in just her underwear and sports bra.

They used a canteen and shared a small basin to brush their teeth. It seemed like Mary was always brushing her teeth. Hope found her friend's meticulous dental hygiene quite annoying at first, but adjusted her attitude once she realized Mary's braces required frequent care. When both girls were done, Mary carried the basin outside to empty it.

Stretching out on her bed, Hope allowed her fingertips to run gently across her chest and neck. Her fingers found her cross; she'd forgotten to take it off and now felt too lethargic to do so.

Mary returned, accompanied by a large fly that somehow eluded the mosquito netting. The black, ugly thing, as big as a moth, whizzed past several times. Hope didn't have the energy to get up and swat at it. "Mary, kill that thing, would ya?"

"I hate flies, they're filthy and disgusting; I'm not going near it."

"You're the one who let it in."

"If I let a jaguar in, I wouldn't go after that either."

"Okay, maybe the friggin' thing will settle down somewhere and I'll take care of him in the morning," Hope said.

"Night, Hope." Mary got into bed and blew out the lamp.

Hope's plan for the fly was nothing more than wishful thinking. Moments later, she heard a loud buzzing around her head. She opened her eyes to find herself face to face with the insect. It had landed in the middle of her cross; its tiny green eyes stared up at her. Black hairs protruded from its back and legs. Two translucent wings lay motionless, poised for flight. She swatted at it with an open hand, but only succeeded in leaving a red handprint on her chest. The pest became airborne in an instant, buzzing in circles around the hut several times before landing once again on the cross, this time near the bottom. Hope repeated her attempt to swat her tiny tormentor, to no avail. The fly jettisoned into the air even faster than before, only to return seconds later, landing near the top of the cross. The ritual repeated two more times. The fly landed on each arm of the cross; she missed it again and again. Hope's chest hurt and her hand felt like it was on fire. *Tired or not, I'm going to kill that S.O.B. if it's the last thing I do!*

Getting out of bed, Hope relit the kerosene lamp, turning the flame up as high as it would go; bright light engulfed the entire hut. She spotted the black menace resting on the wall high above Mary's bed. She was now even more determined to kill it. Hope found a fashion magazine in her bag and rolled it up.

"Eww, don't kill that thing and let it fall on my head," Mary said.

"It won't; I'll smash it against the wall and use the magazine to scrape it up."

With weapon in hand, she slowly approached the repulsive bug. Taking careful aim, she swatted the insect with all of her might, this time she didn't miss. Hope pulled back the magazine from the wall, but the fly showed no physical sign of damage. It wavered for half of a second; its body rippled like mercury. The black image became shapeless, zipped into a corner, and disappeared. Hope's knuckles turned white and all the blood drained from her face.

"Did you get it?" Mary asked.

Hope didn't answer, her right hand burned as if held to a flame. Tears welled in her eyes. She gazed at her palm and saw a red gel-like substance smeared across the skin. It looked very similar to the red sap that oozed from the tree in the forest. *That thing must've left this crap on the cross! That's why it's on my hand!*

Grabbing her canteen, she raced outside the hut and doused her hand in water, emptying the container. The red ooze washed away, leaving angry, red blisters in its place. Hope's suspicions proved correct; she found the same gooey substance smeared on both her cross and bra. After lifting the cross from her neck, she opened the door and tossed it outside the hut. She removed her bra; the gel had dissolved the fabric in several spots, but fortunately, the acid-like substance had not yet bitten into her breasts. Opening the door, she removed her bra and flung it away from the grass structure onto the ground. Reentering the hut, she grabbed Mary's canteen and ran outside. She found her damaged cross lying in the dirt. Opening the canteen, she drenched it in water, flushing away the fly's red excretions. The paint stripped away in places as if someone holding an eyedropper had purposely dripped turpentine across the wooden surface.

She knelt in the dirt as her topless form cast a moonlit shadow over the desecrated cross. Gazing toward the heavens, she folded her hands and prayed to the Lord. "Oh, Father in heaven, please save us!"

Mary appeared at the door. "Hope, what's the matter?"

"Oh, Mary!" she cried.

A reservoir streamed down her face. Hope ran to her friend, latching onto her like some skinned-kneed school girl, sobbing in Mary's arms.

CHAPTER SIX

Hope walked toward the site of the upcoming performance; it was still a good four hours before show time. Everything needed to be perfect despite the fact she had a splitting headache and that walking exacerbated the cramps in her stomach. That time of the month had once again arrived and as usual, it came at the least opportune moment.

As she neared the site, Hope heard the sound of something hard striking wood. The intense pounding made her head throb. She turned the corner to see Tim balanced precariously up on a ladder. Swinging a large sledgehammer, he smacked the top of a large wooden cross, driving the seven foot post deeper into the ground with every swing.

Ryan stood at the foot of the handmade ladder, holding it steady against the thatched roof of the newly constructed open-air church.

Giving the final whacks to the top of the cross, Tim tossed the sledgehammer to the ground; it landed with a thud. He climbed off the ladder and used his forearm to wipe sweat from his brow. "Well, how's it look?"

Hope frowned, "Fine, if you like obstructed views of the play."

Tim draped a white linen cloth over the cross and said, "The final touch."

"Doesn't the white cloth seem a little unorthodox to you? This is a Nativity play; why white linen? The cloth should be purple and only used during Lent."

"Nonsense, white linen is a symbol of rebirth and purity. Isn't that what the Nativity skit is all about? On the contrary, I think that white linen is *very* appropriate."

Hope knew better, but what did she have to gain by arguing with Tim? With the exception of the cross, the skit was her baby and she would be the one to make the final decisions.

Ryan dusted off his hands, smacking them together several times. "You know, I really think that I should be the one to play Joseph."

Oh jeez here it comes! Hope couldn't believe it. *In the eleventh hour Ryan is going to pull this crap!* "You already played Joseph during the Christmas production."

"And did a fine job of it too, I must say. That's why I feel that the role has been miscast. Let Peter play one of the Three Wise Men; he knows the lines. Allow me to give an encore performance."

Egos! I've got to deal with them even out here in the jungle! I wonder if Spielberg has to put up with this crap?

Tim picked up the sledgehammer. "I'll leave you kids to sort out the play; I'm heading back to take a shower." Waving goodbye, he strolled toward the huts.

Hope had lost her patience, her cramps felt worse; and her head felt like it would split in half. This was the last thing she needed. Her blood simmered as she watched Tim stroll out of ear shot. Despite wanting to strangle Ryan on the spot, she took a deep breath, determined to stay calm and handle this delicate situation like a lady.

"I'm sorry, Ryan, but if you wanted to audition for the role of Joseph you should've made your intentions known well before this." Her trial balloon rose into the air, lifted only by her smile, but his anger exploded in quick bursts all around her, never giving her words much loft.

"It's been eating away at me for days. I'm not a one line actor! You know I'm fucking better than that and I don't care if Peter is your boyfriend. For once, make a decision based on talent. I'm sick of your blatant nepotism; just make the goddamn change!"

"First of all, Peter is not my boyfriend."

"Could've fooled me!"

"Look, don't even go there and don't tell me what to do!"

"It's obvious that somebody has to!"

"I don't owe you any explanations, but I'll give you one just the same. Peter's nineteen; this is his last year. You know how some people at church treat him; he's never played the lead in anything."

"So?"

"So despite your obvious talent, I really want Peter to play Joseph. There will be other plays and other leads; you'll get your opportunities."

"Don't patronize me! And don't give me that shit about Peter; he got to direct the fucking play over Christmas."

"I can't talk to you. Look, I've got to go!" Hope pressed her hands against her temples and turned to leave.

Ryan grabbed her arm, "Don't dismiss me!"

With venom in her eyes, Hope grabbed hold of his shirt and yanked his face toward her.

"You've got to be friggin' kidding me, right! Never put your grimy hands on me again. Got it!"

Ryan whimpered, but didn't say another word. Hope released his shirt, giving him a final shove for emphasis. If he had a tail, it would've been situated squarely between his legs as he scampered off toward the huts.

After Ryan left, she felt a tinge of guilt. If her head wasn't throbbing, maybe she wouldn't have been so aggressive. And let's remember he was the one who'd touched her first. He had pushed her buttons and she'd lost control. More than anything, she had disappointed herself. *A true director never would've stooped to his level.*

Hope just prayed that he'd show up and play his assigned role. She took solace in the fact that Ryan was a thespian whore who craved the spotlight more than a junkie craves heroin. *He would totally Jones if he missed the performance.* Besides he'd have to deal with Tim's wrath; she doubted if he had the stones for that.

Expunging all thoughts of Ryan from her mind, she inspected the set. The church's transformation into a manger looked awesome. Straw, cut from the fields, lay strewn across the ground; a few chickens pecked at kernels of corn dispensed from a hidden feeder. Two small piglets tied to a leash completed the scene, vacuuming up their fair share of tribal leftovers.

She turned her attention to a small trunk located behind the church. It housed the gently used Nativity costumes left over from Peter's Christmas skit. She pulled out several of the robes, carefully scrutinizing them. Brenda had done a good job packing them up before the trip and they appeared to be in fair condition. She thought about the many pieces of the show that had to come together as one. It all felt so daunting.

Despite what Ryan thought, her casting was par excellence. Mary would play Mary; Peter, as former director, knew all the lines, making him a natural fit to play Joseph. With great reservations, Hope had cast Ryan, Matthew, and Jason as the Three Wise Men. She knew full well that Ryan would bitch and the other boys' lack of experience would make their roles a tremendous stretch. Despite these obstacles, Hope felt that she could whip them into shape.

Not knowing what to do with Luke, she wrote him into the script as the Little Drummer Boy. The narration would fall squarely on Hope's shoulders with Kuja acting as translator.

The crème de la crème came when Yeki's youngest wife, Aitiak, gave Hope permission to cast their three-month-old son as the baby Jesus, but only after Kuja assured them it would be all right.

Kuja's friend Moxo came through like a champ, the tall, muscular eighteen-year-old appeared less than an hour before show time with a live donkey in tow and an authentic Shuar drum hanging from his neck. Moxo looked strong and powerful as he stood head and shoulders above the rest of the tribesmen; despite his physique, he was kind and gentle, and always willing to help out. Removing the drum from his person, he handed it to a thankful Luke.

Hope, overwhelmed by his generosity, rewarded her newfound Christian knight with the hand-painted wooden cross she'd purchased at the Indian market; the same one damaged by the fly two nights earlier.

Melting Moxo with a smile, she removed the cross and ceremoniously draped it over his head. Hope adjusted the crucifix, centering it on his barrel chest, concluding the spectacle with an exaggerated kiss on his cheek. She gave this performance in plain view of both Peter and Kuja.

Mary laughed when both men stormed off in a huff, "Look what you've gone and done now."

It was just fifteen minutes before show time. Hope knew in her heart of hearts that neither Peter nor Kuja would disappoint her. How could they? They both knew how seriously she took her responsibility. Her womanly instincts proved correct; as if on cue, both boys reluctantly reappeared a few minutes later.

Peter was the last to change into his costume. Hope helped Mary gently tie a large pillow around her midsection, making it easily removable before act two. Everybody else was dressed and ready to go.

The Shuar children began to trickle in as darkness approached. Hope, Kuja, and Moxo distributed a white T-shirt to every child. A colorful, airbrushed scene depicting Jesus nailed to the cross graced the front of the white cotton shirts. The reverse side boldly displayed the phrase, *Got Jesus?* in large block lettering.

Hope was sure that the kids couldn't care less about the Christian message printed on the shirts, just as long as they got a free one. If Tim and Brenda wanted to delude themselves into thinking they were spreading the word with the T-shirts, so be it. Hope didn't care; let them remain delusional. Regardless of the message, this was the bait that brought the kids to the show. Each child spread his or her llama-haired blanket out in front of the manger. The blankets were colorful and tightly woven, providing an adequate barrier from the dirt.

Moxo had acquired five kerosene torches from friends in the modern section. On Hope's instruction, he strategically pushed the bamboo poles into the ground around the set and lit each torch with a burning twig extracted from a nearby bonfire. The fire and the five flickering torches and a flashlight, provided the only theatrical lighting, now that the sun had dipped below the trees.

The time had come, it was now show time. Hope stood before forty-seven children; most of them had come from the modern section, having heard about the show and free T-shirts from friends and relatives in the traditional village. Teja, Keto, and the rest of the Elders stood just beyond the sea of white shirts, watching from afar. Most of the tribesmen and women from the traditional village circled in around them. Carak even made an appearance, standing behind the rest.

Bill Drake, reeking of liquor, passed Hope. He wobbled as he walked, snapping pictures, presumably to print in the church bulletin to show the congregation what a fine job they had all done, thanks to his outstanding leadership, of course. Hope followed him with her eyes as he pushed through the crowd and stopped to chat with a curvaceous, doe-eyed Shuar girl with silky black hair who couldn't have been older than fifteen.

At least he's not eyeballing me, Hope thought.

Yeki stood confidently in between his two wives; they looked as proud as any three parents could; watching their kid's first performance. Moxo stood to their left, fingering the pitted cross hanging from his bare chest. All told, there had to be over a hundred Shuar watching the performance.

A decent turnout for opening night, now let's warm up the crowd with a few songs, Hope thought.

Smiling, Hope raised her hands, as a hush fell over the crowd, "Welcome everyone!"

Kuja translated her words into Shuar.

Brenda sat on a blanket up front with her old guitar; she smiled to the crowd and strummed the first cord.

Hope cleared her throat, "Let's begin with a couple of hymns."

She first sang a peppy rendition of "Jesus Loves Me" accompanied by Brenda, followed by the duo's folksy favorite "Kumbaya."

The children repeated her words in English, followed by Kuja's Shuar translation.

Kuja's strong singing voice came as a big surprise.

Tim switched on his powerful flashlight, producing a strong beam of light that illuminated the silver foiled star hanging in the tree. At that moment, Peter pulled the donkey carrying the pillow-pregnant Mary into view. Brenda played classical Spanish guitar for the musical score.

The play went off better than expected. Most of the actors hit their marks, delivering their lines with near perfection; only Ryan stumbled once on his words, but recovered nicely. Hope's narration, accompanied by Kuja's strong translation, ensured all the children understood the play.

Near the end, Hope had the strangest sensation. The Three Wise Men had already presented their gifts to the baby Jesus. Luke had just started the rump-a pum-pums on his drum when it happened.

Hope felt like someone or something was watching her. Not the audience in front of her or Bill Drake's salacious gaze, it was something else, somewhere in the dark behind her. Call it intuition, that feeling of uncertainty and dread she'd felt many times before. Something was staring at the back of her head; she could feel it piercing her skull. She began to sweat and her hands trembled. The air felt heavy in her lungs, making it difficult to breathe. Her body froze, too scared to turn and look, but too scared to run.

The throbbing in her head intensified with each rump-a pum-pum until it reached a crescendo. It felt much closer now. Hope knew she had to turn and face whatever lurked out there in the dark or it would consume her. She quickly turned and scanned the forest but saw nothing. Still she felt its invisible stare; there was something out there.

Kuja grabbed her arm. "What's wrong?"

Hope remained speechless; the air grew heavier, and she began to choke. Everything went black and she collapsed to the ground, but remained semi-conscious, able to hear the commotion around her. Luke stopped his rump-a pum-pums and actors and audience alike rushed to her side.

"Get back, give her some room!" Tim yelled.

Everyone stepped back except for Keto. The tribal shaman produced a small, bamboo tube. Dipping his finger into the tube, he extracted a thick, white paste and smeared it under Hope's nose. Moments later she opened her eyes; the heavy air lifted and the forest presence had disappeared. Once again she could breathe, inhaling the sweet scents of the forest.

CHAPTER SEVEN

A darker than usual morning gray filtered through the mosquito netting on the door, a clear indication of another sunless day. Hope glanced at Mary resting peacefully, watching her chest rise and fall with every rhythmic breath.

She thought about last night's occurrence, having damn near fainted near the end of the play. Tim, Brenda, and Bill called her strange episode a simple panic attack. Hope knew better, but why waste her breath arguing with the imaginary medical practice of Kirby, Bean and Drake? After all, they knew best.

Hope felt the tree beckoning to her again, calling out, and crying for her return. A great sorrow sliced away at her resistance; it came to her like a beacon emanating from the forest. She tried hard to fight those thoughts, to eradicate them from her head, but the force was too strong; she had no choice. This time she would heed its call. The image of the same gold cross flashed through her head and disappeared, leaving in its place a vacuum of great urgency. But what did this thing want with her? What made her its conduit? Did her *gift* make her more receptive than the others, predisposed to premonitions? Was she the weak link in the chain? Hope knew the answers to all these questions and they shook her to the core; still, she had to go.

Hope rose out of bed and threw on some clothes. She glanced over at Mary resting peacefully, envying her, wishing that she too could just lay there, not having to deal with any of this, but Hope knew full well that this burden was hers alone.

Opening the door, she slipped quietly into the predawn mist. Walking toward the forest, Hope heard the familiar sound of the flowing brook; it appeared in the mist about a dozen feet in front of her. She knelt beside the water and submersed her healing hand into the constant flow. The cool water felt soothing; she wanted to stay there forever, soaking her blisters until all of the pain in her life had disappeared.

The tree called to her as if by name, prodding her forward. Refusal was no longer an option; there would be great consequences if she fought it, consequences far greater than the fly or the skit; those had just been warnings. It would keep coming after her and her friends; this much she knew.

Using the brook as her guide, she walked upstream into the forest. The fine mist became a dense fog further reducing her visibility; she marched on, unable to recognize objects even ten feet in front of her. The moisture-laden vapors diminished the fresh scent of the forest and lay heavy in Hope's lungs.

Despite having been to the tree just once, she somehow knew the way. Her feet involuntarily moved her forward through the ever thickening fog, each step bringing her closer to the tree. Visibility reduced to just three arms lengths ahead of her. She was close now, absorbing the negative energy through her pores. Her heart raced, pumping adrenaline through her veins. Hope's steps slowed; her footing unsure as if she was approaching the edge of a cliff, and in a way she was. Hope extended her arm out in front of her, not wanting to come upon the tree unexpectedly. She took one more careful step and it appeared through the fog, less than six feet away. From this distance, the gray tree looked even uglier than before. The red resin excreting from the deep cracks seemed to be far more prevalent than she remembered, giving the appearance of coagulated blood emanating from opened arteries. The sap appeared to be several inches thick in some places, narrowing down to a wafer thin coating in others.

Tilting her head, she stared at the branches; the right twisted limb ascended only a few feet before it disappeared into the thick, gray cloud. From her closer perspective, the left limb seemed to stretch out even farther than before. The black colored sap still hung in a perpetual drip on the underside of the branch, but seemed to have grown larger in size. She still couldn't make sense of it. How did the sap change color so drastically? The dense fog concealed the black, tar-like puddle that Hope knew lay beneath the drip.

A great sadness radiated from the tree; Hope felt it swelling up inside her, causing a single tear to run down her face. Her fear had diminished; she yearned for understanding; she needed to make sense of this sorrow. The tree drew Hope in like a mosquito to a bug zapper. She stepped closer, wanting to touch the trunk, to somehow eradicate the misery that it emanated.

Standing before the tree, she reached out with both hands, placing them firmly on the cold bark. Her sadness intensified; her single tear transformed into a constant flow.

Without forethought, she ran her fingers across the thickest formation of sap; the thin, amber crust felt hard to the touch. Extending two fingers on her right hand, she pierced the blood red coating with her nails, pressing her fingers deep into the sticky, gum-like sap.

An apparition appeared in the middle of the long, straight branch above her head. The small female form seemed almost human; it knelt across the limb, stretching out on all fours. Blue, yellow, and red feathers covered her otherwise naked body, but they didn't seem to be growing from the body, but rather stuck on with tar. In several places, the black goo dripped to the ground from the gaps in between the feathers. The black coating covered the few exposed areas of skin. Cat green eyes peered through a child's feathered face, glaring back at Hope.

Hope unleashed a shrill scream that reverberated throughout the forest as she tried to pull her fingers from the sap, but they were stuck in a knot hole hidden beneath the red goo. She struggled to free herself, but the harder she pulled, the tighter the tree held its grip. The knot hole seemed to constrict around her fingers and the glue-like sap grew thicker and stickier.

The thing smirked menacingly at her from its perch. Panic-induced hysteria shook her body; she felt like a fly stuck to flypaper, an insect caught in a web. Her racing heart pumped adrenaline through her veins with the force of a high pressure hose. Realizing that she was at its mercy, she screamed again; it was all she could do, knowing full well that nobody would hear her. All of the blood drained from her face and she felt like she might faint, but that thing wouldn't allow it.

The tar and feathers disappeared, revealing a bruised and beaten Indian girl of about thirteen. Dark brown eyes that contained an indescribable sorrow replaced her green orbs. Black and blue marks covered most of her young, thin body. In an instant the bruises disappeared, replaced by burnt skin and scar tissue so thick and wrinkled, it resembled a lava flow. The scalded girl's eyes bulged and her mouth remained open in a silent, continuous scream.

Hope closed her eyes, trying hard to look away, but the scarred image remained scorched into her mind. The image changed into the gold cross that had haunted her for days; it hung on a thick, gold chain around a man's neck. She was close to the object, only inches away, close enough to see hairs on the man's neck and inhale his pungent body odor. The fog had lifted and the cross glittered in the sunlight; the inlaid rubies and emeralds sparkled red and green.

Her perspective changed; she had pulled back from the cross and now looked down at seven men from up in the tree. Physically, her feet remained planted on the ground; her tightly wedged fingers never budged from the red sticky sap, but somehow she peered down from above.

In her mind, she watched a scene unfold through the eyes of the entity, tapping into some sort of residual memory radiating from the tree. Hope felt certain that the girl-like thing wanted her to see it, was forcing her to watch and Hope didn't have the strength or will to fight it. Looking down, she gazed at the seven bearded men marching through the forest. All of the men wore crosses around their necks; several looked like solid gold, while others were inlaid with jewels and pearls. Two crosses were made of silver.

All of the men were oddly dressed; each wore an iron helmet and yellow and black, vertically striped shirts puffed out at the sleeves. A black and burgundy vest covered up most of the shirt. A large, blood red cross woven across a black background covered the right side of the vest. It was the same cloth cross that Hope had envisioned while walking with Mary the night before. The mens' black baggy pants disappeared at the knee, covered by laced, leather boots.

Each man had a long sword sheathed at his waist and many carried small round shields. Some men carried muskets, while others brandished long, iron spears. Two men marched near the front; one proudly waved the old Spanish flag, while the other held a banner displaying a bright red cross contrasted against an all white background, reminding Hope of the Red Cross.

At the very front of the group, two men hacked away at the jungle with large, iron machetes. The rainforest seemed much thicker than she had remembered it being just a few days before. Hope remembered seeing illustrations of men like these in history books; she had even written a report on them. She had no doubt in her mind that these strange looking soldiers were Spanish conquistadors. The man wearing the cross embedded with rubies and emeralds, shouted an order and the other soldiers unloaded their burdens and set up camp. Taking only their spears and muskets, they once again pushed forward with a sense of urgency; it appeared as if they were searching for something or someone.

Why is it showing me this? It was surreal; Hope knew that the last conquistadors trampled through these forests nearly five hundred years ago.

The scene changed and Hope found herself standing among a small tribe of Indians in a clearing deep in the rainforest. Their faces were narrower than the Shuar and their skin color appeared to be a much darker shade of brown; their noses seemed broader, a clear indication of a separate indigenous race.

Could this be the legendary lost tribe that Kuja had described, the Invisible People?

The camp showed no permanent structures, only four small shelters built from leaves and twigs. Hope counted four tribesmen and two women. A thin teenage girl sat on the ground, facing away from Hope at the far end of the clearing.

Blue war paint covered the faces of the bare-chested tribesmen. Bands of colorful feathers adorned their hair, red, blue, and green were the primary colors, with an occasional orange and yellow feather blended in. Beaded necklaces hung from the necks of the two bare-breasted women who wore skirts made from a tanned animal hide. The men wore a thin loin cloth to cover their privates.

Several sharp, wooden spears rested within arm's reach against the surrounding trees. Two iron swords inscribed with Spanish writing near the handles were stuck in the ground near the edge of the clearing. A gold cross lay draped across each sword handle. A pair of iron helmets, identical to the ones worn by the conquistadors, lay on the ground next to the swords.

A small bonfire burned in the center of the clearing. Two blackened heads hung from poles, curing above the fire. Their eyes, noses, and mouths were sewn shut with thick, coarse twine. Burnt stubble was all that remained of what Hope presumed were once full beards. The most elder of the tribesmen danced and chanted around the heads, speaking in an unfamiliar tongue. His headdress seemed fuller and more colorful than the rest; a necklace made from human bones hung from his neck.

A sustained bird-like sound echoed from the forest, coming from a high tree more than 150 yards away. Upon hearing the sound, almost the entire tribe scattered into the forest; even the old shaman vanished in seconds. Hope saw a tribesman slide down the trunk of the tree where the sound had originated; he jumped down the last ten feet and bolted into the forest. He had been the lookout who had sounded the alarm with his bird-like cry.

The clearing was now empty, except for the girl who still sat at the far edge of the clearing with her bare back exposed to Hope. She just sat there, giving no indication of alarm, focusing on the task at hand. Using a rock, she mashed red berries in an earthen bowl, making either war paint or wine. Why didn't the girl react to the warning signal and flee into the forest like all the rest? Hope realized in that moment that the girl was deaf. Unable to hear the warning cry or the sounds of commotion, they'd left her behind. Facing the forest, she hadn't seen the others flee.

Hope heard the sound of machetes hacking their way through the forest, accompanied by the familiar voices of the conquistadors. In a matter of moments, the seven men had made their way into the clearing brandishing spears and muskets.

The girl must have caught a glimpse of them in her peripheral vision, because she suddenly stood and tried to run, but her foot snagged on an exposed tree root and she tripped hard, toppling to the ground, her head slamming into the forest floor. Two of the fastest men were quickly upon her; grabbing the dazed girl by her shoulder blades, they yanked her to her feet. Hope got a good look at the girl for the first time; it was the same bruised and beaten girl that had appeared before her on the tree limb.

"El Capitán Ortiz!" The burliest man said, pointing toward the smoldering flames.

The one called Ortiz became enraged at the sight of the blackened heads of his two men hanging from poles above the fire.

Despite taking four years of Spanish, Hope could only speak simple sentences; fortunately, her comprehension was much better than her speech. She ascertained through the shouting that the two men had been sent out ahead to scout the area and report on the activities of any hostile natives. Now both men lay dead, their blackened faces sewn shut by the very same people they came to observe. Somebody had to pay for this, and that somebody would be the girl. The two men held the struggling girl firmly in their grasp. Hope saw fear swell in her big brown eyes.

Ortiz ordered them to bind the girl's hands and drag her back to camp. They tied the girls hands so tight, her fingers turned purple as they yanked on the rope, pulling the scared child behind them. Hope felt the leather twine cutting into her own wrists with every jerk of the rope. The agonizing pain continued until the Spaniards reached their camp.

The six soldiers salaciously awaited the captain's command; when he gave the order, they attacked the young girl, passing her around like a Barcelona whore; the grunting men repeatedly raped her again and again. Only the captain refused to participate, acting as if he were somehow above it all.

The girl opened her mouth and screamed a silent scream, proving that she was not just deaf, but also mute. Hope felt the girl's physical pain, that thing in the tree forced her to feel it. She felt men inside of her, stretching and ripping her insides. Hope tried to cry out, but her screams also fell silent. One soldier bit into the girl's left breast and Hope felt the pain shoot through her own nipple.

This sexual assault continued for several hours; when they were finished they savagely beat and kicked the girl, tying her to a tree, keeping her alive for future use.

On the captain's orders, the six men grabbed their muskets and went hunting for food in the forest. Only the captain remained behind, cursing and spitting on the girl each time he passed.

Hope heard the sound of many loud gunshots echoing through the trees and after a short while, the men returned carrying several squirrels, a monkey, and more than a dozen macaws. Each man plucked as many birds as he could eat, leaving piles of blue, red and yellow feathers on the ground next to him.

In the center of the clearing, they built a small fire. Impaling the squirrels, monkey, and featherless birds onto the ends of long sticks, they roasted their game over the fire. Hope smelled the strong aroma of cooking meat.

The men laughed and joked as they ate and drank, bragging about their virility with the young girl. Deprived of food and water, the girl's condition deteriorated further. Hope's throat felt parched and hunger pangs grew in her own stomach.

The next morning, only two men raped the girl. Bruised and bloodied, she was far less attractive to look at than she had been the day before.

Afterwards, those same men laughed amongst themselves, grabbed an iron pot, and ventured into the forest. Hope's eyes were able to follow the men as if she were walking just a few steps behind them. They came upon a spot on the ground where black tar bubbled to the surface, having stumbled upon the tar pit the day before while hunting. Dunking the kettle in the gooey muck, they filled the pot with tar and took turns carrying it back to camp. Upon reaching the clearing, they presented the kettle to the captain. One of the men pointed to the piles of colorful feathers lying on the ground. An evil smirk appeared on the captain's lips. Moments later, the two men attached the kettle to its chains and began boiling the tar above the fire.

Hope began to panic; she knew what was coming. She kept telling herself that these were nothing more than shadows of events long past; still, she felt powerless to stop her rising alarm. Hope watched in disbelief as the tar came to a hard boil.

On the captain's order, they untied the bloody, disheveled girl from the tree. Using the same rope, they attached a strand to each wrist. Two men pulled on the ropes, stretching out her arms so as not to splash any of the hot tar on themselves.

The same men who found the tar inserted a pole through the handles of the kettle and lifted it from the fire. Taking deliberate steps, they approached the girl with the black, boiling liquid. With outstretched arms, they lifted the kettle high above the girl's head. The other soldiers scooped up armfuls of feathers in wicked anticipation. The captain himself tied the rope through the loop on the kettle; he alone would revenge the slaughter of his two scouts. The girl's fearful eyes bulged from their sockets; her bruised body trembled like a cowering dog, and her mouth remained open in a silent scream.

Without warning, the captain yanked on the rope, covering the girl with the scalding, black liquid. Her convulsing body twitched, and the whites of her eyes rolled upward in their sockets. Laughing soldiers threw fistfuls of colorful feathers at the hot tar as if they were throwing confetti at a party.

Searing pain shot through Hope's body, scalding every inch of her skin. It was the most intense pain she'd ever felt; she almost passed out, but that thing still wouldn't allow it, forcing her to feel the same agony that it had endured all those years before. Somehow through the pain, Hope opened her eyes. She saw the soldiers sitting on the ground, forming a large circle. They were laughing and drinking, passing several opened bottles of rum between them. In the center of the circle stood a man with a whip; he forced the tarred and feathered child to stagger around the circle, flapping her arms like a bird. If she showed any signs of slowing, he'd whip her, causing blue feathers to fly into the air. Every time he cracked his whip, the drunken men would roar with laughter. After several minutes of torture, she collapsed from pain and exhaustion. He kicked and whipped the feathered girl as she lay on the ground, cursing at her to stand. Nearing death, she could move no more.

In front of the captain stood a tall, ugly tree; he ordered that they hang the girl from the middle of its long, extended branch to make an example of her. He said it would serve as a warning to the rest of the murderous tribe.

They tied a rope around her thin neck and dragged her to the foot of the tree. One of the men coiled the end of the rope and threw it over the limb. The captain slowly pulled on the rope, hoisting the girl off the ground; her legs twitched as she slowly rose toward the branch, a clear indication that she was still alive.

Hope began to choke. The girl's eyes opened; they were nothing more than slits, but Hope could somehow see through those same dying eyes. She panned across the soldiers' excited faces, fixating on the captain's gem-laden cross – the last image she saw before everything faded to black.

Hope lay dazed on the ground; the image of the tarred and feathered girl hanging from the tree jolted her back to her senses. A horrid sound replayed over in her mind; it was the constant drip, drip, drip of large drops of tar falling from the dead girl's fingers and toes, dispersing into the black puddle below.

Opening her eyes, Hope found herself free of the tree, lying on the ground beneath its long branch. The fog had lifted and her face lay just inches away from the black puddle. She felt thankful that the Iwanci had vanished and the tree had released its grip.

Staring up at the branch, she observed the drop of black sap still hanging on the underside of the limb; it seemed to have grown still larger in size. Without warning, it dripped like black molasses and splattered onto the solid puddle beside her. The impeccable timing of the falling sap seemed far more than a simple coincidence; it was the exclamation point of the entire event. Gasping, with widened eyes, she scampered backwards on all fours away from the tree and its black resin puddle.

The sudden movement inflamed her already sore fingers; leaves and twigs stuck to the red sap that still covered them.

The intense pain that she'd endured had diminished; only a slight sting remained around her wrists and neck. Hope saw red rope burns encircling her wrists and knew from her painful touch that a similar line existed around her neck; it was the only physical proof that remained of her encounter, and she took some solace in the knowledge that she wasn't delusional.

Jumping to her feet, she ran as fast as she could away from the tree. Rays of sunlight filtered through the forest as she ran; their straight angles told her that it was almost noon.

She had to find her way back and warn Tim, Brenda, and the others. The group had to leave at once, if they had any chance at all of escaping the Iwanci's wrath. It had kept her alive, but Hope was unsure why. Maybe it was a final warning, her last chance. She needed to make them all understand that they had to leave; it was as simple as that.

The Iwanci hungered for revenge, but for reasons unknown, it had given Hope the chance it hadn't received in life. Still, it watched her. Running through the forest, she felt its venomous stare raining down upon her from the tree tops. Hope scanned the green canopy above her, searching for it. She knew it was there; she could just feel it. Her eyes fixated on a black spot on a high tree branch off to her right more than forty yards away.

A black Nunbird stared back at her through the forest, its hateful eyes spying on her from its high perch. Only after being discovered, did it squawk three times.

Hope's frantic heart pounded harder as she increased her speed; she cried out for joy when the village came into view and she didn't stop running until she'd reached the huts. She gasped a sigh of relief; this time she'd made it, and there would be no second chances.

Mary stepped out of the hut. "Tim and Brenda are looking all over for you; they missed you at breakfast. Where'd you go?"

With tears cascading down her face, she hugged Mary. "I've got to find them; we've got to tell the others and get the hell out of here!"

Mary looked confused. "Why? What's going on?"

"I'll explain later, but right now I've got to find Brenda and Tim." Hope ran through the village in search of the two leaders. She found them interrogating Peter and Kuja up on the knoll next to the canoe project. She caught snippets of the conversation as she approached.

"So when did you see her last?" Tim asked the boys. Brenda crossed her arms, giving a stern look.

Peter pointed at Hope. "I see her right now!"

"Hope! Where the hell have you been?" Tim shouted.

"We were worried sick about you," Brenda added.

Nearing hysterics, Hope sobbed and tears dripped off her chin. The sight of Tim and Brenda released a torrent of emotions; it all came rushing back to her with great fervor and intensity. "We have to leave! Tell the others to grab their things; we must go!"

"Hope, calm down, take it easy, what's the matter?" Tim asked.

"It was horrible. I was in the forest and this thing came after me. It held me captive and forced me to watch horrible images from the past! It tortured me and I nearly died! We must leave right now or it will kill us all!"

Tim gave Brenda a disbelieving glare. His look spoke volumes; it was clear to Hope that neither leader believed her.

"Hope, try to relax; you shouldn't have wandered into the forest by yourself. You could've gotten hurt or lost, and now you come up with this fantastic story," Brenda said.

"But I *was* hurt and this is no story; you have to believe me. It hates outsiders, especially Christians; if you wear the cross you might as well paint a target on your chest!"

"Hope! That will be enough! I don't know what's gotten into you, but I can't stand idly by and listen to you make a mockery of Christ and our religion," Brenda said.

Tim touched Brenda's shoulder. "Let me handle this. Hope, calm down, everything is okay now. Take deep breaths and try to relax."

"Nobody believes me, but it's all true!"

"We're not saying that we don't believe you. I'm sure that something spooked you in the forest and believe me, there are a lot of spooky things lurking out there. Snakes, jaguars, even wild boars."

"But it wasn't any of those; it was an Iwanci. Kuja told me and Mary about it."

Tim looked at Kuja. "Iwanci?"

"Shuar folklore tells of dark spirits that lurk in the forest who seek revenge for past injustices bestowed upon them in life. They can appear as dangerous animals and can even make trees fall on you," Kuja said.

Tim could barely contain his smirk. "Hope, let's take this one step at a time and think about this logically. It was probably one of a hundred animals that spooked you. I don't know what possessed you to waltz into the rainforest alone, but in doing so you left yourself vulnerable to another major panic attack. The creepy sounds of the forest took a toll on your psyche; am I right so far?"

Hope stared at Tim without agreeing or disagreeing.

"And after listening to Kuja's story, your mind began to play tricks on you. The creepy environment seemed inexplicable to you, almost supernatural. The combined effect of your isolation, unfamiliar surroundings, and your recent exposure to Kuja's scary story became the basis for your fears, the perfect recipe for extreme panic, am I right?"

"No, this was real!"

"Okay, okay, if you were held captive, hurt, and tortured, then where are your cuts and bruises, how come you don't have any marks, and how did you get away?"

Hope held her arms out in front of her. "Look at my wrists and neck, isn't this proof enough?"

Brenda grabbed hold of Hope's hands and inspected her wrists. "I don't see anything."

Hope no longer felt the stinging around her neck. She gazed at her wrists; the red circles of pain had vanished.

CHAPTER EIGHT

K uja worked outside his hut making final preparations for the hunt; he ran his finger across the sharp metal blade that he'd honed the day before. Satisfied with the sharpness, he inserted the knife into its leather sheath and attached it to his braided leather belt.

Hunting boar wasn't for the meek; it required bravery and a quiver containing several sharp-tipped throwing spears. Only a fool would venture into the jungle to pursue the tusked beasts without them, and Kuja was no fool. He had made the finest set of spears in the village and his dark eyes gleamed with pride whenever he held one.

As much as he enjoyed the time spent with Hope and Mary, hunting was his true passion. The thrill of tracking prey and making a clean kill made him feel so alive. He always looked forward to his time spent in the forest and today would be no exception. He grabbed a quiver resting against a tree. Sliced bamboo strips glued together with resin made up its circular frame; he'd pulled the head of a small anteater over the bamboo. Sealing one end with leather twine, he had stitched the mouth closed, sewing up its long, whiskered snout.

Six feathered throwing spears protruded from the open end of the anteater. Kuja removed each shaft one by one to inspect them. Holding each up against the sky, he brought the blunt ends to his eye, looking down the three-foot shafts as if to take aim at a distant cloud.

All of the shafts needed to be perfect and four of them were. Hand carved from the hardest trees in the forest, each spear boasted colorful blue and yellow macaw feathers to ensure swift, predictable flights. The whittled wooden points were extremely sharp, capable of penetrating through the coarse bristles of even the toughest boar.

He discarded the remaining two spears; the first one had feathers shearing off the shaft, repairable with beeswax and resin after the hunt, but not before. The second spear showed a slight curvature, making it incapable of straight flight. Kuja's weapons needed to be flawless; he would accept nothing less. He snapped the bowed shaft over his knee, tossing the two pieces aside. Placing the four good spears into his quiver, he swung it across his back and marched off to find his fellow tribesmen.

Ipiak, Yeki, and Moxo were already waiting for him at the edge of the forest. All of the men were bare-chested, himself included. Yeki wore a beaded necklace given to him by the younger of his two wives; it was supposed to bring him good fortune and a fruitful hunt. Moxo proudly wore the wooden cross that Hope had given him. Ipiak and Kuja both wore similar headbands also made from colorful macaw feathers. Orange, yellow, and white plumage adorned Ipiak's band, while Kuja's boasted bright blue and red feathers. The headbands indicated that Ipiak and Kuja were more experienced hunters then Yeki and Moxo and would lead the hunt.

Kuja greeted his friends. Ipiak seemed annoyed by Kuja's late arrival. Appearing anxious to get started, he muttered an inaudible greeting under his breath and waved the group forward. Without banter, the four tribesmen disappeared into the rainforest.

Yeki carried a blowgun and a much shorter quiver that contained several small darts and a thumb-sized bamboo tube filled with curare, the ends sealed with beeswax. Moxo, the youngest and strongest was the least experienced of the four, he carried a burlap sack to carry any small game that they might happen upon along the way.

They had walked for less than half a mile when Yeki spotted a small tree monkey high on a branch roughly seventy feet away. He slowly removed his quiver so as not to startle the animal. Selecting a dart, he pushed the point through the wax, dipping the tip into the bamboo tube of curare before inserting it into the blowgun. Extending his arm, he raised the gun, taking careful aim. He took a deep breath, placing his lips against the mouthpiece. With a quick exhale, he expelled the air from his lungs. The dart shot through the air, hitting the monkey in the chest. The fast acting poison did its job. Moments later, the animal stopped breathing and tumbled from the tree. Moxo ran over to the dead creature and placed it into the sack. Within the hour a squirrel, three macaws, and a toucan all met similar fates and the sack was soon laden with dead animals. A few minutes later, Kuja spotted the first signs of boar; a fresh pile of dung lay on the path in front of them.

Kuja sniffed the air; he could smell the beasts hidden in the brush. The less experienced hunters, Moxo and Yeki, circled around to flush out the wild hogs, while Kuja and Ipiak lay in wait, gripping their sharp, pointed spears. Loud squeals echoed throughout the forest as Moxo and Yeki chased three boars from the brush. Ipiak and Kuja focused on the largest of the brown-haired animals and threw their pointed projectiles; both spears found their mark. The wounded boar squealed in pain, snorting several times before collapsing at their feet. The other tusked beasts scurried unscathed into the brush. Moxo and Yeki closed in from behind, stabbing the squealing pig several more times until it lay dead.

"This will feed our people for two days!" Ipiak said, gleaming with pride.

"The animal is heavy; we must find strong poles," Kuja said, eyeing a thick sapling.

Moxo wiped the blood from his spear with a leaf. "Yeki and I will carry the beast first, then we will—ahhh!"

A tusked boar raced from the brush, shearing off Moxo's right calf muscle. He tumbled to the ground, pressing his now bloody fingers against the gaping wound, screaming in pain. The beast scurried away before Kuja had a chance to throw his spear. It was nothing more than a brown blur as it disappeared under the thick brush.

Two more animals hit Ipiak and Kuja from behind, knocking them both to the ground, just as another boar's sharp tusk pierced Moxo's stomach. The impact sent a splatter of blood into the air. Yeki stabbed at the bushes in all directions in a frantic attempt to fend off the beasts. He failed to draw blood, but it gave Kuja and Ipiak the precious seconds needed to jump to their feet. Neither one of them appeared to be seriously injured; Ipiak bled from a growing circle on his rump, while blood oozed from a thick, razor-like cut across Kuja's thigh.

The beasts attacked again; frenzied boars darted out from the brush in every direction. There seemed to be dozens of them, and they came from everywhere and nowhere, working in tandem as if controlled by a single entity. Kuja's fast reflexes enabled him to side-step two of the charging beasts and stab two others as they passed. Two more tusks penetrated Moxo's upper thigh and back; his screams drowned by the squeals of wounded and dying pigs. The three men stood amongst the carnage, pig blood mixed with their own as they fought together in a tight triangle back to back to back, stabbing and slashing in a flurry at the passing blurs.

"There's too many of them; we have to run," Ipiak said, gasping for breath.

"Over there, let's try to make it to that boulder," Kuja said.

The three men broke formation and bolted toward a large boulder that rose more than five feet off the forest floor. Kuja's heart raced and adrenaline pumped through his veins; never before had a beast forced him to run for his life like a disgraced coward.

The squealing beasts were almost upon him; he felt boar breath on the back of his legs; spastic snorts sprayed slime across his calves. Still several yards from the boulder, he realized that he wasn't going to make it. Coiling his legs, he dove frantically for the rock; his elbows and knees scraped hard against the unforgiving stone. Ipiak grimaced as his body slammed against the rock, landing much harder than Kuja. Yeki's leap fell short, forcing him to cling like a monkey to the side of the formation. Kuja spun around in time to see a tusk penetrate the arch of Yeki's foot; his screams were deafening. Ipiak hoisted Yeki higher onto the boulder out of the animal's reach, just as Kuja stabbed down with his spear, piercing the boar's back. The snorting beast collapsed in a heap. Sensing slaughter, the remaining five boars scurried away into the brush.

Twenty yards away, Moxo rolled and twisted in a pool of his own blood. Kuja saw the fear swell in his friend's eyes. Like a true warrior, Moxo bit his bottom lip, too proud to cry out for help.

All of the wild hogs had disappeared. Only dead animals lay strewn around the path.

Kuja slid forward on the boulder. "I have to help Moxo!"

Ipiak held him back, "No! They're using him as bait; they're lurking in the brush lying in wait."

"I don't care; I just can't leave him out there!" Kuja said.

Yeki grimaced as he applied pressure to his bleeding foot. "We must do something! We can't stay up here forever!"

Ipiak sighed, "Okay, if we go, we go together."

"No, just me and you, Yeki can barely walk. He can't fight or run," Kuja said.

"No, but I can still throw. I will fend off the beasts from here."

An enormous black boar appeared down the path more than thirty yards beyond Moxo. It was the biggest boar that Kuja had ever seen, a true monster; its body weight easily eclipsed the six hundred pound legend that Kuja's grandfather had killed more than sixteen years earlier. A pair of tusks curved upwards for more than two feet, ending in needle sharp points. His thick, bristled hair resembled black porcupine quills; its large, scornful eyes boiled with hatred, piercing deep into Kuja, making his whole body sweat and shudder.

The burly beast snorted three loud times, frothing at the mouth, daring them to come off the rock. Its pungent odor made the surrounding air dank and heavy, and very hard to breathe. Without warning, it charged down the path like an angry black bull; hooves clacked against the path; its strong, muscular legs built speed with every stride. It slammed into Moxo full force; the tusks penetrated deep into his stomach and reemerged out of his back. Moxo moaned clinging to life as the beast raised his head, lifting his impaled body more than three feet off the ground.

Kuja threw his best spear at the beast; its flight seemed true, but it flew high over the animal. The beast whipped his head back and forth and Moxo flew free of his tusks, landing hard on the ground. The dark boar pounced on him, piercing his chest.

A tusk hooked his cross, ripping it from his neck. The wild hog mercilessly gored his mangled body again and again. Bloody tusks stabbed everywhere, tearing out slimy intestines like gray sausage links from his open abdomen. The boar again tossed Moxo several feet into the air.

All three tribesmen threw a volley of spears at the beast. Kuja was sure that his spears would penetrate into the animal; his throws were strong and straight, as were Ipiak's and Yeki's. Each spear missed its target; some flew high or low, while others veered off at the last second to the right or left. They kept throwing until their quivers were empty. It was inexplicable; somehow they had all missed the biggest living target that ever stood before them.

The beast finished its vicious attack as Moxo gasped his last breath and his mauled, blood-soaked body lay motionless. The beast stood triumphantly over Moxo eating his entrails, as blood dripped from his red tusks and snout. Raising his head, the beast stared up at Kuja. For the briefest of seconds, through the bloody froth, the animal seemed to sneer. Had Kuja really seen it? It had happened so fast he wasn't sure, but now wasn't the time for questions.

The beast turned and ran down the path the same direction from which it had first appeared, crashing through the forest, snapping off branches in its wake.

Kuja watched the image of the boar waver in the distance; it rippled similar to the bird he'd seen a few days before. And like the bird, it disappeared before his eyes. It didn't get smaller as it faded into the distance. It didn't make a sharp turn and bolt behind a tree. The image of the beast wavered and rippled, then just disappeared. The heavy stench lifted from the air, replaced by the weaker scent of dead boar.

Kuja couldn't figure out why the boars had attacked. It wasn't in their nature to do so; they'd run before they'd fight. And how could he and his fellow hunters have missed such a big target? It was nearly impossible, but somehow they *had* missed and now their friend lay dead. The realization hit him harder than the beast that had slammed into him. Nothing made sense until he saw the black menace disappear; then he knew.

Liquid fear pumped through Kuja's veins, making his body tremble. Kuja tried to regain his bearings as he climbed down from the rock. Ipiak slid down behind him and both men raced to the broken body of their fallen friend. Yeki climbed down carefully and hobbled along behind them.

Kuja saw the look of horror frozen in Moxo's dead eyes. He ran two fingers down his friend's bloody face, closing the bloodshot orbs. Raising his arms, Kuja began chanting the song of the dead.

Ipiak looked dazed; with teary eyes he grabbed hold of Kuja's arm, stopping the song mid-verse. "This makes no sense, how could this be?"

Kuja stared into Ipiak's eyes. "The *Iwanci* has descended upon us. This is the work of the dark one; it hunts the hunters."

"But why attack *us*?" Ipiak asked.

"The outsiders have stirred its rage."

"But why is it us who feels its wrath?" Ipiak asked.

"Maybe it's because we've allowed this," Kuja said.

"But tales of dark spirits and the *Iwanci* are just legends told to our young ones to make them fearful of the forest," Yeki said.

Kuja angrily pointed at their dead friend. "Does this look like a legend to you!"

CHAPTER NINE

K uja and Ipiak cut down two strong saplings to build a makeshift
stretcher, carving them into two straight poles. They laid them
out about two feet apart parallel to one another, leaving just enough
space to fit the mangled body of their fallen friend. Yeki gathered
reeds and vines and the three men skillfully wove them together con-
necting the poles, filling in the gap until it was strong enough to
support the dead weight.

Kuja and Ipiak, being the strongest and least injured, carried the
stretcher; Yeki hobbled along a few steps behind carrying the burlap
sack filled with the smaller animals. The tribal village depended on
them for food and they would not go hungry; at least they had the
monkeys and macaws to offer them. They would return soon with
more tribesmen, needing many hands to gut and carry away the wild
beasts that now lay dead on the forest floor, but they had to hurry;
the late afternoon sun already hung low in the sky; soon the nightly
scavengers would claim their prize.

First, they needed to bring Moxo back to the village and begin the
burial ritual; otherwise the dark spirit could claim his soul. Ipiak and

Kuja placed Moxo down every few miles to provide a much needed rest from their heavy burden. Yeki didn't provide any relief for the two men, since he couldn't place any real weight on his injured foot.

Soon they arrived at the village and Kuja's strong voice began chanting the song of the dead. Ipiak and Yeki joined in. Upon hearing the somber song, tribesmen and women ran from their huts to see who amongst them had passed on. Tears flowed freely across the cheeks of two young women who walked beside Moxo, caressing his face, comforting his spirit.

The ever growing crowd surrounded the three men as they walked, making it more difficult to carry Moxo's lifeless body back to his hut. Entering the hut, they laid him down on his bed of straw to begin the time of mourning. Soon thereafter, Teja, Keto, and the rest of the Elders arrived.

Keto, the tribal shaman, began his chant to chase away the dark spirits and guide Moxo during his three-day journey into the underworld. Kuja, Ipiak, and Yeki built a large fire outside Moxo's hut; the blaze would burn for three days until his transformation was complete. All of the tribesmen in the village would take turns feeding the flames, keeping a careful vigil over Moxo's body.

With twilight approaching, Ipiak rounded up nine tribesmen. Each man carried a sharp knife sheathed to his belt, some of the men carried strong bamboo poles. They'd have to hurry because with nightfall came the scavengers. Ipiak led them back into the forest to salvage what they could of the slaughtered animals, letting little go to waste. *For this is the Shuar way.*

Hope and Mary climbed up the wooded knoll near the middle of the village where they found the boys hard at work on their canoe project. Ryan, Matthew, and Jason seemed totally engaged, shaving off slivers of wood by cutting into the fallen tree with stone chisels and wooden mallets. Peter and Luke worked at the opposite end of the tree using similar tools to carve out their section of the craft.

Eno, a young Shuar man of about twenty, supervised the two groups, speaking in broken English as he swung a stone axe, skillfully hacking away at the tree's interior. Wood shavings littered the ground surrounding the canoe. The craft seemed to be taking shape, despite the boys' unfamiliarity with the primitive tools.

Everyone stopped what they were doing when Hope and Mary approached.

Peter threw down his mallet and chisel, wiped the sweat from his brow with his forearm, and smiled, "Hey, what are you girls up to?"

"I'm glad that you're all here because I've got something important to tell you."

"You're not going to go on and on about your panic attacks again, now are ya?" Ryan asked.

"Shut up, Ryan, let the girl talk," Peter said.

"Make me!"

"Listen to yourselves; you sound like a couple of five-year-olds," Mary said.

"Listen to me, all of you! I saw the *Iwanci* with my own eyes; these were not panic attacks! Father Ricardo was right; don't go near the woods, there is evil out there. We have to leave, like right now, or something horrible is going to happen to all of us! It knows we're here and it wants us dead!"

"I don't believe you. If you saw this monster how come you're not dead?" Matthew asked.

"Yeah, if this thing is so evil, how come it let *you* live?" Jason asked.

"Look you have to believe me; we have to convince Tim, Brenda, and Bill that we have to go. We don't have much time; I can just feel it!"

"Hope, I believe you," Peter said.

Luke stepped toward the girls, "So do I."

"Of course you guys do, because you're a couple of girls your-selves," Ryan said.

"I'll talk to my dad and try to convince him to cut the trip short," Mary said, putting her arm around Hope.

"And I'll talk to Tim and Brenda; maybe it'll sound more convincing coming from me," Peter said.

"I'll go with you. Maybe if we all voice our concerns, they'll listen," Luke said.

"Why don't you scared ostriches go stick your heads in the sand; me and my buds got a canoe to build," Ryan said.

"Yeah, and here's a news flash for ya; we ain't leaving," Matthew said.

Hope heard Kuja's death song before she saw them carry the stretcher into view. Gazing downhill, she watched everyone rushing from their huts to join the three chanting men.

"What's going on?" Hope asked.

Eno took several steps, turned, and waved them forward. "Come!"

Hope and her friends raced down the knoll, just a few steps behind Eno.

Matthew and Jason looked at Ryan to see if they too should follow.

Ryan shrugged and threw down his tools, "Come on; let's see what's up!"

The three boys followed the others down the hill, walking at a much slower pace. Hope broke off from the others and edged her way through the crowd toward Kuja. He didn't stop chanting even when he saw her approach; the look on his face said everything. With Kuja in the front and Ipiak in the back, they carried two blood-smeared poles, struggling with their cargo of what looked like mauled flesh. As they made their way toward her, Hope assumed they were hauling back a large animal from their hunt.

Hope gasped when she saw Moxo's lifeless body. Ripped flesh and deep gashes covered his upper torso; his face looked like a blood-soaked pin cushion; his nose torn off, replaced by a bloody hole;

only a few strands of cartilage remained. Exposed arteries and tendons hung like burgundy tubes mercilessly ripped from his neck. A maroon cavity the size of a large eggplant, and a shredded spleen were all that remained of his stomach and lower abdomen.

Hope stood whimpering as she watched in horrid disbelief. The reality of Moxo's death had not yet sunken in. The vibrant young man who'd stood before her just the night before now lay dead. This was her Christian Knight that she'd recently ordained with her painted cross, the friendly, thoughtful man who'd literally walked many extra miles for her, the Shuar ambassador of goodwill.

How could he be dead! It seemed impossible. She searched for answers, but nothing made sense. Had another tribe attacked them? Could a vicious animal have done this? If so, why hadn't Kuja and Ipiak come to Moxo's aid? They were among the strongest and most skilled hunters in the tribe.

Hope was vaguely aware of Tim, Brenda, and Bill who'd arrived together and stood behind the crowd. A crying Mary held her concerned father's hand; in that moment Hope wished that she too had a father to comfort her, no matter how creepy or bizarre he might be. The others turned to Tim and Brenda who seemed as confused as everyone else.

Only now did this all seem real and this newfound reality slammed into her like a sucker punch. Tears welled up in her eyes; her heart fluttered, and her breathing became rapid; she felt the onset of a panic attack and tried hard to regain control. She closed her eyes and concentrated on her breathing, trying to relax, having some measure of success, but her world narrowed to thoughts of Moxo and the pain that he must've endured. She wanted to shout out to Kuja over the crowd; only he could provide her with the answers. Listening to his ritualistic chants, she watched him from afar as he and the others built a fire and sensed that she mustn't interfere. She'd have to wait until the ritual was complete. After what seemed like forever, the chanting stopped and the crowd began to disperse. Bill Drake strolled with his arm around his daughter toward the huts. Tim and Brenda walked side by side just a few steps behind Bill and Mary with the others bringing up the rear, reminding Hope of some macabre funeral march.

Still she waited. The Elders huddled around Kuja, and Yeki speaking in Shuar. Kuja stared into Teja's eyes as he spoke, answering in the same native language, making it impossible for Hope to understand what was being said. He spoke slowly, each word carefully chosen seemingly more so then the one before. His words fell heavy across the faces of the Elders, as if he was describing a death blow to the tribe itself.

Yeki hung his heads low as Kuja spoke, only interjecting a word or two here and there. After several minutes Kuja fell silent and tears welled in the eyes of the Elders. With a firm grip, Teja placed his hand on Kuja's shoulder; he gazed into the younger man's eyes and spoke his final solemn words. Kuja returned the stare and gave a nod of understanding. The three other Elders each gave Yeki a pat on the back, an indication that the meeting had come to an end. The group dispersed and Kuja walked past Hope, seemingly lost in his thoughts, oblivious to her presence or the fact that she'd been waiting for him.

Although Hope sensed that the time still wasn't right, she could wait no more.

She stepped in front of Kuja and grabbed both his arms. "Please tell me what happened?"

"Moxo is dead and it is my fault."

"Don't say that. I know it isn't true."

"I was the leader of the hunt and I wasn't able to save him. It was my responsibility to keep him safe and I have failed."

"Whatever happened, I know you tried your best."

"That is not good enough!" He said and his eyes burned with fire.

"You can't blame yourself; Ipiak and Yeki were also there. I'm your friend, please help me to understand. Were you attacked by another tribe?"

"There was no other tribe." Kuja stared at the ground and kicked up dust.

"An animal?" Hope gripped his biceps with all of her might as if latching onto him would somehow lessen the sting of her question; she felt the hurt excreting through his pores.

"This was no animal!" Kuja lifted his head and gazed at Hope; his piercing brown eyes seemed to cut right through her.

Hope shook his arms. "What then? Please tell me!"

"Moxo was killed by an *Iwanci*!"

All the blood drained from Hope's face. It had come to pass, the killing had begun.

CHAPTER TEN

Tim and Brenda walked behind Bill and Mary. The two mission group leaders slowed their pace, purposely increasing the distance between themselves and the Drakes.

"I feel bad about Moxo; he's in God's hands now," Tim said.

Brenda sighed, "I know we're not supposed to, but do you ever question why?"

"Bad things happen to good people, but I guess that's all part of God's plan."

"But why would a gentle, loving God allow that to happen to Moxo?"

"It has to be for a higher purpose, one that we can't understand," Tim said.

"Well, the whole thing frightens me. The rainforest is so serene and peaceful, but it has lulled us into a false sense of security; it takes a tragedy like this to show us just how dangerous this place really is."

"It sounds like a freak accident; I overheard Yeki saying that he'd been killed by a large boar."

"That's what really scares me; these men were experienced hunters, supposedly the best in the village and they weren't able to save Moxo. What if it had been one of our kids who had wandered into the rainforest and met up with this or some other beast? Just yesterday, Hope went off alone. If she'd run into that boar, she'd be the one laying dead out there and we wouldn't even know what happened to her."

Peter and Luke came rushing up the path behind them.

Tim turned when he heard their footsteps, "Hey, guys, what's up?"

"Hope thinks that we should leave early; she predicted something bad was going to happen and it did. What happened to Moxo could happen to us," Peter said.

"I feel bad about Moxo, but it was a freak thing that happened on a hunt. The animal attacked him because it felt threatened or cornered. I don't want you guys to feel scared; the chances of that happening to us are slim to none," Tim said.

Brenda raised her eyebrows at Tim without saying a word.

"But Hope says that there's an *Iwanci* out there and that it's going to kill us," Luke said.

Tim sighed, "I wish that Kuja had never told her that story. Guys, the *Iwanci* is nothing more than Shuar folklore. It's a legend like Bigfoot or the Loch Ness Monster; it simply doesn't exist."

Peter held his elbow and shifted his weight onto his left leg. "Just the same, I'm for going home early."

"Yeah, me too," Luke said.

"Do the other guys feel the same way?"

Peter kicked at the ground. "Well, no but—"

"I think that we should all be in agreement before we make a rash decision like that," Tim said.

"I think that we should talk to Bill and see what he thinks; I personally wouldn't be opposed to going home early," Brenda said.

"Okay, we can talk to him, but I already know what he's going to say."

"At the very least we should hold a group meeting tonight after dinner; I don't want any more of our kids going into the rainforest," Brenda said.

"But what about the canoe? It'll be finished in a day or two. Ryan, Matthew, and Jason want to launch it on the river," Luke said.

"How about they just play with the boat in the brook?" Brenda asked.

"That wouldn't be fair to the boys, especially after all of their hard work. Hey, I know what it's like to take pride in building something; I was once a boy too, you know. How about we let them launch in the river, but make it clear that they can't cross over to the other side and like it or not, they're going to be carefully supervised?"

Brenda rolled her eyes, neither agreeing nor disagreeing; her silence a clear indication that Tim's decision would be his own.

"Okay, it's decided then," Tim said.

⚊⚔⚊

Bill and Mary walked in silence down the path leading to their huts. Tears filled Mary's eyes as Bill searched for the proper words to console his daughter; he never was good at that sort of thing. If Jenny were still alive she'd be the one to handle this. At times like these he missed her more than ever. *Had it already been three years since the accident?*

Clearing his throat, he knew his words would sound awkward before he spoke them. "I'm sorry that you had to see that."

"Poor Moxo, why did he have to die?"

"I don't know. Nobody knows, only God knows why."

"It just doesn't seem fair."

"Life doesn't seem fair sometimes, but it's all a part of growing up." Bill wanted to retract his words as they left his lips. They sounded so stupid; he'd racked his brain searching for a proper anecdote, anything about grief or death, but he came up empty.

"Dad, I don't want to stay here anymore. I think we should leave."

"Honey, I know you're upset, but we have prearranged travel plans, not to mention the others in the group to think about."

"But the others want to go too! I know that Hope, Peter, and Luke want to."

"After a few days you'll feel a little better about this. Time heals all wounds. Think about Moxo; he'd probably want you to stay."

"This is not just about Moxo. Hope says that she saw things in the rainforest, horrible, nasty things."

"In a couple of days my work will be finished. I still have to interview Keto, the tribal shaman, and two of the other Elders. Maybe we can wrap things up a day or two early, but it would be a whole lot of trouble to change our plans; we'd have to make different arrangements for ground transportation, not to mention the costs involved to change all of our flights. It might not be financially feasible."

"I know that it would be a lot of trouble and it might cost money, but please, please let's go home!" Mary wailed.

"We'll see." Bill's remark made it clear that the conversation had ended and his answer was no. Whenever he said "we'll see," the answer was always no and his daughter knew this better than anyone. Mary turned away from her father and stormed off toward her hut.

After dinner, the church group gathered in the clearing where the Elders held their tribal meetings. It consisted of a circle of carefully placed tree stumps that the Shuar used for seating.

Tim, Brenda, and Bill stood in the middle of the circle as they waited for everyone to choose their seats. Hope sat in between Peter and Mary. Luke sat next to Mary, while Ryan, Matthew, and Jason chose to sit on the far side of the circle.

A cool breeze blew in from the forest making the leaves dance in the treetops; a slight chill ran through Hope, causing her to shiver.

Twilight glistened through the green canopy. Hope prayed that their meeting would end before nightfall; they were sitting too close to the trees. She could feel the forest closing in around her, threatening to swallow her up.

Tim stepped into the exact center of the circle and cleared his throat, "We asked you all here tonight to talk about what happened to Moxo and to alleviate some of your fears, but first Dr. Drake will lead us in prayer."

Bill closed his eyes, lowered his head, and folded his hands in prayer. "Moxo, although you walk through the valley of the shadow of death, I pray that you will fear no evil, for thou art with the Lord and He will protect you as He protects all those who have been struck down by the beast. May you know Him as your Lord, as you enter his almighty kingdom in heaven. Amen."

"Amen," the group said in unison.

Bill stepped back and Brenda took her turn in the middle of the circle.

"Thank you, Dr. Drake. Tim has a few words that he'd like to share with you, but first I'd like to take care of a little housekeeping. New rules, nobody goes off into the rainforest for any reason. You must stay in the village at all times."

"But what about our canoe, we're almost ready to launch it in the river!" Ryan said.

"Tim, do you want to address that?"

"Okay, guys, here's the deal. I'm going to let you launch it in the river, but I don't want you crossing over to the other side. Pretend that there is an invisible line running right down the middle of the river; I want you guys staying on this side of that line. Got it?" Tim said.

"Yeah, we got it," Ryan sighed.

"And one more thing, one of us must accompany you while you're on the river."

Three loud groans emanated from the far side of the circle.

"Now let's take a moment to talk about Moxo's untimely death. Although unfortunate, I consider his death to be nothing more than a freak hunting accident. I know that some of you have expressed your fears that something like that could happen to us. Some of you have even requested that we leave early. Let me assure you, we are all safe here in the village."

Hope jumped to her feet. "No, we're not! The *Iwanci* will come for us right here where we sit. We must pack our things and leave right now! What happened to Moxo was no accident; he was killed by the *Iwanci*, Kuja told me!"

"Hope, calm down, you're about to have another panic attack. As I told Peter and Luke earlier, there is no such thing as the *Iwanci*; it's just Shuar folklore. I'm going to have another talk with Kuja about filling your head with such nonsense," Tim said.

"I'm not having a panic attack; I just want you to take me home!"

Peter jumped to his feet. "I want to go home too."

Luke and Mary rose from their seats and stood shoulder to shoulder with Hope and Peter.

"We want to leave too," Luke said.

Mary folded her arms and glared at her father.

"Well, we don't want to hold you here against your will. I guess we could take a vote on it and let the majority rule. Sound fair?" Tim asked.

Ryan, Matthew, and Jason groaned in affirmation, while Hope, Peter, Mary, and Luke simply nodded their heads in agreement.

Tim raised his hands up in front of his chest in surrender. "Okay, all in favor of leaving raise your hand."

The hands of Hope and her three friends shot up immediately.

"Okay, we only have four who voted to go. I'm sorry, guys, but it looks like you're in the minority," Tim said and then his jaw dropped as Brenda's hand slowly rose above her head.

"It seems as though we now have five who want to leave. Okay, everyone who wants to stay raise your hand."

Ryan's, Jason's, and Matthew's hands shot upward, followed by Bill's. Tim's hand was the last to rise.

"It looks like we have a tie. I'd hate to decide this with a flip of a coin, but it seems like the only fair way."

Bill Drake stepped forward. "Tim, let me interject if I may. As Church Council President, I feel that it's my duty to settle the tie. Before I render my decision I'd like to address a couple of issues that I'm sure none of you have considered. It simply isn't financially feasible to change our travel plans. The cost for a group this size changing flights at this late stage in the game would be astronomical. Secondly, it would be no easy task to coordinate ground transportation without the help of Father Ricardo; remember, he's still going to be at his retreat for another week. It would be unfair to ask him to leave early. Therefore, I've decided that we should stick to our original plans. Sorry, guys, you'll just have to make the best of it."

A cheer went up from Ryan, Jason, and Matthew.

Mary stormed off in a huff.

Hope wobbled as if struck by a physical blow. Stunned, she sat back down on the stump; tears welled in her eyes and she buried her face in her hands. Once more, she'd failed to make them understand.

CHAPTER ELEVEN

Three days had passed since they laid Moxo's body out to rest on a bed of straw. Kuja's vigil did nothing to ease the pain in his gut. Despite Teja's kind words, Kuja knew that as the leader of the hunt, he alone bears responsibility for his friend's death.

He kept watch like a sentinel outside of Moxo's hut, wary of the *Iwanci* and any other dark spirits that might intrude during this sacred period of transformation.

Feeding the fire, he kept the flames burning to ward off evil. If the flame burnt out, even for the briefest of moments, it would allow the *Iwanci* to swoop in and capture Moxo's spirit. A momentary lapse is all that it took. Already it had tried to seduce him with sleep. He'd stayed awake by staring into the flames, putting himself into a trance-like state.

After the first night, only he stoked the fire, having dismissed his fellow hunters as well as all other lamenting tribesmen who tried to offer him solace. He had no choice; the *Iwanci* could take any form, even that of a tribesman. It might come to him as a friend and sit on a stump right next to him, using chatter as its weapon, waiting for him to slip up, waiting for a mistake. This was a risk that Kuja wasn't willing to take, choosing instead to hold his vigil alone.

For three days he refused both food and water, knowing that the *Iwanci* could also tamper with that. Determined to at last be there for his fallen friend, he tried his best to protect Moxo as his spirit began his journey into the afterlife.

⊷⊶

Hope tried several times to bring food and water to Kuja, but he just sat on the ground with his legs crossed, staring into the flames in silence. She watched him sporadically lift a piece of dried timber from the woodpile and shove it deep into the inferno, placing his hands in the flames seemingly oblivious to the scorching heat, but his hand would always emerge unscathed. Each night she'd place her canteen and an earthen bowl filled with fish or meat on the ground next to him, and each morning she'd return to find the bowl and canteen untouched.

On the third day Hope approached Kuja, masking her face with her sleeve. The rancid smell of death escaping Moxo's hut had become unbearable. Still Kuja refused to acknowledge her presence, his sunken eyes seemingly mesmerized by the flames. His breathing sounded shallow; he looked thinner than before, and although his arms still appeared strong, they lacked their usual definition. Concerned about her friend's wellbeing, Hope sat in silence next to Kuja, waiting for the time of mourning to come to an end.

Morning became early afternoon and with great patience, she waited in silence. Despite having her nose and mouth covered by the cotton cloth, the smell of Moxo's rotting flesh infiltrated her lungs, making her nauseous, but still she stayed by Kuja's side. An occasional breeze blew from the opposite direction, giving Hope momentary relief from the stench.

As the hour passed, marking the third day of mourning, Teja, Keto, and the rest of the Elders arrived. Kuja rose from the ground chanting the song of the dead. Shuar tribesmen and women hurried from their huts, some accompanied by small children. Many voices blended together. Ipiak arrived, lending his deep voice, as did Yeki.

In the distance Hope saw Tim, Brenda, and Bill approaching at the edge of the crowd. When they neared, they stopped and watched from afar so as not to disturb the tribal ritual. Only then did she see Peter, Mary, and Luke filing in behind them. Jason, Ryan, and Matthew brought up the rear, standing on tiptoes, straining their necks to see what was happening.

The tribal song stopped and Keto entered the hut. His strong shamanistic chants filtered through the walls of the thin bamboo structure as he attempted to help Moxo's spirit transcend into the next world. This went on for nearly a half-hour before the shaman fell silent. He stepped out of the hut and with a wave of his hand motioned to Kuja, Ipiak, and Yeki.

The three tribesmen retrieved the makeshift stretcher they'd built from behind the hut and followed Keto back inside. The stink hit Hope full force when the men lifted the decaying corpse onto the stretcher. Ipiak and Yeki carried Moxo's body out of the hut and down the path that led to the burial grounds. Kuja and Keto followed close behind, seemingly unaffected by the smell.

Hope caught a glimpse of the body as they passed. Dozens of maggots squirmed back and forth feeding on the wounds; the smell of death seared her lungs. After waiting her turn, she joined the slow procession, falling in line behind the Elders. Atiak walked in step next to her; the rest of the tribe followed. Glancing over her shoulder, she saw her group leaders following the crowd, keeping their distance, walking several feet behind the tribe. Hope thought that maybe she too should fall in with the others, but she had been Moxo's friend, more so than the rest. He had helped her with the skit and she had rewarded him with a kiss and by giving him her cross. And wasn't it she who day after day had tried to comfort Kuja? Hadn't she sat vigil with him in Moxo's stench? No, she wasn't going to the back of the bus, not this time. She stepped proudly next to Atiak, feeling very much a part of the tribe.

━╬ ╬━

The burial grounds were located just outside the village near the edge of the forest, less than a hundred yards into the woods. Ipiak and Yeki laid the corpse down on the ground next to a rotted tree. Kuja and Ipiak removed the top half of the trunk; it had been pre-cut prior to the ceremony. The removed section revealed a deep hollow space within the tree. On Keto's command, Ipiak grabbed Moxo's soft shoulders and Yeki hoisted his grey, pasty legs. Together, they gently lifted Moxo's corpse and laid it down inside the tree. This new movement caused a fresh wave of unpleasantness to circulate through the air.

One of two women who had comforted Moxo's spirit on that first day, placed a small cup of *Chicha* behind his head so that he would not be thirsty during his long journey into the afterlife. Next to the *Chicha*, she laid down a handful of edible roots, so that his spirit wouldn't go hungry. Around his neck she strung a necklace made from seeds to protect him. The other woman stepped forward with two of Moxo's spears, a small bow and several arrows, laying them down diagonally across his chest. This was in case he needed to fight the demons of the underworld or use them to hunt when he entered into his new life.

In addition to the maggots, several tribesmen placed live worms, ants, and termites into the stump so that Moxo's spirit would have company and not become lonely during his voyage into the other world.

Keto resumed his chanting and motioned once again to Kuja and Ipiak. Together the two men lifted the top half of the tree off the ground and replaced it back onto its original spot. Both men smeared beeswax and resin into the cracks and crevices, sealing together the two halves of the trunk, interning Moxo's body along with its horrible stench.

The tribesmen had pre-dug a shallow grave next to the tree; Hope estimated that it couldn't have been any deeper than four feet. Kuja, Ipiak, and Yeki, accompanied by seven other tribesmen, lifted the heavy trunk and placed it into the grave. Keto chanted a few more words before giving the order to bury the tree. All ten men used their hands to push dirt into the hole, covering the grave with black soil.

Keto gave a final chant and the tribe slowly dispersed, making their way back to the village. After everyone else had disbanded, Hope and her fellow Christians approached the grave.

Tim stood at the head of the grave, while everyone else encircled the mound of fresh dirt.

"As Christians, I feel that it's our duty to eulogize Moxo by bowing our heads and locking our hands together in prayer as Dr. Drake delivers the passage."

Bill Drake stepped forward between Brenda and Tim; locking his hands with theirs, he closed his eyes and bowed his head. Everyone else did likewise, linking their hands together, completing the electricity of the circle.

After clearing his throat, Bill began. "O Heavenly Father, as the sisters of Lazarus wept over the death of their brother, we weep for Moxo. He was a kind and gentle soul who has left this world way too soon. He is now with Gabriel and St. Peter as he enters the everlasting Kingdom of Heaven. May he too become one of God's angels as we recite the Lord's Prayer."

All ten voices joined in, "Thy kingdom come thy will be done on earth as it is in Heaven. Give us this day our daily bread...deliver us from evil..." With the prayer finished, Dr. Drake shouted, "Amen!" The group responded in kind. With the service now complete, they began the slow procession back to the village.

Hope walked along the path with Peter and Mary. "There really should be some kind of a grave marker."

Peter rubbed his chin. "Yeah, but we don't want to upset the Shuar burial customs."

"Maybe if we did something small, very subtle, you know, not so in your face," Mary said.

Hope smiled. "Let's make a small cross, nothing big; we could even make it out of bamboo."

"But Teja and the rest of the Elders won't like it on the grave."

"We won't put it on the grave; we'll place it about fifteen feet behind the grave; it'll be there, but hardly noticeable."

They hurried back to the village. Peter used his pocketknife to cut two short stalks of bamboo; the first measured less than an arm's length. The second thin stalk measured only half of that. Hope found some nylon twine inside a tool box next to the church. Tying the shorter stalk across the longer one, she crafted a simple cross. She wrapped the remaining cord in a figure eight pattern until almost all of it had been used, binding it with a tight knot before handing the cross back to Peter. He cut the inch of excess cord that hung below the knot and whittled the bottom of the cross into a sharp point.

Hope and her two friends retraced their steps back to the burial ground and Moxo's gravesite. With cross in hand, Hope paced off fifteen steps from the grave and pushed the sharpened end into the moist, black dirt. It was primitive, but it blended nicely with the surrounding forest and after all, that was the point.

Hope smiled. "There! Now Moxo can rest in peace."

As she spoke those words a cold breeze blew in from the forest causing goose bumps to rise on her arms and neck. That dreadful feeling once again fell upon her like cold rain and she sensed the presence of unseen eyes. Her breaths became quick and short, but she forced several slower, longer ones, determined to mask her fear and keep her composure, seeing no need to alarm her friends.

She subtly scanned the treetops, but saw nothing. "Come on, let's head back."

"You're not going to say a few words on Moxo's behalf before we leave?" Peter asked.

"No, let's go, it's all been said."

Mary's nervous laugh revealed her braces. "I wish all services were like this, short and sweet."

Walking back toward the village, Hope remained silent, concentrating on controlling the panic within. Her brisk pace more easily hid her irregular breathing. Both Peter and Mary struggled to keep up with her. The breeze continued to blow at her back and she could feel invisible eyes piercing the back of her skull with every step.

Hope walked into the clearing of the village and in an instant that heavy feeling lifted off of her; no longer did she feel eyes upon her and her breathing soon returned to normal. She stopped and turned, allowing Peter and Mary to gap the dozen or so yards that now separated her from them; they came huffing and puffing up behind her.

"Hey, what's the hurry?" Mary gasped.

"Yeah, where's the fire?" Peter said.

"It's good to walk fast, keeps the blood flowing."

⚔⚔

Several days had passed since Moxo's funeral and Kuja remained quiet and withdrawn. Hope decided to leave Kuja alone for awhile, allowing him to lament his loss in his own private way.

Hope and Mary heeded Brenda's words, staying within the confines of the village, vowing to never enter the rainforest alone or otherwise, opting instead to teach bible studies to the Shuar children; after all, that's what they were there for. Still, Hope didn't feel safe even in the village, so she sought out the company of men in a protective, big brother sort of way.

Ipiak, having bounced back from the tragedy rather quickly, seemed eager to fill the void created by Kuja's absence, even offering to help Hope and Mary conduct Bible Story class with the children. His English was nowhere near as good as Kuja's; still, he did his best to translate Hope's and Mary's words into Shuar. One day he even helped out with the finger painting class, using a drawing as his guide, he painted a pretty good Noah's Ark.

Peter and the boys, with Eno's guidance, neared completion of their canoe project, making Peter unavailable by day, but willing to spend time with Hope at night. Still their relationship never evolved beyond friendship. So Hope split her time almost equally between Ipiak and Peter.

⪥⪤

After dinner, a pale moon appeared like a ghost in the eastern sky, growing brighter with each passing moment. A warm, gentle breeze flowed through Hope's silky hair, caressing her face.

"Do you want to go for a walk?" Peter asked.

Mary shot Hope a disapproving glare.

"Sure." Hope's smile widened.

Both she and Peter rose from the stumps they'd been sitting on and strolled away from the group. Hope wondered if Peter would try to hold her hand once they were out of sight. A part of her wanted him to, but another voice said that it would feel awkward and weird. *If it hasn't happened already, it's probably not going to.*

As they turned the corner, Hope was glad that they were now out of view.

"You know, we should do this more often," Peter said, with his hands on his side.

"Yeah, it's such a nice night for a walk."

"Hope, you mind if I ask you a question?"

"Not at all."

"When we first got here, you spent all your free time with Kuja, and now you're spending it with Ipiak. Why?"

"Why Peter, are you jealous?" She smiled coyly.

"No, it's just that I wish you'd spend more time with me."

"That's so sweet, but you're not always around."

"I'm around now." Peter placed his hand in hers. It startled her at first, but it didn't seem weird. They walked on, hand in hand, having crossed that line for the first time. They were in that fragile moment, the one where it would either move forward naturally or shatter forever into a million pieces. She analyzed everything; if he uttered the wrong word, even the wrong syllable, they'd crash headlong into brother and sisterhood forever. And after that, no matter how hard he tried and no matter how many times he asked, they would never get back to that moment.

What if he kisses me? And what if the kiss is awful? Worse yet, what if I don't feel anything? Hope knew it was now or never. She stopped suddenly and gazed into his hazel eyes; they seemed to sparkle in the moonlight; why hadn't she noticed them before? With both hands she grabbed hold of his biceps and leaned slowly toward him. Peter seemed startled, even embarrassed by this, but he regained his composure and leaned toward her. It was going to happen; the kiss was inevitable. His lips met hers and they came together as one. And it was a great kiss; no, it was an amazingly fantastic kiss. The kiss made her tingle. Not that she'd kissed a lot of guys, but this was the best kiss she'd ever had. Peter kissed her again, then again. Gentle kisses led to deeper, more passionate ones. Strolling down the moonlit path, they made their way to the footbridge and kissed some more. Peter placed his hand in hers and led her down to the banks of the brook. A smooth flat rock, large enough for them to lie across, jettisoned from the bank. They sat down next to each other on the cool stone. Hope giggled, feeling giddy. Peter wrapped his arm around her waist. The pressure of his arm felt good; she snuggled up closer to him, pressing her head against his chest. He wrapped his other arm around her, holding her tight, gently rocking her back and forth. The warm breeze remained constant, keeping the mosquitoes and gnats at bay. Crickets and tree frogs chirped in the woods around them, serenading them with song.

Hope gazed up at the stars and Peter pointed out several constellations, including Orion, Taurus, and the Big Dipper. Still in his arms, she turned to face him, almost nose to nose, she smiled, gazing into his eyes; his lips gapped the short distance between them. He leaned back, laying her down on the rock next to him. The curve of her hip pressed hard against the stone surface causing discomfort, but his kisses numbed her pain.

Peter's hands caressed her face and neck; her body yearned for his touch. Several hours had passed, but it seemed like only minutes. She never wanted the moment to end.

The easterly moon had leaped into the southwest sky, a clear indication that it was time to go; they strolled together hand in hand toward the heart of the village. Hope was thankful that everyone had already gone to bed. When they reached Hope's hut, Peter leaned in and gave her a soft lingering kiss, the perfect ending to a perfect night.

CHAPTER TWELVE

The morning sun filtered into the hut through the mosquito netting; the bright, friendly rays offered the promise of a glorious day.

Hope lay in bed, having just awoken from a beautiful dream. She ran a finger across her chapped lips, physical proof it hadn't been a dream; her wonderful night with Peter had really happened.

Hope smiled, gazing up at the thatched roof. She breathed in deep before releasing a blissful sigh.

"So, where did you and Peter go last night?" Mary asked, her head propped up on her arm.

"We just went for a walk and it was w-o-n-d-e-r-f-u-l!"

"Where'd you walk to? Macas? I *heard* when you came in. You were gone for almost four hours!"

"Who are you, the official time keeper?"

"No, I lay awake in bed for hours worried about you. Hey, I was just asking; don't tell me, I don't care."

"He showed me the different constellations and we just sort of lost track of time." This statement was partially true.

"You kissed him, didn't you?" Mary flashed a devilish smile.

"That's none of your business." Hope bit her bottom lip.

Mary slapped the bed, "I knew it!"

Hope's smile widened, remembering that last sweet kiss.

"He didn't...You didn't...?"

Hope blushed, "Mary! Please!"

Before Mary could answer, Peter called to Hope from outside the hut, "Hey, I'm here, are you ready?

"Be there in a minute!" Hope shouted, and then turned to Mary, "Come pick flowers with us."

"Flowers?"

"Yeah, we're going to place them on Moxo's grave."

"But I thought we weren't allowed in the forest?"

"We're not going into the forest; I spotted some beautiful white orchids along the edge of the woods. Believe me; our feet will remain planted firmly in the village."

Mary's smile quickly faded, "Are you sure you want me to go? You know—since you're going with Peter and all."

Hope smiled, "Don't be silly; you're my best friend, of course I want you to go. Besides, I don't think floral arrangements are exactly Peter's strongest suit, if you know what I mean."

The smile returned to Mary's face.

Peter's voice rang out again, "Hope, ya coming?"

"Don't get your panties all in a bunch. I'll be there in a second."

Mary giggled.

Both girls slipped on jeans and T-shirts. Mary used a brush on her hair, then a second one on her teeth. Hope ran a comb through her hair, and took a swig of mouthwash opting to swallow it. After applying a generous coating of lip gloss, Hope pushed open the door. Peter stood waiting.

"Hi." Hope smiled, gazing into his hazel eyes.

"Good morning."

"Yes, it's a *wonderful* morning," Hope's smile widened.

"I would even go so far as to say it's a beautiful morning, but not as beautiful as you two ladies."

Mary stepped outside, "Okay, are we ready? Let's go pick some flowers." She fidgeted, seemingly uncomfortable with Peter's lovey-dovey talk.

As Hope followed Mary through the door, Peter mouthed the words, "Is *she* coming?"

Hope smiled and gave a quick nod. Peter lips pursed, but he quickly recovered.

"I found a soda bottle the other day and I saved it. I want to use it as a vase." Hope said, picking up the clear plastic bottle next to the hut.

Mary seemed excited. "We're going to need water for the bottle—I mean, vase."

"Do you have your canteen?"

"It's in the hut, let me grab it."

"Do we need to go down to the brook?"

"Nah, filled it yesterday."

Mary ran into the hut and reemerged seconds later holding her canteen; she adjusted the strap and slung it across her shoulder. Peter offered to carry Hope's bottle and she let him do so.

Walking along the outskirts of the village, they came upon the white orchids that Hope had spotted the day before. The girls picked the flowers leaving more than a foot of stem on each one. Mary discovered some green ferns along with several purple lilies; Hope thought they'd provide a nice contrast against the white orchids, so they picked them as well. Having collected more than two dozen flowers, they headed off toward the burial grounds; reaching the path, they walked the short distance to Moxo's grave.

The mound of dirt looked drier than the day before, but undisturbed. Peter used his pocket knife to cut off the neck of the bottle, widening the opening, allowing all the flowers to fit. He handed the bottle to Hope, who placed it at the head of the grave. Mary removed the canteen from her shoulder, unscrewed the cap, and half-filled the bottle. Both girls knelt next to their *vase* and helped each other arrange the flowers into a beautiful bouquet.

Hope bent over to smell the flowers as did Mary; the unique floral blend offered a sweet, aromatic scent. Hope stood to admire their handiwork. The green, textured ferns and delicate, purple lilies accentuated the arrangement, making the orchids look amazing. Mary smiled, seemingly satisfied.

Hope gazed beyond the grave toward the forest; the bamboo cross was nowhere in sight.

In that same moment, Peter noticed it too. "Where's the cross?"

Hope scanned the woods; the vegetation surrounding the site remained undisturbed. Whoever took their cross had come from the same direction as they had. Did the Elders discover the cross and remove it? Was it Ryan and his two mindless *buds* up to some shenanigans? No, even they knew better than to disrespect the dead.

"Let's check out the site," Peter said.

Hope really didn't want to; it was too close to the woods. The theft frightened her. She wanted to go back to the village, but she felt less scared with her friends by her side. Together they crept forward pacing off the fifteen steps behind the grave. The circular hole in the dirt proved that someone had pulled out the cross; no one had knocked it over or snapped it off at the base.

Peter pointed to something in the weeds, "Look!"

The remnants of the cross lay partially hidden beneath the ferns. He used his foot to brush back the vegetation. The two short stalks of bamboo had separated, lying almost parallel to one another on the forest floor. The nylon twine had dissolved away in spots; a red gel-like substance, very similar to the goo excreted by that fly-thing, covered the frayed remnants. It looked as if somebody had smeared cranberry sauce all over the twine.

Peter bent over to pick up the two stalks.

"Don't touch it!" Hope shouted.

"Why?"

"Just get back!"

Hope's sharp words startled Peter, but he took a step backward.

"That stuff is like acid, look!" Mary said.

The three friends watched in disbelief as the red goo ate away at the remaining nylon.

Hope's eyes widened. "Come on, let's go."

"Ah! My foot!" Peter screamed.

Hope looked down at the tip of his sneaker and discovered a dime-size hole. The red goo had eaten through the thin rubber and was now biting into his toes.

"Quick, get that shoe off!" Hope screamed.

Peter lifted his right leg and pulled at the laces. Steadying himself on Hope's shoulder, he grabbed the heel and flipped off the sneaker. A dissolved sock revealed three bloody toes, the big one being the worst.

"Take off your sock!" Hope shouted.

Peter used his thumb to flip off what remained of his stocking, and grimaced as he did so.

"Mary quick! Your canteen!" Hope snatched the container and poured the water over his foot, flushing the gel away from his toes.

"Gimme your knife," Hope said, holding out her palm.

Peter fished around in his pocket for a moment before pulling out his pocket knife. Hope grabbed the red-handled knife from his hand and flipped open the well-oiled blade; it snapped easily into place.

Placing the blade under her T-shirt, she poked a hole through the cotton about three inches above her navel. Cutting in a circular pattern, she worked her way around the shirt, only handing the knife to Mary when she'd reached the back. Mary made quick work of the remaining section, completing the shirt's transformation into a half-T. The loose band now hung freely around Hope's waist. Taking back the knife, Hope cut the cloth from her body.

Hope bent over and patted her knees as if she were calling a puppy. "Gimme your foot."

Peter placed his bare heal just above her knee. She cut the cloth into several strands and wrapped up each injured toe individually. Blood soaked through the cloth, producing three red stains of various sizes. Pleased with her quasi-bandages, she used the remaining cloth to cover as much of his foot as possible. Peter lowered his foot to the ground.

"Okay, try taking a step," Hope said.

Peter's face contorted as he hobbled forward.

"Stop, we'll try taking the weight off of it."

"Where'd you learn First Aid?" Mary asked.

"In Health, you'll learn it too your senior year. Now come on and give me a hand."

Peter draped an arm around each girl's shoulder. A swarm of gnats hovered over them, seemingly determined to follow them home. The black, silent cloud descended onto their heads. Before Hope could swat them away, she breathed several of them in through her nostrils, causing her to choke and cough.

That fly-like thing had melted away the twine; Hope was sure of it. A hot flash caused her to wobble; creases formed on her forehead.

The swarm of gnats once again descended to eye level, causing the girls to swat at them with their free hands. Despite the pesky insects, Hope and Mary, taking one step at a time, helped Peter hobble the short distance back to the huts.

No sooner had they gotten Peter settled down on Hope's bed when the shouting began. Growing louder by the moment, the frantic voice belonged to Luke. "The cross is gone! The cross is gone!"

Hope and Mary left Peter and went outside to see what the commotion was all about. Tim and the boys had already gathered. Panting for breath, Luke stood bent over with his hands on his knees.

The other boys stood in various stages of undress. Ryan buttoned up his shirt. Matthew zipped his fly and tugged at his jeans. Jason stood shirtless with his arms folded across his bare chest.

"Somebody stole the cross!" Luke said.

Tim placed his hand on Luke's shoulder. "Relax, what cross? What are you talking about?"

"The cross next to the church, it's gone!"

By this time Brenda and Bill had also arrived.

"Why all the shouting?" Brenda asked.

"Yeah, what's the matter?" Bill asked.

"Luke says someone stole the cross next to the church," Tim said, placing his hands on his hips.

"That's impossible; I saw you hammer that thing deep into the ground. I tried to shake it, but it was as solid as cement," Ryan said.

Bill pointed in the direction of the church and said, "Well, let's go see for ourselves!"

The professor led the way with Hope and the others marching close behind. Tim raised his eyebrow, pointed at Hope, and whispered something into Brenda's ear.

"I'll talk to her about it later," Brenda said.

At that moment, Hope remembered she was still wearing her half-T; apparently her bare midriff was far too risqué for the likes of Tim and Brenda.

When they approached the church, Hope saw that the cross truly was missing.

"It's gone, sure as shit," Ryan said.

Tim glared at him, "Hey, Ryan, watch your mouth; there are ladies present."

Ryan hung his head. "Sorry."

"It's gone all right, but who would've taken it?" Bill asked.

Tim peered down into the deep, square hole where the cross had been. "A better question is, who *could've* taken it? The post was in there good, more than three feet deep. I hammered it into the ground myself; it would've required herculean strength or a bull-dozer to remove it."

Hope stared toward the woods, following a straight line in the dirt where someone had dragged the cross into the forest. A trail carved through the bushes, separating them into two distinct halves. Farther ahead, large branches lay strewn on the ground, snapped off of the low hanging trees. Whatever had made that path through the woods must've been strong. Something white caught her eye just in front of the parted bushes. Without saying a word, she walked toward the forest.

"Hope, where ya going?" Tim shouted.

"Just a sec."

On the ground, several feet before the bushes, Hope found the cloth that until recently had hung neatly draped over the cross. She picked it up and inspected it. Stamped onto the white linen was a large, dirty, black footprint. Whoever or whatever left the print walked barefoot; she could see the distinct lines across the ball of the foot, perfectly formed toes, and a rounded heal. A fierce smell emanated from the print; it was an odor that Hope had become all too familiar with, the stink of rotting flesh, the stench of death.

CHAPTER THIRTEEN

Peter hobbled up the knoll just as Jason chiseled the last chip of wood from the canoe. After all of his sweat equity, Peter wanted to be present to witness that moment of completion despite being AWOL from the project due to his foot injury. All of the boys hooted and hollered, drunk with excitement, united in their feelings of achievement. With just a half hour of daylight remaining, they made a pact to launch the dugout craft first thing in the morning.

⊨⊨

Ryan rose from his cot. Matthew and Jason slept sprawled out across their own bedding, both boys breathed rhythmically. Ryan shook Jason first, placing his hand across his mouth; the sleeper awoke in a wild-eyed panic. Bringing a finger to his lips, Ryan shushed him into silence. Moments later, he woke a startled Matthew in the same muffled fashion.

Peter, who'd been lying awake, observed this strange behavior. When Ryan glanced in his direction, he'd feigned sleep, closing his eyes, breathing heavy. Lying still, he listened to the boys' futile attempts to creep out of bed unnoticed. They tiptoed over to their clothes and quietly got dressed.

It was apparent that Ryan and his friends had made alternate plans from the ones they'd agreed upon the night before, new plans that didn't include Peter or Luke. Opening one eye, he watched the boys slip through the crack in the door; one by one, the three rats scampered into the morning light.

Peter sprang from bed and leaned over Luke's cot, giving him a firm shake, "Wake up and get dressed; those morons just left."

Luke opened his eyes, startled, "What?"

"Those imbeciles are launching the canoe without us!"

"No way!"

"Way! Get your butt in gear! We're going after them!" Peter already had one leg through his jeans, hopping on one foot; he frantically worked on the second one.

Luke sat up, still half-asleep, showing no sense of urgency; his motions were slow and lethargic.

Peter pulled his T-shirt over his head; it was one leftover from the skit. "Come on, get dressed!"

Luke finally got moving. Peter, now dressed, waited for Luke, his patience growing thin. "Ready, Snail Boy? Let's go!"

Luke smiled, "Ah, that's Mr. Snail Boy to you."

Peter smirked at this, but still felt agitated, not so much with Luke but with those other assholes. Together they left the hut and marched off toward the knoll. Despite his foot injury, he wasn't about to let Ryan and his feeble friends steal all the glory for themselves, especially after all of the tough elbow grease that he and Luke had put into building that canoe.

Three days had passed since the red gel had tried to devour his foot. Atiak had been a big help on that first day, removing Hope's makeshift bandages and applying a dark brown salve to his bloody toes. It had the consistency of thick molasses, but it felt good, squelching the sting. She made the soothing mixture using a combination of several plants including aloe, guava, and manioc. Whatever it was, it worked. By the third day, new, pink skin encircled his shrinking scabs, evidence that his toes were on the mend.

Peter spotted them up on the hill next to the canoe; Ryan flailed his arms, belting out orders to his two lackeys. Jason and Matthew each crouched down in a squat position holding opposite ends of the craft.

"Ready! Lift!" Ryan shouted.

With interlocked hands, both boys strained to lift the canoe and after putting their backs into it, they managed to hoist the craft up to their crotches. They wobbled back and forth several times before finding their balance, succeeding in taking several small steps down the modest grade.

Peter, pleased that he'd caught them red-handed, marched up to the foot of the knoll looking for bear. Luke trailed several steps behind.

"Hey, what's up assholes?" Peter yelled as he approached.

Upon hearing the words, Jason and Matthew placed the canoe back onto the ground. Looking toward Ryan, they awaited his response.

"Hey, bud, why the name calling?" Ryan said.

"You know why, dick-weed! Couldn't wait for us, huh? Had to sneak out behind our backs? You know, Ryan, you're a real shithead."

Ryan rubbed his chin, hesitating a few seconds before he spoke, making it appear as though he was giving the matter some thought. His smile widened. "Don't cry, little girl, we were just thinking of you and your injured foot. You've been hobbling around here for a good three days now, not even touching the canoe. We just didn't want to see you get hurt, that's all."

"You know that's bullshit; we discussed all this last night and I said I was in!"

"Hey, when you came up lame *we* were the ones who picked up the slack," Ryan said.

Jason nodded. "Yeah, we're the ones who finished it."

"We did most of the work; it's only right that we be the ones to launch it," Matthew said.

"Oh yeah! What about Luke? He was here every day. How come you didn't bring him along?" Peter asked.

Ryan smirked. "Well, we were going to bring Sleeping Beauty here, but he was resting so peacefully, we didn't want to disturb him."

"You lying sack of shit, how 'bout I come up there and twist your head off!"

Ryan took a step toward Peter, but remained on the high ground. "Bring it on, asshole."

"Yeah, bring it on!" Matthew yelled.

Jason pointed toward Luke, "And when we get done with big asshole, we'll ream little asshole too!" This brought on a chorus of laughter from both Ryan and Matthew.

Peter's blood boiled, turning his cheeks apple red. Despite his injured foot, he stormed up the slight grade after Ryan, having to run a gauntlet of wood chips that rained down upon him like hail. Matthew and Jason heaved the small chunks of tree, by-products from the canoe. Luke stayed behind Peter, using him as a shield, and followed him up the knoll.

⊷⊶

Hope and Mary saw Ipiak walking along just ahead of them, heading toward the main cooking hut when they heard the commotion coming from the knoll. Peter's cursing triggered an abrupt turnabout, causing the breakfast goers to reverse their course. Mary and Ipiak tried to keep pace with Hope as she raced to the hill to investigate.

Passing the huts, she turned the corner. Hope now had a clear view of Peter and Luke standing on the bottom of the knoll, shouting up at Ryan. Jason said something inaudible. Whatever he said must've been funny, because Ryan and Matthew appeared to be laughing.

Peter shook his fist and charged the hill. Ryan stood in a ready position defensively holding up his fists, while Jason and Matthew threw handful after handful of wood chips down on Peter as he approached.

Eno, who'd walked up the back side of the hill, dropped his carving tools and broke into an all out sprint. He got there just in time to step in front of the two boys. Ipiak bolted up the knoll; Hope and Mary climbed the short hill just a few steps behind him. Ipiak got there in time to grab Peter from behind, dragging him away from Ryan.

After several minutes, Peter calmed down, but he demanded that Ryan make a full apology. Ryan agreed, saying sorry; albeit halfhearted, it was an apology nonetheless.

Blending his English with Shuar, Eno suggested sharing some *ayahuasca* with the boys in order to free their spirits of any remaining hostilities. Ipiak acted as translator helping Eno get his point across, describing the tranquil, calming effect produced by the herbal concoction.

Peter clenched his jaw and rubbed his chin.

Receiving no objections, Eno proceeded. Removing a leather pouch from his belt, he untied the strings and pulled out a small earthen jug. It was no bigger than one of those pint size bottles of blackberry brandy that Hope had sipped on last winter at the ice skating pond. Eno reached into the pouch again, this time producing a small earthen cup no bigger than a shot glass. He uncorked the small bottle and poured out a measure of the syrupy brown liquid, offering it to Peter.

"I don't know about this," Peter said, making no effort to reach for the cup.

"Girly man doesn't want it, so give it to me, I'll try it!" Ryan held out his hand.

Peter glared at him.

Eno handed Ryan the ceramic cup filled to the rim. Ryan took the cup from his hand without spilling a drop and tossed it back with one swift motion. "Ahhhh," he said as he stared at Peter and smiled.

Next, Jason the follower stepped forward. "Can I try some?"

Eno filled the cup and handed it to Jason who slugged it down in one gulp, but not without a grimace. "This is great; try some," Jason wheezed, handing the cup to Matthew.

Matthew held the cup, allowing Eno to pour out another measure of the brown liquid. He too threw it into the back of his throat and winced without saying a word.

Blood once again rushed to Peter's cheeks. Ryan's girly man comment had clearly relit his fuse. With his manhood in question, Peter demanded the cup.

Why do guys act like such little boys? Hope thought.

She hated these testosterone-fueled mind games and didn't want Peter to drink the syrup on her accord. She touched his arm and said, "You don't have to do this if you don't want to."

"Thanks, but I gave it some thought. I'll give it a try."

Matthew, still wincing, handed Peter the cup. Eno filled it to the brim and Peter, this time without hesitation, slammed it back. Glaring at his nemesis, Peter feigned a smile.

Eno refilled the cup, handing it to Mary. It took her more than ten, tiny sips and several coughs to finish the cup, but somehow she got it all down.

Pouring out more, Eno offered the dark syrup to Hope, who held up her hand in protest.

"No, thanks, I think I'll pass."

"You really should try some," Mary said.

"I don't do drugs."

Mary smiled. "Come on, Hope, we're here to learn about the Shuar and their customs, aren't we?"

"Yeah, a little bit won't hurtcha," Ryan said.

Now it was her turn to buckle under peer pressure; she took a small sip. It tasted bitter, almost unbearable.

Hope sipped the drink, pinching her nose to dull her senses until it was gone. The herbal concoction was warm and tingly as it slid down her throat and into her stomach.

"This really warms you up," Mary said, rubbing her tummy.

"I don't feel anything; give me another shot," Ryan said.

Ipiak shook his head, "It takes a while; you shouldn't have anymore." Ryan grabbed the cup. "Come on, I'm all right; I can handle it."

Eno looked at Ipiak, shrugged his shoulders and refilled his cup. Ryan glared at Peter, raising his cup in a mock toast, downing it even faster than the one before.

Peter grabbed the cup from Ryan and demanded another shot as well. Once filled, he too slammed it back.

Peter's behavior angered Hope. *Why is he allowing Ryan to bait him like that?*

Eno and Ipiak poured out a cup for themselves and downed the drink; they too refilled the cup and drank that as well. Ipiak explained their need for the second dose, saying that both men had built up a strong resistance to it.

Ryan smiled, looking like he'd just had an epiphany, and turned to Luke. "What about you, sissy boy? Aren't you going to try some?"

"No, I don't think so." Luke held strong, the only one in the group who had not sampled the strong hallucinogen.

Matthew waved his hand at him and said, "Don't be a wuss your entire life."

Jason pumped his fist in the air and chanted, "Luke! Luke! Luke!"

Soon, Ryan and Matthew joined the mantra.

Hope, appalled by the peer pressure, shouted, "Leave him alone!" But the boys' frenzied chants drowned out her words.

Peter shouted, "Screw those guys; don't do it if you don't want to."

Each repetition of the chant seemed to chip away at Luke's psyche. At about the half minute mark, it appeared that they'd broken through, shattering his resistance. When he reached for the cup, a cheer of approval went up from his hecklers.

Eno poured out the last of the *ayahausca*, turning the bottle upside down and shaking out the last drop. Despite his efforts, the remaining brown liquid only filled the cup halfway. He handed the half-shot to Luke, who reluctantly accepted it.

Luke held the cup out in front of him, staring at the brown liquid; he took a deep breath looking like a man about to drink hemlock. Raising the cup to his nose, he sniffed the fluid and grimaced.

Ryan resumed the chant, "Luke! Luke! Luke!" The two other boys followed suit.

After taking a final breath, Luke closed his eyes and downed the bitter concoction.

This final act of submission brought on another round of cheers from Ryan and his two friends.

Hope shook her head in disgust, and then looked to Mary for her reaction. When their eyes met, Mary just shrugged. Eno said something in Shuar; everyone looked at Ipiak for a translation.

Ipiak waited for him to finish before he spoke. "Eno said that we must stay seated during our individual journeys while we commune with the spirits."

With those words, both Eno and Ipiak slunk to the ground and sat with their legs crossed. They closed their eyes and remained motionless, except for their rhythmic breathing.

Hope followed Eno's instructions and sat on the ground next to Ipiak. Peter sat next to her. Mary, in a show of solidarity, also took a seat amongst the wood chips. Luke did likewise, forming a loose circle.

Ryan, Matthew, and Jason refused to sit with the group, opting instead to stand outside the circle making snide remarks from afar, most of them directed at Peter. Matthew pulled a pack of cigarettes from his shirt pocket. After smacking the pack against his hand several times, he removed one and placed it in his mouth. He struck a match and lit the cigarette. Taking a big drag, he released a huge cloud of gray smoke into the air. Under normal circumstances, Matthew would never be so bold, but these weren't normal circumstances.

Hope felt odd; she ran her fingers across her arm and her skin felt rubbery. After pinching it, she gave it a tug; the skin seemed to stretch, showing great elasticity. When released, it seemed to snap back into place like a rubber band.

This strange sensation gave her goose bumps across her arm. Needing a better understanding of what was happening to her, she shouted, "Ipiak! Eno!" but received no reply. Both tribesmen sat in silence, having fallen into a trance.

CHAPTER FOURTEEN

S itting around the circle, Hope became very aware of her surroundings. The leaves on the trees seemed much greener than they had
been just a few minutes before. The sunlight filtering through the
canopy offered an array of spectral colors that seemed to jump out
at her.

The ferns were more defined than usual, almost fluorescent with
clearer lines and more depth, almost like wearing special 3-D glasses.

She squinted and said, "Everything's so bright, so alive!" Even the
flat hands and numbers on her watch seemed multi-dimensional and
it was only 8:20; she couldn't have been sitting there for only twenty
minutes.

Mary laughed, "We should take some of this stuff home with us!"

"Only if you want to be strip-searched and thrown in jail by
Mr. Customs Man," Peter said.

A large black butterfly fluttered in a circle above Hope's head,
floating on a breeze; each rise and fall left a sparkling trail in its
wake. A bright red spot accentuated each black wing, as if dabbed on
with a fine paint brush.

The butterfly stopped circling and began to flutter away down the knoll. Startled by its unexpected departure, Hope had an overwhelming desire to follow it. Without hesitation, she leaped to her feet and gave chase.

Peter called out for her to stop, but his words failed to register; they sounded like nothing more than white noise. Catching the butterfly became her obsession, although she hadn't given much thought about what to do with it once she'd caught it. It flew faster, flying erratically through the village. At times it seemed to allow her to catch up to it, only to flutter away again at the last second, always staying just out of reach. Its pull on her psyche was strong, it made her feel like a little girl again, bringing her back to those lazy summer days when she used to chase butterflies across the grounds of the swim club. This in itself was intoxicating. How old had she been when she'd gotten her first butterfly net and the little plastic cage that accompanied it, five?

Peter and Mary's shrill shouts sounded dull in her ears, compared to the sounds of her childhood that echoed through her head. She heard the laughter of children and kids splashing in the pool, and the sounds of a kickball game in full swing; she could even smell the barbecued ribs cooking on the grill. Peter's voice sounded like background noise in comparison, making it easy to dismiss. She couldn't stop now, not without running the risk of erasing her memories. Thoughts of her father flashed through her mind; he was alive then and she could see him standing in front of her, bare-chested, wearing his navy blue swim trunks. She jittered with excitement, bouncing on her toes as he grasped the net with one hand and delicately removed the black and red butterfly with his other. She held out the cage with its door wide open, while her father gently released the winged creature into the aerated container.

Coincidentally, that first butterfly looked a lot like the one that she was currently chasing. Her friends pursued her, but she was only vaguely aware of them as she ran faster and, like the butterfly, she fluttered free, avoiding capture.

The butterfly crossed the footbridge. Veering left, it danced along the banks of the brook. The sparkling water mesmerized Hope, but only for a brief moment. The butterfly fluttered in place again, seemingly waiting for her. Her focus returned to the winged bug. Like a silent Pied Piper it danced in circles as it lured her down the path that led to the rainforest.

Hope found herself past the boundaries that Brenda had set for the group, but she didn't care; catching the butterfly was all that mattered. The forest seemed more vibrant than before, almost fluorescent. And the lines, those beautiful lines that detailed the trunks and branches were so clear and crisp.

Each step brought her deeper into the jungle; she was determined now more than ever to catch the elusive insect. Try as she may, the butterfly always seemed just out of reach. The jungle thickened, but still she pressed on. The familiar bug started down one path, then switched to another, then jumped again to another. She stopped for a moment and spun around, having lost sight of the winged creature. *Where's that butterfly?*

It reappeared as if on command farther down the path. It seemed larger than before and its black spotted wings now appeared to be a deep translucent blue.

This stopped Hope in her tracks; all the blood drained from her cheeks and she began to hyperventilate. Despite being as high as she was, she didn't think the insect's transformation was natural. Was it the *ayahausca* that made the butterfly change size and color? Was she just hallucinating or was this something more sinister?

When she'd lost sight of the butterfly it had suddenly reappeared, as if it had forgotten which species it had been impersonating and hastily transformed into a similar one, hoping that she wouldn't notice. But, she had noticed, and her hands began to tremble. She tried to calm herself by taking slow, deliberate breaths; she prayed that it was the drug that altered her perception or perhaps it was simply a different butterfly. This thought satisfied her for the moment; her hands stopped shaking and her breathing returned to normal.

She gazed down the path and adrenaline shot through her veins. She swallowed hard as her throat sunk into her heart. The butterfly fluttered in place, and there was no denying it, the black winged insect waited for her. Yes, the black winged insect! She'd watched it transform before her eyes back to its original size and color. It hovered in place about eye level above the path; it moved two feet backward toward Hope, then two feet forward. It acted like a dog trying to coax his master forward, but this was no Lassie and she knew that its intentions were anything but good.

Hope stood frozen on the path; when it became apparent that she wouldn't budge any farther, the butterfly wavered and vanished, like the Nunbird and the fly.

Hope second guessed herself. Had it been nothing more than an apparition? Was she tripping out on *ayahuasca?*

Gazing down the trail; it appeared that a red, slick, wetness spattered the leaves of the green ferns that surrounded the path on both sides. It was if a large wounded animal had staggered down the path spurting blood everywhere across the greenery. What if it wasn't an animal? What if it was a man or a woman slaughtered on the path and carried away by killers to do God knows what? At that moment Hope noticed the blood spatter on her own shirt and began to tremble. She must've somehow brushed against the ferns, but she didn't remember doing so.

She felt scared and alone. She never should've taken that drug, a hard lesson learned. It was all too much for her; she dropped to her knees, buried her face in her hands, and began to cry. After several minutes, she realized that her tears were getting her nowhere. Using the back of her hands, she wiped them away.

Nearly an hour had elapsed since she'd first checked the time sitting in the circle; it seemed like only minutes. She'd spent most of that time running aimlessly through the forest; having switched paths so many times, she'd lost all sense of direction. Her friends had been fifty or so yards behind her; she'd somehow lost them and now *she* was lost. *Which path had I come down?* She closed her eyes and pressed her hands against her temples.

Hope lifted her head; the blood had disappeared from her shirt and there was no longer any trace of it on the surrounding ferns. She thought she'd heard a faint voice in the distance. It had to be the *ayahausca* once again playing tricks on her mind. Then she heard it again. It sounded a little closer this time. It was a voice, Peter's voice! He shouted her name; her boyfriend had come to rescue her!

"Peter! Peter! I'm over here!"

"Don't move! Stay there! I'll come to you!"

He must have been a good distance away, because it took him several minutes to fight his way through the brush. Mary and Luke were right behind him. Much to her astonishment, Ryan, Jason, and Matthew were walking just a few steps behind the others.

Peter pushed away several low hanging branches to get to Hope; he wrapped his arms around her and held her tight, giving her a big kiss. "Are you all right?"

Hope fidgeted in his arms, feeling sheepish and stupid for running off. "I'm okay, I guess."

Now that her relationship with Peter was exposed, she wondered how the others would react. Everyone seemed to be okay with it, except for Ryan whose look of disgust equaled that of a child forced to eat lima beans. He folded his arms in a disapproving manner and belched loudly, "That says it all!"

Jason and Matthew both chuckled.

Mary crinkled her nose at Ryan. "You revolting pig!"

Her comments brought on another round of laughter, this time from all three of them.

Mary placed her hands on Hope's shoulders. "Why'd you run off like that?

"I guess I got carried away chasing that butterfly."

Mary raised her left eyebrow, "Huh? Butterfly? What butterfly?"

"You must've seen it. It had black wings with a red spot in the center."

"I didn't see it either," Luke said, sounding disappointed.

Ryan reached into the pocket of his jeans, turning it inside out. After unzipping his fly, his hand disappeared inside his pants. "No, but I did see a one-eared elephant with a long trunk. Want to see it?" Ryan said, threatening to expose himself.

This brought another round of laughter from Matthew and Jason.

"If you think your elephant has a long trunk, then you really must be hallucinating," Hope said.

Normally reserved, Luke glared at Ryan through glazed eyes. "Oooh! She dressed you down!"

Ryan punched him hard on the shoulder. Luke cowered, rubbing his arm.

"Ryan, cut the crap; touch him again and I'll bash your head in so far, you'll be blowing your nose through your zipper," Peter said.

Jason and Matthew giggled.

Ryan stepped toward Peter, "Anytime you think you're man enough."

Peter gritted his teeth, clenching his fist, and stepped toward Ryan.

Hope jumped in between them. "I'm tired of this macho bullshit from both of you! I know it's a stretch but pretend like you're in a church group working together on a mission trip."

"I don't get it! Why'd you guys follow us, just to act like a bunch of jerks?" Mary asked.

Ryan pointed at Luke, "Hey, he's the one who started with me; I was just trying to lighten things up, that's all."

Mary raised one eyebrow. "You haven't answered my question. Why'd you follow us?"

"When Hope bolted, I figured we'd better give chase; it was better than standing around with our dicks in our hands, waiting for those Indian zombies to wake up."

"They didn't follow you? They could have guided us back," Hope said.

Jason shook his head in disgust, "No, they didn't even budge."

"Shit! I've lost my cigarettes!" Matthew said, patting the front of his shirt.

"Matt, what about you, did you see them get up?" Hope asked.

Matthew pointed down the path, "They're still sitting there as far as I know."

Luke dry heaved several times before vomiting yellow chunks onto the forest floor.

Mary and Ryan gagged at the sight of this. Hope also nearly vomited before turning away.

Moments later, Jason flailed his arms, yelling, "Fire ants! Get them off, they're all over me! Get them off!" He frantically swatted at the nonexistent insects.

Ryan slapped him across the face. "Get a grip, there's nothing there!"

Unconvinced, Jason continued shouting and jumping. Matthew tackled him and held his legs while Ryan sat on his chest, pinning down his shoulder blades until he calmed. Soon, Jason stopped shouting and his tone changed. "I'm okay, guys; you can get off me anytime now."

After what seemed like longer than necessary, Ryan rolled off of him, allowing him to sit. Matthew grabbed his hand and pulled him to his feet.

Hope's throat felt parched; she needed a drink, but no one had brought a canteen. "I think it's best if we head back," Hope said, dreading the walk.

Everyone seemed to agree and turned to start walking in the other direction.

Hope and Peter held hands now that their relationship was out in the open. Together, they led the group back down the path from which they'd come—or so they thought.

Nothing looked familiar, and she was becoming thirstier by the minute. Once again she had that eerie sensation. The hairs stood up straight on the back of her neck and despite holding Peter's hand, her heart raced.

Hope scanned the forest floor in all directions, but saw nothing. She looked up high into the trees—still nothing. Her uncompromising thirst replaced her anxiety. *We're in the rainforest, so where the heck is all the rain?*

They'd walked for only a few minutes when Ryan and his crew started bitching. She chose to tune them out. *Who asked them to come along anyway?* Right now she needed water and she needed it soon.

After what seemed like forever, the winding path led to a ravine. At the bottom of the ravine flowed a brook. Hope led the way down to the water, praying that it was drinkable and that it wasn't a mirage.

The clear, shallow water moved fast across the algae-covered stones as it cascaded downhill. Some of the water filled small pools between the rocks. Hope got down on her hands and knees to drink from one of the still pools. The others spread out along the bank, finding their own points of access to the water.

Hope cupped her hands, ladling the cool water, bringing it to her lips. She drank for several minutes until she had her fill. The cool drink soothed her throat. With her thirst now quenched, she allowed the ripples to dissipate, returning the pool back to its smooth, pond-like surface.

Hope peered into the pool to look at her own reflection, concerned for the first time about her appearance. She hoped her perspiration, lack of makeup, and disheveled hair didn't turn Peter off. *Maybe I can spruce up a bit.*

When she leaned over the pool to get a better look at herself, something appeared above her shoulder. Her shrill screams echoed throughout the ravine. The reflection of a man stared back at her. Blue war paint covered his face; orange and black feathers protruded from his hair; he stood bare-chested with a bone necklace hanging from his neck; his large hand gripped a long spear.

Hope spun around in a ready position to defend herself against her would-be attacker—but no one was there. She turned back to the pool and his reflection was gone.

CHAPTER FIFTEEN

B renda took a deep breath, holding it for a second before releasing a long sigh; it had already been more than a week since her romantic interlude with Tim. She found herself on an emotional rollercoaster, analyzing everything, resolving nothing, each moment since their midnight rendezvous magnified under a microscope, dissected into a thousand pieces, carefully examined then reassembled back into that same pile of shit.

The *morning after* at breakfast, she couldn't even summon up the courage to look him in the eyes. Their conversation was superficial at best; a part of her felt stupid. Despite her promises to herself and God, she'd become weaker than the watered down drinks served at the strip bar where she used to dance. She could always blame it on the alcohol, but this wasn't even close to the truth. She wanted this, even more so than Tim.

And afterward she'd once again found herself craving coke. She thought she'd locked away her demons forever in rehab back in New Jersey, but somehow they'd escaped, finding her here in the jungle, sucking away her resistance just like the drug itself. She'd been kidding herself the whole time; that was the undeniable truth, as she realized only now that her cravings never left.

Her mind shifted back to Tim; with time she'd be able to put this whole sexual escapade behind her; at least that's what she kept telling herself, but it seemed to get worse with each passing day instead of better. Tim pined for her, making several attempts to woo her since their liaison, professing how much he cared for her time and again. She kept him at arm's length, always steering their conversation toward their mission work, avoiding anything personal.

She kept telling herself that's the way it had to be, that voice within told her that she didn't deserve Tim or any guy like him. Why would any guy want damaged merchandise when they could get something brand new right off the shelf? And she couldn't describe herself as slightly damaged; severe damage seemed to be a far better description, in more ways than one. Tim was sweet, honest, and wholesome, and she was morally corrupt. What was she supposed to do, hide her past from him forever? Live a lie for the rest of her life? *No, it's better to avoid entanglements now.*

Another fainter voice glowed within, like a smoldering ash that refused to die, the voice that allowed her to remember how good he'd made her feel, by the footbridge—in her bed. She called it her *what if voice.* What if somehow all of this was fate? What if she was meant to be with Tim? What if she did kiss him and it felt great? What if one day she could have a normal relationship with a man, perhaps this man? What if she told him about her past and he forgave her for it, promising to never question her about it again? And he did so because he loved her and for no other reason. Shouldn't she at least explore those possibilities? It seemed like a pipedream.

Breakfast came and went, but she stayed in her hut lying on her bed, having no desire to make meaningless small talk with Tim, knowing full well that she would never be able to discuss anything of substance, especially around the others. She'd rather go hungry than subject herself to that.

Brenda carefully chose the words that she'd speak to Tim; never satisfied, she'd toss them aside again and again, only to begin anew. She got dressed, knowing that she couldn't hide out there forever. It would only be a matter of time before someone stopped by to check on her. She had to act now or forever lose her nerve.

Taking a deep breath, she found the intestinal fortitude to carry out her plan. After leaving her hut, she walked toward the men's quarters. She passed Bill Drake with a small recorder in his hand, presumably off to conduct yet another interview. She offered him a big hello. He attempted to insert new batteries into the device, grunting a gruff hello as he passed.

In the far distance she saw the kids up on the hill; they were all together; she wouldn't find this fact strange until much later. She continued on, thankful that she and Tim would be able to talk alone.

Brenda knocked on the bamboo door, "Tim? Are you in there?

Tim emerged shirtless from the hut rubbing a towel through his wet hair, "Good morning, I missed you at breakfast."

"We have to talk."

"Oh? It's never good when a woman says, *we have to talk.*"

Brenda stood speechless.

Tim disappeared from the doorway only to reappear moments later wearing a blue polo shirt with his hair now combed. A small group of Shuar boys approached with sticks in hand, pretending to be on a boar hunt, taking up positions around the hut.

Tim smiled. "There's too much traffic around here; let's go for a walk."

"Fine."

Brenda strolled along next to Tim, her arms folded across her breasts as if to hide them.

"So what is it that you want to talk about?"

"About the other night."

"Hey, you've made your point, you're not interested. I get it. You don't have to bang me over the head with it."

"No, I just want to talk."

They took a path that originated beyond the huts, a path with which Brenda was unfamiliar; it led into the rainforest.

As they walked, Brenda tried to collect her thoughts, searching for the proper words. Forgetting everything that she'd rehearsed, she decided to just lay it on the line, get all the cow shit out there and let the chips fall where they may. "I've been thinking about some of the things that you've said over the past week. Did you mean any of it?"

"Every word."

"Well, I've been giving it a lot of thought."

Tim's smile widened, "And?"

"And there are a lot of things about me you don't know. I have a very sordid past. I've kept my distance from you because I was afraid that if you ever found out the truth, you wouldn't like me anymore. The truth is I used to suck cock for cocaine. I'm nothing more than your run of the mill coke slut. I'm hiding from myself here in the jungle behind a wall of Christianity."

And there it all was, everything exposed, hanging out there like stained g-strings pinned to a clothesline, and there it would stay; there was no taking it back, no sugar coating, just the sordid truth.

They walked in silence and the color left Tim's face; his skin grew pale, almost gray. He seemed to digest each word, letting it absorb into his system. He stopped after a few steps and looked at her as if he were about to speak. After stammering on his words, he stared down at the path and resumed his walk, maintaining a methodical pace as he rubbed his chin and took deep breaths.

She walked beside him for more than fifty yards, tears flowing freely down her cheeks; she had told the truth, exposing her heart in the process, only to have it crushed under the weight of his silence. But what had she expected? She didn't deserve him and now she'd bared her soul, exposing her wicked underbelly, revealing the sinful creature within.

Stopping again on the path, he turned to face her, pointing his finger toward the sky as if to rebuke her or make a point. Instead, he grabbed her by the shoulders and gazed into her eyes as her stream of tears became a full-fledged sob.

"Look at me! Look at me!" He violently shook her shoulders.

Brenda peered into his bulging eyes; he looked crazed. Taking a breath, he inhaled deeply before he spoke, "Listen to me; please listen to me!" Grimacing as if each word pained him, tears filled his eyes as he said, "I don't give a damn about your past; all I care about is the here and now, you and me, nothing else matters. Can you understand that?"

Brenda smiled, "Yes! Yes!"

And with those words now spoken, Tim wrapped his arms around her and held her tight for a good long time, and then they kissed. This time Brenda didn't turn away; she kissed him back, and his lips felt soft against her own, just the way she had imagined it. She continued crying, but they were now tears of joy. She resigned herself to at least giving it a try; that's all she could ask for. They walked hand in hand along the path and this time their fingers meshed perfectly like a pair of gears. The path led down to a fertile meadow; his smile widened as they approached. Tim opened his arms wide. "Behold Eden."

Brenda took in her lush green surroundings. Wild purple flowers poked through a patch of yellow orchids creating a sweet, unique scent.

Several orange butterflies fluttered, back and forth in between the flowers. A small hummingbird jockeyed for position around the flying insects, hovering in place to collect its nectar.

Brenda smiled. "This really is like the Garden of Eden; how'd you find this place?"

"Never you mind, my dear." Tim took Brenda by the hand and led her to a tree swollen with small, purple berries. "Come and taste the forbidden fruit."

Tim picked several berries and popped them into his mouth.

"What is it?" Brenda asked.

"Acai." He picked a ripe one that looked like it was about to burst and fed it to Brenda. She held it in between her lips for a moment before biting into the sweet, juicy berry and saying, "This is really good!"

"It's a known aphrodisiac. I'll show you just how well it works." Tim leaned forward and kissed Brenda gently on her now purple lips.

Without hesitation, she kissed him back; it was intoxicating.

They stepped off the path to lay in the tall grass, matting it down with their bodies. Basking in the sunlight in the beautiful garden, they removed each other's clothing, caressing each other, and without reservation, Brenda made love to her Adam for the rest of the afternoon.

═╬═ ╬═

Brenda and Tim walked hand in hand through the forest, only breaking their grip when they'd reached the village. Sunburn stung Brenda's skin, especially those tender parts that had never before seen the light of day. She didn't care; with Tim by her side, she felt strong and confident.

Brenda looked around. Something felt strange; she noticed it right away, "Where are the kids?"

"I don't know. They could be hiding anywhere," Tim smiled.

"I'm serious, there's nobody around."

"Did you see any of them before we left?"

Brenda thought for a moment, "Yeah, they were all up on the hill by the canoe."

"Let's check it out."

Together, they made their way to the top of the knoll. Only Eno and Ipiak sat with their eyes closed and their legs crossed; no one else was in sight. An earthen flask and a tiny ceramic cup rested on the ground beside them.

"What's this?" Tim picked up the bottle and took a whiff. Both tribesmen remained unresponsive.

Brenda gave Ipiak a firm shake. "Wake up! Where are the kids?"

Ipiak began to stir; it took him a moment to acclimate to his surroundings.

Brenda repeated herself, shouting, "Where are the kids?"

Ipiak scratched his head, "I don't know; they were here when I sat down."

"What was in the cup?" Tim asked.

"*Ayahuasca.*"

"Did the kids drink any of it?" Brenda asked.

Ipiak nodded, "They had a little."

"Oh, Christ!" Tim said.

"What's the matter?" Brenda asked.

"*Ayahuasca* is a strong hallucinogen; they could be anywhere."

Eno began to stir, shouting something in Shuar.

"What's he hollering about?" Tim asked.

Ipiak shook his head in disgust. "He said that he told them to stay seated to commune with the spirits."

A large vein bulged from Brenda's neck; she pointed at Eno and yelled, "Tell him to save it!"

⊷⊰⊹⊱⊶

Brenda was beside herself; she had a headache and felt sick to her stomach. They'd searched the entire village for the kids and came up empty. Logic told her they had to be somewhere in the rainforest, but where? They'd disobeyed her rules, but why?

"We've got to find them! We just have to," Brenda said.

"Take it easy, we'll find them. The tribesmen are jungle experts; let's ask them to help us."

This idea made Brenda feel a little better, and the pounding in her head subsided for the moment, although her stomach was still upset. Together they searched for Teja, who was nowhere in sight.

Yeki sat on a stump whittling a spear outside his hut; he said he'd seen Teja less than ten minutes before strolling toward the Shuar ceremonial site. Brenda and Tim quickened their pace. They found

Teja sitting on a stump next to Bill Drake who held a microphone in the Elder's face. Apparently, the good professor was conducting yet another interview.

"Teja, all of the kids are missing; we need your help!" Tim said.

"What do you mean missing?" Bill put down the microphone and turned off the recorder.

Brenda felt sheepish, "They're not in the village; we've searched everywhere!"

"Mary too?" Creases formed across Bill's forehead.

Both she and Tim nodded.

The professor's face turned red. "Goddamn it, weren't you two supposed to be watching them?"

"We turned our heads for just a second and they were gone," Tim said.

Nothing could be further from the truth. Tim had told an outright lie; they'd been away for hours enjoying a romp in the woods, shunning their responsibilities, and now they all were gone, and it was all her fault, but Brenda said nothing. She stood by her man in silence.

Bill turned to Teja, speaking Spanish, the only language that they both understood.

"*¿Nos pueden ayudar a encontrar a nuestros muchachos? Ellos están perididos en el bosque.*" he asked

"*Si.*"

"I asked him if he could help us find the kids and he said yes," Bill said and then turned back to Teja.

"*Necesitamos sus mejores rastreadores.*"

"*Kuja y Ipiak son mis mejores rastreadores,*" Teja replied.

"What did he say?" Brenda asked.

"I told him we needed his best trackers and he said that Kuja and Ipiak are the best."

"Tell him Ipiak is no good to us; he's under the influence of *ayahuasca,*" Tim said.

"Ipiak no es bueno porque está bajo la influencia de ayahuasca," Bill said to Teja.

Teja sighed; and rubbed his forehead. *"Entonces, yo voy a recoger a Yeki."*

"He said I will pick Yeki then!" Bill said.

They headed back into the main part of the village. Teja called over two small boys and asked them to find Kuja and Yeki.

Bill, Tim, and Brenda hurried back to their huts to gather supplies, agreeing to reassemble in ten minutes outside their huts. Brenda emerged last from her bamboo structure; everybody else was there waiting for her. She hated being last, but she had felt like she was forgetting something; she didn't want to venture into the jungle unprepared. She'd stuffed a knapsack with food, mostly fruit and beef jerky.

At the last minute she grabbed a first aid kit, in case they found the kids and somebody was hurt. This thought horrified her; if anybody was hurt it would be her fault.

Bill paced back and forth showing his impatience; beads of sweat formed across his forehead, his bloated head looking like it might explode at any minute. Brenda didn't have to remind herself that *his* daughter was among those lost in the rainforest.

Bill held a large flashlight, the kind that attaches to a 12-volt power pack, and a can of insect repellent. Tim held a flare gun; around his waist he wore an ammo belt that contained six flares.

"Bill, can I have the bug spray?" Brenda asked.

"Here! Take it!" Bill shoved it toward her with such force, she flinched.

After taking the can from his hand, she managed a meek, "Thank you" and applied the aerosol to all exposed areas of her skin. She then applied a generous coating to Tim's bare arms and legs. With Tim protected, she turned her attention back to Bill. He snatched the can away from her in the same rude fashion, opting to apply the insecticide himself. Neither Kuja nor Yeki requested the spray; Brenda assumed that they had their own tribal remedies to repel mosquitoes.

"My daughter's out there; let's go, we're wasting time."

"Follow us!" Kuja waved the group forward.

Kuja and Yeki led them down to the footbridge and found a small path leading into the forest.

Kuja brought the procession to a halt, saying, "We will begin here."

After moving forward, the group soon found themselves under a green canopy of tall trees; Kuja and Yeki stopped along the path every now and again to inspect the dirt. On occasion, they knelt down to examine a crushed fern or broken twig.

Kuja stood and faced the group. "We're on the right path."

Brenda found some solace in the knowledge that they were heading in the right direction.

Bill shouted, "Mary!" again and again. Brenda and Tim called out in a similar fashion, alternating names. There was no reply.

The search party walked deeper into the jungle; it was late afternoon and the path led out of the forest, into a field of tall, brown grass. The Ecuadorian sun hid behind a blanket of clouds, offering minimal daylight before fading into total darkness. Bill clicked on his flashlight.

An owl perched in a dead tree, alarmed by the sudden brightness, hooted several times before flying off into the hazy night. Brenda's voice grew hoarser with every shout. Tim's and Bill's voices also seemed greatly diminished.

"Let's try the flare gun," Tim said and unsnapped the leather holster strapped to his belt.

Loading the gun, he pointed the pistol toward the starless sky, squeezing the trigger. The projectile rocketed more than a hundred yards into the air, lighting up the surrounding fields as it made its slow, parachuted descent, burning out just twenty yards above the ground. The smell of burnt sulfur lingered in the air.

They called out again, repeating the names of the lost—the jungle remained silent, except for a large capybara that scurried into the brush. Brenda jumped backward when she saw the giant rodent, despite having Tim by her side. She wondered how Hope and Mary must feel alone in the jungle; this thought kept her moving forward.

Tim repeated his ritual with the flare gun every mile or so. Brenda glanced at her watch, using the light of the flare to read the time. It was now past 9:00 p.m., they'd been searching for more than four hours. Brenda ate a banana to keep herself going; she offered food to the others but they all declined. Feeling spent, she didn't know how much longer she could go on.

Now and again Kuja would stop to ask Bill for the flashlight. Kneeling down on the path with Yeki, they'd inspect a partial footprint or a patch of matted down grass. Both seemed confident that they were still heading in the right direction.

Brenda's vocal cords ached; she now sounded like she had laryngitis. Tim loaded up the gun for his final shot. Before he could do so, Bill grabbed the gun from his hands and said, "Give me that damn thing!"

Bill raised his arm like the Statue of Liberty and fired. The flare lit up the sky and began its parachuted descent. A sinking feeling fell over Brenda; the glowing light illuminated Bill's face as he looked skyward, and there was no mistaking his look of despair. The burnt out flare extinguished all hopes of finding them, at least on that gloomy night. Bill's once powerful flashlight now grew dim. Everyone agreed to call off the search until morning. They were exhausted, having searched for miles without any luck. Brenda needed all of her remaining energy to hike back.

"Maybe the kids found their way and they're all waiting for us back at the village," Tim said.

Maybe that is the case, it's at least possible, Brenda thought and it lifted her spirits, giving her the strength to trudge through the forest. *And if they are there, I'll never take my eyes off of them for the rest of the trip.*

The dim flashlight burnt out during the last mile, forcing them to walk back in total darkness. As she neared complete exhaustion a voice rang out in her head. *The sins of a few lead to the slaughter of the innocent.* She thought about Hope and Mary lost with the others in the rainforest, innocent kids forced to spend the night alone in the jungle. *Maybe they were back in the village, maybe.*

She'd shunned her responsibilities for a romp in the woods with Tim. *If anything happens to them it will be my fault.* There was nothing else in her life that she was sure of, but she was sure of that. A trickle of light appeared through the trees; it was the bonfires from the village. Together they staggered out of the forest. Brenda's feet felt like caked cement, but that didn't matter; she rushed into the village calling out their names, "Hope, Mary, Peter, Ryan!" But nobody responded; none of them had returned. Tears welled up in Bill's eyes and the sight of that made Brenda cry too. Her mind went numb, left with nothing to rest her hopes on, except for the confidence in Tim's hoarse voice.

"Let's get some rest; we'll resume our search in the morning."

CHAPTER SIXTEEN

Hope couldn't decide if the reflection of the warrior was real or another *ayahuasca*-induced hallucination. Her shrill screams had brought Peter running and he held her tight until her trembling stopped. She felt foolish having cried wolf, trying to convince herself that her mind must've been playing tricks on her. *Nobody could disappear that fast, could they?*

The forest surrounding the brook was thinner than the thick canopy of green they'd marched through earlier. The rocky ravine proved difficult to navigate; huge boulders littered the landscape, hindering tree growth. Large patches of blue Ecuadorian sky were visible through the sparse green cover. Hope glanced at her watch confirming what she already knew—it was past noon.

The others climbed their way across the rocky terrain back to Hope and Peter. Water drenched the fronts of Ryan's and Matthew's shirts. Hope didn't know why that bothered her; maybe it was her way of keeping her mind off the things that really mattered, like where the hell were they and how would they find their way back.

The sun sat in the sky almost directly above them. Peter used his hand as a visor to study its exact position; he squinted as if making a difficult calculation. Without hesitation, he pointed to his right. "The village is east; we must head east to get back."

"Are you sure?" Ryan asked.

"Of course I'm sure." And with those words, Peter and Hope led the others out of the ravine, following a path to their right. Once again they found themselves in the thick forest. The trees were much denser here, their trunks positioned next to one another like hundreds of soldiers standing at attention. And they came in different sizes; some were old and rotund, while others were thin saplings, but they grew in tight, so tight that a rifle shot would travel less than thirty feet before it slammed into bark.

They pressed on for another two hours; Hope wished they'd remained by the brook, having grown thirsty once again. Despite having Peter by her side, she felt the thick forest closing in on her. Once again she felt eyes upon her.

Stopping on the path, she spun around, scanning the forest floor, and then the canopy above. In the distance, hiding high in the branches, a troop of red monkeys stared back at her—she counted nine.

The monkeys stood less than three feet tall with tails of almost the same length. Despite being small in stature, they looked menacing; red fur covered their muscular bodies with the exception of their faces and the ends of their tails, which were black and leathery.

Hope didn't trust what she saw. What if the monkeys were like the butterfly and the reflection? What if this was just another drug-induced illusion? She tugged on Peter's shirt, pointing toward the tree tops. "Tell me what you see."

"Huh?"

"Tell me what you see!"

Peter squinted, his eyes scanning the forest. "I don't see—wait a minute! Holy shit, it looks like we have company."

Mary turned to look. "What? What is it?"

"A pack of red monkeys," Peter said.

"Thank God! You *can* see them!" Hope giggled almost giddy.

Ryan turned to look. "Where? I don't see anything."

Mary pointed, "Look there, right along the tree line."

Ryan squinted, his face contorting as he strained to see the red primates; his facial muscles relaxed at the first sign of recognition. "Cool! Now I see them."

"Well, fry me one; I'm hungry!" Matthew said.

Ryan and Jason, still high, giggled hysterically.

A monkey much larger than the rest glared at them from his tall perch just left of the path. Hope presumed it was the dominant male, the troop leader, because the other primates didn't move forward until he did.

"Come on, let's go!" Peter waved the group forward.

Hope followed Peter's lead, deciding it was best to turn around and ignore the ugly creatures.

After walking more than fifty yards, Hope glanced over her shoulder. The monkeys had closed the gap between them; they lurked in the green canopy, jumping from tree to tree following from above, less than forty yards behind them.

Hope grabbed Peter's arm, "Look!"

Peter stopped and turned, and when he did, the dominant male also stopped, bringing the entire troop to a halt.

"How come they're not howling?" Luke asked.

"Huh?" Peter asked.

"I know my monkeys and these are Red Howlers, the loudest animals on the planet; how come they're not howling?"

"The loudest animal? Come on, you're shitting me, right?" Ryan asked.

"No, I'm not, as you put it, *shitting* you."

"They do seem suspiciously quiet," Hope said.

A mumble of agreement passed among the group.

Hope could see the leader's face much clearer now; his expression looked anything but friendly; she would even call it hostile. The red fur that encircled his black face lent him a satanic appearance. A devil surrounded by his troop of red demons.

Peter started forward again as did Hope and the others, but so did the monkeys. After several dozen steps, Peter stopped short and the monkeys did likewise. When they moved forward again, the monkeys followed. This went on for some time.

Every time she glanced over her shoulder, they appeared to be closer than before. They were now less than twenty yards away and they seemed to have spread out wider, forming a loose net across the forest.

The dominant male looked even uglier and angrier at this closer distance, as did his lieutenants that flanked his sides. They were so close; Hope could see several long strands of hair growing from a mole on the leader's face. *Is that foam dripping from his mouth?*

Her heart raced and her breathing felt labored; that familiar feeling of panic began to churn in her gut. "Peter, they're getting close; we must do something!"

"Just keep walking; they'll tire and give up after awhile."

"Or maybe we'll tire first; maybe they're waiting for us to take our final steps, then they'll pounce on us and rip us to shreds!" Ryan said.

Hope allowed Ryan's words to sink in; her hands trembled. *Could it be true, could this be our fate, ripped limb from limb by a pack of angry monkeys?*

Peter grabbed her shaking hands. "That will be enough, Ryan!" he said.

"Yeah, yeah," Ryan said, too exhausted to snap back at him.

Hope glared at the lead monkey; he had only moved slightly closer, maybe less than a yard, but the apes at both ends of the line seemed to be circling in on them, forming an irregular horseshoe. The monkey on her far right was almost parallel to her now, having jumped over to a tree less than twenty yards away. The dominant male stared down from his high perch; he seemed to be smirking at her as if he had some secret knowledge that only he was privy to. This was far more than Hope could bear, and she pulled her hands back from Peter. "Do something! Now!" she said.

Peter swallowed hard. "Okay, guys, grab some sticks, we're going to come right at them; don't hit them unless you're forced to; we just want to chase them away."

Ryan, Jason, and Matthew were quick to oblige, picking up thick sticks the size of clubs. At first, Luke picked up a much thinner stick, but after comparing it to the others, he tossed it aside in favor of a bigger one. Peter found a thick, bat-sized branch and turned to face the lead monkey.

The alpha male had moved down from the higher branches to a much lower one. All of the monkeys followed him downward; some stood on tree limbs; others hung from branches, and one hung from his tail. Crazy as it seemed, it was as if they were preparing for battle.

Peter shook his stick. "Okay, when I say go, we chase those red bastards back into the forest."

Mary looked petrified upon hearing Peter's words; she stood next to Hope and grasped her hand. Hope returned her squeeze, saying, "Don't worry, it's gonna be okay," but her words sounded shallow and weak. Mary's knees wobbled as both girls took several steps backward, away from the battlefield.

Ryan and Matthew stood in a crouched position holding their clubs. Jason stared at the troop leader and smacked his stick against the palm of his left hand again and again. Luke took a deep breath, holding his stick against his side.

Peter swallowed hard. "Ready! Go!"

They charged forward, screaming at the monkeys with raised sticks in hand.

The lead monkey stood up straight with arms raised above his head. He snarled, baring his teeth; more foam dripped from his mouth and he let out a low, nasty growl. The sound shook the forest, stopping the boys where they stood.

Jason with venom in his eyes, swung his stick at the enraged monkey, but missed. The animal snapped at him several times.

"Get back, he might have rabies!" Peter shouted.

Jason leaped backwards, but one of the soldier monkeys scratched his hand, leaving a red line of blood across his knuckles.

The remaining eight monkeys leaped to the ground, their roars reverberating through the forest. The ungodly sound shook Hope to the core. The deep growls sounded like they emanated from the bowels of hell. Their roars grew louder to the point where Hope and Mary had to cover their ears.

A thick froth formed around the mouths of three of the monkeys. They snapped at fleshy arms and legs just out of reach. Foam flung from their faces, hitting Luke and Matthew on their legs as they jumped backward. The boys retreated from the rabid animals, afraid to turn, afraid to take their eyes off them. They were back to where they'd started, having accomplished nothing, huddled together around Hope and Mary.

The monkeys neither attacked nor retreated; they just stood, maintaining their distance. After several minutes, the alpha monkey climbed back up into the trees. One by one the others followed his lead until they were all perched again high up in the branches.

To Hope the message was clear; they were being herded like cattle in one direction. As long as they moved forward everything was okay; just don't try to reverse course and head back. They were still watching her, she could see them staring.

The forest grew darker as the late afternoon sun trekked across the sky. *Soon it will be dark and then what? Are they waiting to attack in the dark?*

After several minutes, Peter waved them forward again. They all pushed on through the jungle—and so did the monkeys.

Up ahead, a tree laden with heart-shaped fruit fought for its share of sunlight against the foliating giants that surrounded it. The fruit's green, leafy skin resembled that of an artichoke.

Peter was the first to reach it, plucking a hand grenade-sized specimen from the tree. Using his pocket knife, he sliced it in half exposing a white, fleshy interior dotted with black seeds. He sniffed it first before tasting it.

Hope turned once again to look at the monkeys; it had become her ritual—every time they stopped she'd turn to look at the monkeys. They were always there. Each time she prayed they wouldn't be, hoping they'd gone off to harass some other helpless creature. But they were there all right, still lurking in the trees in all their ugliness. The foam dripping from the leader's mouth splattered on the ground, making a sickening sound. *Thank God they've stopped moving forward.*

She turned her attention back to Peter, back to the fruit. Her parched throat felt like she'd swallowed cotton; she needed a drink, as did the others. She prayed that the fruit was edible, craving to suck out any juices from its flesh. What a cruel joke it would be if it wasn't.

Ryan, Matthew, and Jason watched like vultures in silent anticipation, seemingly waiting for their human guinea pig to either drop dead or give them some sort of a positive indication to indulge in the fruit.

Peter sunk his teeth into it. He chewed it several times and swallowed. "It's good!"

He handed the other half to Hope. She tore off a tiny portion of skin and placed it in her mouth.

Using her tongue, she pressed the sliver of fruit against the roof of her mouth, extracting the tiny droplets of juice.

"How's it taste?" Mary asked.

"Tangy and tart, try some." Hope bit into the fruit wholeheartedly.

Mary picked her own green heart from the branch; Peter sliced it open for her. Ryan and his crew gorged themselves, not bothering to ask for the knife. Only Luke appeared hesitant, allowing the big dogs to eat first before claiming his own morsel from the back of the tree. Like the rest of them, he bit through the thick skin as if it were an apple.

Peter picked more than a dozen pieces from the tree; he then sliced each one in half, handing the cut fruit to the girls. Hope consumed several halves of the delightful fruit, and only then was her thirst quenched. When she couldn't eat another bite, she tilted her head back and squirted the juice directly into her mouth. When he had finished eating, Peter began shoving as much of the fruit as he could into his pockets; upon seeing this, everyone followed his example. Hope knew that this might have to sustain them for awhile. There was no telling when they would find food or another water source.

Twilight descended upon them; still Peter waved them forward, "Let's try to push on just a little farther; it will be less ground we'll have to cover in the morning."

"Screw it, let's stay here," Ryan said.

At that moment the alpha monkey let out a howl that shook the forest. Ryan's eyes bulged and he said, "Okay, let's do it your way."

They walked on for less than a quarter-mile before complete darkness crept in.

Peter stopped. "This seems like as good a place as any. Let's make a clearing."

Hope scanned the trees behind them; it was too dark to see the monkeys, but they were still there. She could hear them jumping through the trees.

Peter and Luke began pulling out ferns and plants. In a rare show of cooperation, Ryan and his cronies pitched in, helping to create a small circle of dirt; its circumference measured less than twenty feet. Hope spotted several decent-sized tropical plants a few yards in front of them. She and Mary picked the large leaves and laid them down across the circle to provide a thin layer of bedding. With the dirt now covered, everyone claimed their spot on the circle. Hope felt a little safer sitting in the middle surrounded by the boys. Mary plopped down next to her, followed by Luke. The rest of the boys made up the perimeter of the circle, keeping their clubs within arm's reach.

Empting his pockets, Peter placed the fruit near Hope in the middle of the circle. "Let's keep all of the fruit together; we'll wait until morning and ration it out."

"I'd rather hold onto my own fruit, thank you very much," Ryan said.

Hope, Mary, and Luke emptied their pockets and placed their green hearts on the ground next to Peter's pile.

Matthew and Jason seemed undecided as to what they should do; each boy held two hearts. They stared at the fruit, then back at Ryan.

"Suit yourselves; but let's at least count them up and see what we've got," Peter said.

This seemed to be acceptable to everyone. Ryan placed his fruit down in front of him. Matthew and Jason created their own separate piles. A final count of twenty-eight pieces of fruit lay in separate piles around the circle.

Darkness had arrived and Hope looked at her watch. The illuminated hands indicated that it was only 6:18 p.m., but she felt exhausted. They'd marched through the forest shadowed every step of the way by those horrible monkeys and they hadn't seen anything that looked even remotely familiar. She prayed that Peter was guiding them in the right direction, but felt far less confident than she had before. Her arms itched, pocked with mosquito bites. She wanted nothing more than to lie down and put an end to this miserable day, but how could she sleep with those rabid monkeys lurking in the forest just out of sight? She heard them moving through the trees all around her; now and again she'd catch the shadow of a monkey leaping into a still closer tree. They seemed to be everywhere now. Hope heard the red demons shuffling in front of her, completing their circle. The look on Peter's face told her that he knew it too, but the words remained unspoken. What good would it do, other than upset Mary and Luke?

Ryan and Matthew hoarded their fruit like a couple of starving refugees. Jason sat in silence studying the scratch across his knuckles, rotating his fist back and forth, leaving Hope to wonder if he might be losing it.

Matthew produced some matches from his back pocket and they were able to light a small fire using the dead wood that lay around them; nobody dared venture more than a few feet away from the circle. They constructed the fire near the left side of the ring to give them ample sleeping room.

The trees rustled above them. Tiny beads of sweat formed across Peter's forehead. "I think that one of us should remain awake to stoke the fire and stand guard while the rest of us sleep."

"Since you're the one who brought us here, I think it should be you," Ryan said.

Hope tried to play peacemaker, having no patience to play referee, "Why don't you guys take turns, rotating shifts every two hours."

While Ryan thought about this, Peter answered for him, "I'll take first shift, followed by Matthew, Jason, and Ryan."

Ryan pointed at Luke, "What about sissy boy here, how come he doesn't have to stand guard?"

Peter shrugged, but everyone knew the answer, including Hope. *If the monkeys attacked, what could Luke really do to protect them?* Luke must have known the answer too because tears welled in his eyes.

An earth shaking growl echoed through the forest; the source was close from the near left. Moments later another growl blasted them, this one coming from the opposite side of the circle. Hope stood in the center of the ring with Mary clutching her tight. Hope's heart raced and her body trembled as Mary sobbed in her arms.

The boys grabbed their clubs, even Luke. With their backs against the girls they formed a tight circle.

Mary kept repeating, "We're going to die, we're going to die. I just know it."

Ryan's eyes bulged in their sockets as he screamed, "Shut her up! I can't think straight!"

Another deep growl echoed through the forest, this one coming from in front of them.

Hope pulled Mary down with her to the ground, rocking her back and forth in her arms, trying her best to calm her fears while attempting to mask her own. If only she could stop shaking; her voice cracked as she spoke words that she didn't believe, "Shush, it's going to be all right, I promise."

Two more animals growled in the dark sounding closer than the others. The sound shook Hope to the bone; it was so loud it hurt her eardrums. She tried again to soothe her friend, but her words were just gibberish; she no longer made sense. Mary just whimpered and buried her face in Hope's bosom; she felt the wetness of Mary's tears soaking through her T-shirt.

The roar of monkeys came from everywhere. Hope and Mary crouched down as low as they could; Ryan pressed his trembling leg against Hope's side each time the monkeys roared. This audio onslaught designed to intimidate them was working. This was nothing less than psychological warfare.

Then the howling stopped just as suddenly as it had begun. The forest fell silent; even the crickets stopped chirping. The silence, like the darkness, closed in around them. Hope didn't know which was worse.

Ryan's legs stopped trembling and he stepped away from her, a clown-like smile transformed his face and he bounced on his toes. "They're gone! They've headed back into the forest!"

Hope knew better; she felt their presence all around her despite the eerie silence, but why frighten the others? Ryan seemed happy for the moment and that was a rarity she didn't want to upset.

"Okay, get some rest, I'll take first shift. At daybreak we'll find our way back to the village," Peter said, confident.

Hope and Mary lay down together head to foot like Ying and Yang in the middle of the circle. Peter sat with club in hand near the left edge close to the fire, peering out into the darkness.

Ryan, Matthew, Jason, and Luke formed a loose square around the girls. Hope lay awake for almost two hours listening to the rhythmic breathing of the others; it was better than the silence and she was glad that at least someone was able to sleep.

She opened her eyes to glance at Peter who had just added a piece of wood to the fire. His eyes looked heavy, closing for a brief moment before popping back open again. His shift would soon be over and he could then get some rest. She hoped that he would snuggle up next to her, wanting to feel his body against her own, making her feel safe, as safe as possible under the circumstances, safe enough to finally get some sleep. While Hope savored those thoughts, a red, furry arm reached out from the shadows with the speed of a pit viper, grabbed Peter by the ankle, and dragged him toward the darkness.

"Ahh! Help!" Peter shouted.

Hope saw the panic in Peter's eyes. He kicked and screamed, clawing at the ground, fighting frantically to stay in the circle, but there was nothing for him to hold onto, nothing to grasp as the red devil pulled him toward the forest.

CHAPTER SEVENTEEN

G rabbing Peter's ankle, the three-foot tall primate yanked him toward the forest; its loud snarls jolted the others awake. Peter screamed and clawed at the dirt, digging in with his nails, raking the soil for more than a yard, desperate to latch onto anything.

Hope dove at Peter's arms with the quickness of a cat. Grabbing hold of his wrists, she added significant weight, making it impossible for the troop leader to drag him off. The infuriated animal bit down hard several times on Peter's shin before gnawing away at his ankle. Peter cried out; his shrill screams echoed throughout the forest.

Jason fought off an attack of his own from the far side, managing to kick free of the ferocious animal. His heel struck the monkey hard, shattering his nose, bloodying its leathery face. The injured beast's howls shook the earth as it retreated into the darkness.

Matthew, now fully awake, grabbed his club and raced to Peter's aid. Ryan, who had been in a deep sleep, seemed disoriented as he tried to find his bearings, while Mary sat up covering her ears with her trembling hands. By this time Jason had grabbed his own club and followed Matthew, running just a few steps behind. Both boys beat the enraged primate, hitting it again and again, slamming their clubs into its head and back. Their blows should have shattered its skull, but the red monkey didn't seem fazed. Jason cocked back his arm and slammed the club full force into the animal's forehead. The blow knocked its jaw loose from Peter's bloodied ankle, ripping away a chunk of flesh. Still the red menace didn't collapse and instead rolled backward across the ground, leaped to its feet, and scampered up a tree. Lying across a high branch, he showed no signs of injury.

Hope watched in disbelief as the image of the monkey began to waver. Within seconds it had transformed itself into the feathered form of the young indigenous girl. The feathered face of a child gazed down upon Hope, sneering at her from above. Black tar dripped from her thin, frail body. Matthew and Jason saw it too; both boys stood staring in silence, open-mouthed.

Ryan stumbled over to them and said, "What the fuck is that?" But no one answered. Its green, cat-like eyes seemed to pierce right through Hope, draining all of her energy. She felt weak, so weak that her fingers loosened, no longer able to maintain pressure on Peter's wrists. An overwhelming sense of sadness washed over her and through her. The images of the Conquistadors and their hideous acts once again flashed through her mind.

The aura surrounding the *Iwanci* seemed to weaken. The manifestation wavered for several seconds, and then disappeared. Hope began feeling better immediately. The sadness lifted off her like a thick fog rising up into the trees; her strength returned to something that resembled normal.

With the controlling entity now gone, the other *real* Howlers found themselves leaderless. The pack retreated into the forest; each howl seemed farther than the last, and even the ones foaming from the mouth wandered off.

Peter rolled back and forth on the ground screaming in agony. Hope still lay on her stomach with her arms stretched out in front of her gripping his wrists; now that her strength returned, she didn't want to let go. She reluctantly did so when it became necessary to drag Peter toward the middle of the circle. Luke and Jason each grabbed an arm, slowly pulling him forward. Peter bit his bottom lip, grimacing in pain as they dragged him the half-dozen or so feet forward.

Hope removed Peter's sneaker and sock to inspect his ankle; there were no broken bones, but several teeth marks pierced his shin and a three-inch patch of flesh hung from his ankle.

Peter's voice cracked, "I'm infected; that animal had rabies!"

Hope pointed at the pile of heart-shaped fruit. "Luke, grab me the ripest ones you can find."

Luke scurried over to the fruit, squeezing each piece; he selected two of the ripest ones before bringing them over to Hope.

"Hold his legs down; this might hurt a bit," she said.

Jason and Matthew each grabbed a leg and held it just above the shin. Cutting the fruit in half, Hope squeezed the juice into Peter's open wounds. Muscle spasms shot through his leg; he grimaced as the acidic liquid cleansed the gash.

"There, that might disinfect it," Hope said. *It's worth a shot and it certainly can't hurt.*

Still holding the knife, she cut a sleeve off Peter's T-shirt. She then cut the cloth in half to create strips to use as bandages.

Hope pointed at the tropical plant that they had used for bedding. "Mary, could you pick me some fresh leaves?" she said, giving Mary something to focus on other than her fear.

Mary, still trembling, seemed surprised by the request, but she stopped crying, walked over to the large plant, and picked several leaves.

"Good job, thanks." Hope flashed Mary an encouraging smile.

Taking the leaves from her friend, she wrapped several of them around Peter's leg and ankle, and using the cloth strips, she tied them in place.

Luke paced back and forth, rubbing his chin. His expression changed from solemn and serious to one of excitement; his face lit up like a beacon as he approached Peter.

"If the pack leader isn't real, if it is just a creation of the *Iwanci*, then maybe the rabies aren't real either!" he said.

Hope digested Luke's words. "He's got a point. Maybe there never were any rabies; maybe the foaming from its mouth was just to rattle us."

Jason, hands on hips, said, "But I saw two other monkeys frothing from their mouths and they were real; the foam hit my leg."

"I saw it too and maybe those monkeys were rabid, but they weren't the ones that bit Peter, and neither one of them transformed into something else. This one did!" Luke said.

Peter managed a smile. Luke's line of reasoning seemed to cheer him up. "I guess time will tell," he said.

"Yeah, a lot of time," Luke said. "Even if you're infected, the incubation period is more than a week; you'll be back in Macas getting shots at the hospital long before that happens."

"How the hell do you know?" Ryan asked.

"I assume we'll find our way out by then."

"No, not that, how'd you know the incubation period is more than a week?"

"My cousin got bit by a rabid skunk; he got seven shots in his butt over seven days. His doctor told him that without the shots, he would've seen symptoms in about a week."

The creases in Peter's forehead relaxed; he breathed in deep before releasing a long sigh, looking like a man reprieved from a death sentence.

⊶⊷

Hope curled up next to Peter; the cool, leafy bandages seemed to soothe his pain allowing him to doze peacefully. The others also slept with the exception of Matthew; it was his turn to be the senti-nel. Hope watched him add a few more branches to the fire; his eyes seemed heavy and she hoped that he could stay awake. Her thoughts turned to Mary; she wondered how her younger friend was holding up after her horrible ordeal. Glancing over at her, she watched her chest rise and fall with each rhythmic breath, glad that she, like the others, could get some rest.

Hope turned toward Peter and draped her arm around him. The warmth from his body comforted her, giving her a sense of close-ness that she hadn't felt before. This filled her mind with happy thoughts, thoughts about her and Peter, allowing her to drift away into a euphoric, peaceful bliss.

⊨⊱ ⊰⊨

A twig snapped just outside of camp, waking Hope. She felt groggy and lightheaded as if she was still under the influence of the *ayahuasca*, but the drug had worn off before they'd eaten the fruit. Hope sat up; a white fog covered the forest floor. The first gray light of dawn filtered through the thick jungle covering. The fog was so thick; she couldn't see more than two feet around her. Peter still lay on the ground next to her. Their bodies had separated during the night, but he was still close enough to see, close enough to touch. She heard the sound again; another slow snap of a twig, it sounded like a careful footstep trying to blend into the forest, but Hope heard it, then again. She grabbed Peter's shoulder and gave him a firm shake, "Wake up."

Peter stirred, mumbled something, and rolled over on his side. Hope shook him harder.

"Okay, okay, I'm awake." Peter sat up, "I feel like I'm in a daze."

"You too?"

Mary crept toward them through the fog. "Did you say you feel like you're in a daze? So do I, my head is so fuzzy. What do you think is going on?"

159

"It can't still be the *ayahuasca*," Peter said.

Hope pointed into the woods. "I heard a noise, like cracking wood, it woke me up."

Peter stood, grabbing each of their hands; he pulled the girls to their feet. Hope found herself standing waist high in a shallow sea of white, thick fog.

"Well, let's investigate. It's probably just some small animal passing through. But let's take a look; maybe it's Tim and Brenda out looking for us," Peter said.

"They'd have to come looking for us once they realized we were missing, wouldn't they?" Mary appeared hopeful.

"They'd come, but not without Shuar guides," Hope said.

"But they'll come. My father will come, right?"

"Don't worry, they'll come; that's if we can't find our way back first. Now let's go check out that sound," Peter said.

The fog was so thick, Hope couldn't see her sneakers. After walking only a few steps, she tripped over a tree root and fell to the ground. In the mist, laying inches from her face, were seven small figurines. The crude objects made from palm leaves looped together, formed leafy, stick-like figures. Two of the figurines were clearly female, having shredded leaves that resembled long hair, and two loops indicating breasts. The remaining figurines had a loop in the groin area, representing male genitalia.

"Pull me up! Pull me up!" Hope screamed.

The commotion awoke the others; Hope heard Luke's voice coming toward her, just as Peter grabbed her arm and yanked her to her feet.

"Hey, what's going on?" Luke asked.

Peter and Mary both shrugged.

"Look!" Hope's trembling finger pointed downward.

"At what?" Peter asked.

"Just look!"

Peter knelt down, disappearing into the haze. "Holy crap!"

Hope, still shaken, began to cry. "Somebody was here last night while we slept!"

Luke gasped, "Your clothes! Look at your clothes!"

Hope looked at Mary's outfit, then her own and gasped. They were wearing each other's clothing. This realization hit her full force; it seemed impossible, but they wore the proof.

Someone had violated them while they slept; there was no other explanation. Someone or something had stripped them both during the night and redressed them in the other's clothes, but who and for what purpose?

Hope wondered what had happened to her. Whoever it was, had they done *that? Was I penetrated or, worse yet, impregnated?*

The thought of this made her sick; she dry heaved several times before spitting up a mouthful of sour. She tried to be rational. Did she feel any different? Her insides felt the same; being a virgin it should have hurt, but she felt nothing—but she'd been unconscious. But she felt no discomfort, no itching–nothing. *So maybe that didn't happen.* She clung to this idea because it made her feel better; nevertheless, she still felt violated and she screamed. "What do you want from us?"

Mary began to cry. "They're going to kill us! I just know it."

"I just want to go home!" Hope sobbed into her hands.

Peter wrapped his arms around her and kissed her forehead. "It's going to be all right," he said, his voice reassuring.

Ryan, Matthew, and Jason emerged from the fog; their sudden appearance startled Hope.

"What's all the screaming?" Ryan asked.

Luke pointed to the ground, "Look at the dolls!"

Ryan ducked into the fog and reemerged a moment later. "Holy shit, where the hell did they come from?"

Luke pointed to the two girls, "And look, they're wearing each other's clothes!"

"Why? I don't get it," Ryan said.

Luke shrugged. "They just woke up that way."

"That's really messed up," Matthew said.

Peter glared at Matthew, "Well, you're the one who was supposed to be watching."

"Not the whole night! It's true I did doze off, but my shift was just for two hours; no one came to relieve me."

Jason's face turned red. "You mean me, don't ya? Why don't you just say it! You know if you weren't sleeping on the job you could've come over and woke me up! What was I supposed to do, stay awake during your shift just so I'd be ready for my shift when it came along?"

"Hey, buds, knock it off. What's done is done," Ryan said.

"Who do you think is screwing with us?" Jason asked.

Peter shrugged.

"Well, whoever it is, I'm not sticking around to find out," Jason said.

Mary's eyes were wide with fear; Peter wrapped his arms around both girls. "We're okay now, let's keep our heads and stick to our plan. Ipiak and Eno must've told them what happened by now. I know that everyone's out looking for us."

His words comforted Hope, but she still felt unsure about their safety.

Peter led the boys from the clearing to give the girls privacy so that they could change back into their own clothing. The mist was still thick, so they didn't have to go very far.

While changing, Hope inspected her underwear for any spotting or semen. She prayed to God that she wouldn't find any evidence of this and thanked him out loud when He answered her prayers. There was no soreness, no bruising, not even a rash, but her skin felt oily as if someone had rubbed her down with baby oil.

Mary clenched her teeth and made a similar inspection, she, too, seemed thankful there was no physical evidence of rape. The creases on her forehead disappeared and her jaw relaxed, but she'd missed something important—they both had.

CHAPTER EIGHTEEN

Hope spotted the small, red dot on the back of Mary's thigh. It looked as though someone had pricked her with a needle. After seeing this, Hope discovered a similar wound on the back of her own leg. She showed the marks to Mary. "This explains why we feel drugged."

Mary sniffled, "I'm scared."

"Does your skin feel oily?"

"Yeah, it's all over me."

Hope held Mary's hands together in front of her. "It's okay to be scared; I'm scared too, but don't worry, somehow we'll get through this."

They finished dressing and after a few minutes, the boys returned to the clearing. Feeling embarrassed, Hope decided not to mention the thin film of oil that covered their bodies. Mary also remained silent.

Peter looked at the gray sky. "Let's follow the sun; it always rises in the east. I'm pretty sure that the Shuar village is to the east."

Ryan pointed at the patches of dark clouds peeking through the tree tops, "Hey, nimrod, I don't know if you noticed, but there is no sun."

Jason and Matthew cackled.

Peter mumbled something under his breath that sounded like *fuck you, asshole.*

Despite not wanting to side with Ryan, Hope realized that he was right; the sun remained hidden behind thick, black clouds that hung low over the rainforest. The white fog seemed to be getting thicker, rising higher off the forest floor. Regardless of the weather, Hope was determined to find her way out of the forest.

Peter looked up at the dark sky. "I think east is that way," he said, pointing straight ahead.

Ryan pointed in the opposite direction. "I think you're wrong; east is that way."

"I agree with Ryan," Matthew said.

Jason looked in one direction, then the other. "Ryan's got to be right."

Luke pointed to a large tree. "Look at the moss on the back of that tree. Moss always grows on the north side of the trunk because that's where it gets the least amount of sunlight. If that's the north side of the tree, then Peter's right and east is that way."

Matthew laughed, "If you say so, Mr. Wizard." Luke didn't respond to this indignation.

"Let's follow Peter," Hope said.

Mary agreed, "I'm with you guys."

Ryan scoffed, "Damn it, Peter, you better be right."

"Yeah, you better be right," Matthew said.

Hope walked beside Peter, who appeared to be favoring his injured ankle; she wouldn't call it a limp, but he walked with an uneven gait. The others followed them as they headed off in what seemed to be an easterly direction. After walking several miles, the fog began to dissipate. The forest began to thin and the tall trees gave way to a field of tall grass. The exposed vegetation grew much thicker there, spilling over the path in some places. Up ahead, to the left of the path, she saw a small clearing barely visible through a sea of reeds. She grabbed Peter by the shoulder and pointed. "Take a look over there, I think it's man made!"

"Let's check it out," Peter said.

Hope noticed a slight grimace cross his face as he hastened his pace but he appeared eager to reach the clearing despite his discomfort. Only a few steps behind, she watched him fight through the overgrowth, pushing down reeds, forging a thin path for her and the others to follow. After reaching the clearing, he froze in his tracks, stopping so short that Hope nearly slammed into him. It took her a second to see what had caused his sudden stop.

A field of shrunken heads stood impaled on long poles before her; many of them appeared to be those of native children. Most of the black heads were no larger than baseballs. Sharp, wooden pins pierced the lips holding them together. Coarse twine, woven tightly through the pins, sealed their mouths. The same twine had been used to sew shut the eyes and nostrils. Two adult heads stood out amongst the sea of smaller ones, reduced to the size of large apples.

Her mind could barely process the amount of carnage displayed before her. She just stood there with her mouth ajar while everyone else scattered screaming into the forest—that is, everyone except for Peter and Mary.

Hope's cries turned into loud sobs.

"Look away!" Peter shouted.

"I can't, I must bear witness to the slaughter. Look at those poor children with their small heads stuck on those poles forever."

Mary too began to cry.

Peter pulled Mary toward him and wrapped his arms around both girls. "We've got to think about ourselves right now or we'll never get out of here." His sobering statement quieted them down, at least for the moment.

CHAPTER NINETEEN

Tim awoke to the shouts of Shuar tribesmen running outside his hut. His stiff legs proved heavy and hard to move, still aching from last night's marathon trek through the forest. It took several seconds for his eyes to adjust to the dim, gray light that filtered in through the mosquito netting. Bill Drake's loud snores thundered in Tim's ears even though he lay more than six feet away.

Despite Bill's snoring, Tim felt a great void. Emptiness filled the hut; it took him a moment to remember why. The unforgiving truth banished any thoughts of additional sleep as his eyes opened wide. *We've got to get back out there and find those kids.*

More excited voices hurried past the hut; he glanced at his watch; the iridescent hands read *5:47*. The date in the little box showed a miniature 19; they were supposed to return home on the 25th. He felt anxious, knowing that they were running out of time. Jumping to his feet, he pulled on his jeans, laced up his hiking boots, and reloaded his ammo belt with flares. Grabbing an extra flare from the box, he shoved it into the gun. *Maybe that one extra flare will make a difference.*

As soon as he stepped out of his hut, he tried to see what the commotion was about. Dozens of Shuar men ran back and forth shouting. Four Jeeps and two pickup trucks pulled into the village. Frenzied tribesmen climbed into the vehicles, while men with crew cuts and army fatigues handed each of them a rifle. After the last man climbed in, the vehicles sped off.

Tim had learned many Shuar words over the last three weeks, but the tribesmen spoke too fast for him to understand anything. Kuja's grandfather, Pepe, walked toward him at a rapid pace; his English wasn't as fluent as his grandson's, but still understandable.

Tim stepped in front of him, motioning for him to stop. "Whoa, whoa, whoa, what's going on, Pepe?"

"We're at war!"

"At war with whom?"

"Peru!"

Tim tried to grasp the scope of the conflict. "Is it the Shuar people who are at war?"

"Not just Shuar, also army of Ecuador. Our warriors will fight with army to defeat our common enemy!"

"Why are you fighting?" Tim asked.

"Peruvians have crossed our borders. They claim the forest as their own! Our warriors will drive them out of the forest and back across the border!"

"Thanks, Pepe!" Tim ran off to find Brenda.

She had just stepped out of her hut when he approached.

"We've got to find those kids and fast!" Tim said.

"Why? What's going on?"

"War has broken out."

"With another tribe?"

"No, between Ecuador and Peru, some kind of border dispute. We've got to find those kids and get everybody out of here!"

"You get Bill, I'll round up Kuja and Yeki, and we'll get started!"

"I don't know about Kuja, but forget about Yeki. I just saw him climb into the bed of a pickup and speed off."

"What a screwed up time for this to happen! We'll just have to pack up our things and head out on our own."

⚔⚔

Tim returned to the hut just as Bill emerged through the doorway buttoning his shirt. Agitated, he said, "Time's a wasting, let's get out there and find my daughter!"

"Just a second, let me grab the flare gun."

"Jesus, what for? It will be daylight in a few minutes and nobody will be able to see the damn thing anyway."

"But it might come in handy if we haven't found them by nightfall."

"Look, let's get something straight, buster, if we haven't found my daughter by nightfall, I'll shove that flare gun up your ass and pull the trigger! Got it?" His words cut deep. The blame placed squarely on Tim's shoulders was almost too much for him to bear.

Tim stared down and kicked at the dirt, "Yes, sir, I got it."

"Now come on, let's get moving!"

Tim reluctantly left the flare gun in the hut and followed Bill, walking several steps behind.

⚔⚔

When they reached Brenda's hut, Tim was surprised to find Kuja standing by her side, eager to help, packing supplies. *At least Kuja hasn't abandoned us.*

Tim and Brenda strapped the knapsacks onto their backs and followed Bill and Kuja into the rainforest.

After walking for miles through the thick jungle, Kuja picked up the trail where they'd abandoned their search the night before. He stopped every so often to bend down and inspect a broken twig or run his fingers across the loose dirt inside a footprint. By noon they didn't seem any closer to finding the group. The trail led them to a large tree. Kuja once again stopped to inspect the dirt.

"Look at that imprint; someone's been sitting in the dirt, a female, her footprints are out in front of her, she must've been leaning hard against her knees to cause that."

"Can you tell if it's Mary?" Bill asked.

"I don't think so, it's probably Hope; for awhile now I've noticed two sets of footprints, ones coming in and others going out. This means they backtracked down the same path. A little ways back, I saw a female footprint smaller than this one. I think it belonged to Mary."

The bulging veins in Bill's neck and forehead retreated upon hearing Kuja's words.

"Why do you think they stopped here and backtracked?" Tim asked.

"I think they found who they were looking for—I think they've found Hope."

"Now if only we can find them," Bill said.

Instead, the mosquitoes proved to be the most successful people finders. Brenda pulled out a spray bottle of insect repellent and applied it to her exposed skin. She passed the spray to Bill and Tim, both of them coating themselves thoroughly. Kuja's genetics gave him a natural resistance to the bugs.

After awhile, Bill needed to rest; they stopped for a moment and ate some fruit and bread that Brenda had packed for them. The repetitive boom of artillery fire thundered off in the distance. A few minutes later, a squadron of warplanes flew low overhead, shaking the forest with a sonic boom. Brenda jumped at the sudden sound and grabbed hold of Tim's arm.

"This is a real war!" Brenda's voice cracked.

"Let's find them and get the hell out of here!" Tim said.

Bill rose to his feet, "Then let's hop to it!"

The rest of the group cautiously returned, peering at the field of heads from a safe distance. Luke crept behind Peter and Hope.

Ryan seemed impatient, fidgeting back and forth, "Come on, let's move out."

"Give us a minute," Peter said.

"We don't have a minute. We have no idea where the hell we are and it might take us all fucking day to walk out of here," Ryan said.

Jason parroted Ryan's words, "Yeah, it might take all fucking day."

Peter turned to Hope, "Are you okay?"

"I'm all right now, let's go," Hope said, too exhausted to argue.

Peter turned to Mary, "How 'bout you?"

"I'm ready," Mary said.

"Okay, let's move out." Peter waved the group forward.

Ryan's face turned red. "Hey, hotshot, I don't think you should be the leader."

"Yeah, who died and made you boss?" Jason asked.

"Why are we listening to this asshole in the first place?" Matthew asked.

"Well, what do you pricks propose?" Peter asked.

"I think that I should lead the group," Ryan said.

Peter stepped toward Ryan and bumped his chest. "Oh, do you now?"

Ryan bumped back. "Yeah, I do."

Hope stepped in between them and said, "Why don't we take a vote to see who should be the leader?"

"Yeah, take a vote!" Mary said.

"That's fine with me!" Peter said.

"Okay hotshot, let's take a vote," Ryan said.

Hope stood in the middle of the group, "Okay, everyone who wants Peter to be our leader, raise your hand."

Hope, Mary, and Peter raised their hands high into the air.

"You only got three votes; you can't win. Do we have to continue with this charade?" Ryan asked.

Hope gave one quick nod. "Let's continue in an orderly fashion. Okay, now everyone who wants Ryan to be our leader, raise your hand."

Ryan's, Matthew's, and Jason's hands shot into the air.

"It's a tie, three against three," Mary said.

Ryan pointed at Luke, "He didn't vote!"

"I abstain," Luke said.

"You can't abstain, you have to vote!" Matthew said.

"Yeah, you have to vote," Jason said.

Hope touched Luke's shoulder. "It really would be for the best."

"Okay, I'll vote," he said.

"Just say it; who do you want as our leader, Peter or Ryan?" Hope asked.

"Um, um," Luke stammered.

"Just spit it out already," Matthew said.

"Um—Peter."

Matthew pushed Luke to the ground and shouted, "You little pussy!"

Peter gave Matthew a shove. "Leave him alone!"

Matthew's eyes burned with hatred. Ryan stepped forward and said, "Matt, leave him be."

"There are only so many hours in a day; we should go," Hope said.

"That's what I've been saying all along!" Ryan said.

The skies remained dark, but it didn't rain. Peter once again led them in an easterly direction. Hope kept an eye on Ryan and Matthew, wondering when the next mutiny would take place. They walked for miles, stopping on occasion to eat berries. The field gave way to yet another forest. The thick clouds hovered over the jungle, growing darker as nightfall approached. The terrain became rockier under their feet. Faced with the reality of spending a second night in the forest, they decided to set up camp next to a small spring.

Despite the earlier confrontations, they tried to work together as a team. Matthew and Jason spent the next hour clearing the ground, using the same method from the previous night.

Hope and Mary gathered large palm-like leaves for their bedding. The menial task took Hope's mind off the horrors she'd endured earlier in the forest. She prayed that it provided the same therapy for Mary; sooner or later she'd have to deal with it, both of them would, but not now, not if she wanted to maintain her sanity. Peter was right; they had to focus on their own survival. She forced herself to compartmentalize, placing all of the heads in a little box.

She took a deep breath and spread the leaves across the circle. "We're starting to become old pros at this."

Mary seemed aloof. "If we stay out here any longer, we'll have to form our own tribe."

⚔ ⚔

Ryan and Matthew collected firewood near the clearing while Peter, Luke, and Jason ventured much deeper into the forest in search of food. The food gatherers returned an hour later struggling to carry a large stalk of green bananas. Their pockets bulged with walnut-sized mountain coconuts. Peter and Jason placed the banana stalk down in the center of the circle; there had to be more than three dozen bananas attached to the thick stem.

"They're not ripe, but I'll bet they're edible," Peter said.

Hope snapped off a banana, peeled back the green skin, and took a bite. Peter was right; the unripe banana was hard, but edible. All three boys emptied their pockets, handing the miniature coconuts to the others. Matthew and Ryan smashed the nuts with rocks, cracking the shell to expose the tender white meat. Peter cracked enough nuts for Luke, himself, and the two girls. Everyone ate until they had their fill.

Matthew pulled the box of matches from his pocket and succeeded in starting a small fire.

Thunder rumbled in the distance, Hope looked up at the dark, angry rain clouds forming in the eastern sky, just a few short miles away. The clouds seemed to be floating parallel to their location, but not overtaking them. *With any luck, the rain will pass us by*, Hope thought, allowing them to maintain their fire.

A twig snapped off in the distance and Peter scanned the forest. "I think someone should stand guard while we sleep."

"I second that, especially after last night," Hope said.

Ryan extended his open palm to Peter, "Be my guest."

"It's Jason's turn, remember? Matthew never woke him up," Peter said.

"Okay, I'll do it, but only for two hours, then it's someone else's turn."

⇉⇇

Hope lay on her side next to Peter on a bed of leaves closest to the fire; she felt like her mental state was somewhere between exhaustion and insanity. Mary's steady breathing indicated that somehow she'd fallen asleep. Hope wished that she too could doze off, but her wretched memories grew inside her. She wished she had some Prozac or Xanax; even a double shot of whiskey would suffice and Hope hated whiskey. She thought about anything to relieve her anxiety, her mother, Peter, the Shuar children, the day they'd leave this Godforsaken place, but those thoughts only fluttered through her mind, and she always came back to the day's events. She watched the fire burn and felt Peter's arm reach across her. Pulling his hand into her bosom, holding it tight against her, she prayed that somehow he'd protect her.

She glanced over at Jason who diligently stood guard, flinching at every sound, staring into the darkness, staring at his hand. Several hours must have passed because Jason walked over to Ryan and shook him awake. *The changing of the guard,* Hope thought, just before she fell unconscious.

⟩⟨ ⟨⟩

Hope lay naked on the ground in the middle of a small clearing. She felt drugged, vaguely aware of others lying on the ground around her. She strained to see, but her eyes were just slits.

Dozens of poles rose up above her. A shrunken head crowned each pole. She recognized the faces above her; she lay in the same field of heads. A drum beat pounded somewhere behind her. The heads glowed orange, illuminated by the flicker of several handheld torches. The pungent odor of burning animal fat made her gag.

Many hands held down her arms and legs, stretching her body out across the ground. Through the shadows she saw the red painted faces of her captors staring down at her. *I must be in Hell,* she thought as she faded in and out of consciousness.

In the darkness, unfamiliar voices chanted in a strange language all around her. A much older, bare-chested man wearing a feathered head-dress stepped from the shadows chanting the loudest. Holding a small, earthen bowl in his hand, he mixed the contents with a long, thin stick.

The drum beat ceased and the shaman's chanting stopped. He approached Hope with his vaporous mixture. Using the thin stick like a quill, he drew precise markings across her stomach. The mixture burned like acid across her abdomen and she cried out in pain. Using a thin, bronze needle, he punctured her below the navel, inserting something under her skin. The shaman dabbed the acid-like mixture into the wound to seal the puncture.

⟩⟨ ⟨⟩

Hope awoke to her own screams, jolting Peter out of a sound sleep, his arm still tightly clutched against her chest. Her stomach stung as if stabbed by a thousand needles.

"Wake up, Hope, you must've had a bad dream," he said.

"No, it was real!"

All of the others awoke, including Ryan who had been dozing next to the fire at the time. Luke rushed to her side.

"Are you okay?" Luke asked.

"I dreamt that I was being held captive and tortured by a strange tribe."

"That's weird; I dreamt something very similar to that myself," Jason said.

"You've both had a nightmare, that's all," Peter said.

Hope touched her tender belly through her shirt. "My stomach feels all tingly."

"Mine too," Jason replied.

Mary gingerly touched her own stomach and grimaced, her face pale and drawn.

Hope raised her shirt up above her navel. Mary and Peter both gasped.

"What's the matter?" Hope asked.

Peter stood speechless; he could only point.

Hope sat up and gazed at her midsection. The blood drained from her face when she saw the strange symbols written across it.

The drawings resembled hieroglyphics, scrolled with great care, etched in a perfect line.

Jason raised his own shirt and gasped when he found symbols scrolled across his own stomach. Mary, still sitting on the ground, hesitated before lifting her shirt; she too discovered the strange markings etched across her skin. She rushed over to Hope, buried her face in her bosom, and bellowed. Hope held her in her arms, rocking her like a baby, reducing her cries to a hiccup.

"Holy shit!" Ryan said after checking his own stomach and that pretty much said it all.

Peter, Matthew, and Luke also discovered symbols drawn across their midsections.

"We've been branded like cattle!" Peter said.

"Goddamn it! Let me just catch that son-of-a-bitch who wrote on me," Ryan said, "If I could have five minutes with him, it would have almost been worth it."

"Hey, tough guy, too bad you weren't tough enough to stay awake last night; if you had, none of this would have happened," Peter said.

Ryan stepped toward Peter. "You know, I am really getting sick of your shit!"

"I'm getting sick of you being an asshole."

Both boys stepped forward, but Jason and Matthew stepped in between them. Jason led Ryan away from Peter while Matthew led Peter away in the opposite direction. After several minutes, Peter had calmed down enough to hold a normal conversation.

Hope turned to Peter, breaking the silence, "Do you think it's permanent?

"Excuse me?"

"The markings, do you think they're permanent?"

"Let's try to wash them off," Peter said.

Hope pulled Mary to her feet, and together they followed Peter and Luke into the shallow spring. Ryan, still grumbling, watched from afar with Matthew and Jason standing by his side.

Using water and sand, they scrubbed their stomachs vigorously. Hope grimaced as she scrubbed, her skin turning red and raw. Mary whimpered with every stroke; tears dripped off her chin into the water.

Despite the pain and their best efforts, the bold symbols remained.

CHAPTER TWENTY

Kuja led the way through the jungle; Bill, Tim, and Brenda trailed close behind. Together they tracked Mary and the others for many hours; the terrain became rockier and the green canopy thinned out, revealing heavy rainclouds. The footprints led them to a rocky ravine with a strong flowing brook running through it.

Kuja scrambled down the slope to the water while everyone else remained at the top of the ravine.

Jumping from rock to rock, he made his way to the bottom. Bending down along the banks of the brook, he inspected several of the flat rocks and yelled up to them, "I see footprints, they were here, and they stopped to drink."

"Why couldn't they've just stayed here and made camp? They had fresh water, didn't they realize that we'd come looking for them?" Brenda asked no one in particular.

"Why do teenagers do anything?" Bill muttered.

"At least they're not dehydrated," Tim said.

Kuja scurried up the slope just in time to hear Tim's comment. "They'd have to find more water before too long; one drink won't be enough. Let's get a drink ourselves and refill our canteens."

⇥ ⇤

Kuja's words didn't sit well with Brenda. The thought of thirsty kids in the heat magnified her guilt; if only she'd kept an eye on them, none of this would've happened.

She followed Kuja and Bill into the ravine. Distracted by her thoughts, she stepped on a loose rock and slipped, twisting her ankle. The pain was instant and intense and she cried out. Tim, who'd been following her down the slope, grabbed her arm and braced her from falling; they were still more than twenty yards from the bottom.

"What's the matter?" Bill asked, turning around.

"My ankle, I twisted it."

"Oh, Christ!" Bill yelled.

"Wrap your arm around my shoulder; let me help you down to the brook, and maybe we can keep the swelling down by soaking it in the water," Tim said.

But it was too late; the ankle had already begun to balloon. Brenda clung to Tim and together they hobbled down to the rushing water, each step more painful than the last.

In a way, she welcomed the pain, it was a form of penance for her sin, and it was God's way of punishing her. There'd be more punishments to come, of this she was sure.

Upon reaching the brook, she eased herself down with Tim's help onto a flat rock; he untied her boot and carefully pulled it off. Despite Tim's gentleness, Brenda grimaced, crying out from the fresh jolt of pain. This seemed to startle Tim, who stopped for a moment.

"You hanging in there?" he asked as he peeled off her sock and rolled up her pant leg.

"Yeah, I guess I'll be okay," Brenda said, even as her contorted face showed otherwise. She dipped her foot into the cool brook; at first the water hurt, but the sting lasted only a moment. The current rushed past her ankle with the force of Jacuzzi jets, numbing the pain.

Tim emptied his canteen and refilled it with fresh water before he handed it to Brenda. She took a long drink. The water felt great going down her throat; she hadn't realized just how thirsty she'd become.

"We're never going to find those kids now!" Bill said, pacing back and forth like a caged animal. He glanced at his watch, shaking his head. Brenda looked at her own watch; it was a little past noon, and they'd been hiking for more than five hours.

"Did you bring flashlights? We're halfway through the day; we'll run out of daylight in less than six hours," Kuja said, staring up at the cloud-covered sky.

"I packed two into one of the knapsacks," Brenda said.

"Her ankle's pretty bad; I don't think she can walk," Tim said.

"Okay, here's our best shot at finding those kids. Tim, you stay here with Brenda and the knapsacks, and Kuja and I will take the flashlights and continue the search," Bill said.

"Do you think it's wise to separate?" Tim asked, kicking at the ground.

"She can't walk; you've said so yourself. We'll set up camp here tonight; that should give the swelling a chance to go down. I've got those kids to think about, that's my first priority."

Bill's tone said the topic was no longer open for discussion.

"So you just want us to sit here until you get back?" Tim asked.

"No, I want you to find some flat ground for us to sleep on, clear the ground if you have to, gather some dry wood, and light a fire after it gets dark. That should keep the animals away and if our flashlights burn out, it will act as a beacon to help us find our way back," Bill said.

"What do you want me to do?" Brenda asked.

"I want you to keep on soaking that ankle, young lady. Fifteen minutes in the water, fifteen minutes out. Keep doing it until we return—hopefully with our kids."

⊷╬ ╬⊶

Peter stepped out of the spring grumbling, and yelled at Ryan, "You should've kept watch! That's all you had to do, especially after what happened to the girls!"

"You can kiss my ass, how' bout that! You haven't exactly been watching over things yourself."

Here we go again! Hope thought.

She stepped from the spring and grabbed Peter's arm, "Let it go, what's done is done."

Despite her words, she felt the muscles tense in his arm; there was no way he was going to let this go.

"Was staying awake for two lousy hours too much to ask?" Peter said.

"It's your dumb ass that brought us out here in the first place. I told you we should've gone in the other direction."

"Both of you guys stop your bickering and just shut up!" Hope said.

"No, Ryan's right. If we had followed his lead we would've gone off in a different direction and probably found our way back to the village by now," Matthew said, looking back at Jason for agreement. Hope had seen Matthew give that look before; it was Jason's cue to jump into the fray, but Jason didn't seem to care; he stood disinterested several feet behind Ryan, inspecting his arm and flexing his finger.

Hope filled the void created by Jason's silence. "It's easy to say that now, but you don't know for sure."

Ryan wagged his finger at Hope, "All I know is, if I were the leader, none of this would've happened! Nobody would've had stupid

180

symbols drawn on their skin, and your stomach would've stayed as pristine as your lily white ass."

"How about I shove my size fourteen boot up *your* big fat ass?" Peter said, taking a threatening step toward Ryan.

"Shut up! Just shut up!" Jason yelled, holding his arm out in front of him. "All you dumb fucks care about is yourselves, look at my goddamn hand!"

His swollen hand resembled a small lemon; a line of yellow puss oozed from the monkey scratch he'd received across his knuckles the day before, a clear indication of a staph infection.

The argument now forgotten, everyone circled around Jason and stared at his hand. Hope didn't say anything, because what could be said? They had no antibiotics and without them, the infection would spread and Jason would die. Jason must have realized this too."Just don't stare at me, let's get moving. Peter, you wanted to be the leader, now fucking lead! Let's go!"

Bill followed Kuja through the forest, finding it hard to keep up with the young tribesman, and having to stop and catch his breath every hundred yards or so. Each time Bill stopped, Kuja retraced his steps and waited. During those rests, Bill had time to think; he felt bad leaving Brenda and Tim behind, but what could he do? He had his daughter and the rest of those kids to think about.

Kuja bent down and picked up what looked like a piece of shit and inspected it carefully. Breaking it in half, he brought it to his nose and inhaled. "Day old monkey dung, I've seen it for awhile now, it's all around the path." Kuja stared up into the canopy, "It's almost if the monkeys are following them."

"Why would they do that?"

"I don't know; it's not in their nature to do so."

Bill took a deep breath, thought about Mary, and found the strength to push on.

⊷⊶

Ryan and Matthew grabbed the few remaining bananas as the group started off again. Peter, with Hope by his side, led the group through the thick greenery. "If we keep walking in a straight line, we're bound to cross over a logging road at some point; anyway that's what they taught us in Boy Scouts."

"Ah, Peter, that logic only holds true in New Jersey; out here you could walk for weeks without crossing a road," Luke whispered, leaning toward Peter.

"Ah, thanks," Peter said.

Hope had also heard Luke's whispered words, and was thankful that he hadn't made the others aware of Peter's error; she wanted to avoid a mutiny at all costs.

They walked for several miles under the tall trees; everything looked as it did before. Every once in a while Hope looked back at Mary, her friend stared straight ahead, unblinking. Her dull expression remained constant as if she were on a death march; her speech was sporadic at best. They had been through so much; everything had taken its toll.

Hope wondered how much longer she could stifle her own pain. It was a constant battle to keep from slipping into oblivion. She flashed a hopeful smile at Mary, who remained unresponsive, staring straight ahead, placing one heavy foot in front of the other.

Jason walked last in line, staring at his swollen hand, rotating it back and forth.

After awhile, the forest gave way to a field of reeds and tall grass and Hope got a sense of déjà vu. Up ahead just left of the path, she saw a familiar clearing through the reeds.

Stepping with caution, Peter led the group forward, stopping just short of the circle. Hope gasped, not wanting to look, but neither could she look away. The sea of miniature faces stared back at her. Somehow, they'd circled around to the same spot where they'd been the day before.

The impaled, shrunken heads stood like macabre sentinels. One face stood out amongst the rest. It was that of a young indigenous girl, she looked Shuar; it was hard to tell her age, but Hope guessed that she must've been about thirteen. Her baseball-sized head was black as tar; long strands of silky black hair flowed from her scalp; three short wooden spikes pierced her lips. Unlike the other heads, there wasn't any twine tying the spikes together. Hardened clay plugged her nostrils; her eyes were sewn shut, but the twine looked frayed and broken in spots. Hope stood by Peter's side, and with her arm looped around his bicep, she pulled him closer, determined to stand her ground.

Hope became transfixed on that one head; if she'd blinked she would've missed it, but she didn't blink—now she wished she had.

The expression on the face changed. It happened so fast, Hope wasn't sure that she'd seen it at all, but after looking closer she had no doubt. The sharp spikes still sealed the front lips, but the left corner of the mouth rose into a frozen sneer. The frayed stitching across the eyes had snapped in several more places and they were now partially open, revealing the dark, empty sockets within. Hope flinched, and tried to scream but only mustered up a pathetic whimper.

"What's the matter?" Peter asked.

"Come on, let's go back. I can't bear to look another second," she said. Her fingers trembled as she pulled on his arm. She felt the panic rise within her; her breaths became quick and shallow. Peter led Hope away from the morbid spectacle; the others were quick to follow.

They hadn't gotten a hundred yards away from the clearing, when Ryan grabbed Peter's arm from behind and shouted, "Hey, Magellan, we just spent two days walking in a big circle!"

Peter pulled his arm back. "I don't understand it. We've always walked in the same direction."

"Or so you thought!" Matthew said.

"You have no idea where the hell you're taking us, do you?" Jason asked, looking away from his hand for the first time since his earlier outburst.

"I'll tell you what; you guys pick our direction and let's see if *you* can do any better!" Peter said, flushed.

"Well, we certainly can't do any worse!" Ryan said.

"Stop fighting, all of you! We've got to stick together," Hope shouted.

"I'll tell you what. You stay here with Magellan, the boys and I have had enough. We're forming our own tribe and now *I'm* in charge. Were heading off in a new direction; you girls are welcome to join us or stay here with this loser, the choice is yours."

"Ryan, that's just plain stupid; we've got to stick together," Hope said.

"What are you talking about? If we split up into two groups we have twice the chance of being rescued," Matthew said.

"Jason, what do you think?" Hope asked.

Jason stared at his hand for a long moment before looking up at Peter. "I'm with Ryan," he said, lacking emotion.

"What about you, Luke? You staying or coming?" Ryan asked.

"Staying."

"I always knew you were a big pussy," Matthew said.

"You three girls can stay here with Peter," Ryan said, waving his group forward. "Come on tribe, let's move out."

Ryan marched in a westerly direction toward the forest; Matthew followed, and Jason lagged several yards behind.

Hope watched them walk off, Jason once again stared at his hand, rotating it obsessively; he looked back over his shoulder at her just once before disappearing into the jungle.

"Good riddance!" Peter said, as he turned and headed off in a new direction with Hope and the others following. They walked south through the woods, bypassing the field of shrunken heads, picking up the path again on the far side of the clearing. The terrain became rockier as they walked; still they pressed on for more than an hour. The dark clouds that lurked just above the treetops discharged a light drizzle.

Ryan and his tribe had forged their way through the forest for little over an hour. He had guided them down a thin path that led into a gully. The self-proclaimed leader could hear the sound of rushing water a few seconds before he could see the small brook cascading over and around hundreds of rocks and boulders.

"You guys thirsty?" Ryan asked, turning around.

"Yeah, I'm dying," Matthew said.

"What about you, Jay?"

"I could use a drink," Jason said, still studying his hand.

"Okay, let's climb down there."

Jason and Matthew followed Ryan down into the gully, climbing from rock to rock, trying to be as sure-footed as possible. Reaching the brook, Ryan and Matthew cupped their hands and ladled the cool water, gulping it down. Jason used his good hand to bring the water to his lips, taking many smaller sips.

After drinking their fill, the three friends rested for several minutes, stretching out across the flat rocks surrounding the brook.

"Now we have to climb out of here," Ryan said, gazing up at the steep grade.

"Piece of cake," Matthew said, pulling off his shirt.

Ryan also removed his shirt and tossed it onto a flat rock.

Jason got up to sit by the brook, submerging his swollen hand into the rushing water, seemingly satisfied to sit by himself for awhile.

"I'm in no hurry to climb up that hill; let's explore around here a little first," Matthew said.

Ryan liked that idea; a half hour should allow them enough time to explore and still give them enough daylight to find their way back to the village. Together they walked along the banks, heading farther downstream. Jason stayed behind to continue soaking his hand in the water.

After several minutes the two boys came upon a small waterfall. The rushing water cascaded down about eight feet before crashing into a clear pool below. Matthew noticed several long branches wedged in between the rocks at the top of the falls. Holding his arms out for balance, he tiptoed across several partially submerged rocks, making his way to the branches. Yanking out three long, straight branches, he heaved them toward Ryan standing on the bank. Matthew retraced his steps back to his friend.

"What are you going to do with these?" Ryan asked.

"Make spears."

"Do you think Jay will want one?" Ryan asked.

"Maybe not, you know with his hand and all."

"It's getting worse, you know that?"

"Yeah, he needs a doctor."

"The swelling is starting to creep up his arm; he's not rotating his hand anymore because it hurts too much; it's in his wrist."

"Let's get back to him."

They grabbed their branches and made their way back to Jason. Ryan and Matthew returned to the large, flat rock were they had been sitting and stripped off all of the branches until they had two long, sturdy poles. Matthew was right; Jason continued soaking his hand, showing little interest in making a spear, but that didn't stop Matthew and Ryan from scraping the ends of their poles against the flat rocks, creating two sharp points.

Ryan touched the tip of the point. "Let someone try and fuck with us now!"

"I'll stab them in the gut!" Matthew said, making a stabbing motion with his spear.

"Make one for me," Jason shouted. Beads of sweat formed on his forehead; he attempted a smile, but it looked more like a grimace.

"Sure, Jay, I'll make one for ya," Matthew said. Picking up the third stick, he stripped off the branches and scraped the end against the rock, producing a point even sharper than his own.

On the far side of the brook, the bank rose up exposing several layers of rich, black soil. Matthew spotted a light green layer in between the dark soil. He waded though the shallows to investigate. Upon reaching the bank, he poked his finger into the green muck.

"What is it?" Ryan asked.

"Green clay."

Matthew scooped out enough of the muck to press into a ball, and then waded back across the pool and climbed out onto the rock.

"What are you going to do with that?" Ryan asked.

"Watch!" Matthew said, using his finger like a paintbrush, smearing three lines of clay onto both of his cheeks. "This will help with the mosquito bites."

"Let me try some," Ryan said and painted several lines across his forehead and cheeks.

Jason, using his good hand, broke off a piece of clay and drew on his own face as well.

Matthew smiled, "Now we have a real tribe!"

A light rain began to fall, spotting the surrounding rocks.

"We're in for a downpour, we'd better—ouch! I just got stung by a bee!" Matthew screamed.

Ryan also felt a sharp sting on the back of his own leg. He ran his fingers over a bump on the back of his calf. It felt like a small piece of wood embedded in his leg. He pulled out the small object and inspected it. It appeared to be a small dart.

"Goddamn it! I've been stung too!" Jason yelled.

"Take cover! They're darts!" Ryan yelled as he felt the same stinging sensation on the hamstring of his other leg.

All three boys raced for the safety of a large boulder, but Jason and Matthew both took shots to their backsides before reaching cover.

Ryan scanned his surroundings but saw nothing. His vision blurred; he felt lightheaded and short of breath. Speckles floated through his field of vision and he thought he might pass out. That's when they first appeared. Four bare-chested men emerged from the foliage on the far side of the brook. Blue war paint covered three of their faces; blood red paint covered the fourth man's face. Two of the men carried long spears; the other two held blowguns. They walked toward him, having already crossed the brook. Ryan had thoughts of grabbing for his own spear, but became paralyzed by fear as spots flashed before his eyes. They were almost upon him, close enough for him to smell their awful body odor. He tried to scream, but no words came out, and then everything faded to black.

CHAPTER TWENTY-ONE

Brenda soaked her ankle in the brook while Tim went off to collect firewood. She passed the time by tossing small pebbles into the water, *kerplunk—kerplunk*; each one sank beneath the surface. A part of her wished that she too could sink below the water and disappear. Her lower leg felt numb, having been submerged in the brook on and off for nearly three hours. She lifted her leg from the water; the swelling had gone down considerably. Brenda eased her foot back into the current; she leaned back on her arms and tilted her head toward the sky.

The dark rain clouds loomed above her, growing darker by the minute. Soon it began to drizzle. Fine raindrops rippled on the water, but she made no attempt to seek shelter. The rain grew stronger and large drops fell down upon her, splattering everywhere, soaking her arms, her face, her hair. Still she sat there, wishing that a downpour of biblical proportions would consume her. Tim's voice soon broke her thoughts of a watery demise.

"Get out of the water, I'll grab the tarp and rain gear. All of this firewood is going to get soaked," he said, dropping his armful of wood on the ground. Hurrying to the knapsacks, he found the rolled up tarp and unraveled the large patch of blue nylon. Three foot lengths of rope tied to each corner through small, brass eye-rings made it easy to set up the tarp.

"These four trees will do," he said, standing on his toes; he reached up and tied the first rope to the trunk. Tying quick knots, he secured two more corners, but had to pull hard on the last rope to make it reach, having just enough excess to tie the final knot. "Come on! Get under the tarp!"

Brenda, who begrudgingly pulled her foot from the water, hobbled under the ten-foot by ten-foot canopy. Tim hurried to collect the wood and dropped his armful of semi-wet timber on the ground under the shelter. The rain pounded down on the tarp, making a loud splattering sound as it hit the nylon.

⊷⊶⊷

The light drizzle continued to spit down on Hope and her three friends.

"Look! There's smoke coming out of the ground!" Hope said, pointing down at a small formation of jagged rocks. A wisp of white smoke rose up through the cracks; she sniffed the air; it smelled like rotten eggs.

Luke knelt down to touch one of the rocks emitting smoke from its crevices. "It's warm; these vents are releasing what smells like burnt sulfur."

The clouds released their heavy burden, unleashing a torrent. Hope tried to cover her head with her hands; Mary and Luke did likewise, but it did little good. The raindrops were so big and forceful, they stung Hope's arms.

"Come on! We got to find some shelter!" Peter shouted, running headlong into the driving rain.

Hope, Mary, and Luke followed Peter down the path. A small mountain rose out of the forest ahead of them, partially visible through the rain-soaked treetops. They stopped at the foot of the slope; its peak disappeared into the low hanging clouds.

"Maybe we can find a stone overhang," Peter said, using his hand as a visor to shield the rain.

"Look there!" Hope pointed at a small opening about a dozen yards up the rocky hill.

"Perfect, let's go!" Peter shouted.

Peter and Luke scaled the mountain with relative ease, making their way to the opening. The girls struggled up the slippery grade, taking much longer to reach the dark circle. Peter extended his arm and pulled Hope up the final few feet. Luke latched onto Mary's hand and hoisted her forward through the deluge. Hope looked at the opening and had second thoughts about climbing into it; *God only knows what's in there.*

The hole looked small, much smaller than Hope had estimated, only a few feet in diameter. Watching Peter stick his head into the black circle made her feel claustrophobic.

"Peter, wait! What if there's some sort of vicious animal in there?"

Peter's head reemerged, his hair covered in dirt. "No, it's okay, it opens up into a larger area."

Hope wondered how he could see that in the dark, but the pounding rain made it difficult to ask.

Once again Peter climbed in headfirst, shimmying forward on his stomach; he disappeared into the black hole. Mary went next, hesitating for a moment before crawling into the opening. Peter reached back, grabbing her by the hands, helping her through the narrow entrance.

Luke followed Mary and Peter into the darkness; making his shoulders small, he moved forward until he disappeared, reminding Hope of a guinea pig being swallowed by a boa constrictor, a thought that didn't make her feel any better as she approached the opening.

No longer did she see the point of crawling into the dark circle; she was already soaked.

She would have stayed put if Peter hadn't called out to her.

"Hope, come on! It's okay, I promise," he said.

Taking a deep breath, she felt more claustrophobic than ever as she climbed into the darkness. Loose dirt fell into her wet hair as she moved forward, and the feeling of tightness closed in around her. The tunnel was only a few feet long, but it felt much longer. Peter's fingers interlocked with hers as he pulled her through the tight opening into a vast cavern.

Once inside, she found herself able to stand. Brushing the dirt from her hair, she picked out small clumps of mud as if they were lice. To Hope's surprise, the cave wasn't pitch black. A bluish glow emanated from the back of the cavern.

"Look at that!" Peter said, taking a few steps toward the light.

"Let's just stand by the opening and wait until the rain stops," Hope said, folding her arms across her chest.

"Don't you want to know what that is?" Peter asked.

"Not really," Luke said.

"Me neither," Hope said.

Mary didn't offer an opinion either way.

"Come on, let's check it out," Peter said.

"This isn't a game!" Hope shouted.

Peter ignored Hope and began walking toward the blue glow.

"Well, we should probably all stick together," Luke said, swallowing hard.

"Luke's right; maybe we should follow Peter," Mary said.

"I can't believe this," Hope muttered, stepping forward against her better judgment.

Hope held Mary's hand and together they crept up behind Peter who hadn't walked very far. Luke followed just a few steps behind the girls.

Exploring the cave proved difficult even with the dim blue light. Peter's steps were slow and deliberate. Hope grabbed his belt loop; touching him somehow made her feel safer. But *why are we doing this?*

She felt Mary's fingers resting on her shoulder. Hope turned to see Luke complete the chain, holding onto Mary's shirt.

Peter kicked a small pebble forward; it fell off a ledge somewhere in front of them. It dropped for several seconds before making a loud *kerplunk.*

"I think we should turn back," Hope said, tugging on Peter's belt loop.

"Our eyes are beginning to adjust to the dark. Let's go just a little farther," Peter said.

Peter was right; their night vision had improved. Hope found herself approaching a ledge overlooking a vast, dark chasm. Carved into the rock face, was a narrow walkway no wider than Hope's sneakers placed end-to-end. It seemed less than thirty feet long, but it bulged in the middle, making it seem much longer. A larger plateau connected the walkway on the far side.

"There is no way in hell I'm stepping out onto that ledge and you're not either," Hope said, releasing her grip on Peter's belt.

"Come on, it's plenty wide, don't you want to see what's on the other side?" Ignoring her, he inched forward along the narrow walkway with his back pressed against the stone wall.

"I'm not going out there either. You don't have to do this!" Luke said.

"Just come back!" Mary yelled.

Peter stopped when he reached the middle of the span. He gazed at the large plateau on the other side, then back at Hope. Letting out a huge sigh, he started to inch his way back toward her. He'd taken just a few steps when the blue light disappeared, engulfing them in darkness.

"I'm scared! Let's get out of here!" Hope shouted.

A foul odor came from the direction of the plateau overwhelming Hope; it smelled rancid, like rotten meat, getting stronger by the second. She coughed several times, choking on the stink.

"Ah! Look out!" Peter screamed from the ledge.

"Peter!" Hope shouted, but received no reply.

Before she could call out again, someone grabbed her from the darkness. Many unseen hands groped her body; her curdling screams blended in with the others' echoing throughout the chasm. She struggled with her invisible attackers, but there were arms and hands everywhere. Long, bony fingers ran across her flesh. She struggled in vain exhausting herself.

The blue light reappeared. Hope now saw her captors. A tribesman held her arms behind her back, while four others incapacitated Peter, Luke, and Mary in a similar fashion. After pressing their faces against the cold stone wall, the tribesmen bound their hands with twine. Tattoos covered their chests and backs. The strange symbols looked similar to the ones scrolled across Hope's own stomach.

Blue paint covered four of the tribesmen's faces; red war paint covered a fifth face, and some carried spears. The red-faced man carried a bronze machete. The smell grew worse; their bodies reeked, and Hope nearly fainted from the stench. She looked at Peter; a trickle of blood dripped from his nose.

The tribesmen pushed and jostled Hope and the others across the stone walkway to the large plateau. Then with a sudden jerk, Hope found herself and the others pulled along a narrow passageway until they reached a small chamber that emitted the blue light. In the center of the room a small fire burned in a hearth built into a natural rock crevice. A translucent, turquoise dome covered the fire, carved from a single slab of blue quartz. A circle cut into the center of the dome emitted smoke from the blaze. Hope saw animal skins piled up next to the fire.

So that's how they did it! They used the fire and quartz to create the blue glow and used the animal skins to cover the quartz, creating total darkness.

Mary stood sniveling next to her. Peter and Luke stood silent.

Their captors spoke amongst themselves in a strange tongue, as they led them out of the stone room through a second opening. They descended deeper into the cavern; their captors pushed and shoved them forward at spear point through a natural tunnel formation.

Hope caught a whiff of burning animal fat permeating from the many torches embedded into the cave walls. The rancid odor almost overpowered the pungent body odor emanating from the tribesmen, but not quite.

The ground leveled off as the stone corridor opened into a vast chamber. Prodded away from the chamber, the group veered to the left. The tribesmen herded them down another stone passageway that proved to be a semicircle around the main room.

A large bamboo pen appeared at the end of the corridor, the dim torchlight made it difficult to see, but the prison cell looked occupied. The thick bamboo poles ran from the floor to the ceiling. Three long poles securely latched a door made from the same material. Each step brought Hope closer to the occupants of the cage. She stood close enough now to see three sad faces peering through the bamboo bars. The green lines smeared across their cheeks and foreheads fooled Hope for a brief moment. Looking closer, she discovered that the caked clay faces belonged to Ryan, Matthew and Jason.

⚒ ⚒

The tight twine dug into Hope's wrists. Mary stood somewhere behind her out of view, but her whimpers told Hope that her hands were also tightly bound.

The red-faced man holding the machete placed the tip on the floor and leaned the handle against the stone wall; he removed the three bamboo poles latching the door and swung it open. Grunting loudly, he pushed Ryan and Matthew away from the door. They fell backward, landing hard on their tied hands. Jason avoided the shove because he stood far enough away from the door. The taller blue-faced man pushed Hope and Mary into the cage; they stepped over Ryan and Matthew and walked toward the back next to Jason.

The tribesmen shoved Peter and Luke into the cage with such force, they fell forward tripping over Ryan and Matthew. Peter's knee landed in Matthew's gut knocking the wind out of him. The red-faced man erupted in laughter, watching Matthew gasp for air. Closing the cage, he barred the door by slipping the poles back into place. All five tribesmen disappeared down the corridor from which they'd come.

"Are you guys all right?" Hope knelt down next to the disheveled pile of young men.

Peter's limbs intertwined with Matthew's and Luke's. He unraveled his legs and tried to stand, but with tied hands, he lost his balance and fell over again. Ryan had a gash above his eyebrow and Matthew continued to gasp for air. Luke, free of Peter's legs, stood first. Peter found his footing on his second attempt. Ryan and Matthew chose to remain seated.

"We've been better," Ryan said.

"Hang in there, we'll think of something," Peter said, backing into Hope, touching her numb fingers. Standing back to back, she looked at him over her shoulder and feigned a smile. Despite their desperate situation, she felt glad that Peter was with her; touching his fingers brought her some level of comfort.

Jason stood near the back wall grimacing. He looked feverish, and beads of sweat formed on his face and ran down his cheeks. The staph infection had spread, moving through his forearm, causing it to grow larger than a ripe zucchini. His purple fingers looked like sausages and his hand ballooned to three times its normal size. The taut twine cut into his wrist, making it bleed. The cage amounted to a death sentence. The infection would consume his body. Jason's eyes told her he knew it too. He needed fast medical treatment, but how? Escape seemed impossible.

Hope scanned her surroundings looking for a way out. Solid rock made up three of the walls. A long slit cut several inches wide through the stone provided a primitive window into the main chamber. The bamboo bars that held them looked thick and sturdy. Most of them appeared to be at least three inches in diameter.

The latched door offered the only means of escape, but the three poles were thick and strong. Their only way out would be if someone let them out and that wasn't about to happen.

Mary sat in the corner whimpering. Hope sat on the stone floor next to her, but could no longer find words of comfort. Luke found a space next to Mary; she turned her face into his chest and sobbed.

Ryan, Jason, and Matthew sat together near the left wall; all three stared at each other and the bamboo bars. Peter lay next to Hope, twisting and turning like a contortionist, digging his thumb into his pocket.

"What are you doing?" Hope asked.

"My knife is in my pocket, but I can't reach it."

"Sit up and turn around, let me give it a try," Hope said, but the red-faced man reappeared from the corridor, staring at them through the bamboo. She withdrew her hands so as not to draw attention to herself or Peter.

Just beyond the bars, the tribesman sat on a flat slab of cut stone placed there for that purpose. His long spear rested across his lap.

Without warning, he stood and jabbed at Hope and Peter with his spear through the bamboo, causing them to scurry away backward on their hands like a pair of hermit crabs. The guard sat there for hours staring into the cage, never taking his eyes off them, making it impossible for Hope to retrieve Peter's pocketknife.

Hours past and hunger pangs caused a rumbling in Hope's stomach. Not being able to see her own watch, she looked at Peter's; it was 11:10 p.m.

No one had brought them food or water, which wasn't a good sign. All kinds of scenarios raced through her mind, like why waste good food on people who wouldn't be alive very long? But the big question remained. *What do they want with us? Whatever it is it can't be good.* This thinking didn't serve any real purpose. She rolled onto her side and pressed her body against Peter's. Fighting back tears, she drifted off to sleep.

CHAPTER TWENTY-TWO

B ill and Kuja pressed on through the jungle as a light drizzle began to fall.

"Look over there!" Kuja said, pointing to the remnants of a campsite. After reaching the small circle, he searched for signs of Mary and the others. Bill, out of breath, came up behind him through the reeds.

Large leaves covered most of the circle; some leaves looked ripped and pressed flat, Kuja held one up. "They slept here last night."

"Thank God they made it this far."

Kuja knelt down next to the pile of gray ash near the middle of the clearing. He inserted his finger into the cinders. "This fire is cold for more than five hours."

"Could they be that far ahead of us?" Bill asked, looking at his watch.

"Hard to say, depends if they kept walking or stopped to rest."

Kuja picked up several cut halves of cherimoya, carefully inspecting what remained of the white fleshy fruit. "They've found food."

Bill walked across the patch of dirt and inspected the leaves strewn along the edge of the clearing. "What happened here?"

Kuja knelt down and ran his finger across the nail marks raked into the dirt. Moving toward the edge of the circle, he discovered several leaves speckled with dried blood. "There was a struggle, someone was dragged toward the forest; he's hurt."

"You said *he*, how do you know it wasn't one of the girls?"

"By the nail marks and the space between the fingers, a girl's hand is much smaller."

The drizzle continued and Kuja glanced up through the breaks in the canopy at the dark clouds. He closed his eyes and rested with his hand on his chin.

The drizzle turned into a light rain. "Come on, let's go, we're losing time," Bill said, once again looking at his watch.

"I'm ready," Kuja said, his eyes wide.

Together the two men trudged through the forest.

⇥ ⇤

After walking for two more hours, they broke out of the forest into a large field of reeds and grass. A patch of bamboo appeared on their left. The rain fell harder; Bill now wished he'd brought the knapsack containing the raingear. Wet and tired, they pressed on. Thinking of Mary, he suppressed his discomfort, praying that she and the others were faring better than they were.

Kuja stared down at the path and saw many tracks, but the wet trail made footprints harder to read. He noticed something to his left and stopped. Someone had knocked down a row of reeds. After following the trail of broken reeds, they came to a small clearing.

The rain fell heavier. "I think we're getting closer," Bill said, his tone hopeful.

Row after row of small holes covered the entire clearing. Each hole appeared evenly spaced from the one next to it. Clumped mud surrounded each hole.

"What's the meaning of this?" Bill asked.

Kuja knelt down in the rain and inserted his fingers into one of the holes. Extracting a pinch of loose dirt, he rubbed it between his thumb and forefinger, "Poles."

"What?"

"Poles, hours ago a field of poles stood here."

"Why would somebody plant a field of poles and then pull them out?" Bill asked.

Kuja found a green feather lying in the mud next to several barefoot prints. They belonged to men with callused feet. "This is the work of the Invisible People."

The wind picked up and the cold shower turned into a driving rain, making it difficult to move forward. The main path split into four thinner ones; puddles covered the dirt making it impossible to track any further. Darkness set in and it became obvious that they'd have to abandon their search.

Without saying a word, Kuja began climbing the tallest tree.

"What are you doing?" Bill asked.

"Marking the tree," he said, climbing higher.

The branches thinned near the top and Bill wondered if they'd support Kuja's weight, unsure of the tribesman's purpose. Kuja, now within arm's reach of the top, removed his orange headband and wrapped it around the highest branch. Bill, puzzled by his actions, watched him descend down the tree, and seconds later he was back on terra-firma.

"You must be crazy climbing up there in this rain!" Bill said.

"I marked the tree so they can find where we left off."

"They?"

"Men who fly," Kuja said.

"You mean search and rescue?"

"Yes, our flashlights will only last a few hours; we must start back. And tomorrow we can't start anew. We must start where we left off, we need, how do you say it? H-e-l-i-copters."

"I must find my daughter!" Bill shouted, feeling defeated, having come to the realization that Mary and the others would have to spend yet another night in the cold, rainy forest. His eyes welled up; the hard rain washed away his tears.

Darkness arrived and he now wished that he'd brought Tim's flare gun. At least that would offer them one last chance before they turned back. Why had he been so pigheaded? Did he need to show Tim who was boss? Whatever the reason it didn't matter now; they'd finished their search, at least for the night. They were left with only one option, make their way back to Tim and Brenda and spend a wet night in the forest. In the morning they'd hike the five hours back to the Shuar village and contact the authorities.

Both men unclipped their flashlights from their belts and clicked on the strong beams. The powerful lights illuminated the path along with a torrent of raindrops that appeared and disappeared like phantoms before the light.

══╬ ╬══

A lone, tattooed warrior watched in silence through the rain as the two intruders walked with their moonbeams in hand into the night. Lurking in the shadows, he'd gone unnoticed, having tracked them for hours through the wet forest.

The white man had looked right at him as he stood motionless; blending in with the trees, but the tainted brown man gave him reason to wait. More than once he thought the man had seen him, but he was mistaken.

If they'd continued on, he would have used his blowgun to stop them. Using his bird-like call to summon the others, they would have carried them into the caves. There, Kalku, the mystical one would sacrifice them to Chon-Chon, the feathered child of death. This must wait for another day because very soon seven offerings will fill the sacrificial chamber. How easy it had been to apply the sacrificial ointments. *Tonight, Kalku will mark their stomachs, etching seven sacred prayers to Chon-Chon across their skin. The simple trickery of moving the field of heads to another clearing will make them believe they'd walked in a circle. Kalku's magic will drive them like animals!*

Soon there will be another row of seven fresh heads in the field of poles.

The moonbeams moved farther away. *Let them go,* he thought, *tomorrow we find them. Chon-Chon is always watching, giving guidance to Kalku, and always leading him to the offerings. Whatever shape Chon-Chon took, she never stopped watching.*

Now satisfied with the distance between them, he fought through the rain and scampered up the tree like a wet monkey, plucking the feathered headband from the top branches. Climbing down the tree much faster than the brown-skinned man had done several minutes before, he stood with his prize and smirked as he watched the moonbeams fade into nothing.

Tim tried to start a small fire under the tarp, but the wood wouldn't light. After striking several matches and watching them fizzle out against the damp kindling, he decided to give up, at least for now. Even under the tarp, the air felt damp and cold; Brenda shivered, crossing her arms against her chest, and her lips turned a deep shade of blue.

"We should huddle together for warmth," Tim said.

"Don't even try it."

"Believe me, that's the furthest thing from my mind."

"Oh, is it?"

"Don't flatter yourself; I'm just trying to warm you up, that's all."

Brenda sighed, "I guess it does make sense."

"Let's at least get under the same poncho to trap our body heat," Tim said, lifting the front of his plastic raingear, allowing Brenda to duck her head underneath. The poncho stretched then ripped across the seam, but not enough to matter.

They sat together on the ground, face to face. Brenda straddled his lap; he thought about her barroom days and how she'd earned her money in that same position. He hated himself for being judgmental.

With their arms wrapped around each other, they held each other tight. Tim felt Brenda's thighs pressing against his kidneys, but he didn't care. It felt good, even through her damp clothes, but not in a sexual way. This surprised him, especially after his thoughts of lap dancing and having been her recent lover. It felt more spiritual than sexual as their bodies came together. Never before had he felt this close to anyone; he drank in her warm breath and absorbed her body heat.

She had listened to him; at first she didn't want to, but she had; he'd earned her trust and this fact wasn't lost on him. He kissed her forehead, and she gazed up at him; looking into her eyes, he could see the little girl hidden deep within and that little girl returned his smile.

⋖⊹ ⊹⋗

Together they lay on the ground under the poncho for several hours. The torrential downpour continued, pounding the tarp louder, as darkness started to fall.

"The wood should be dry by now; let me give the fire another go," Tim said, remembering Bill's instructions.

"Keep it small, you don't want to roast us or smoke us out."

"I'll try, but it has to be large enough for them to see it when they come back."

Near the middle of the floor, Tim stacked a small pile of wood; he struck a match and lit the kindling.

"Success!" he shouted.

He'd started a small fire, but the flat tarp held in the smoke, choking them.

Stepping out into the rain, he adjusted the ropes, raising one side of the tarp, allowing the smoke to escape. The drawback to this feat of engineering was the waterfall it created; rainwater cascaded off the low end of the tarp, creating a puddle large enough to claim several feet of covered ground.

The fire provided adequate warmth, eliminating the need for the poncho. Brenda rested next to the fire, while Tim stoked the flames.

Watching her sleep, he thought about the warmth of her body, wanting to once again wrap himself around her, but that was no longer possible. Bill and Kuja could return at any moment. What would the good professor think about the two of them snuggled close to one another? He couldn't risk that, not now, not with those kids missing.

Time passed slowly; Tim looked at his watch and saw it was already past eleven. He wondered where they could be. Had they found them? He doubted that they could find anything in this rain. Moments later he wondered no more; Bill's approaching cough announced their arrival. Tim stood to greet the dripping men as they stepped under the tarp. Nobody accompanied them and Tim wasn't about to ask the obvious.

"Welcome back," Tim said instead, offering his hand.

Bill weakly shook his hand and grunted his greeting as he stepped past Tim to warm himself by the fire. Brenda stirred, sitting up; she looked confused, perhaps wondering where she was. Tim watched for that moment of realization to cross her face. When it came, she looked at Bill and frowned, but recovered nicely. "Are you guys hungry? Do you want something to eat?"

"That would be great," Kuja said.

Bill grunted something that could've been a yes. Brenda reached into the larger of the two knapsacks and pulled out a package of beef jerky, handing it to Kuja. The tribesman tore open the plastic packaging and ripped off a small piece of beef for himself before handing the rest to Bill.

Kuja ate slowly, savoring each bite, while Bill wolfed down the remainder of the jerky before anyone else could ask for more.

"We tracked them deep into the forest, but we were stopped by the puddles and darkness," Kuja said.

With the jerky gone, Bill moved closer to the fire to continue drying. "We had to give up for the night, but we marked the spot; Kuja tied his orange headband to the top of a tree."

"So what's the plan for tomorrow?" Tim asked, now completely confused.

"We get up early and hike back to the village, maybe catch a ride to the modern section and call the authorities. Hopefully, this damn rain will stop by then."

"So why the headband in the tree?" Brenda asked. Tim was glad she'd asked instead of him; the question wouldn't sound so stupid coming from her.

"Search and rescue can come in with helicopters and find the spot where we left off."

"Helicopters! Do you think they will?" Her tone changed; she sounded almost jovial.

"If they're available," Bill said, looking at Kuja, and patting him on the back. "How I wish I'd brought that flare gun."

I bet you did, fat man! I bet you did! Tim thought.

CHAPTER TWENTY-THREE

Hope awoke to the smell of urine and the sound of distant voices. Everyone else still lay on the floor unconscious. Wet stains were evident on all of their jeans, hers included. She felt dirty and disgusting, but that was the least of her problems.

Peter breathed heavy, facing her with his eyes closed and his back against the rear wall. She looked at his watch; it was already 1:30 p.m. *How'd I sleep so long?* The tiny red mark on her forearm provided her with the answer. They had drugged her once again. She glanced over at Jason; the swelling on his arm had ballooned further and now reached his bicep. At least he wasn't suffering at the moment. A blood red dot on his good arm provided evidence of an injection site.

Leaning toward her boyfriend, she whispered, "Peter wake up!"

"I'm awake, been so for over an hour now," Peter said, his eyes still closed.

"Do you hear those voices?"

"Sounds like it's coming from the main chamber. Listen, I've got—" Just then the red-faced guard jumped to his feet and poked the spear at them through the bamboo.

"*Gulamingumba!*" he shouted at them with piercing brown eyes. His boisterous voice caused the others to stir, but they seemed dazed as they lay on the ground; only Jason remained asleep.

The tribesman had told them to shut up; she could discern that much from his tone. They dared not speak, but she tried to communicate with Peter by nodding her head and using rapid eye movements.

Leaning against Peter's shoulder she tried to stand, bringing up first one knee, then the other. She found her footing and was surprised that she had enough strength left in her legs to accomplish that feat. After one failed attempt, Peter also managed to stand. The guard again shouted something at them, but this time made no threatening gestures with his spear; still they dared not speak.

Hope made no sudden motions, but took slow steps toward the long, rectangular slit that allowed her to peer into the main chamber. For whatever reason, the red-faced man made no effort to stop her. Peter stood against the back wall fidgeting, never taking his eyes off the guard.

Peering through the slit, the cavern looked much brighter than the day before and an array of torches lit the room. Many tribesmen and their families filled the large space; men, women, and children sat together in rows on the hard stone floor. The room filled quickly and more than three-quarters of it was already full. Hope saw many others filtering in through several different entrances near the back.

It must have been hot in the cavern because the tribe wore minimal clothing. Even the women sat almost naked, small patches of loin cloth covering their private parts providing their only clothing. A similar cloth covered the men's genital area, but nothing else. Tattooed symbols not unlike her own; covered their upper torsos, including their faces and necks, and many wore necklaces made from what looked like human bone. Some of the women also wore necklaces made from colorful beads and quartz. Women with small children sat behind their men. Hope counted three babies suckling on their mothers' breasts.

At the front of the chamber, a plateau rose up about twenty feet above the floor. The flat stone surface cut deep into the rock, resembled a stage. A carved stone formation stood about two feet high in the middle of the platform; it looked like a sacrificial altar. The surface was flat, with two long blood groves cut into the stone that allowed for runoff down the sides of the altar. Dark maroon stained the narrow troughs.

On the left, a stone stairway cut into the rock led up to the plateau. To the right, the rock platform fell off into a glowing abyss. Its orange hue presumably came from an unseen pool of magma circulating below. *We must be inside the volcano,* Hope thought.

A large, translucent statue stood behind the altar at the rear of the plateau. When Hope looked closer, her eyes widened, beads of sweat began to form on her forehead. The statue stood over twenty feet tall and was cut from a single slab of aqua blue quartz. The astounding workmanship and attention to detail rivaled pictures of Michelangelo's David that she'd studied in Art History class. Perfect feathers carved into the quartz covered the entire statue. Muscles rippled through the feathers on the arms, legs, and stomach.

A child's face gazed down upon the crowd; a sneering face that looked all too familiar. The tribesmen stood, raising their spears high into the air at the statue, chanting, "Chon-Chon, Chon-Chon." The women bowed, chanting together in prayer to the crystal idol.

A deity by any other name is still the same, Hope thought. Make no mistake; the *Iwanci's* crystal face stared back at her.

⚔ ⚔

The last of the tribe entered the chamber, taking their seats on the floor. A tall, muscular man in his twenties stood on the platform. A necklace of human teeth hung across his tattooed chest. He held a torch in his left hand and a long spear in his right.

The red-faced guard left his post and walked down the corridor. He stood in the first entrance to the main chamber to observe the ceremony.

Hope turned her attention back to the man on the platform. The young warrior raised his long spear and shouted, "*Kalku!*"

On that command, a loud roar rose from the crowd. All of the men stood again and raised their spears as the cheer went up. In the front row, a tribesman began beating an animal skin drum, creating a steady methodical rhythm.

A shaman stepped from the darkness onto the platform wearing a brightly colored headdress made from blue and gold feathers. A necklace of assorted bones hung across his chest. Hope stared at his face; he was the same shaman haunting her dreams. The younger warrior bowed to the older shaman and began a chant that soon resonated with every tribal voice. "*Kalku! Kalku! Kalku!*"

The shaman held a large, bronze machete in his hand, changing his grip several times before deciding to hold the shiny blade with both hands. He extended the blade out in front of him, standing motionless as if he were praying or meditating.

The younger man held a figurine. Hope recognized the palm leaf doll; it was identical to the male versions that she'd stumbled upon the day before in the mist. Walking in step to the drum, the younger man stopped at the edge of the abyss and tossed the leafy stick figure into the fiery pit. The orange glow became much brighter for a brief moment, illuminating the tribesman's body, revealing his determined face and rippling arm muscles.

The shaman broke out of his trance, and began a slow dance to the steady beat, dancing faster as the rhythm increased. The glowing lava combined with the flicker of torch light gave his skin an orange hue, making him look demonic.

The younger man raised his spear and pointed it toward the red-faced man, shouting orders. Upon hearing his instructions, the guard bowed slightly, stepping back into the corridor. He hurried to the cage and grabbed his own spear that had been resting against the wall. After removing the bars, he unlatched the door and entered the cage.

Grabbing Peter by the arm, he tried to pull him forward. Peter lunged backward away from the man, pressing his back against Hope. "Hold my fingers!" he shouted, as he pressed something hard into her hands. The guard slapped Peter several times in the face before dragging him from the cage.

"Please, no, stop! Let him go! Peter!" Hope screamed as she watched her boyfriend dragged away. Mary and Luke had come to their senses, shouting for the red-faced man to stop.

After sliding the three bamboo bars back across the door, the guard smirked at Hope and her two friends. Prodding Peter forward with his spear, he led him down the corridor toward the main chamber. Moments later Hope, Mary, and Luke watched through the long slit as the guard pushed and shoved Peter into the main chamber.

The beating of the drum intensified, and the shaman hastened his pace.

Hope stared at Peter's tormentor; the red war paint covering his face now made sense. *He's part of the show.* Jabbing Peter in the rump with his spear, he forced him up the long stone staircase leading to the raised platform. Each jab penetrated Peter's jeans; he grimaced, biting his lip with every poke. Hope saw the red wetness soaking through his pants and gasped. Peter and the guard reached the top step, walking onto the stone stage that overlooked the crowd. The drumbeat intensified as the shaman danced himself into a frenzy.

The young warrior yanked Peter away from the red-faced guard. With his hands still firmly bound, he dragged the nineteen-year-old to the altar, while Peter struggled in vain. After forcing him to kneel, the tribesman wrapped his hand around Peter's hair and pulled his head down, holding his face flat against the worn stone. The shaman approached Peter, raising the machete high above his head with both hands.

Hope came to the sudden realization of what was about to happen. Her throat contracted and her voice quivered as she tried to force out the words, "Oh, my God! Oh, my God!" But her syllables were barely audible.

The drumbeat came to a sudden stop. The chamber fell silent just as Hope regained her voice. Through the slit she shouted, "No!" Her gut-wrenching screams echoed throughout the cavern, but her plea fell on deaf ears. The shaman, with one swift blow, separated Peter's head from his shoulders. A dull thump resonated throughout the chamber as Peter's head fell onto the hard rock plateau. Hope tasted the sour rising in her throat and vomited the contents of her stomach onto the stone floor. Out of respect for Peter, she stepped back to the slit and continued to watch, like a wife at a hanging.

The shaman placed the machete on the altar. Picking up Peter's head, he held it by the hair, raising it high above his own. A loud cheer erupted from the crowd. Hope saw Peter's facial muscles still twitching, refusing to die; blood dripped from his neck. Turning her head, she could bear no more.

Hope's trembling hands steadied her against the wall; her vision became spotted. Feeling like she might faint, she bowed her head, fighting hard to remain conscious. The moment passed, and when she looked up again, she saw that all movement had stopped on Peter's face. Tasting her tears, she whispered a prayer through salty lips, "May his soul rest in peace."

Tears also streamed down Mary's face. She stared down at the floor. The cheering crowd drowned her wails. Luke appeared to be in shock, staring in silence.

The familiar rhythm of the drum started again and the shaman began his blood dance. Holding Peter's head, he smeared his arms, face and chest with blood dripping from the open neck.

Hysterics set in; Hope sobbed. Peter was dead; she'd seen him butchered before her eyes, but she couldn't come to terms with this harsh reality.

By this time Ryan, Matthew, and Jason began to stir and after a couple of minutes, they struggled to their feet.

"Where's Peter? What's going on?" Ryan asked.

Unable to speak, Hope pointed toward the slit. All three boys bellied up to the wall; Matthew stood in Hope's vomit. Their jaws dropped and the color left Ryan's face. Jason's face had already looked peaked, but Matthew's face turned a new shade of green.

"He's dead! They've killed him," Matthew said.

Ryan dry heaved. "They chopped off his fucking head!"

Jason looked dazed, not saying a word.

"We're next!" Mary said, her sobs becoming much harder.

The drumbeat increased in tempo. Hope approached the stone window and watched the shaman dance wildly with Peter's head. Hope squeezed her hands tight, pressing her fingers against the hard object still lodged in her deadened hands. It gave her a form of release, similar to biting a bullet.

She watched Jason grimace and the sweat dripping from his face; she could no longer bear to look at his infected arm. Instead, she closed her eyes and pressed harder against the object in her hand.

The object! Peter had given it to her; he wanted her to have it. Everything happened so fast; her entire focus had been on Peter, and she hadn't given the object much thought. Holding it in her palm, she ran her blood-starved fingers over it, but they lacked sensation and hardly moved, making it difficult to determine what it was. *The pocketknife!* Somehow he'd finagled it out of his pants. Maybe it was when he laid on the ground next to her. Or maybe he did it while he stood near the back wall fidgeting against the rock. It didn't matter; somehow he'd done it, giving them a chance, albeit a long shot.

Using her nails, she picked at the groove in the blade; after many attempts she flicked open the knife and it clicked into place. She needed someone to help her. Luke had slunk to the floor, sitting in the far corner with his legs bent, his forehead resting on his propped knees.

The other boys stood with their backs to Hope, peering through the long rectangle. The shaman's blood dance mesmerized them. Jason's sweat-soaked shirt and dampened hair indicated he wasn't doing all that well himself.

Mary, standing by her side, seemed like the logical choice to assist with the knife; she'd helped her once before, cutting through her cotton shirt.

"Mary, turn around."

"What?"

"Turn around and touch my hands."

"Why?" She looked confused.

"Just do it. I'm going to try and cut you loose."

"But how–"

"Just do it!"

Mary and Hope stood almost back to back, leaving enough space between them to allow for finger movement. Hope held the knife in her hand, gripping the handle backward with the point facing Mary. Placing the blade on the coarse twine that strangled Mary's hands, she shuffled back and forth and began to saw. The blade slipped once, slicing into Mary's skin; she whimpered, taking a reflexive step away from the knife. Drops of blood dripped from her wrist onto the floor. Mary, despite her injury, stepped back toward Hope.

"Not much further," Hope said. After finding the notch in the twine, she continued to saw. The twine snapped, surrendering its hold on Mary's hands; she wiggled her fingers and pressed her palm flat against her cut.

"Here, take the knife and cut me loose," Hope said.

Mary grabbed the blade and made fast work of the cord digging into Hope's wrists. With the twine cut, Hope pulled her hands apart, letting the cut rope fall to the floor. The freed veins and arteries throbbed from the sudden release of blood, bringing her hands back to life. She flexed her fingers several times to allow feeling to return.

Grabbing the knife from Mary, she stepped toward a surprised Luke; he raised his head, watching her cut through his ropes in seconds.

By this time Ryan and Jason turned to see what was going on.

"Holy shit! You're free, but how?" Ryan said.

Hope didn't say a word; she'd let Peter's knife do the talking for her. The sharp blade cut first through Ryan's ropes, then Jason's, then Matthew's.

Sliced rope lay strewn everywhere across the floor.

"Our hands are free but what fucking good is that going to do?" Ryan asked, massaging his wrists.

"Yeah, we're at their mercy stuck in this prison," Matthew said.

Jason stared at his swollen arms, speaking matter-of-factly, "If Peter is any indication, they'll show no mercy."

"Maybe we can use that knife and cut through the bamboo bars," Mary said.

"They're too thick," Luke said, shaking the bars. "It'll take too long."

"Shush! Do you hear that?" Hope asked, pressing her extended arms against Ryan and Matthew.

"I don't hear nothing," Ryan said.

"Exactly! The drumbeat stopped," Hope said and strained her ears to listen.

The distinct voices of the young tribesmen echoed throughout the cavern. Hope, Ryan, and Matthew ran to the sound, taking their positions along the long stone window.

"Keep your arms down! Don't let them see your hands!" Hope hissed.

Ryan and Matthew dropped their arms to their sides and took their positions next to Hope.

The Shaman had stopped dancing; still he held Peter's head, dangling it by his hair. The younger tribesman stood to the shaman's left, a few feet from the glowing pit. He shouted, "*Chon-Chon*," and this time the tribe responded in kind, repeating their mantra over and over.

When the chant neared its crescendo, the tribesman stepped toward Peter's headless body. Picking it up off the ground, he hoisted it over his shoulder in what looked like a fireman's carry. With each rhythmic chant of "*Chon-Chon*," he stepped methodically toward the fiery abyss. Reaching the edge, he widened his stance. Bending his knees, he raised the corpse over his head, locking his arms into a v-shape. Blood poured from the open neck, running down the tribesman's arm, splattering onto the stone floor. The tribal mantra electrified the crowd. After leaning backward, he thrust forward, heaving Peter's remains into the lava pit. The headless corpse took several seconds to fall. Hope heard the body splash into the magma where it incinerated in a flash of fire that lit up the cavern. All of the tribesmen sitting below stood and shouted, raising their spears high into the air.

The young tribesman took a few steps toward the old shaman and began a new chant, "*Kalku! Kalku!*"

All the voices in the cavern resonated as one, repeating the new mantra. Kalku, with his fist still tightly wrapped around Peter's hair, again raised the head. The chanting rose to a fever pitch. Pressing the head against his right palm, he took a long breath and heaved it like a shot-put into the crowd.

A near riot ensued on the floor; Peter's head bounced from hand to hand across the top of the crowd as each tribesman fought and jostled trying to claim it for himself. It reminded Hope of a bunch of single women fighting for a bouquet at a wedding or a foul ball bouncing across a sea of hands at a Big League game before the fan with the fastest reflexes hauled it in. And like that fan, a young, quick-handed tribesman snatched Peter's head. Securing it against his chest, he pushed through the crowd, disappearing with his prize through a rear exit.

The crowd fell silent and once again the young tribal warrior shouted commands from the stone stage, pointing at the red-faced man who stood in a side doorway. Their guard raised his spear in homage to the shaman before stepping back into the corridor. The pounding of the drum started up again; its slow tempo sounded like a death knell.

A hundred thoughts raced through Hope's mind. They shouldn't have just stood there like a bunch of idiots; they should've used the time wisely to devise a plan, plot some means of escape, and now it was too late.

In another minute their jailer would return and see the ropes scattered across the floor. After beating them into submission, he'd tie them up again and choose another sacrificial lamb. Hope trembled, wondering who that might be. A part of her wished it would be her; she almost welcomed death, not wanting to watch her friends' senseless slaughter.

She'd meet Peter in God's kingdom and, like Romeo and Juliet, they'd be together in heaven forever. These thoughts were euphoric, but another part of her knew it was wrong. This other part told her to fight to stay alive.

CHAPTER TWENTY-FOUR

H ope crouched to the floor, moving at a frantic pace. "Quick, grab the ropes and stuff them into your pockets!" she shouted.

The others snatched strands of twine from the floor, shoving them into their pants, their pockets, anywhere they could. Jason staggered and moaned as he bent over; creases formed on his forehead, and grabbing just one handful of rope with his good hand, he managed to push most of it into his pocket.

"Put your hands behind your backs and act like you're still tied up," Hope said.

Who will be the one? She thought. Strong Matthew seemed like a good choice. Placing her hand on his shoulder, she stared into his eyes and handed him the knife, "You know what to do," she said, her lips pursed.

Matthew nodded, taking the knife from her hand.

The red-faced man reappeared just beyond the bars. They all stood facing him with their hands hidden behind them. He came upon them quickly.

The man grinned, revealing his yellow and crooked teeth. Jabbing at Hope with his spear, he taunted her through the bars. She reflexively took a step backward, making sure she was out of reach. He yelled at her, shaking his spear. After snorting like a pig, he turned and leaned his weapon against the rock wall. Without the spear, he no longer presented an immediate threat which allowed Hope to step forward and stare at him through the bars. He returned her gaze, focusing his attention only on her; she could see the evil glistening in his dark eyes.

Hope sensed her fate; she'd be the one separated from the herd, the next lamb to the slaughter. Holding his stare, he never took his eyes off her; he slid back the first pole, followed by the second, then the third.

Pushing open the door he lunged at her, grabbing for her neck, but missed. Hope had stepped backward just out of reach, forcing the guard to enter the cage. Again he tried to grab her, but she staggered back into the corner, her body slammed hard into the cold stone wall. Dazed, she collapsed to the floor. Her eyes darted back and forth looking for the others, looking for help, but they all stood frozen in place. Matthew's mouth hung ajar, his feet planted as if rooted to the ground. Nobody came to her aid and her heart raced; she stood powerless with nowhere left to run.

His bony fingers wrapped around her throat; she gagged and choked as he tried to lift her off the floor. Spots danced before her eyes; she felt like she might pass out at any moment, but still she had the wherewithal to keep her hands hidden behind her back.

Ryan moved first, stepping forward, he grabbed the guard from behind, holding him in an arm lock. This broke the guard's grip on Hope's throat, but he strained and bucked, turned and twisted, struggling to break free. Ryan wouldn't be able to hold him for long; the man was too strong. Hope just sat there, gasping for air, helpless to aid Ryan in any way. Thick veins bulged through the war paint on the guard's neck, his already large biceps grew bigger still.

The man tried to call out for help, but barely uttered a syllable before Jason grabbed the guard's face with his good hand, covering his mouth and nose. The man bucked like a bull, twisting to his left then right, but still Ryan held on.

Matthew broke out of his trance. Stepping forward, he plunged the knife deep into the tribesman's gut; the blade disappeared up to the handle. Withdrawing the blade, he stabbed him again and again and again. Blood splattered everywhere, covering Matthew's arms, chest, and face; large drops speckled Hope's shirt, and still the red-faced man fought on.

Jason yanked back the man's head, revealing his neck. Matthew sliced his throat, cutting him ear to ear. His throat gurgled for several seconds before his body went limp, Ryan tossed him into a heap on the floor. A maroon puddle formed around the dead man's head.

Drenched in blood, Matthew stood in a daze still gripping the knife. Hope found her footing and stepped toward Matthew, prying the knife from his shaking hand. She wiped the blade on her shirt, folded the knife, and shoved it into her back pocket.

"Good job!" she said, gazing into Matthew's vacant eyes; maybe there'd be more time to thank him later. Her only focus was that open door and their chance for freedom.

"Come on, let's go!" Hope waved the group forward. Mary and Luke followed her into the corridor; the other three boys were just steps behind. Matthew grabbed the dead man's spear as they passed, carrying it by his side. They hurried forward, coming to the first opening that led into the main chamber. Hope crouched down low near the floor and peeked around the corner, and saw a multitude of people standing with their backs to her just a few feet away. They all seemed mesmerized by the shaman's chants and the methodical drum beat.

Hope weighed her options; if they crawled on the floor across the opening, the two stone steps leading up into the cavern might provide enough of an obstructed view should anyone turn around. They could make a run for it, but not without going undetected.

"Follow me!" Hope whispered, hugging her body against the steps. She crawled on her stomach across the gap, easily making it to the other side. One by one the others safely crawled across the entrance, but the entire process took far too long, and they'd have to pick up the pace if they had any chance of escape.

"Okay, here's the plan. We're going to run through this corridor like an obstacle course. We need to sprint to the next opening, dive onto our bellies in silence, and then come up running again on the other side," Hope said. "You think you can handle that?" Everyone nodded with the exception of Mary and Jason, who stood expressionless.

Hope took off running, reaching the second opening; she slid across the entranceway on her stomach; jumping to her feet, she sprinted toward the third, glancing over her shoulder. Everyone was right behind her, even Mary and Jason. Matthew brought up the rear, worming his way across the gap, still holding the dead man's spear. At the end of the corridor, Hope slunk against the far wall, hiding in the shadows. She took a sharp right, running up the natural tunnel formation, straining her legs against the steady grade. Glancing over her shoulder, she was pleased to find everyone sucking wind right behind her.

Hope hesitated when they'd reached a fork in the tunnel.

"Which way?" Ryan shouted from somewhere behind her.

"Toward the blue glow," Hope replied, now using the blue light as a beacon.

The blue glow intensified as they ran toward it, as did the tempo of the drums behind them. Hope had almost reached the small room projecting the light when the drum beat stopped and a roar went up from the tribe.

"I think we've just run out of time," Hope said in between breaths, surprised that they'd gotten that far. They raced into the room housing the hearth and the blue crystal dome; it was empty, except for an elderly woman left to tend the fire. She shouted frantically at them, flailing her arms, trying to block the doorway. Hope lowered her shoulder and bowled her over; she never stopped running. They ran out of the room and along the long passageway, taking several minutes to reach the plateau and the narrow ledge beyond. Gasping for breath, Hope stopped at the ledge to survey the situation.

Coming in, they'd been jostled and pushed by the tribesmen across the stone walkway, but their captors weren't about to let them fall, where was the fun in that? This time they'd have to find their balance and bridge the span unescorted.

Ryan stepped toward the ledge and said, "Holy shit!" Making it apparent that Ryan and his two friends were viewing the span for the first time.

"Come on!" Hope said, holding Mary's hand.

Luke and the rest of the boys followed a few steps behind. Together, they shimmied out onto the narrow ledge, but they were moving too slow. Hope knew they'd have to bridge the chasm much faster.

"Hurry!" Hope said, tugging on Mary's shaking arm.

"If we fall off the ledge, this will have been for nothing!" Mary said, her voice cracking.

"If they catch us, we're dead! You've got to take your chances on the ledge!"

Luke grabbed hold of Mary's other hand, enabling them to inch across the ledge quicker than before, but still far too slow for Hope's liking. With their backs to the wall, they slid forward, trying to keep in sync with each other as they stepped.

We're almost there, Hope thought, looking toward the other side.

At that moment, the vast cavern went black. A sinking feeling washed over Hope who couldn't see anything in the darkness.

Mary began to cry, "I'm going to fall; I just know it!"

"Just calm down," Luke said.

Hope knew the tribesmen were closing in on them. They've made it to the room with the blue dome, covering the quartz, creating darkness.

She heard their shouts and their not so distant footsteps. "We've got to move faster!"

The tribesmen will make it across this ledge in no time, she thought.

"Follow my lead. Take a deep breath and step," Hope said, attempting to relax Mary and get her moving.

"Okay," Mary whimpered.

Matthew tried to coach her, "Everybody breathe deep and take a giant step as far as your legs will bend."

Hope and the boys took their giant steps, but Mary took only a few giant steps before reaching the bulge near the center of the span, and there she returned to her baby mouse steps.

"Breathe and step. Breathe and step," Hope repeated as she slid sideways, coaxing her friend along. Mary somehow found the courage to get back in step with Hope and the rest of the group. Hope felt a sense of relief, having now reached the other side.

"I can see a speck of light in the distance. That's got to be the opening!" Hope said.

They were able to pick up their pace by feeling their way along the wall. The speck of light grew bigger as they approached. Hope led the group toward the light; she increased their pace to a jog, knowing that there weren't any major obstacles in front of them.

Running through the dark, the warriors reached the plateau and the narrow ledge, bridging the chasm in seconds. Making their way across, they quickly closed the gap between themselves and the white ones ahead.

Hope reached the opening and the rest of the group gathered around her. Cupping her hands, she boosted Mary into the tight tunnel. Mary squirmed forward, using her knees and elbows; she crawled several dusty feet before pulling herself to the outside.

"Hope, you go next!" Luke said.

Hope climbed into the opening; it seemed tighter than before and dirt clung to her sweaty arms making it difficult for her to move forward. Her bulging veins swollen with blood made it tighter still. Loose dirt fell into her hair and eyes, but she crawled like a worm, squirming her way through the opening.

She fell out into the daylight squinting as the bright sunshine blinded her. After sliding on her stomach downhill for several feet, she found her footing and scurried back up to the entrance to assist the others.

Luke was already halfway through the short tunnel. Hope reached in and grabbed his arms; with Mary's help, she pulled Luke through the opening. Jason went next, his swollen arm proved useless, forcing him to struggle forward with just one hand. Each movement caused a new contortion of his pained face.

"Hurry up, I hear them coming!" Ryan shouted, his voice muffled inside the cave.

Luke climbed headfirst back into the tunnel, latching onto Jason's good arm. The girls grabbed hold of Luke's ankles; and, using their weight, leaned back and pulled with all their might. The small rock tube muffled Jason's screams. They pulled harder like a couple of midwives assisting with a difficult birth. After another hard pull, they succeeded in birthing the odd twins, extracting both Luke and Jason from Mother Earth herself.

⊨◁+ +▷⊨

"Move to the side!" Matthew shouted and Hope and Luke did as instructed. Mary and Jason also moved away from the opening. Matthew threw his spear; it shot through the hole like a javelin rising into the air, and landed a half dozen yards or so down the mountain.

"Get moving! They're almost here!" Ryan shouted.

Matthew clawed his way through the opening faster than the others. Grabbing his arms, Hope and Luke yanked him through to the outside. Matthew sprinted down the hill to fetch his spear, and after grabbing it, he climbed back up the mountain to the dark hole. Poking his head inside the opening, Matthew saw Ryan struggling to move forward; being much larger than the rest, his mid-section became wedged against the sides.

"I'm stuck!" Ryan shouted.

Matthew stuck his spearhead deep into the ground and squirmed his way back into the hole, gripping Ryan's hands.

"They're here! They're fucking here!"

"I got him, pull us out!" Matthew shouted.

Matthew felt his friends' hands yanking on his legs and ankles but Ryan didn't budge.

"Suck it in!" Matthew shouted. Giving a last ditch effort, he tightened his own stomach muscles and summoned all the strength in his arms, curling Ryan's wrists toward him like a dumbbell.

Ryan moved an inch forward, then two.

"Pull!" Matthew shouted.

The hands pulled hard on his legs, almost dislocating his femur, but they were moving forward. The tunnel released its grip on Ryan and they both popped out into the sunlight.

Matthew heard shouts coming from inside the opening; he pulled his spear from the ground and cautiously peered inside. A blue-faced tribesman holding a machete stared back at him less than three feet away. The warrior jabbed the blade at him with the speed of a coiled viper. Matthew pulled his head back, saved only by his quick reflexes. The point narrowly missed his face; the tip stuck four inches out of the opening, the bronze blade glistening in the bright sun.

"Run!" Matthew screamed. Hope, Mary, and Luke were already down the hill running for the forest. Ryan and Jason took a few steps down the mount, but hesitated, seemingly waiting for him to join them.

Matthew made no attempt to follow. "Go! I'll hold them off."

"Not without you!" Ryan said.

Matthew shook his head in defiance, still holding his spear; he climbed higher, positioning himself above the opening, looking down upon the faces of his worried friends.

More of the blade emerged from the hole, five inches, then six, then eight, a fist followed clenched around the handle. Matthew's heart pounded in his chest; adrenaline shot through his veins; he looked at his own hands and saw the blood had already dried from his kill. Gripping his spear, he cocked it back, holding it next to his ear.

A forearm emerged, followed by an elbow. How easy it would've been to pierce the tribesman's limb, slicing tendons, rendering his arm useless, but he stood fast, knowing that at any moment better targets would emerge. It took patience to hunt a headhunter; this thought scared and excited him at the same time. After being at their mercy for so long, he was now in control.

A second arm appeared followed by the top of a head; loose brown dirt lay sprinkled through black hair. He now saw the entire head; it looked like a turtle emerging from its shell. Matthew stood frozen in place, hesitant to deliver the blow. This time nobody was there to hold his victim; this time he was on his own.

Come on, just a little farther!

The tribesman inched forward, revealing his neck. Matthew focused on a small tattoo that resembled a tiny bird just above the base and thrust his spear downward with such force, his arm seemed spring loaded. The sharp stone point pierced the back of his neck. The tribesman screamed. Matthew leaned on the shaft with his body weight, driving the tip through flesh and cartilage. Piercing the Adam's apple, he buried the point deep into the dirt.

The machete fell from the tribesman's hand as he choked and gagged; now clutching both hands to his throat. Blood spurted from his neck into the dirt below, creating a muddy red paste.

The impaled man's hands moved to the shaft. Gripping it below his neck, he tried to pull the point from the ground, but his blood-drenched hands slipped on the slick shaft and he seemed unable to maintain a proper grip. Matthew pushed harder on the spear, forcing the point deeper into the dirt.

The tribesman's head twitched on the pole as he gurgled on his own blood. Matthew enjoyed the sound; it was the sound of helplessness, the sound of imminent death. He pressed harder still on the shaft. Using his body weight, he leaned on the spear, moving the wood farther through the dying man's neck. More than two feet of shaft now lay hidden beneath the ground. The man stopped twitching and gasped his final, bloody breath. Adrenaline pumped through Matthew's veins; killing this man seemed much easier than the first. Like the headhunters, he demanded his prize; he touched the dead man's throat, dipping two fingers in his blood. Matthew brought his fingers to his face and smeared two red lines across each cheek. The wetness felt good on his skin; never before had he felt so liberated, so powerful.

Picking up the dead man's machete, he raised his arms above his head, locking them into a "V." Tilting his head toward the sun, he felt the warmth on his face and released a war cry that curdled even his own blood.

CHAPTER TWENTY-FIVE

The impaled tribesman's body rose several inches off the dirt, and then fell back to the ground. The spear pinning his neck to the earth became tight across the mouth of the cave, forming a large T. It then relaxed again, leaving about a half-inch gap between the spear and the mouth. This process repeated itself again and again—the gap grew wider.

Matthew realized that many unseen hands pulled on the dead man's legs from inside the cave. Lifting his body off the ground, they only succeeded in manipulating it a tiny distance back and forth. The muffled grunts of many tribesmen echoed from within the cavern as they struggled to unplug the opening. If Matthew hadn't pierced the thick cartilage of the man's Adam's apple, they might have already torn the dead man free. It would only be a matter of time before they dislodged the corpse and cleared the tunnel.

Matthew jumped down from his perch above the mouth of the cave, picked up the machete, and slid downhill to join Ryan and Jason at the base of the mountain.

"That was awesome!" Jason said.

"Way to go, bud," Ryan said, giving him a firm pat on his shoulder.

"We better get moving!" Matthew said, waving the group forward with his bronze blade. He tried to remember which path Hope and the others had ran down, hoping to reunite with them somewhere in the forest.

Hope had been right; there was strength in numbers, and they'd stand a better chance if they stuck together. Matthew only hesitated a second before selecting one of the many paths leading into the rainforest, praying that he'd chosen the right one.

Together the three boys began a steady jog. Matthew led the way into the jungle; Jason followed clutching his useless arm with his good hand, pulling it tight against his body. Ryan, being the slowest of the group lagged farther behind.

Hope ran side-by-side with Mary following Luke down the path. Somehow they'd made it out of the cave; fueled by adrenaline she ran onward. She was free and nothing felt better than freedom, but how far could they run and where could they hide from the Invisible People? This was their forest and it had been for thousands of years; they knew every inch of it. Hope knew that if they had even the slightest chance of escape, they'd have to become like the tree frogs and the chameleons, blending in with their surroundings; they too would have to become invisible.

Right now, distance was the key to their survival and she wanted to put as much of it as possible between themselves and their pursuers, so they kept on running.

Hope glanced over her shoulder; Ryan and the other boys were nowhere in sight. Why hadn't they followed them? Had they chosen a different path?

Once again, they were deep in the forest; they'd been running hard for more than fifteen minutes. Hope felt her heart pounding in her chest, but she knew they couldn't stop running—not yet.

The main path branched off into three separate ones.

"Which way?" Luke shouted.

"Left!" Mary shouted, gasping for breath.

Luke veered left; Hope and Mary followed him running side-by-side, their hearts pumping faster still. The new path found a break in the forest and opened up into a large meadow. After running into the grassland, Mary began to fall back. Hope heard her footsteps and heavy breathing just a few yards behind her—a quick scream broke her stride, followed by complete silence.

Hope stopped and turned, Mary had disappeared!

"Luke, stop! Stop! Mary's gone!"

Luke stopped, gasping for air; he turned and hurried back to Hope.

"Let's go back!" Hope said, out of breath.

They'd raced back a little more than twenty yards when Hope spotted what looked like an open pit a short distance ahead; it was only a step off the path, and she would've noticed it had it been there before.

Hope feared the worst and she called out to Mary. A loud moan came from within the pit. Hope reached the edge, fearful of what she might see. Mary lay at the bottom, surrounded by twigs and leaves that had fallen in with her. Five sharpened bamboo spikes impaled Mary through her midsection. After piercing her back, they ripped through her stomach, protruding outward more than six inches. Blood squirted from her belly, pumped vigorously by her racing heart.

"Oh, Mary! No!" Hope gasped.

"Oh, my God!" Luke screamed.

"Save yourselves, it's too late for me!" Mary whimpered.

Hope's eyes filled with tears; Mary was right; her injuries looked fatal. A thick white paste covered the tips of two pristine spikes that had missed Mary; even if her wounds didn't kill her, the poison certainly would. *Probably curare, the poison Kuja uses during his hunts,* Hope thought. Tears now streamed down her cheeks because she knew just how quickly the poison worked on the nervous system. Kuja had explained it all to her; now she wished he hadn't.

Luke looked at Hope, speaking to her only with his eyes and his message was clear. Mary's situation was hopeless, but Hope would be damned if she was going to leave her dying friend. No, Mary wouldn't die alone; she'd stay with her till the end, no longer caring about the consequences.

"Luke, you go, I'll try to catch up with you later."

"No, all three of us will stay together."

There was only room for one more in the pit and Luke agreed it should be Hope who climbed down. Holding her arms, Luke eased her in, guiding her feet away from the remaining spikes.

Hope turned and stepped toward Mary. Kneeling down next to her, she leaned over her, gazing into her flickering eyes. She squeezed her arm and wiped away her tears, trying to provide her friend with a final moment of comfort. Mary's breathing became shallow and she coughed up blood. Hope stroked her forehead, speaking to her in a soothing voice.

"It's going to be okay, soon there will be no more pain and you'll be in a wonderful place."

Mary tried to smile. "Hope, you're an angel. You're my—" And with those final words Mary's head fell to the side and she exhaled her last breath.

Hope made the sign of the cross. Using her fingers, she made a peace sign, running her hand down Mary's forehead, closing her eyelids. Folding first Mary's hands across her chest, then her own in prayer, she asked God to look after Mary and Peter and gave thanks that the poison had done its job and Mary no longer suffered.

She stroked Mary's cheeks as tears flowed down her own. Here lay her best friend and now she was gone. A little more than a year ago she'd attended her sweet sixteen birthday party. Mary still wore the silver heart-shaped locket she'd given her around her neck. Inside the clasp it read *Best Friends Forever.* Hope removed the pendant from

Mary's neck and placed it over her own head. She bent over Mary and kissed her on the forehead. "Best friends forever," she said as tears dripped off her chin.

"Let me pull you up; we really should be going," Luke said, teary eyed himself.

Hope wanted to pull Mary from this God-forsaken deathtrap and give her a proper burial, but she knew that Luke was right and that under the circumstances, that wouldn't be possible; at least she'd always be able to keep a little piece of Mary close to her heart.

Luke grabbed Hope's hands and hoisted her from the pit. Together they ran across the meadow and didn't stop running until they found themselves under the green canopy of the rainforest.

Matthew, his cheeks streaked with blood and with machete in hand, led the charge into the forest. The bronze blade glistened in the sun as he ran, carrying his bounty, his spoil of war, a proud symbol of victory over his enemy.

Glancing over his shoulder, he saw Jason grimace with every step, his swollen arm tucked against his stomach, held there by his good hand. It looked much larger than in the cave. *Maybe it just looked bigger in the sunlight,* Matthew thought. Or maybe it really had grown bigger; either way, if the infection travelled any farther it would spell the end. *Running can't be good for him,* he thought. Pumping the blood through his veins would make the infection spread all that much faster, but what choice did they have? They needed to get as far away from that cave as possible, having once again become the hunted.

Behind Jason lagged Ryan, their former leader. Matthew scoffed at this, wondering why he had followed him in the first place. What good did it do him, any of them for that matter?

Matthew was the leader now; everyone knew it. The words remained unspoken, and he'd taken matters into his own hands and led by action; for the second time today he'd killed a man—and he liked it. If given the opportunity, he'd kill again.

They ran on, never stopping, the scent of the forest filling Matthew's lungs with the sweet scent of freedom. The path in front of them became three; Matthew thought it wise to get off the main path, and chose the path to the right. Waving them forward with his machete, he veered off in that direction, Jason and Ryan following him; of course they did, because he was their leader.

⊶✛⊷

The sound of artillery fire echoed in the distance. Tim felt Brenda flinch every time the cannons bellowed. He had supported her weight for hours, allowing her to lean on him, using his shoulder as a crutch.

Brenda's lame ankle had slowed them down considerably; it had taken more than seven hours to hike back to the Shuar village. At least the rain had stopped and the hot sun had dried their damp clothes.

Kuja carried both backpacks; making frequent stops, he allowed them to catch up, but every time he did, Bill stared at his watch and released a huge sigh. The professor's insensitivity irked Tim and by the fourth sigh, he was ready to strangle him.

Two o'clock came and went by the time they'd reached the brook that led to the village. Tim and Brenda followed Kuja and Bill the final yards, and together they crossed over the bridge and staggered up the slight grade that led to the open air huts. Sitting on cut wood stumps, the group rested. Kuja unloaded his burden, placing both knapsacks down on the dirt floor. Bill and Brenda released loud sighs as they eased their bottoms down onto the hard wood surface.

Atiak, along with two other women, had been boiling anaconda in an iron kettle when they'd arrived. Tim recognized the women as the ones who'd cried over Moxo at his funeral. As hard as he tried, he couldn't remember their names; maybe he was just too damn tired or never properly introduced. What did it matter? Atiak fished out four thin pieces of snake with a long wooden spoon and served them on earthen plates to the weary members of the search party.

The thinner of the two women handed Tim a wooden mug filled with *Chicha*; he thanked her and took a long drink. After supporting Brenda's weight for so many miles it felt good to sit and eat. He'd only taken a few bites, which tasted surprisingly good, before Bill jumped on him again to get moving.

"It's already 3 o'clock; don't you think you should head out for the modern section and make that call?" Bill asked.

Tim put his plate down and looked at his watch; it was only 2:45, but why argue with the good professor? Bill decided that Tim would be the one to trek the extra four miles to the modern section; after all, he was the logical choice; still he resented Bill telling him what to do. But why prolong the inevitable; he wanted to get away from that insensitive clod anyway.

"Come on, Kuja, let's go," Tim said, rising up from his seat, knowing that he'd need Kuja to translate his English into Spanish. *What good would it do to call the authorities in Macas, if no one understood English?* he thought.

Kuja shoved the last bites of anaconda into his mouth and chugged downed the *Chicha*. He placed the mug down and jumped to his feet, "I'm ready!"

"Good luck!" Brenda said, giving Tim's arm a firm squeeze as he passed.

Bill mumbled something under his breath in between bites of snake, but Tim wasn't sure what he'd said. Maybe, "Good Luck," or "Hurry up." Knowing Bill, it was probably the latter. Tim gave a half-hearted wave to anyone who cared and headed off with Kuja for the modern section.

—◄+ +►—

Tim placed an ace bandage and a roll of white surgical tape on the counter next to the cash register as he removed a crisp ten dollar bill from his wallet. Kuja stood behind the counter at the Santos General Store with his ear pressed against the phone. Senor Santos, the store's proprietor, stood next to Kuja and rung up the sale, accepting Tim's money and handing him back $4.20 in change. The Shuar man looked to be in his mid-fifties; he wore jeans and a multi-colored tie-dye T-shirt, fidgeting nervously.

Kuja sighed; as they transferred him from one department to the next, and after the third transfer, Tim lost all patience.

"Goddamn it! Tell them we got seven kids lost in the rainforest; we need helicopters and search and rescue!" Tim shouted.

Kuja spoke Spanish into the phone and waited, he then nodded his head, "Si, senor!"

"What'd he say?"

Kuja pressed the receiver against his hand. "He said that all the helicopters have been reassigned to the military to help transport troops to the border, along with every available man."

"Are they saying they have absolutely no one to help us find those kids?"

Once again Kuja pressed his ear to the phone, speaking rapidly in Spanish; he fell silent waiting for his reply, "Si, senor."

"Well?"

"He said yes, that is correct, they have nobody in Macas," Kuja said, covering the mouth piece with his hand. "The best he can do is check on the availability of the helicopter and crew in Riobamba, but he said that he could make no promises."

"Ask him if they *are* available, how long will it take?"

Kuja once again spoke and waited for his reply, "Si, Si." He pressed the phone against his bare chest. "Twenty-four to forty-eight hours."

"Those kids don't have that kind of time!"

"Should I hang up?" Kuja asked.

"No, get his name and tell him to call Riobamba; it's better than nothing," Tim said, and Kuja did as instructed. "Now hang up and ask the operator to put me through to the U.S. Embassy in Quito!"

"It's ringing," Kuja said. Tim grabbed the phone from his hands. A woman's raspy voice bellowed through the earpiece, "U.S. Embassy, how may I direct your call?" *Thank God I have somebody who speaks English,* Tim thought.

"Give me the State Depart—" A barrage of artillery fire boomed in the distance, causing static on the phone line; it sounded like it came from the direction of the border. The volley of exploding shells that followed startled Tim, and a second later the line went dead.

"Do you have a cell phone?" Tim asked. "Ours doesn't work out here." He grabbed Santos by the shoulder.

Kuja translated Tim's words to Santos. The shopkeeper used a lot of frantic hand motions as he tried to explain. After a quick burst of wordage, he fell silent.

"He said that Peruvian saboteurs destroyed the communication towers; cell phones were the first to go."

"Great! That's just fucking great!"

CHAPTER TWENTY-SIX

Six tribesmen struggled to free the dead man from the mouth of the cave. Twelve hands firmly gripped his legs at the thighs, knees, and ankles. On the leader's command they pulled and pushed together as they tried to remove the corpse from the short passageway.

"*Klua!*" the leader shouted. The tribesmen leaned back on their heels and pulled forcefully, but the dead man didn't budge and the spear moved very little as it pressed hard against the cave opening.

"*Malki!*" the leader commanded and the tribesmen pushed the corpse forward as hard as they could, but the spear only returned to its original position. After several more attempts, the tribesmen succeeded in elongating the tear in the neck; the wooden shaft now rested up against the dead man's chin. The hard bone of the skull gave the tribesmen better leverage against the shaft. Another hard pull caused the vertebrae in the neck to crack and then break; flesh and cartilage tore away as the head separated from the body. The sudden release of tension caused the body to jettison backwards through the tunnel. The headless corpse landed on the ground next to the six tribesmen who'd fallen in a heap around it, thrown off balance by the swift and unexpected movement.

"*Famook!*" the leader shouted, shaking his spear point toward the opening.

The tribesmen obeyed his command, hurrying to their feet. The strongest of the warriors entered the blood-slick tunnel first; he reached the opening in seconds.

The head had slid down the pole and rested on the ground, but the shaft blocked the opening, and the spear still stood planted firmly in the dirt. The lone tribesman grabbed the shaft; his prone position offered very little leverage, but still he worked the spear back and forth, and from side to side. The hole surrounding the spear grew until the shaft became loose enough to pull the tip from the ground. After tossing the spear and head aside, he pulled himself out of the hole.

One-by-one the others made their way through the opening, and the leader was the last to emerge. His face looked determined; his eyes burned with hatred; he held a machete in one hand and a long spear in the other. Raising them both high above his head, he released a shrill war cry as he led the charge downhill. The other tribesmen lifted their spears and cheered, following their leader down the rocky slope, toward the path that led into the rainforest.

Matthew pushed forward through the jungle. The path narrowed, becoming nothing more than a boar trail. Swinging his machete, he chopped at the vegetation growing across the path.

Stopping for a moment to rest, he tossed his machete onto the ground and looked at his opened hand; several blisters rose off his palm, and only now did he feel the pain. He turned to check on his two friends. Ryan stood bent over with his hands on his knees, trying to catch his breath. Jason groaned behind him, pale and drawn.

"You hanging in there?" Matthew asked.

"It hurts like hell," Jason said.

Matthew placed his hand on Jason's forehead. "You're burning up with fever!"

Jason grimaced, "What? Are we playing let's state the obvious?"

"You're doing good bud. Keep the faith," Ryan said.

Matthew picked up his machete. "Are you still able to walk?"

"Yeah, it's better when we move; it makes me delirious and I forget about the pain."

"I'm dying of thirst; can't we rest a bit more?" Ryan asked.

Matthew glared at Ryan, "Rest when you're dead and if we don't move, you soon will be, now come on, let's go." He grabbed the blade with his blister-free hand and resumed his hacking of the overgrowth. Jason and Ryan fell in line behind him.

Hope and Luke pushed on under the green canopy; both were exhausted, but they moved forward the best they could. Once again, Hope sensed eyes upon her. She scanned the treetops but saw nothing. There was something out there all right; she could feel it. Her heart pounded hard within her chest and her breathing became erratic; she began to hyperventilate, and this time it didn't go unnoticed.

"Are you okay?" Luke asked.

"It's the *Iwanci*, it's out there."

"How do you know?"

"I can feel its presence; it chills me to the bone."

"Try to put it out of your mind."

"I can't, it's—there it is!" Hope pointed to a long tree limb more than fifty yards away.

The feathered child sat in the middle of the limb, swinging her legs back and forth with the ease of a young girl pumping her legs on a swing. Tar dripped from her body, falling to the ground. The black goo flung off her legs with each movement, arcing upward for a moment before splattering on the forest floor. The feathered face stared back at Hope; the *Iwanci's* mouth stood frozen in its familiar smirk, and then it was gone. The apparition disappeared; it had only been there for a few seconds. The chill left Hope and she no longer felt its presence.

"Did you see that?" Hope asked.

"I just caught a quick glimpse before it vanished," Luke said.

"It's toying with us, like a child playing with a couple of dolls." Hope covered her face with her hands and sobbed, "I can't take it anymore! What's the use, it knows our every move!"

"We've got to keep our heads and stay calm. It wants us to panic; it seems to feed on our fear."

"It doesn't matter, I've seen what head games it can play. I'd rather die than go through that again."

The tribesmen had reached the spot where the path became three. The leader knelt down to study the vegetation. Touching the over-growth with his fingers, he discovered freshly broken twigs, and grass that had been matted down along the paths to the right and left. He instructed his six warriors to break up into two groups of three.

"I'll lead one group myself," he said and pointed at the others. "Return with three heads. If you fail it will be your heads I offer to Kalku."

"The white devils have killed two of our tribesmen and their deaths must be avenged. The killing must be slow and agonizing. Tie them to a tree and skin them alive, only then can you take their heads." Drool dripped from his mouth at the thought of this. "I will take them to Kalku and he will offer the goddess the heads of the six white devils."

He glared at the three tribesmen before giving his final command, "Leave their headless corpses tied to the tree, slice them open, and leave them for the jaguar. The big cats and the red ants must also eat; this is the way of the forest. Now be gone!"

The two groups separated; he and three others took the path to the left, while the remaining three tribesmen disappeared down the path to the right.

⚔

The leader ran at a good pace, trying to gap the great distance between the hunters and the hunted. The path led them out of the forest and into a long meadow. His tribesmen had dug several boar traps there just a few days before. Up ahead, a pit lay sprung less than an arm's length off the path.

"We will come back and gut the animal after I've collected my heads," the leader shouted.

Reaching the pit first, the leader gazed down at the body of the dead female. The other tribesmen raised their spears in celebration high above their heads. They whooped and hollered as one, having caught the first of their prey.

"Soon we will have the others!" the leader said.

A leather sheath hung from his beaded belt. Drawing his bronze blade, he climbed down into the pit. Wrapping her hair around his fist, he pulled upward, making the neck taut, allowing him to slice through flesh and arteries, severing the final stubborn strands of cartilage and bone.

The pale, white head separated from the neck and he held it high above his own. The three tribesmen surrounded the pit, and once again raised their spears and cheered as the female's metal teeth glistened in the late afternoon sunlight.

⚔

Matthew slashed his way through the jungle, looking back to check on Jason every few minutes. Jason's face grew paler by the moment; his steps were uneven and he wobbled like a drunk from side-to-side. Ryan walked behind him, holding him steady; more than once he'd kept him from falling.

The overgrown path led to a stream, and Matthew felt a sense of relief; it had been more than a day since any of them had even a sip of water; at least they would not die of thirst. They all knelt along the bank and scooped handful after handful of cool, crisp water. Jason splashed his face several times before dunking his head in the stream.

That should help bring down his fever, Matthew thought.

Ryan drank for several minutes before he stopped to catch his breath.

"We've gone far enough for one day, let's stop here," Ryan said.

Nothing could be further from the truth; they hadn't gone anywhere near far enough and Matthew knew it. The Invisible People might hunt them down at any moment. After losing two of their own, they'd be more determined than ever to seek their revenge.

Jason was his biggest concern. Even if he caught a second wind, he couldn't go on much further. He had to find a way to keep him alive, but still keep the group moving.

Matthew realized that even with a healthy Jason, there'd be no way to outrun the Invisible People, but this time he wouldn't go down without a fight; he'd go down swinging his machete—that much he could promise. He needed a way to elude them, but how?

Matthew smacked his palm against his forehead as a flash of revelation came to him. It probably wouldn't work, but what choice did he have?

"Ryan, drape Jason's arm over your shoulder, then I want both of you to walk right down the middle of the stream," Matthew said.

"What?" Ryan asked.

"Just do it! Walk as far down the stream as you possibly can."

"Where're you going to be?" Jason asked.

"I'm going to try and throw them off our trail; don't touch the banks and don't stop walking until I catch up to you."

Ryan helped Jason into the water and together they sloshed up stream. Matthew crossed the stream and pressed his sneaker hard into the mud as he climbed onto the far bank. Using his machete, he hacked at the overgrowth and continued down the path for about fifteen minutes. He then reversed his course, walking backwards, purposely creating a second set of tracks that appeared to be moving forward. Beads of perspiration formed across his forehead; he prayed that this wouldn't become an exercise in futility. He'd already lost way too much time; he might back right into them at any moment. This thought made him walk backwards faster; his calf muscles burned, and his steps became spastic and uncoordinated.

Come on, where's the stream, he thought. After many glances over his shoulder, the stream finally reappeared. Walking backward down the bank, he felt relieved once he submerged his feet into the cool water.

Matthew trekked upstream, trying his best not to muddy the waters as he walked. Ryan and Jason were nowhere in sight and that was a good thing; it meant that they'd covered some distance from where they first entered the stream, making it more difficult to be tracked.

The twists and turns of the banks led him farther upstream, but it became increasingly more difficult to go any faster on the algae-slick rocks. After splashing through the stream for more than a half hour, he spotted Ryan and Jason trudging through the water up ahead of him. Ryan tripped, causing both boys to fall face forward into the stream. Ryan tried to find his footing while Jason splashed and struggled in the shallow water.

Matthew hurried through the stream as fast as he could. Ryan managed to stand; his hair and clothing were soaked. Jason, no longer having the strength to stand, floundered in the shallows. Matthew grabbed Jason by his shoulder and pulled him to his feet.

Jason shouted out from the sudden movement of his infected arm; his skin now took on a grayish hue, and his knees buckled as he tried to keep his balance in the moving water. Matthew came to the realization that Jason had taken his last steps. His fatigued, infected body could move no more. His body suddenly went limp in Matthew's arms; it took all of his strength to support Jason's dead weight.

"You did good! You did real good!" Matthew said to his semi-conscious friend. "Ryan, give me a hand!"

Ryan splashed over to them and helped Matthew support Jason.

"Let's try and make it to that path on the other side of the bank," Matthew said.

Ryan draped Jason's good arm over his shoulder, "Hang in there, bud, we'll get you across."

Matthew wrapped his arm around Jason's chest, trying his best to avoid his swollen, pus-filled arm. Together, they dragged Jason up the far bank and more than a hundred yards down the narrow path.

Ryan breathed heavily, his crimson face puffed out, resembling a blow fish, and veins bulged on his neck and forehead as he struggled with Jason's weight. "How much farther?" Ryan asked in between breaths.

"Not too much, the path looks like it widens up ahead. We'll set up camp there."

Upon reaching the area where the path widened, they laid Jason onto the ground; he drifted in and out of consciousness. Matthew felt Jason's forehead, and his temperature seemed much hotter than before.

"Ryan, pull out those ferns until you have a dirt floor, then cover the area with leaves," Matthew said, pointing to a large tropical plant. "Get some leaves underneath him and try to make him as comfortable as possible."

"Why, what are you going to do?" Ryan asked.

Matthew didn't answer; instead he went right to work. Ryan would figure out what he was up to soon enough. Using his machete, he cut down a Rosewood sapling, slicing off leaves and branches, creating a long pole. He then cut the pole into eight sections, each one just shy of six inches. He whittled the ends into sharp hardwood points, similar to the ones he saw Kuja make back in the village. *Christ, that seems like a lifetime ago.*

Jason now laid unconscious, globs of yellow pus draining from visible cracks on his elbow. Matthew picked a small leaf and smeared Jason's pus onto it. He then spread the gunk onto several tips. Needing additional pus, he squeezed the elbow, milking it until he had enough to cover six of the eight points.

"Ryan shook his head in disbelief, "You're a sick bastard, you know that?"

"This is tribal warfare; we need to use every means possible to defeat the stronger enemy. Here, take these and kill those bastards, if for some reason I don't make it back," Matthew said, tossing the two remaining spikes into the ground at Ryan's feet.

Ryan swallowed hard, "Don't even talk like that."

"If he wakes up, keep talking to him until I get back."

Wrapping his six hardwood points together in a large leaf, he walked back down the path to set his traps.

Ryan felt exhausted; he looked over at Jason who still lay unconscious. *It wouldn't hurt to catch a little shut eye myself.* He'd just stretched out on the ground next to Jason when he heard his voice.

"I'm going to die aren't I?" Jason asked.

Ryan sat up and stared at his friend; Jason's eyes were now wide open, and sweat poured off his face, dripping onto the tropical leaves underneath his head. He seemed as if he was having a moment of clarity.

Ryan hesitated before speaking, not knowing how to answer him. "Just try to hang in there, bud, that's all you can do."

Projectile vomit shot out of Jason's mouth. He choked a couple of times, before clearing his airway. He gasped for breath, dry heaving several times, proving that his stomach was now empty.

He cried out again, screaming—no, hollering. It sounded almost as loud as those red bastard monkeys that had infected his hand in the first place. Ryan fidgeted, concerned that his friend's screams would give away their location.

"I know it's hard, but try to stay calm," Ryan said.

"Cut it off!"

"What?"

"My arm! Fucking cut it off!"

CHAPTER TWENTY-SEVEN

Tim glanced at his watch; it was already past seven by the time he and Kuja trudged the four miles back to the village. His stomach churned at the thought of having to report their failure to the others. *Brenda will take the news hard, she's already blaming herself—along with me.* He couldn't bear to once again watch her withdraw into herself, giving him her sinking look of despair.

He saw Bill and Brenda sitting under the open air hut, pretty much in the same place that he'd left them. They both rose as he and Kuja approached.

"Well, let's get this over with," Tim said, his tone grim as he gave Kuja a light pat on his shoulder.

Kuja nodded at Tim before staring down at his own feet. A moment later they ducked under the thatched roof.

"Welcome back!" Brenda said, her eyes sparkling with eager anticipation.

"How'd you make out?" Bill asked rubbing the back of his hand.

"Not good," Tim said. Bowing his head, he took off his hat and held it in front of his stomach as if that somehow would make the news more palatable.

"What do you mean? You did call the authorities in Macas, didn't you?" Bill asked.

"Yeah, we called them."

"Well, what the hell did they say?" Bill asked.

"They said that the search and rescue helicopter has been commandeered by the military along with the entire rescue crew because of this goddamn war!"

"Tim, there's got to be someone that can help us. Tell me you found someone who can help me find Mary and the rest of those kids," Bill said.

"There are no helicopters, no search and rescue, not even a reliable police force, they're all gone."

"Well, get your ass back out there and call the U.S. Embassy; we're Americans for Christ sake, they've got to help us!"

"Already tried, I'd just connected with them in Quito when the line went dead, a mortar shell exploded somewhere outside of town, didn't even get past the operator."

Bill turned his back on Tim and took several deliberate steps away from him. Staring toward the forest, Bill wiped his tears in silence.

"Oh, my God! What're we going to do?" Brenda asked, her voice cracking.

"It looks like we're on our own." Tim said.

Brenda flinched as cannon fire once again thundered in the distance.

Hope pushed on through the forest at a hurried pace with Luke by her side. Adrenaline pumped through her veins; her eyes scanned everywhere, high in the canopy, in the lower branches, on the forest floor. Every bird and animal of the forest became suspect; any one of them could be the *Iwanci*. Several blue macaws and a toucan perched in the trees looked down upon her. Avoiding their gazes, she pressed on.

Despite their pace, she watched each step, never stepping off the path, afraid that if she did, she'd suffer the same fate as Mary; any misstep could be her last.

The forest became darker; she glanced at her watch. A quarter past four, they'd only have a couple more hours of daylight and then what?

⇒╫ ╫⇐

Matthew had done what he could to make things difficult for their pursuers, and with the job complete, he rushed down the path that led to their camp. Jason's moans revealed their position well before he'd reached the clearing.

Jason's going to give us away, Matthew thought, *but fuck it! What can I do about it?*

Jason lay on his back as Matthew stepped into the clearing. Sweat ran off his pale gray face, like condensation running down the side of a glass. His head moved from side-to-side, his eyes were open, but glazed. Through his moans he mumbled a word or two, but they were mostly incoherent. Ryan knelt over him, wiping sweat away from Jason's eyes; his own face white with worry.

Matthew hadn't been gone more than an hour, but Jason's condition had worsened. The swelling in his arm had increased drastically; it had swollen his bicep to herculean proportions; globs of yellow pus excreted from his elbow and the infected redness marched onward toward his shoulder.

Jason released a scream, followed by another guttural moan.

"There must be something we can do," Matthew said, as much to himself as to Ryan.

"I'm glad you're back, he's been yelling crazy shit since you left—this really sucks," Ryan said.

Jason moaned again, this time louder than before.

Maybe I should just put him out of his misery, Matthew thought, giving the matter some serious consideration. He dismissed the idea as being too self-serving. *Would that really be in Jason's best interest—or my own?* He looked deep within himself. Was he just worried about self preservation, knowing that Jason's screams would give away their position? *He might as well be yelling with a megaphone, "We're over here, come and get us!"*

But why not kill him? Would I let a dog suffer like this? He's going to die anyway. It certainly would relieve them of their burden, he thought, allowing them to move faster through the jungle, giving them both a better chance at survival.

I'm the leader and it is my decision to make, I have to think of what's good for everyone.

If he has to die, let it be now.

⊨⊹ ⊹⊨

The three tribesmen had tracked their human prey for more than two hours. The most seasoned of the hunter's led the way carrying a blowgun. A small quiver strapped across his back contained a dozen darts and a sealed bamboo tube of curare. One dipped dart was strong enough to kill his human prey ten times over. He was only a few years older than the other two, and the best tracker. Stopping every now and again, he knelt down to observe the trail.

The other two tribesmen were brothers, both men carried long spears and were strong, fast runners more than capable of gapping the distance between the hunters and the hunted.

Three sets of fresh tracks covered the path. Cut vegetation lay strewn on the ground everywhere. The senior hunter knew they were not that far ahead of them. It wouldn't be long until they'd seek their revenge. As the leader ordered, they'd make them pay for the two deaths, first skinning them alive and then taking their heads. This was the only way to restore honor to Kalku and the tribe. *We must find them, it will be our heads if we do not,* he thought, heeding the leader's words.

The path led to a shallow stream, the seasoned tracker could see where they had crossed. Footprints were clearly visible on the far bank. All three tribesmen splashed through the water and climbed up onto the far side. Two sets of tracks led down the path, but there was no sign of the third.

"One has split off," the lead hunter said to the others.

"He's in the stream," the older brother said.

"But which direction?" the younger brother asked, looking first upstream and then downstream.

"We will find and kill these two first and then we will come back for the man in the stream," the older tribesmen said, rubbing his chin before starting down the path.

All three tribesmen hurried forward at a brisk jog. After several minutes, the lead tracker came to a stop. The trail of footprints had vanished; he knelt down to inspect the last two prints on the path, and only then did he realize that the footprints were identical, made with the same foot.

"We go back! All the white ones are in the stream!"

They turned and ran down the path at a full sprint; this time the two brothers led the way, and the lead tracker trailed behind, shamed by his mistake. They reached the stream in half the time it took them to travel down the path the first time. All three men splashed into the water and stood shin high in the shallow stream.

"Which way?" the younger brother asked.

The lead tracker stared into the water and pointed upstream, "That way."

"This time there can be no mistakes, this time we must be sure! You go downstream and me and my brother will travel upstream," the older brother said.

The shamed tracker reluctantly agreed and started to wade downstream. The two brothers, holding their spears, splashed upstream through the water at a frantic pace in search of their human quarry.

━═╬ ╬═━

The brothers searched the banks as they ran, looking for any disturbance in the soft, black soil. Finding none, they pressed on, their hearts pounding harder in their chests with every step.

"There!" the older brother said, stopping mid-stride in the now ankle-high water. He pointed to a set of footprints on the far bank. The younger brother also stopped. "Some of the footprints are still wet and I can see a trail leading into the forest."

Both men splashed their way to the far bank. The younger brother reached the bank first; the soil under the wet footprints appeared looser than the surrounding dirt, but he paid it no mind. Stepping hard onto the bank on that very spot, he screamed out as a sharp jolt of pain shot through his foot. The shrill sound reverberated through the forest.

Four sharp, wooden spikes pierced his bare foot, ripping through his arch and heel. A carefully placed footprint camouflaged the spikes in the loose soil. They penetrated deep, cutting through flesh and bone up to his ankle.

With great effort he pulled his foot free of the trap screaming louder still. Two of the spikes remained embedded in his foot; he fell backward into the shallow water. His brother grabbed his ankle. One-by-one he yanked the spikes from his soft flesh, causing two more high pitched screams. Blood spurted from the bottom of his foot, causing a red cloud to dissipate into the slow moving water.

His brother pulled him from the stream, wrapping his arm across his shoulder; they hobbled to the bank together, being cautious not to step or sit on anymore hidden spikes. His brother then picked the leaves of a large tropical plant known to stop bleeding and wrapped them around his foot.

"I will avenge you, my brother; rest here and I shall return with their heads!" the older brother said, pounding his chest hard once with his fist.

"Beware of their trickery," the injured man said, grimacing with every word.

Jason cried out again, and his eyes cleared for a moment. "Cut it off!" he shouted.

Matthew sat in silence then looked at Ryan.

"My arm, cut it off!"

"He shouted that several times when you were gone, crazy talk, huh?" Ryan asked.

Matthew rubbed his chin for more than half a minute.

Jason shouted again, breaking the silence, "Cut it the fuck off!"

"Okay!" Matthew said.

"You got to be fucking kidding me?" Ryan asked.

"No, I'm not kidding, now go get some firewood; let's get this party started."

Jason seemed more coherent than before; he tried to grin, but only grimaced.

Ryan walked through the ferns picking up dead branches. After collecting an armful of wood, he returned to the clearing.

Matthew sighed, knowing that Jason's chances weren't good and that he'd probably die anyway, but at least he wouldn't be killing him outright—and there's always that shred of hope. This was Jason's best and only chance. Matthew would give it his best shot and if Jason died, he could live with that.

Ryan dropped the firewood into the middle of the clearing, shoving kindling in between the bigger branches. Matthew snapped some of the larger branches in half and added them to the pile of wood. Removing the waterproof cylinder of matches from his back pocket, he pulled off the top and was relieved to find that he still had three left. He struck the match and lit the kindling; it burnt slow at first and then the flames began to catch onto the dry branches above. Soon he had a raging bonfire.

Jason moaned again, seeming to be more coherent now. Matthew could see the fear in his eyes.

"Hang in there, pal, it will be over before you know it," Matthew said.

Ryan squeezed Jason's good arm, "We're here for you, bud."

Jason tried to smile but his face twisted and he moaned louder still. Sweat continued to pour off his face.

Matthew unbuckled Jason's belt and slid the leather from the loops. Using the tip of the machete, he poked another hole through the leather farther down the belt. Wrapping the thin leather strap around Jason's arm, he pulled the belt tight around the only remaining portion that wasn't yet infected. He still needed another quarter inch to reach the new hole. Matthew stepped on Jason's shoulder and pulled upward with all his strength.

"Ahh, fuck!" Jason screamed.

"Quick, buckle the belt!" Matthew shouted.

Ryan pressed the thin brass pin toward the hole, "I can't reach; I need a little more."

Matthew gritted his teeth and pulled. Jason's shrill screams were louder still, as his face contorted and twisted into something unrecognizable.

"I got it!" Ryan forced the brass pin through the hole.

"Great, now let's sterilize the blade." Matthew picked up the machete and inspected the green-edged blade, stained by the cut vegetation. *The fire should take care of that too.*

Picking up the remnants of Jason's sleeve, he wrapped it around the bronze handle to protect his hand from the heat before placing the blade into the fire. The green coating quickly burned away leaving the edge of the blade a pristine black.

Matthew removed the blade from the fire and swallowed hard; he couldn't believe that he was going to do this, knowing full well that Jason would probably bleed to death. But what choice did he have?

"Hold him down!" Matthew said.

Ryan pressed on Jason's chest and good shoulder.

Matthew grabbed Jason's infected arm and stretched it out away from his body. He stood behind him to get the proper angle. *This is no good.* To make a clean cut, he needed a chopping block under the arm. Matthew walked out of the clearing still holding the machete, searching for a suitable rock.

"What the fuck are you doing?" Ryan asked panting, sweat dripping off his own forehead.

"Keep your shirt on, I'll be right there," Matthew said as he pushed away ferns with his foot. Spotting a thin, flat rock, he picked it up with his free hand and carried it back to the clearing. He slid the rock under Jason's upper arm and shoulder, propping him up off the ground.

Jason stared up at him, fear glistening in his eyes. Matthew inspected the tourniquet; it looked tight. He used the large blade to cut about three inches of leather off the end of the belt.

"Bite down hard on this," Matthew said, bringing the chunk of belt up to Jason's mouth.

Jason opened his mouth, accepting the leather, and clamped down hard with his teeth on the makeshift bit. Sweat drenched the leaves beneath his head. Creases formed on his forehead, his squinting eyes now determined and prepared.

Jason understood every word of Matthew's instructions, proving he was lucid. Matthew wished he wasn't, the pain would be unbearable. If he was unconscious he might fare better—and then Matthew wouldn't have to look into his eyes.

Matthew was procrastinating and he knew it. *You're over thinking this—just do it!*

He took another deep breath and released the air from his lungs. Ryan, still holding Jason down, glared up at him, looking more frightened than Jason.

Matthew gripped the machete with both hands and stepped behind Jason. He felt like some medieval executioner and realized that he probably was. He slowly lowered the blade onto the arm, just below the shoulder, choosing the exact spot, and made a thin cut, scoring the skin, giving him a thin, red line to aim for.

Satisfied with his mark, he gazed one final time at Jason. "Bite down hard!"

Slowly, Matthew raised the blade off Jason's arm and cocked it above his own head. Concentrating on the bloody line, he studied the thickening mark for several seconds until he could see nothing else. He needed to be precise; he'd get just one shot at this, and there'd be no room for mistakes. The blade began its downward thrust, feeling like a muscular reflex, an involuntary action. The blade severed flesh and arteries, missing the red line by less than a quarter of an inch. Jason's screams echoed throughout the forest, but Matthew had purposely blocked them out. Blood spurted from Jason's arm, but despite Matthew's best effort, the arm remained attached. Bone stopped the blade halfway through the arm.

Jason's screams didn't stop; his body reeled back and forth while Ryan did his best to hold him down.

"Hold him still! I'm going to have to try again!" Matthew said.

Matthew once again raised the blade above his head. He knew that he'd have to come down in the same exact spot if he had any chance of making a clean cut, but this time he had no clear target to aim for, as blood flowed from the wound covering the arm. It was no good; he had to see the gash. Matthew removed his own shirt, switching hands with the machete to complete the maneuver. Using his shirt as a rag, he wiped the blood from Jason's arm, giving him only a brief second to see the gash before the arm covered itself in blood.

Once again he raised the blade and prayed, focusing on the area where the gash had been moments before. He brought the blade down with one swift motion. Jason screamed out again, but this time Jason's arm lay on the ground separated from his body. Matthew grabbed the detached arm and tossed it aside. Despite the tourniquet, blood spurted everywhere; it would only be a matter of minutes before Jason bled out.

"Don't let him move, keep holding him," Matthew ordered. He shoved the blade into the fire as he watched Jason's life blood drain from his body.

Come on! Come on! Get hot! Matthew thought. After several minutes the thick blade glowed yellow. Wrapping the bloody rag around the handle, he pulled the machete from the fire. He pressed the flat blade against Jason's gushing stump, searing arteries and blood vessels. Jason passed out. The smell of burning flesh permeated the air. Matthew had only succeeded in sealing half the stump, as blood still flowed freely from the rest of the wound.

Once again he placed the blade in the flame until it glowed yellow. He then pulled the machete from the fire and pressed the hot metal against the bloody mess, searing the other side of the stump. Matthew felt nauseous from the smell of burnt flesh—but most of the bleeding had stopped.

"Grab some more leaves and cover him up; we don't want him going into shock," Matthew said.

CHAPTER TWENTY-EIGHT

The lone tribesman left his brother's side and hurried down the path to seek revenge.

A shrill scream came from up ahead bringing his jog to a sudden halt, and he listened closely. It happened again, this time longer and louder—it sounded close. The smell of burning wood filtered through the trees, carrying with it a trace of cooked meat. Scanning the trees, he discovered smoke hovering in the canopy in the not so far distance.

I'll attack and kill the strongest man first. The fat one and the one with the swollen hand will then fall by my spear. He gripped his spear tighter as he crept forward toward his prey.

His foot caught on a vine that lay strewn across the path, causing something to whip toward his face; it happened too fast for him to react, too fast to even know what hit him. His left eye exploded in its socket, and the pain lasted only a few seconds, long enough for him to cry out and gasp his last breath as his spirit left this world.

Matthew and Ryan heard the scream that came from down the path.
"What the hell was that?" Ryan asked, his face again drawn and pale.

"Grab your spikes, and use them if you have to; we're sitting ducks if we stay here. Come on, let's bring the fight to them. We have to protect Jason," Matthew said, his cheeks still caked with blood, his eyes flecked with excitement. Grabbing the machete, he marched down the path; Ryan gripping his spikes, trailed a few steps behind him.

After creeping forward for less than fifty yards, Matthew came to a stop and held up his hand, signaling Ryan to do likewise. Something looked strange, but he wasn't close enough yet to determine what he was looking at.

"Yes! It worked!" Matthew shouted, signaling Ryan to follow him. They crept forward. Matthew firmly gripped his machete while Ryan's knuckles turned white, holding the spikes out in front of him.

A man lay dead hanging more than a foot above the path, his head impaled by a six inch spike through his left eye. He had fallen forward, leaning on top of the spike and the strong sapling that killed him. The flexible branch bent almost to the ground, but still supported his body weight, creating the illusion of suspended animation. His arms hung down, seemingly defying gravity. Blood dripped from the eye socket into a growing puddle below him.

Matthew, charged with adrenaline, was pleased with his handiwork. He'd killed another man and he basked in the glory. He'd found the perfect sapling; its flexible branch grew across the path at eye level. Using several thin vines, he'd tied two of his tainted wooden spikes to the branch making them taut, spacing them inches apart, using his own face for measurement. After bending the branch back, he rigged a trigger device by tying a single strand of vine to the end of the limb, running it down the sapling, around the trunk, across the path, and securing it to the trunk of another tree.

The slightest disturbance along the path would trigger his lethal device—and it did. Only one of the two spikes hit its mark, but that proved to be all that was necessary.

Matthew knelt beside the body, dipped two fingers into the pool of coagulating blood and smeared two lines across his face, reinforcing the cracked streaks of maroon that were already there. He repeated the process, marking the other side of his face in a similar fashion. He did it with the ease of a woman re-applying lipstick in a powder room.

"You're a sick bastard, you know that!" Ryan said.

"Come on, let's get back to Jason," Matthew said, picking up the dead man's spear; he turned toward Ryan, and after giving him a menacing look, he smiled and moved forward.

Hope and Luke pushed on through the jungle, hungry and thirsty, not having had anything to eat or drink in over a day. The hunger in Hope's stomach paled the dire thirst that parched her throat. Every step she took seemed to increase her need for water, but she knew they couldn't stop, not if they wanted to avoid capture. She snapped off a leaf as she walked and placed it in her mouth. The bitter tasting plant provided little moisture, but it caused her mouth to salivate, allowing her to move forward. Food she could do without, but every cell in her body craved water. Her thoughts turned to the spring were they camped the night before their capture. *It must be somewhere up ahead, but how far?* Hope guessed it had to be more than two miles. *If only we can hold on that long.* This oasis in her mind became her only focus; each step they took meant that they were one step closer, at least that's what she kept telling herself as they trudged forward, trying to keep ahead of the headhunters and away from the *Iwanci*.

The tribal leader handed Mary's dripping head up to the waiting hands of the fastest runner. Another tribesman grabbed the leader's bloody hand and hoisted him out of the pit.

"Take this head back to Kalku and tell him that we shall soon have the rest!" the leader said, pointing down the path in the direction from which they'd come.

The tribesman held Mary's head upside down out in front of him, gripping her silky hair, cupping it like a bowl to keep it from dripping; Mary's silver braces glistened across a perfect set of white teeth. Bowing to the leader, the tribesman gave a nod. Tucking the head under one arm, he bolted down the trail toward the mountain. Moments later he disappeared from view.

"Her body is not yet stiff; they're not far ahead of us!" the leader said, waving the two remaining men forward. Together, the three tribesmen, with spears and machete in hand, hurried down the path after their human prey.

The lone tracker, having sloshed through the stream for more than a mile, found no evidence of the white ones. *They must've traveled upstream. I'll go back and help the brothers.*

After reversing his direction, he splashed upstream for more than an hour until he heard low moans coming from the bank up ahead of him to his left. He could barely hear them above the sound of the flowing stream. He spotted the youngest brother sitting on the bank, pressing leaves against the bottom of his foot.

"Why do you sit there?" he asked.

"I have stepped on a trap and I cannot walk."

"Where is your brother?"

"He has gone off alone after the white ones."

"How long?"

"He's gone awhile, but I heard him scream out."

"I will help him kill the white ones, then we will come back for you."

The injured man grabbed his arm, "Bring back their heads!"

The tribesman nodded and after climbing up the bank, he headed down the narrow path. He hadn't walked very far when he stopped in his tracks. The older brother hung off the ground with a long spike piercing his left eye—he lay dead, with a pool of thick blood soaking into the ground below him.

The tribesman stepped toward him and saw that the dead man's spear was missing. *The white ones have done this!* He scanned the trail ahead of him, looking for any sign of the white ones, looking for more traps.

Thunder echoed off in the distance; it sounded again and again and again. *The Thunder God is angered.* The thunder shook the forest louder than before, repeating itself every few moments; the tribesman had never heard the Thunder God so angry. He turned around and headed back toward the stream. It didn't take him long to reach the injured man.

"Why have you returned so soon? Did you find my brother and kill the white ones?"

"Your brother is dead; the white ones have killed him."

"What? But how?" His lip quivered, but only for a moment as his sorrow turned to anger. "We must avenge my brother!"

Another series of booms echoed through the forest.

"I will avenge him, but first I must watch and wait."

"Until when?"

"Until they are at their weakest, then I will strike like a snake coiled in the bushes."

━═╬═━

The loud, repetitive thunder made the leader stop. It echoed again, repeating itself in rapid succession five times, then six, then seven. The wrath of the Thunder God was upon them.

"We must find the white ones and kill them now. Only that will appease Chon-Chon and the Thunder God," the leader said.

⊶ ⊷

Hope's legs felt heavy and her throat began to close, forcing her to breathe through her nose. The spring that she'd been obsessing over for miles appeared before her. At first, Hope thought that the lack of water had made her delusional, and that delirium had caused her to see a mirage, but she could see the burnt remnants of their bonfire. Only then did she know it was real.

They knelt down in the dirt next to the spring and ladled handful after handful of cool, crisp water, bringing it to their lips. This was their first drink in nearly two days and to Hope it felt like a taste of heaven going down her throat. Tears rolled down her face. God had answered her prayers.

After catching her breath, she drank more, scooping the water to her mouth. Some went down the wrong pipe causing her to gag.

"Are you all right?" Luke asked, slapping her on her back several times.

"Yeah I'm al—"

A loud boom shook the forest, startling Hope. She saw patches of dark sky peeking through the canopy; daylight was fading fast, and heavy rain clouds loomed above them.

"That thunder sounded close; we're in for another downpour, we should try and find some shelter," Hope said.

Luke stared up at the sky, rubbing his chin, "I'm not sure that was thund—"

Another loud boom echoed through the forest, followed by another, then another.

"That sounds like artillery fire!" Luke said.

"But how could that be possible?" Hope asked.

"Maybe there's a military proving ground somewhere out there," Luke smiled. "But do you know what this means?"

The artillery sounded again, then several more times in rapid succession; this time they could distinguish the distant sound of exploding shells. To Hope, it was music to her ears.

"Yeah, it means there's an army out there, an army of men who can take us out of this God forsaken hell hole!"

Another boom echoed in the distance; this time Hope got a bearing. It came from the forest in front of them, but off to the right. They found a path that led them in that direction. Hope was determined to follow the sound as it continued to reverberate through the trees. With Luke by her side, they pressed onward, each step bringing them closer to nightfall until they found themselves immersed in total darkness.

⋖⊢ ⊣⋗

Matthew and Ryan returned to camp. Jason still lay unconscious, his body covered by the large leaves. Matthew knelt down next to him to inspect what was left of his arm. The seared arteries and blood vessels looked slimy, but only small amounts of blood oozed from the stump.

With some effort, Matthew unbuckled the tourniquet and laid the belt at Jason's feet.

A loud boom echoed through the forest. "Was that thunder?" Matthew asked.

"Yeah, I guess," Ryan said, confused.

The sound repeated itself and then echoed again. Matthew strained his ears. The booming repeated at regular intervals.

"That sounds like cannon fire!" Matthew said.

"Cannon fire?"

"Whatever it is, it's man-made!"

Ryan smiled, "You mean?"

"Exactly, that's our ticket out of here!"

"What about him?" Ryan asked, pointing to Jason.

"Remember when Kuja and Ipiak carried Moxo from the forest on a homemade stretcher?"

"Yeah."

"We're going to do the same thing."

"You have the know-how?"

"It's easy, especially with this blade."

Matthew and Ryan walked out of the clearing and into the forest, and before long they came upon several strong saplings growing together just a few feet apart, their trunks no thicker than broom handles. Using the machete, Matthew chopped down two thin trees.

"We're running out of daylight. I'll strip off the branches; you go pick some reeds; keep them as long as possible and try to find some vines so that we can weave everything together. Hurry back; remember, we're working against the clock," Matthew said.

"You got it, anything for my bud Jason," Ryan said, walking off on his scavenger hunt.

Matthew sliced off all the branches on the saplings, creating two long poles. He tried to bend one, but it didn't budge. *These will be strong enough to hold Jason.* He cut notches into the poles to make it easier to weave the reeds and tie the vines together. After a short while, Ryan returned with an armful of long reeds and light green vines that he had spooled around his hand, just as darkness descended upon them.

"Come on, we can build the stretcher by the light of our fire," Matthew said.

The two boys gathered up their materials and headed back to camp, using the glowing embers of their fire as their only beacon through the darkness.

Matthew placed his poles next to the fire and knelt down next to Jason. Ryan unloaded his armful of reeds and vines, placing them farther away from the fire; he too knelt in the dirt next to Jason. Their friend still lay unconscious; beads of sweat formed on Jason's forehead like water beading on car wax. Matthew felt Jason's forehead; it still burned with fever and he'd lost a lot of blood. He wondered if his friend would make it through the night.

"Come on; let's get to work on that stretcher," Matthew said, trying to take his mind off Jason's grave condition. *At least I've done all I could.*

Jason's body began to shake. Matthew pushed the large leaves against Jason's body, tucking them underneath him as if he were tucking in a sheet.

"I hope that he's not going into shock," Matthew said.

"If he is, there's not much else we can do."

"Come on; let's weave that thing together," Matthew said, looking for an excuse to turn away from Jason, unable to look at his shaking friend a moment longer.

"I told you, I don't know a damn thing about basket weaving," Ryan said.

"It can't be that hard. It doesn't have to look pretty; it just needs to hold his weight."

"Show me what to do; I'm willing to give it a shot."

"You just hand me the reeds and I'll slap that damn thing together."

Both boys walked the few steps over to the poles. Matthew picked them up and then laid them out parallel to each other about two feet apart. Ryan handed him reeds, one at a time. Matthew looped each horizontal strand around both poles, and then tied them together underneath. When he had finished, he wove more reeds, this time vertically through the contraption, creating a tight pattern. Using long strands of vines, he reinforced his creation by stretching and then tying them across the bottom to strengthen the entire design. The makeshift stretcher looked strong if not impressive; Matthew hoped that they'd get the opportunity to use it, but based on Jason's condition it seemed like a long shot.

Thunder boomed again above the canopy, accompanied by flashes of lightning—this time it was the real thing.

"The rain will be here any minute," Ryan said.

"We have to keep Jason dry and warm," Matthew scanned the forest floor and gathered up dozens of small pebbles and piled them into the fire.

Matthew grabbed the machete and pushed it into the ground using the tip to pry away the dirt. He stabbed the blade into the soil next to Jason again and again. Using the width of the blade like a shovel, he scooped out the loose grains. A slight drizzle began to penetrate the defenses of the green canopy.

"What are you doing?" Ryan asked.

"Trying to keep Jason warm."

"But how's digging in the dirt in a rain storm going to keep Jason warm?"

"You'll see, now go gather more rocks and pick me some more of those big leaves."

Matthew worked at a frantic pace, digging out a long trough equal to the length of Jason's body. Its width equaled that of the bronze blade and it measured more than six inches deep.

Ryan returned with the rocks and leaves as Matthew scooped out the last of the dirt. The drizzle transformed into a steady rain. Raindrops sizzled into steam as they hit the fire.

"Hurry up! Weave the leaves through the reeds of the stretcher, we have to try and make that thing waterproof." Matthew said, as he placed the additional rocks into the fire.

Ryan looked confused, but did as instructed. Matthew knelt down and inserted the flat blade deep into the base of the fire. Removing the blade, he extracted a wedge full of hot stones. Rising to his feet, he approached the trough and dumped the heated rocks into the gap.

Thunder rocked the cover above, followed by a quick flash of lightning. The dark, angry clouds released a torrent of rain; the large drops penetrated through the canopy as if the leaves weren't even there.

Matthew scooped blade full after blade full of hot rocks from the fire, laying them along the bottom of the long trough. After lining the trench with stones, he pushed the dirt back into the hole. Patting the soil down with the flat blade, he made it level with the ground. Pressing his hand against the soil, he felt the warmth rising up through the ground. *Perfect, not hot enough to cook him but warm enough to keep him toasty.*

Matthew glanced over at Ryan; he'd woven the last leaf through the reeds. Green covered the bottom of the stretcher.

"Quick, help me lift him onto the stones," Matthew said.

Ryan grabbed Jason's legs, while Matthew grabbed Jason's good shoulder and pressed a hand against his back.

"Ready, lift!" Matthew said. Ryan lifted Jason's legs with ease, but Matthew strained with the bulk of the weight. Together, they lifted him, moving his body over the bed of covered stones. Matthew's hand slipped and Jason landed harder than Matthew would've liked. Jason moaned and tried to open his eyes, but they were nothing more than slits. Both eyes closed again as he fell back into unconsciousness.

"Hand me that stretcher!" Matthew said.

Ryan handed him the woven mass of reeds and leaves. Taking the stretcher from his hands, he placed it over Jason with the leafy side facing up. He propped up one side against the tree, angling it a foot above Jason's head. The tilted stretcher allowed the rain to run off the leaves and onto the ground beyond Jason's feet. Both boys were soaked, but they had to finish the job. They returned to the grove of tropical plants and picked a dozen or so more leaves. After hurrying back, they pressed the thick stems into the reeds of the stretcher, draping the green foliage over the sides, providing their injured friend with as much protection from the weather as possible.

"He looks pretty warm in there. I wish I'd built one of those for me," Ryan said as the rain splattered off his face.

"Ya done good!" Matthew said, gripping Ryan's shoulder. Streaks of blood ran down Matthew's face like red tears. "Come on; let's get out of this rain."

They returned to the grove of large plants and slipped beneath the leaves, hunkering down for a cold, wet night.

⥼ ⥽

The lone tribesman waited in the heavy rain. Remaining motionless, he blended in with his surroundings, standing close enough to see the clearing, while keeping his distance, fearful of springing another trap. The strong one and the fat one were no longer in sight, only the injured one lay under a canopy of hanging leaves, but he couldn't shoot without moving closer—and he dared not move closer. No, he would become one with the forest and wait for their weakest moment, only than could he kill all three and avenge the tribe.

CHAPTER TWENTY-NINE

Thunder shook the dark forest like angry Howler's roaring above the canopy. Hope flinched every time the clouds bellowed; the boom shook her to the core, vibrating through her bones. Sporadic lightning flashed across the path, providing just enough light for Luke and Hope to move forward. Luke's face lit up for the briefest of moments, long enough to betray the fear in his eyes.

A light mist filtered through the canopy, becoming a steady drizzle. After several more thunderclaps, it transformed into a full-fledged downpour.

"We must get out of this rain," Hope said, but there wasn't much shelter to speak of. Nothing but tall trees and small ferns populated the forest, not much else.

On their left, a small cluster of larger tropical plants sprouted from the forest floor, their giant leaves silhouetted against a flash of lightning.

"Let's get under those plants," Luke said. The patch of enormous plants could easily conceal the entire church group. Hope's tears blended with the rain. It was now the *church group* minus two—and not just any two. The savage murders of her best friend and boyfriend slammed into her gut like a kick to the stomach.

Wiping away the rain and tears, Hope followed Luke under the green leaves. The plant provided some protection from the deluge. Together, they prepared to spend yet another miserable night in the rainforest. The constant sound of rain splattering against the leaves brought with it an uneasy calm; a calm that allowed Hope to lament for the first time over the deaths of her fallen friends—only now did it seem real to her. Gripping the stem with both hands, she pulled herself into a fetal position, wondering in silence why it had been Peter and Mary who met their end instead of her.

Luke laid down next to Hope, separated by the thick stem, contorting his body in such a fashion as to keep it covered by the large leaves.

Hope shivered from the dampness against her skin, and the thoughts of her butchered friends. "Why did they have to die?" she asked, staring into Luke's eyes as if he might somehow know the answer.

Luke hesitated before answering. After stammering on his words, he fell silent again as if searching for the *right* words. He cleared his throat, "Maybe it's all part of God's plan."

"It seems more like Satan's plan. It makes you wonder if there even is a God."

"Hope, don't talk like that; you know you don't mean it."

"I'm sorry, it just seems like bad things always happen to good people."

"Not always, Hope, not always. You just have to keep the faith—our faith—your faith."

"You're right; I'm just hungry and tired and sad, very sad." Hope feigned a smile and grabbed hold of Luke's hands as her eyes welled up again.

⚔ ⚔

Tim lay awake in bed listening to the rain. He glanced at his watch; it was already past four. The sound of thunder blended with distant cannon fire. Bill snored a few feet away from him, oblivious to the constant pounding.

Tim knew that the chances of finding those kids alive diminished with each passing moment. *What can we do different today?* He wracked his brain, but came up empty. The only resources they had were their scant supplies and their hiking ability, but even that was limited to how far they could walk in a day. *I should just be thankful we have Kuja.* Brenda's lame ankle didn't help matters much either. *If only I had gotten through to the U.S. Embassy in Quito.*

A drop of rain leaked through the thatched roof and splattered onto the dirt floor, followed by another and then another. Soon a small, muddy puddle formed in the center of the hut; the constant splatter felt like Chinese water torture to Tim's ears, but he made no effort to stop it.

Father Ricardo spent a sleepless night, tossing and turning in bed at the religious retreat outside of Macas. Earlier that evening at dinner, he'd received disturbing reports that the ongoing border dispute between Ecuador and Peru had escalated into a full scale war.

Despite the pounding rain, he heard the distant sound of artillery fire booming throughout the night as the war raged into its second day. The young priest glanced at the digital clock on his nightstand; the crimson display read 5:10. He rose from bed and paced the floor. The rain pinged hard against the window pane and splattered into large puddles on the sandy driveway.

The mission group might be in harm's way. I've got to get them out of there!

Father Ricardo got dressed and grabbed a small travel bag. The screen door to his cottage creaked open and slammed hard behind him as he stepped into the heavy rain. Despite taking less than a dozen steps, his clothes were drenched by the time he'd reached the van. After finding his keys, he started the engine, shifted it into gear, and sped off into the night.

His skin felt cold and clammy; the windshield wipers swept back and forth rhythmically as he drove, each swipe of the blade dispersing a sheet of water. He pushed the button to turn on the heater, but the air blew cold and continued to do so as he drove. Only after several minutes did he remember that the heater didn't work.

Poor visibility and bad weather forced him to drive much slower than he wanted to. The nine miles to Sucua seemed to take forever. His heart raced as both the pounding rain and artillery fire increased in intensity. The rain began to dissipate as he entered the modern section, but not the cannon fire. After several minutes he slowed his wipers and then turned them off. The gray haze told him it was almost morning. At last he'd found the muddy road that led to the traditional area. The van rocked back and forth as it splashed through a gauntlet of deep puddles until he reached the Shuar village.

Brenda awoke to the sound of rain and cannon fire. By the time she got dressed, the rain had almost stopped. She looked at her ankle and squeezed it; there was still some pain and discoloration, but the swelling had gone down considerably. Somehow she was going to get back out there and help with the search, yet she didn't want to become a burden to the others. Startled by a sudden knock on the door, she closed the last two buttons on her shirt.

"Who's there?"

"It's me, Tim."

"Come in."

Tim entered her hut and pulled a wrinkled paper bag from the pocket of his blue windbreaker. He motioned for her to take a seat on her bed and she did so reluctantly.

"Let's take a look at that ankle," he said.

He pulled up the crude stool that he'd built for her during that first week of construction. Brenda removed her sock and placed her bare foot in Tim's lap; his cold fingers tickled, but she didn't fidget or complain. Opening the bag, he pulled out an Ace bandage. He tightly wrapped her ankle, fastening the bandage with two serrated metal clips. Using strips of white surgical tape, he further reinforced her ankle.

"Where'd you get that?"

"At the store in the modern section."

Brenda was about to thank him when they heard a vehicle pull into the village.

"Hey, wait for me!" Brenda said, following Tim who was already out the door. Her ankle felt stiff, but she was able to support her weight and walk in a brisk robotic fashion, feeling much like the just-oiled Tin Man in *The Wizard of Oz*.

Bill popped out of the men's hut, pulling a shirt on over his sunken chest and his roll of belly fat as he hurried toward the approaching vehicle.

Brenda instantly recognized the van and its occupant; she burst into tears when she saw the priest approach, remembering his stern warning about not letting the kids wander off into the rainforest, along with his ominous message that, "the sins of a few will lead to the slaughter of the innocent." Words that raced through her mind over and over. Once again, she became overwhelmed with self-blame.

The van rolled to a stop and the engine shut off. Father Ricardo climbed out, offering a friendly wave and a warm smile.

Bowing her head as Father Ricardo approached, she stared at the ground unable to look the priest in his eyes. Her eyes welled with tears.

Father Ricardo stared at Brenda; creases formed on his forehead and his eyes glistened with concern. "What troubles you, my child?"

Brenda didn't answer as her tears turned to sobs.

Turning toward Bill, Father Ricardo shook his limp hand. "Why does she weep?"

Bill shrugged his shoulders and mumbled an inaudible response.

"I'm afraid I've got some bad news. I'm sure you've heard about the war. I'm sorry, but I've got to cut your trip short. It might become dangerous for you and the others to stay. I suggest that we make preparations to leave at once," Father Ricardo said.

Bill looked solemn as he listened to Father Ricardo's words, but offered no response.

"We've got a group of lost kids; we can't leave until we find them," Tim said, breaking the uncomfortable silence.

"How long have they been missing?"

"Three full days."

"What? And you didn't contact me? Have you at least notified the authorities?"

Bill let out a sigh, rolled his eyes, and shook his head in disgust as he turned away from the priest.

"We tried; we called Macas from the modern section, but every available man is off fighting the war, including search and rescue. We had just connected with the U.S. Embassy when the lines went dead," Tim said.

"What about your cell?" Father Ricardo asked.

"We can't get any service out here and even if we could, I've heard that Peruvian guerillas blew up the cell towers."

The priest unclipped his own cell phone from his belt and stared at it, "You're right, no bars. The phones went dead last night at my retreat. Are they also down in Macas?"

"Don't know," Tim said.

"I'm heading to Macas; if the phones are working, I'll try to raise Search and Rescue in Riobamba. I'll also try to contact the U.S. Embassy; maybe they can get some men and military helicopters in here."

"What if the phones are dead in Macas?" Brenda asked in between sobs.

"Then I'll keep driving until I find a village where the phones do work!" Father Ricardo said.

"I'm going with you!" Bill demanded.

Father Ricardo gave a nod goodbye to Tim and Brenda before he and Bill climbed into the van. The priest fired up the engine, and slapped the shifter into reverse. The van backed up a dozen or so feet, as burnt propane spewed from the exhaust, lingering in the air. Lurching forward, the van bumped, bounced, and splashed its way down the muddy road until it disappeared from view.

Kuja arrived just as the van pulled away. "Was that Mr. Bill in the passenger seat?" he asked.

"Yes, he and Father Ricardo are going to try and call the authorities from Macas," Tim said.

"That's if the phone lines are working," Brenda added.

"What about us? Are we going back out there, just the three of us?" Kuja's eyes glistened with determination; his words sounded more like statements than questions.

Tim looked at Brenda, "How's your ankle? You feel up to it? Or should Kuja and I go it alone?"

"My ankle's fine; let's grab our stuff and get the hell out there!"

CHAPTER THIRTY

E xhaustion washed over Hope as she lay under the plant. Luke lay next to her with his arms and legs wrapped around hers to provide comfort from the dampness. The thick stem of the plant separated them which somehow made it all right. Hope would never allow herself to be this cozy with Luke under normal circumstances, but these weren't normal circumstances and this wasn't the time to be squeamish. His body felt good next to hers and she felt protected in his arms in a brotherly sort of way. After lying there for some time, they both drifted off to sleep. While they slept, the huge leaves provided adequate protection from the rain.

Hope began to dream. She was eight years old again sitting in a swing, pumping her tiny legs back and forth as her father gently pushed her from behind. The swing was the old fashioned type, just like the one her grandfather had built for her. He'd made the seat from a thick leather strap, like the ones barbers used to sharpen straight edge blades. Strong rope fastened the seat to the long, straight limb of a tall oak tree.

Her father smiled as she laughed with nervous excitement, swinging higher with every leg pump. In the bright sunlight, he looked just the way she remembered him from his pictures, dressed in a denim shirt and blue jeans, his brown straight hair flowing from a floppy leather hat. Without warning, he stopped the swing with both hands and knelt down in front of her; his smile was gone as he sternly gazed into her eyes.

"Follow the morning sun. Become one with the sun and you'll find your way out!"

The image of her father disappeared and she found herself sitting alone on the swing, feeling hollow and empty. This disturbing scene jolted her awake; she remembered the day her father died; she felt abandoned by him on that day too. Luke's limbs intertwined with hers made her feel safe and she was glad he was there.

The birds of the forest serenaded her with their morning songs. It was a good omen; today was going to be different from the rest. She was about to crawl out from under the plant, but she hesitated; her senses told her to freeze. A faint scent filtered in beneath the leaves. It was a smell she'd become all too familiar with. The pungent odor grew stronger by the moment. Luke silently slept; she prayed that he'd continue to do so. She strained her ears to listen, but heard nothing except song birds somewhere in the trees above her. She inched closer to the stem, pulling her legs close to her chest, making herself as small as possible. Still she heard nothing.

A brown foot descended slowly to the ground in front of her, less than six inches away from her face. The smell was overbearing and she saw sweat coming from his pores. Hope inched backward away from the ankle, fearful her warm breath might betray her. A second foot came down in front of the first, brushing back the leaves of another plant. Two more feet appeared to her left, moving forward, brushing away the surrounding vegetation with a slow, sweeping motion.

The foot stopped and took a step backward, nearly stepping on her face. She held her breath—ten seconds—twenty seconds, the foot didn't move—thirty seconds—forty seconds, her lungs were about to explode, she could hold her breath no longer—the foot stepped forward, followed by the second. The feet on her right also took several steps away from her. After several more torturous seconds, all of the feet disappeared from view. Hope silently released the air in her lungs and took in another slow breath, then another.

The stench began to dissipate as the tribesmen moved away from her. Soon, the smell had disappeared. Luke began to stir and he was about to speak when Hope shushed him with her finger. Together, they lay motionless under the plant for a long time, fearful the headhunters might return. After awhile, Hope peeked out from under the leaves and scanned her surroundings. They were gone, at least for now. The rain had disappeared, but her angst remained. Once again, the air smelled fresh and clean. A powder blue sky peeked through the green canopy. Prism-like rays of morning sunshine filtered through the trees, illuminating the surrounding ferns.

Luke appeared from beneath the leaves and whispered, "Which way?"

"Toward the sun," Hope whispered without hesitation, as she stared up through the trees at the rising dawn.

Together, they crouched low in the ferns and headed off in a new direction, one that led them toward the sun and away from the Invisible People. Hope now walked with renewed vigor and confidence, feeling her father's guidance with each new step.

Brenda glanced at her watch; it was already past 11:00 a.m., she and Tim had been following Kuja for nearly four hours. They had retraced their steps from the day before, but still hadn't reached virgin territory. They hadn't even reached their old camp site. Her ankle had begun to swell, making each step more painful than the last, but she wasn't about to let them know that. She had come out here to find those kids and damn it, that's just what she was going to do, because if she didn't... She wasn't prepared to come to terms with that possibility, not now, not ever.

They'd stop every so often to cup their hands and call out to the kids. Their voices sounded meek and pathetic, absorbed quickly by the vast jungle, becoming hoarser with every call. At least they were doing something instead of just waiting in the village. That would've been unbearable. During each of these stops, Brenda pressed a pair of binoculars against her face and scanned the forest. On occasion she'd see movement in the distance, but it always turned out to be a macaw or a toucan or a squirrel monkey. Mostly, she saw trees, row after row of fucking trees, as far as the eye could see. After this trip, if she never saw another goddamn tree it would be too soon.

Late morning turned into late afternoon, despite exhaustion, they kept on searching. They reached their old camp site and boldly forged ahead through a light drizzle, trudging an additional two miles into virgin territory before darkness set in. Tim pulled the blue tarp from his knapsack and quickly set it up. Several thunder claps turned the sprinkle into a heavy downpour. Kuja managed to start a small fire under the tarp, while Brenda rationed out an ample supply of manioc root and beef jerky. The two men chatted amongst themselves, planning out their search strategies for tomorrow, but Brenda was in no mood for conversation. Another day had passed and they had failed once again. The *not knowing* was worse than anything. *Where are those kids?* Tears streamed down her cheeks as she crawled into the sleeping bag to hunker down for another cold, wet, sleepless night.

⊷⊷ ⊷⊷

Matthew awoke to moans coming from the direction of their camp. *Jason's awake.* He gave Ryan a shake, "Come on, wake up!"

"Huh?"

"Come on, let's go, Jason's awake."

After crawling out from the foliage, they hurried back the fifty or so yards to camp. They found Jason still lying in his shelter. His eyes were slits and he moaned after every breath, his stump looked wet and nasty, but there was no sign of bleeding and color had returned to his cheeks.

Matthew shooed away several flies feeding on the wound. "Jason, can you hear me?"

Jason feigned a smile.

Matthew placed his palm on Jason's forehead. "His fever broke, that's a good sign."

"How you feeling, bud?" Ryan asked.

Jason pursed his lips as he tried to speak. Matthew lowered his head and placed his ear above Jason's mouth.

"Thanks," Jason whispered.

"We did what needed to be done," Matthew said.

"You thirsty?" Ryan asked.

Jason nodded his head.

"I can go back to the stream to get some water, but I have nothing to carry it in," Ryan said.

"I saw some pitcher plants over there; they must be filled with water after all this rain," Matthew said.

"Pitcher plants?" Ryan asked.

"Yeah, they're like water pitchers; they hold water to drown bugs so they can eat them. Come on, I'll show you."

Matthew led Ryan back toward the tropical plants with the large leaves; off to the right there were more than a dozen plants whose petals formed a small pitcher, each one filled with rainwater. They picked several of them, taking care not to spill the water, and brought them back to Jason.

Ryan tilted Jason's head, while Matthew brought the first of the soft plants to Jason's lips. He drank eagerly until the plant was empty. Matthew repeated the process until Jason had drained all of the plants of their precious liquid.

"Feel better?" Ryan asked as he lowered Jason's head.

Jason nodded.

"Where'd you learn about the pitcher plant?" Ryan asked.

"We saw that video about carnivorous plants in science class. Don't you remember? You were sitting right next to me."

"Must've been studying Suzie Hamilton that day; she sat only two seats over. Hey, you study plants and bugs; I'll study Suzie Hamilton."

Jason tried to smirk, another good sign.

"Okay, here's the plan; yesterday we built this stretcher," Matthew said pointing to the roof of the shelter. "We're going to carry you through the forest and hopefully back to the village."

Jason feigned a smile.

"But there's no cannon fire to guide us," Ryan said.

"That's all right; I still have a bearing on the direction from which it came."

Matthew and Ryan disassembled the shelter and laid the stretcher down next to Jason.

"All right, we're going to lift you, are you ready?"

Jason nodded. Matthew grabbed Jason behind the shoulder blades and Ryan gripped his legs.

"On three! One, two, three, lift!"

Jason unleashed a long moan as they lifted him and placed him down gently on the stretcher. "There, the hard part's over," Matthew said. "I'll take the front, you take the back."

Matthew and Ryan grabbed the handles and lifted Jason, and then started to march.

⇥⊹ ⊹⇤

Brenda awoke to a new day determined to find those kids. The rain had stopped and the first light of dawn filtered through the lush, green, canopy. Tim and Kuja had already taken down the tarp and extinguished the fire. Brenda packed up her belongings, slung the backpack over her shoulder and draped the binoculars around her neck. She followed Kuja and Tim as they started down the narrow trail. They walked for less than an hour under the forest canopy, serenaded by songbirds.

The path led Kuja and Tim out of the woods and into an open field, as Brenda lagged several steps behind. Long reeds and high grass rose up several feet on both sides of the path. The sun shone bright in the open space and Brenda's eyes took several seconds to adjust. The area was about the size of two football fields. At the end of the grassland, the path led up a slight grade and into a new forest. In the middle of the field, a second path cut to the left through the tall grass, entering the forest less than thirty yards away.

Kuja stopped suddenly at this crossroad and knelt down to inspect the soil.

"Any sign of them?" Tim asked.

"No, last night's rain washed away any footprints," Kuja said.

"So which path do you think is best?" Brenda asked.

Kuja rubbed his chin for a moment. "Let's go to the left, it will bring us back under the canopy, maybe the trees protected some of the prints."

They started down the new path and hadn't taken more than twenty steps when Brenda felt overwhelmed by a sudden need to stop.

Tim glanced back over his shoulder and said, "Come on, Brenda, quit lollygagging, let's go."

Ignoring Tim, she turned around and pressed the binoculars against her face, scanning the field. Tall grass hid most of the original path, but a small section remained visible near the top of the grade at the point where it entered the forest. Something caught her eye—quick movement in the shadows.

Another damn squirrel monkey, she thought.

A figure stepped from the shadows, but this was no squirrel monkey. A man stood before her, a white man who appeared to be in his late twenties. Brenda couldn't believe it, but there he stood clear as day, wearing a denim shirt and jeans. Brown, shoulder length hair flowed downward from a floppy leather hat.

How could this be? Brenda thought. *We're miles deep in the jungle. What's he doing out here by himself?*

The man gazed back at Brenda, making eye contact through the binoculars; it looked as if he was standing right in front of her. Removing his hat, he used it to wave her forward. After flashing a momentary smile, he stepped back into the shadows and disappeared. He was there one moment and gone the next. Brenda began to wonder if she'd really seen him at all.

"Will you come on?" Tim yelled.

"I just saw a man standing over there." Brenda pointed toward the path.

"What? Where?" Tim asked.

"Right where the path meets the forest."

Tim grabbed the binoculars still draped around Brenda's neck. Not bothering to remove them, he pressed the field glasses against his face, pulling her toward him, "I don't see anything."

"He's not there now—but he was, I swear it."

"Okay, let's check it out," Tim said with a sigh.

Kuja reversed his course and headed back to the original path. Brenda and Tim followed him through the field and up the grade, stopping at the point where the path met the forest.

"Nobody's here," Tim said.

"But he was, I swear."

Kuja knelt down to inspect the sandy soil. "There aren't any footprints; if someone was here, I'd see fresh tracks."

"But he *was* standing there. I saw him clear as day."

"Okay, if you say so, but since there are no footprints of either our mystery man or the kids, I suggest we head back down the other path," Tim said.

"I agree," Kuja said.

"Whatever!" Brenda said gritting her teeth.

Brenda followed Tim and Kuja back in the direction from which they'd come. After reaching the point where the two paths intersected, Brenda again felt the urge to stop and look around. She pressed the field glasses to her face and gazed at the spot where they'd stood just moments before. Nothing looked out of the ordinary, but as she removed the binoculars from her face, she again saw movement.

Tim's voice growled in the background, "Give it up already, and let's go!"

Brenda gazed through the binoculars—someone had emerged from the forest and was moving toward them; another figure appeared, walking close behind the first.

"I see someone!"

"You won't give up, will you? We have to go!" Tim shouted.

"But there are people out there and they're coming this way! A girl with dark hair and a boy! It's Hope! And Luke is with her!"

Brenda threw down her binoculars and despite her bad ankle, hobbled toward Hope in a rapid fashion, as if she was in a three-legged race. She cried out to Hope, screaming her name as she moved forward; Tim and Kuja followed close behind her.

⇒⃫ ⇐⃫

Hope heard a voice call out to her; she had to be imagining it. The voice grew louder. She gazed down the path and saw someone hobbling toward her, a woman—Brenda!

Hope's eyes filled with tears as she ran to meet her on the path and Luke also began to run. Hope and Brenda came together in a strong embrace.

Tim hugged Luke and patted him on the back several times. "Thank God we found you."

Hope clung to Brenda, not wanting to let her go, sobbing over the loss of her friends, feeling guilty that she and Luke were the ones who'd made it out of the forest alive. But mixed into those tears of sadness were tears of joy. They were safe.

Brenda stopped crying long enough to ask the dreaded question, "Where's everybody else?"

Hope glanced at Luke, hoping he'd be the one to tell the tale of murder, but instead he cowered, staring at his feet. No, the burden rested on her. After taking a deep breath, she told the story about her two friends and their savage murders.

※

The news of Mary's and Peter's deaths sliced through Brenda's frontal lobe like a lobotomy. Her legs wobbled and she could no longer speak. Her vision narrowed; she was now unaware of her surroundings. Her belief system had shattered like shards of glass across blacktop.

What kind of God allows this to happen? She cursed God and after remembering *why* it happened, she cursed herself. *She* was the one who brought this upon Mary and Peter, nobody else. She felt personally responsible for their deaths.

The sins of a few will lead to the slaughter of the innocent. This reality suffocated her conscious thought, making her retreat into her own dark world, the only world in which she could now exist. Voices of others surrounded her, but no longer could she comprehend their meanings.

The memory of it all came rushing back to her, the coke; the sex. She felt like her life was one long conveyor belt, like those fast moving walkways at the airport. As hard as she tried to reverse her course, she was never able to. Instead, she ran headlong into her demons. All her life she tried to avoid them, step around them, but they always blocked her path, getting in her way, pushing her further into despair. In the next moment, she felt herself descending into the lowest level of Hell.

She had fornicated with the serpent in the Garden of Eden, had been fucked by the devil himself, and now she must pay with the lives of the innocent and her very soul.

CHAPTER THIRTY-ONE

The horrific details of Peter's and Mary's death had been more than Brenda could bear. The telling of those events gave Hope a sense of relief, but moments later she came to regret it.

Tim dropped to his knees and pressed both hands against his temples, trying to squeeze the gut wrenching news from his head. Brenda withdrew in silence as she processed the information; her face grew pale and her eyes glazed over. Looking into those empty eyes, Hope knew that something within her had forever changed.

Tim grabbed Brenda by the shoulders and gave her a violent shake, but she remained unresponsive. "Brenda, Brenda! Snap out of it!" Tim yelled, as she gazed into the forest.

―❖―

There wasn't much that Tim could do about Brenda, but his desire to find the missing boys became his obsession. *Two are dead*, he thought, *I'll be damned if we lose any more.* He silently vowed that he wasn't leaving the jungle without Jason, Matthew, and Ryan.

Tim turned to Hope and Luke, "With Kuja's help, do you guys think you can take Brenda back to the village without me?" Tim asked.

"Of course," Hope said, "But where're you going?"

"I've got to find the boys."

"What if you get lost yourself?" Luke asked.

"That's a chance that I'll just have to take. But don't wait for me; when you get back to the village, I want you to gather all of your belongings. When Father Ricardo and Dr. Drake return, I want everybody to pile into the van and leave at once, understand? Don't wait for me; I'll catch up with you guys in Macas."

"What if you never make it to Macas?" Hope asked.

"Then fly home without me."

"But—" Luke said.

"No buts—just do it!"

Tim's eyes met Kuja's, "Take good care of them."

Kuja picked up a jagged rock and scratched a large X across the bark of a tall Kapok tree; he then drew a circle around it.

"Now that I don't have to track; I know a shorter, easier path through the forest. It will save us a few hours. I will mark the trail for you, look for my X."

"Thanks Kuja, I will."

"Come on, let's go home," Kuja said, waving the group forward, taking the first steps of what still proved to be a grueling hike back to the village. Hope and Luke draped Brenda's arms across their shoulders to support her weight. Brenda could walk, but only when her two escorts pulled and prodded her along.

"God speed!" Tim shouted, as he watched them cross the field and disappear into the jungle.

Tim took a deep breath and headed off in the opposite direction. Walking through the field and up the grade, he entered the forest at the exact spot where Brenda claimed to have seen the mysterious man. This time there were two clear pairs of footprints in the sandy soil, but these belonged to Hope and Luke. Still, he felt that this path gave him as much chance as any to find the three boys.

<hr/>

The machete lay flat against Jason's stomach for lack of a better way of carrying it. Matthew and Ryan had already carried the stretcher for more than two hours. Jason moaned every time a sudden slip or misguided step jostled the stretcher. When the jostling became too frequent, Matthew brought the procession to a halt. This became Ryan's signal to ease Jason down to the ground.

The rest periods lasted just ten minutes. Few words were spoken during these breaks, because speech required energy and energy was in short supply. Matthew designated himself the official time keeper. Each time, he'd glance at his watch and jump to his feet to signal the end of the break. This ritual became Ryan's cue to grumble about needing a longer rest, but he always resumed his position at the rear of the stretcher. Together, on Matthew's command, they'd lift Jason and continue their long journey through the jungle.

<hr/>

Blending in with the trees, the tribesman took careful aim at the fat one. Filling his lungs to capacity, he placed his lips over the mouthpiece. He could easily kill him with a quick burst of breath, but he hesitated. The strong one proved to be a fierce warrior and the machete was always within arm's reach, he couldn't risk a charge. He'd never be able to reload, aim and shoot before the strong one cut him down with his blade. No, he must still wait.

<hr/>

Most of the time, they walked under a cover of tall trees. The thick foliage diminished the sunlight, dwarfing the ground plants and ferns, allowing them to move easily through the forest. At other times, the path led them out of the jungle into fields and meadows. Thick plants grew over the path in many of these open areas. Here the going was slow because it required the use of the machete to move forward.

Matthew swung the blade freely, hacking away at the vegetation until a path had been cleared wide enough to allow them to pass. Ryan was nothing more than a passive observer during these unscheduled breaks. Jason remained conscious watching Matthew hack away at the overgrowth. After fighting their way through one of these fields, they found themselves back under the jungle canopy. They hadn't walked more than fifty yards through this new section of forest, when Matthew heard the sound of rushing water somewhere in front of him. The path led down to the bank of a fast moving river. Together, they placed Jason down. Matthew gazed at the white water, then the far bank. Scratching his chin, he tried to estimate the distance across the river and figured it would take more than a strong slingshot to reach the other side. The distance, combined with the rapid moving water, guaranteed a dangerous crossing for anyone who tried. The path resumed on the far bank, cutting back into the forest.

After weighing all their options, Matthew decided on a course of action.

"We've got to get across that river," he said.

"That water's moving pretty fast and I'm not a great swimmer," Ryan said.

"It's fast but shallow," Matthew said as he pointed toward the water. "Look, you can see the bottom."

"You can't see the middle; what if it's deeper there?" Ryan asked.

"Just hold onto the stretcher; we can use it for support and it might even float."

"But what if we dump Jason in the water? I don't like it. I say we find another way."

"Let's ask Jason, we'll let him decide," Matthew said. "What do you think, pal, should we try and cross the river?"

Jason lay silent, tilting his head; he stared at Matthew, as his eyes opened wider than before. His voice sounded hoarse, but for the second time since the amputation he spoke, "Cross the river."

"And so it's decided!" Matthew said.

"Give me another minute to rest," Ryan said.

Matthew thought for a moment and decided that it would be the wise thing to do, "Okay, we'll rest for a full twenty minutes before attempting our crossover."

This seemed to satisfy Ryan for the moment, but as the time elapsed and the deadline approached, his forehead became dotted with beads of sweat. After several more minutes, Matthew looked at his watch, thankful that it was waterproof. He announced, "It's time!"

Ryan grunted as he struggled to his feet.

"We need to secure Jason to the stretcher so he doesn't fall into the water. Buckle your belt to his, strap it around the stretcher and pull it tight around his mid-section," Matthew said.

"I need my belt to hold up my pants," Ryan said. "Why don't we use your belt?"

"Because my belt isn't long enough, even with it tied to Jason's. Once you're in the river you won't need it; the wet fabric will cling to your skin. You can put the belt back on once we make it across."

Ryan stood silent, seemingly stymied by Matthew's logic. He removed his belt and buckled it together with Jason's. Matthew tilted up his end of the stretcher to make it easier for Ryan to tie the elongated leather strap around it. Ryan pulled the belts tight around Jason and tied the ends together into something resembling a knot. If he'd been a boy scout, he certainly wouldn't have earned any merit badges for this effort. Despite the half-assed knot, Jason appeared to be secure against the stretcher.

With Jason tied down, they lifted him off the ground and carried him to the water's edge. Matthew, without hesitation, stepped boldly into the river. Ryan, forced to do likewise, splashed into the river behind him.

As he watched them enter the river, the tribesman knew his moment had arrived. Crouching low on a rock, he reached into his quiver and removed the sealed bamboo tube and a dart. Piercing the beeswax, he dipped the point deep into curare and pulled it out—the white poison covered the tip. After inserting the dart in the gun, he took careful aim at the fat one. In another moment he would be dead.

The river was shallow, less than knee high, but Matthew could feel the force of the cool water against his legs. As he moved farther into the river, the water began to get deeper, now rising up several inches above his knees. The force of the rapids increased, but he could still see the riverbed through the current and decided to continue on.

"I don't know about this!" Ryan shouted.

"Come on, we'll make it, we're almost halfway there." Matthew took several more steps, the water was almost up to his waist and strong enough to physically push him several feet downstream. He strained to keep Jason and the stretcher out of the water. Glancing over his shoulder, he saw Ryan struggling to do the same.

Matthew's legs felt like rubber in the water, weakened by hunger and exhaustion, fighting what seemed like a losing battle against the river. He crossed the halfway mark, still determined to make it to the other side. Again glancing over his shoulder, he saw an equally exhausted Ryan fighting to maintain his balance. Something on the bank caught Matthew's attention.

A camouflaged tribesman, crouching on a flat rock, took aim with a blowgun. Green and brown markings covered the man's face chest and limbs allowing him to blend with his surroundings like a chameleon. He sucked in a lungful of air and blew hard into the mouthpiece, launching a dart.

Acting on instinct, Matthew shoved the stretcher, causing Ryan's body to twist in the water. The small dart stuck into the end of the pole, missing Ryan's hand by inches. The tribesmen quickly reloaded his weapon. Matthew, thrown off balance, took a step backward and fell into a deep hole, plunging underwater. Clinging to the handles of the stretcher, he pulled Ryan forward, causing him to lose his balance and fall into the torrent. The machete slipped off Jason's stomach and fell into the river, swirling through the water as it sunk to the bottom.

The buoyant properties of the stretcher might have enabled it to float with just Jason's weight, but with both Ryan and Matthew pressing down on the handles, it didn't stand a chance. Jason lay helpless, strapped to the stretcher more than a foot underwater. Matthew, still submerged himself, saw him struggling for a breath.

If only I can regain my footing, Matthew thought, but each time he tried, his foot slipped on algae-covered rocks. The force of the rapids pushed them into still deeper water. Matthew's legs no longer touched the riverbed. The stretcher swirled around in circles with Jason still trapped underwater. Matthew gasped a quick breath when the rapids pushed him to the surface, only to submerge his head again beneath the whitewater.

We must let go or Jason will drown, Matthew thought. Even if he did let go, he knew that Ryan would never give up his life preserver. If Jason had any chance at all, he'd have to act now.

Matthew let go of the handles and his end tilted toward the surface, but Jason remained submerged, forced down by Ryan's weight.

The stretcher continued to spin in the water and Ryan's form rapidly approached. Matthew knew what he must do. As Ryan spun toward him, he clothes-lined him across the neck, knocking his hands free of the stretcher. Ryan's eyes bulged and he clutched his throat underwater with both hands. The stretcher popped immediately to the surface and shot through the rapids, racing downstream with its helpless passenger.

Matthew placed Ryan in a headlock and pulled him lifeguard style to the surface. They both managed to take a breath before the rapids pushed them back underwater, tossing them around like twigs, pushing them farther downstream.

The fat one twisted at the last second and he had missed! He reloaded fast, but his prey had fallen into the whitewater. He shot again, but the dart missed as they spun in the river. *At least I'll watch them drown.* This thought satisfied him, still he needed to take their heads. Grabbing his blowgun and quiver, he raced along the bank chasing the white ones as they shot through the rapids.

Early morning became 10:30 and Tim wasn't any closer to finding the boys. He'd pushed on though the rainforest with great fervor, but after walking for three hours without even the slightest trace of humanity, his enthusiasm waned.

Kuja and the others must be more than halfway back to the village by now. At least that thought gave him solace.

Walking under the never ending canopy of green, he felt a sudden sensation like he was being watched. After scanning the trees, he spotted a blue Macaw about thirty yards away, perched on a tree limb. *I must have walked too long alone in the forest,* he thought. He could've sworn that the bird had smirked at him, but it happened so fast he couldn't be sure. It felt like the time he drank too much *Strong Bull Whiskey* and swore that the ring-nosed bull on the label had winked at him, but this time he was sober. When he looked again, the bird was gone, but he didn't remember seeing it fly off. The entire incident sent a chill through his body, but he put it out of his mind and pressed on.

The path snaked through a large patch of ferns. Something caught his ear and he stopped for a moment to listen—it was the unmistakable sound of rushing water. He didn't know why he felt a sense of urgency, but he did, so he walked briskly toward the sound. After traveling a short distance, he stood on the edge of what he'd later describe as a large boulder that overlooked a raging river. The water swirled less than ten feet below his feet.

Tim gazed upstream and spotted something half submerged, shooting through the rapids toward him. It looked like a miniature raft made from matted reeds of some sort and something lay across it. The river pushed the object underwater again, but it reappeared several yards closer. This time he could see the form of a man on top of the reeds—and he wasn't moving.

Acting on instinct, Tim sprang from the cliff and dove into the raging water. He swam hard to a spot where he stood a chance of intercepting the man. Nearing exhaustion, he saw the raft appear before him; in another second it would be beyond his reach. After giving one last stroke, he lunged for a wooden pole that jettisoned from the rear of the primitive craft. Tim's hand locked onto it like a vice; his left hand found the second pole, enabling him to steer the contraption. He rode behind the man, kicking his feet, guiding the tiny raft toward the bank like a boogie board in the Jersey surf.

Upon reaching the bank, he dragged the man from the river, pulling him to higher ground. Only then did he recognize the man as Jason. His face took on a bluish tone and he began to cough up water, but he was breathing.

Tim gasped, startled by Jason's stump. *Where's his arm?* He had only begun to ponder this question, when he heard cries for help coming from the river. Leaving Jason strapped to the platform, high on the bank, he raced to the river and scanned the water. He looked upstream but didn't see anybody. While gazing downstream, he heard another shrill cry for help. This time he was able to pinpoint the location. About fifty yards downstream, a man clung to a tree limb, hanging above the water. Closer inspection revealed that it was Matthew grasping the limb. Ryan twisted in the water behind him, with his arms wrapped around Matthew's waist.

Tim cupped his hands and shouted, "Hang on! I'll be right there!"

Racing along the bank, Tim reached the tree branch that supported Matthew, it sprouted from the bank about two feet above the water, but the limb was far too thin for Tim to crawl out onto.

Matthew's fingers began to loosen under the strain of Ryan's weight. Tim watched helplessly as Matthew readjusted his hands, fighting to maintain his grip on the thin branch. A tiny dart fell from the sky, its white tip stuck into the branch less than a foot away from Matthew's hand.

"I can't hang on much longer!" Matthew shouted.

Tim gazed across the river and saw a bare-chested tribesman angling a blowgun high into the air. With a quick burst of air, the green faced man rained another dart down on Matthew, this one landing in the water next to him. The man hurried to reload.

A frantic search of the surrounding flood plain produced a long, dead branch. *It might just be long enough to reach,* Tim thought, sprinting with it back to the river. With outstretched arms, Tim extended the branch toward Ryan, but he'd underestimated its length; the branch fell short by almost a yard.

"Ryan, you're going to have to let go of Matt's legs and lunge for the branch," Tim said.

"I can't, I'm not a good swimmer!" Ryan said.

"You're going to have to try."

"I can't, I'm scared!"

"My fucking hands are slipping, and that asshole's shooting at us. If I let go, we're both going to drown, just do it!" Matthew shouted.

Ryan took a deep breath and lunged for the dead branch. His right hand grasped the limb, followed by his left. Tim pulled the branch toward him, hand over hand with Ryan struggling to hold onto the end. Within seconds, Tim had pulled Ryan to safety, leaving him to wallow in the shallows, like an exhausted hippopotamus

Once again, Tim extended the dead branch toward Matthew. More than three feet separated Matthew from the branch. Using the tree from which he hung to push off, he lunged for the dead limb. He reached it with ease, but the branch snapped when he grabbed for it. The foaming white water began to pull him away. Still holding the broken branch in his right hand, he lunged again with his left and somehow managed to grab the tip of the much shorter stick. Tim took great care not to break the brittle branch further as he pulled Matthew to shore.

With Matthew safe, Tim extended his hand to Ryan, pulling him onto the bank. Matthew climbed out of the river unassisted. All three men collapsed in exhausted heaps next to one another in the tall grass. Matthew spun around to face his attacker. The tribesman, now out of range, stared back at them with his piercing brown eyes. With a final sneer, he turned and melted into the forest.

CHAPTER THIRTY-TWO

E arly afternoon had arrived by the time Hope and the others had reached the Shuar village. Kuja had led them through many miles of jungle, over streams and across meadows. Their journey neared its end and Hope couldn't have been more grateful.

Her eyes welled as she and Luke helped Brenda across the bridge; never before had a bridge been so pleasing to the eye. There were times when Hope thought she'd never see that bridge again, and now she boldly marched across it with Kuja leading the way. In that moment, she realized that this was more than a simple bridge; it was the bridge to her salvation, her ticket home.

Her mother would be there waiting for her at the airport, helping her to resume her battered life, but it would never be the same. At least she had a life; Mary and Peter were far less fortunate.

They passed the knoll where the nightmare began. Hope remembered it all, the fight between Peter and Ryan, the canoe, the hallucinations. Everything changed in those moments after they took the *ayahuasca*, and nothing would ever be the same.

After walking for several more minutes, they'd reached the huts. Hope helped Brenda to the latrine, while Luke and Kuja waited outside. Afterwards, she and Luke walked Brenda over to a large tree, easing her down, resting her back against the trunk.

Hope waved her hand in front of Brenda's face, but her unblinking eyes remained unresponsive. Atiak approached carrying a basket filled with purple mangosteen, offering one each to Hope and Luke, who readily accepted the tasty fruit. Atiak held one out for Brenda, who offered no response. The Shuar woman raised an eyebrow.

"What wrong?" Atiak asked.

Brenda's face looked drawn and expressionless.

"We don't know. She could be in shock," Hope said.

"It happened after hearing very bad news," Luke added.

Together, they told Atiak about Brenda's unexpected reaction to Peter's and Mary's deaths. Atiak offered to help anyway she could, and Hope gratefully accepted her offer.

"Stay with her, I come back." Atiak said. She walked to her hut and returned almost a half hour later with a leather pouch. After opening the drawstrings, she reached in and produced a short piece of bamboo about three inches long, filled with a thick yellow paste.

Using a twig, she applied the ointment, painting it onto Brenda's forehead, chanting in Shuar as she did so. It didn't seem to do much good because Brenda remained in a trance-like state. *Atiak's remedy might just be Shuar superstition, but what could it hurt?* Hope thought.

"Stay with her, we come back," Hope said, mimicking Atiak's broken English.

Hope and Luke left Brenda with Atiak and retreated to their respective huts to gather their belongings. But first, Hope was in desperate need of a shower and a change of clothing. She grabbed a clay vessel large enough to hold a sufficient amount of water and headed down to the brook. After filling the container, she carried it back to Brenda's makeshift shower and filled the watering can.

Removing her clothes, she stepped into the stall and pulled the rope to tilt the can down. The water felt cool and refreshing against her skin. Using soap that she'd *borrowed* from the dormitory in Macas, she scrubbed away dirt and grime, sweat and urine—and a collage of blood—her blood, Mary's blood—a dead man's blood.

The last drops of water emptied from the can. Hope closed her eyes and ran her fingers across her chest. Mary's heart-shaped locket still hung from her neck. She rubbed it between her fingers and whispered a prayer of peace.

Hope wrapped a towel around herself and walked the dozen or so feet back to the hut she'd shared with Mary. She changed her clothes. The clean cotton underwear felt good against her skin. Never before did she appreciate something as simple as clean underwear. She finished dressing by pulling on a fresh pair of jeans and a V-neck top, proudly displaying Mary's locket on her chest. After slipping on a pair of sandals, she packed up their belongings. She tried not to cry as she slowly folded Mary's things. Holding each article of clothing out at arm's length, she envisioned Mary wearing the outfit before placing it neatly into the duffle bag. More than once, she felt overwhelmed by the task, forcing her to stop for a long while to fight back tears. After what seemed like forever, she placed the last article in the bag. She didn't know why she had folded everything with such care and precision; it would probably just go to Goodwill anyway. Finally, she decided that she'd done so out of respect. When she'd finished, she left everything near the door and headed back to check on Brenda.

By the time Hope returned, almost two hours had elapsed. They had moved Brenda to a long table under an open air hut. A group which included Teja, Carak, and the rest of the Elders, gathered around the hut. Kuja stood next to them, speaking in Spanish; he explained what had happened to Brenda.

Keto hovered over Brenda with Atiak standing by his side. A beaded necklace hung across his bare chest. He was clearly in charge now, probably summoned by Atiak after her ointment failed to produce a cure. The group stood quiet with the exception of Keto, who spoke in Shuar, his shamanistic chants resonating through the crowd.

Hope politely forced her way into the circle, standing next to Kuja. Together, they watched Keto perform some type of healing ritual.

"Do you know what he's saying?" Hope asked in a whisper.

"He's chanting about an evil spirit, the *Iwanci*. He says that it has attacked her mind," Kuja said.

Keto held a brown chicken egg in his hand and rubbed it across Brenda's forehead, down her cheeks and around the base of her neck, but she remained still and expressionless. A half-filled cup of water rested on the table next to her head.

"Why is he doing that?" Hope asked.

"He's trying to remove the evil spirit from Brenda. If he's successful, the egg will absorb the evil. He won't know if it worked until he cracks it open and drops it into the water. If the yolk sinks, it has done its job. If the yolk floats, it means that the *Iwanci*'s evil is very strong and it will be difficult to help Brenda," Kuja said.

After rubbing the egg several more times across Brenda's skin, Keto cracked it open against the edge of the table, allowing the yolk to drop into the cup. Everyone inched forward to see what would happen, Kuja and Hope included. The yolk first sank toward the middle, but then it shot to the top of the cup where it remained floating on the water's surface.

A gasp arose from the crowd. Creases appeared on Keto's forehead and beads of sweat formed on his face. A large vein bulged across his neck. A leather pouch similar to the one Atiak had used earlier lay on the ground at Keto's feet. He grabbed the pouch and pulled open the strings. Reaching in, he pulled out a long, clay pipe and a pinch of tobacco. After packing the bowl, he placed the pipe in his mouth and struck a match. He took several quick puffs, drawing them in before inhaling deeper, filling his lungs with smoke. Keto exhaled, blowing the bluish cloud into Brenda's face and hair. Turning his attention to Brenda's ears, he filled her left ear with smoke, followed by her right.

Brenda didn't cough or fidget, her unblinking eyes stared blankly at the thatched roof above her head.

"What's that all about?" Hope asked.

"He's using the smoke to summon good spirit guides to help him expel the *Iwanci* from Brenda's head."

Keto bent over Brenda and placed his mouth on her forehead. She gave no indication that she could see or feel the shaman. He made a slurping sound, creating suction. After removing his mouth, he spit on the ground. He repeated the process several times in rapid succession, acting as if he were sucking venom from an open wound.

Hope looked at Kuja in amazement, but didn't say a word. She didn't have to; her expression said it all.

"He's trying to suck the evil spirit out of her head, but he must immediately spit it out, otherwise the *Iwanci* spirit will leave Brenda and enter him."

Keto's chanting became louder and he waved his open hand over Brenda's head and in front of her face, reminding Hope of a priest giving a blessing to a parishioner during Holy Communion.

The shaman's chants reached a crescendo, and he then fell silent. Brenda remained in a trance, showing no visible change.

"He's finished; he's done all he could," Kuja said.

Hope stared at Brenda looking for a sign, anything that might show some improvement. And then a change did occur, but not one for the better.

A familiar smirk crossed Brenda's lips, but the smirk wasn't her own. It happened so fast, lasting less than two seconds before sinking back into Brenda's expressionless face, but it lasted long enough for Hope to be certain of what she saw. She might have dismissed it outright under normal circumstances, but not after having seen that same smirk many times before. No, that smirk didn't belong to Brenda, despite it being forced upon her face. It belonged on the face of a feathered child, a child long dead. And that child spirit conveyed a message, one that was all too clear. The smirk silently screamed, *I'M STILL HERE!*

Hope felt like she was suffocating. A feeling of panic rose within her, and she began to hyperventilate. She had a desperate need to get away from the crowd, away from Brenda and the *Iwanci*. Breaking away from the circle, she ran toward her hut, hanging a sharp left around the thatched shelter of the common eating area. As she leaned into the turn she ran right into someone. A man with strong hands grabbed her shoulders, stopping her dead. Those hands belonged to Bill Drake. Father Ricardo stood near the van several feet behind him, both men having arrived moments before.

"Hope! Thank God! You're alive! You made it back!" Bill said.

Hope felt shocked and bewildered, offering no response.

Bill gazed at Hope's chest, "That's Mary's locket you're wearing! Where's Mary, back at the hut?"

Hope tried to answer, but stammered on her words, and fell silent. She could only stare at the ground and shake her head.

"Is she somewhere in the village, did she make it back?"

Hope again shook her head no.

"Oh, Christ, she's still out there? You left her out there?"

Hope didn't want to be the one to deliver the bad news, not this time, but she saw no way around it. After all, this was Mary's father asking about his daughter and he deserved an answer. The cruel words escaped her mouth, "Mary's gone; she didn't make it out."

"Is she—"

Hope nodded her head yes.

"No! No! It can't be! My baby, my little girl! It can't be, how? There has to be some mistake!" But there was no mistake, Mary and Peter were dead. Hope saw the pain in Bill's eyes and could no longer hold back her tears. Hope relived the pain of Mary's death, her final moments playing like a movie in her head, cutting her to the core.

"I'm so sorry," Hope said.

"What about everyone else?" Father Ricardo asked, his voice cracking with concern.

"Peter's dead... Luke made it back. Brenda's in the village, but she isn't well. Tim is still out in the jungle looking for Ryan, Matthew, and Jason," Hope cried.

Bill dropped to his knees and began to shake violently; it looked like he might be having a seizure.

Father Ricardo lifted him from the ground. Wrapping his arms around him, he held him in a strong embrace, patting his back several times.

"The Lord will keep you and guide you during this time of mourning."

Bill buried his face in the priest's brown tunic and sobbed incessantly.

The echo of cannon fire thundered through the village, followed by a close barrage of exploding shells. The war sounded much closer than before, just a few short miles away. Sucua and the Shuar village seemed to lie in the path of the Peruvian aggressors. Hope knew that if they didn't get out of there soon, they might never leave.

Bill seemed oblivious to the danger. "Goddamn it, shit! Assholes! They should've been watching!" He shouted, kicking at the dirt as if he suffered from Tourette's. In the next instant, the creases on his forehead disappeared and he looked far more subdued.

"Oh, Mary, my sweet, sweet Mary." He buried his face in his hands and cried hysterically; he wasn't in any condition to make decisions concerning the group. No, that burden fell on Father Ricardo, who stressed the urgency of the matter.

"Grab your bags and meet me at the van. Only take your own belongings, don't waste time packing up everyone else's things; it took several trips to get everything out here and it will take several trips to get everything back. Oh, pack a bag for Brenda, just her essentials. We'll leave as soon as possible."

Hope and Luke obeyed the priest, racing back to their huts to pack Brenda's duffle bag and gather their own belongings. They returned to the van several minutes later, struggling with their heavy baggage.

Father Ricardo had found Brenda and was helping her into the van. He sat her down in the seat behind the driver and rested her head against the window. Seeing this, Hope reached into her duffle bag and pulled out a small pillow. She gently wedged it between the window and Brenda's head.

Bill paced back and forth near the van, making no effort to board the vehicle. The priest opened the rear doors and loaded up the bags into the three-foot space between the doors and the last seat. There was plenty of room to pile in more bags, but time was of the essence.

"Okay, get in the van, we have to get moving," Father Ricardo said.

"But what about Tim, we can't just leave him out there!" Hope said, pointing toward the forest.

"He said that we shouldn't wait for him, we should just go," Luke said.

Another shell exploded in the not so far distance. "We must go now!" Father Ricardo shouted.

Hope reluctantly climbed into the van. Brenda's smirk still spooked her so she sat away from her, taking the last seat in the rear. Luke took the seat behind Brenda, close enough to prop her up should she fall off the seat. Father Ricardo stood next to the front passenger door, and motioned for Bill to get in as if he were waving in a reluctant dog. "Come on, Bill, it's time to go."

Dr. Drake must have taken offense to this, because he ignored the priest, opting instead to climb into the back of the van, plopping himself down in the seat in front of Hope.

Father Ricardo was about to slide the door closed, when Hope heard a voice.

"Hey, wait for us!"

Hope turned her head and saw Tim and Matthew hurrying toward them carrying a makeshift stretcher. Jason lay on the stretcher and Ryan trailed several yards behind them.

A feeling of jubilation cascaded over Hope as her heart pounded with joy. She and Luke would not be the only ones to have escaped the jungle. Jumping out of the van, she ran to greet them. Luke, who was already in front of her, wrapped his arms around Tim. Luke's extra weight forced Tim and Matthew to place Jason down.

Hope nearly tackled both Matthew and Ryan, giving them each a hard embrace. Turning her attention to Jason, she took a step back, gasping at his slimy stump. After taking a deep breath, she regained her composure. Kneeling down next to Jason, she gave him the hug he so rightly deserved. Jason cracked a smile and seemed glad to be back, as did Tim and the other two boys.

Another artillery shell exploded, sounding even closer than before. This had a sobering effect on the happy reunion. Everyone fell silent except for Tim.

"Matt and Ryan, give me a hand with Jason; we're going to lay him out flat right behind Brenda," Tim said.

Jason grimaced as Tim lifted his shoulders, and Matthew and Ryan each grabbed a leg. Together, they carried him toward the open door of the van. Tim strained and hoisted Jason up onto the seat. Everyone breathed a sigh of relief, especially Jason, who now lay flat on his back on the seat cushion.

"Okay, Hope and Luke, it's your turn, take your seats in the van," Tim said.

Hope climbed back into the van and returned to the backseat. A still grumbling Bill Drake didn't even acknowledge her as she passed. Luke sat next to Brenda in the first seat, now that Jason lay across the seat he formerly occupied.

"Should we go get our bags?" Matthew asked.

"Matt and Ryan, just get in the van! Sit behind Jason. I'll grab your bags," Tim said.

Another boom echoed, this one closer still.

CHAPTER THIRTY-THREE

Tim reached the hut and flung the door open, nearly knocking it off its bamboo hinges. He shoved armfuls of clothes into three duffle bags. He tossed his tool belt and flare gun into his own bag, almost as an afterthought.

Closing the bags, he flung two of them over both shoulders and carried the third in his hand. Hurrying out the door, he raced through the village toward the van, jostling the bags several times on his shoulders, thrown off balance by the bulky weight.

The van's engine cranked as he approached. Moments later, he saw Father Ricardo trying to start the vehicle. The frustrated priest turned the ignition key again and again; the engine turned over but refused to start. Each time the pistons sputtered for a few seconds before falling silent.

"Stop! Don't kill the battery," Tim said, shouting at the priest through the open window.

Father Ricardo banged on the steering wheel with his open palms. "I can't understand it. It has always started fine."

"Maybe you flooded the carburetor," Matthew shouted through the open window.

"The van runs on propane, you can't flood the engine," Father Ricardo shouted back.

"Pop the hood and let me take a look," Tim said.

"You need help?" Matthew asked.

"Nah, stay in the van, if I get this thing running, we're outta here."

The priest pulled the lever to pop open the hood. Tim opened the rear doors of the van and loaded in Matt's and Ryan's bags, piling them on top of the others. He crowned the pile with his own bag.

Tim opened his duffle and touched the hard metal surface of the flare gun. He yanked the gun from the bag and tossed it on top of Ryan's duffle. Again he reached into the bag, this time fishing out his tool belt. Tim hurried with tools in hand to the front of the van; twilight was almost upon them and he knew he'd have to work fast.

The hood latch proved to be elusive, hiding deep within the grill. After making several attempts, he found the latch with his outstretched fingers and lifted the hood.

Tim was far from being a mechanic, but he had once worked on a small propane lawnmower at the church. He remembered fiddling with the broken engine long enough to get it running. *This one can't be much different*, he thought, but after inspecting the engine, he quickly realized just how wrong he was. This engine looked far more complex, hoses, wires, and intake valves ran everywhere. *Maybe it's something simple, like a dirty air filter*, he thought.

Locating the air filter, he loosened the wing nut and removed the cover. He lifted the filter from its metal holder and inspected it. Brown dust covered the entire circle of paper grooves; dirt was visible in every crevice. Tim banged the filter against the quarter-panel several times creating a cloud of dust. After reinstalling the filter, he replaced the cover and screwed on the wing nut.

"Try it now!" Tim said.

The priest turned the key; the engine cranked and spurted a bit longer than before, but quickly died.

Tim spotted the carburetor resting below the air filter. *Maybe it would help if I turned the idle adjustment screw,* he thought, having read an article about carburetors in *Popular Mechanics* more than two years ago.

Pulling his head out from under the hood, he removed a thin flathead screwdriver from his tool belt and placed the blade in the groove of what he thought was the idle screw. He was about to make the adjustment when two military jeeps roared into the village. With their tires locked, both jeeps slid in the soft dirt, skidding to a stop less than half a dozen yards away from the van.

Eight soldiers climbed out of the two vehicles, emerging from the plume of dust. Tim recognized the soldiers; they were Shuar tribesmen, and Ipiak and Yeki were among them. They now had crew cuts and wore camouflaged army fatigues, looking quite different from how they did just a few days before. Gone were their traditional Shuar clothes and long hair.

Their sudden transformation shocked Tim; if he didn't know better they could've been mistaken for U.S. Military Personnel.

Hope watched the soldiers through the windshield. Yeki retrieved a traditional Shuar drum from the back of a jeep. Sitting on the ground with folded legs, he beat the taut animal skin with his hand. The rhythmic pounding seemed to summon the rest of the tribe. Shuar men and women of all ages stopped whatever they were doing and gathered around the soldiers, forming a loose circle. Kuja, Atiak, and Teja were amongst them; so was Keto and Carak, along with the rest of the Elders. Young children and mothers carrying babies walked briskly to watch the soldiers.

Ipiak pulled a large burlap sack from the back of his jeep and swung it over his shoulder, his feet shuffling in time with the melodic beat. He poured the contents of the bag out into the center of the circle. Hope gasped as seven bloody heads rolled onto the ground. All of the heads had short, military-style haircuts. *They must be the heads of slain Peruvian soldiers,* Hope thought. Adrenaline fueled her panic and blood raced through her veins as thoughts of Peter and Mary came rushing back.

Hope dry heaved and stared at the metal floor, wanting to look anywhere except out her window. Luke gagged, while Matthew and Ryan sat in stunned silence. Jason was the lucky one; lying flat on his back, he couldn't see a thing.

Bill Drake offered a, "Holy shit!" from his seat in front of Hope, but not much else.

Brenda stared straight ahead, her mind incapable of absorbing the macabre spectacle.

"We've got to get the hell out of here!" Tim shouted from under the hood. A clicking sound followed. "Try it now!" Tim yelled.

Father Ricardo turned the ignition key; the engine sputtered several more times and backfired. The engine again fell silent, sounding as if it had gasped its final breath.

"Shit!" Tim shouted.

Hope's attention turned to the scene unfolding outside her window; she didn't want to look, but she couldn't help herself. It was like watching a train wreck, and she couldn't look away. The soldiers removed their uniforms and stripped naked. They began dancing around their human trophies with their privates flapping in the breeze.

Each tribesman, including Ipiak, selected a head by picking it up and inspecting it. It had to be the same one he'd taken in battle. At least that's what Kuja had told her the day they picked mushrooms together. *God! It seemed so long ago.*

The beat grew faster and the naked men moved the heads up and down as they danced, reenacting their kills for the entire tribe.

As the tribesmen danced in a circle, Hope stared at each head as it passed. Their facial expressions looked different, some of their eyes were open, and others remained closed. Fear froze the faces of two of the soldiers, while another appeared to be resting peacefully in death. Those seven faces seared Hope's mind forever, because they were more than just dead soldiers. They were sons and brothers, husbands and fathers, loved and cherished by mothers, wives, and children who would never see them again.

Hope continued to watch as the tribesmen worked themselves into a frenzy as they smeared maroon blood from the open necks all over their brown bodies.

"Try it now!" Tim shouted.

The priest cranked the engine; the pistons sputtered twice and died.

"Try it again, but this time, don't step on the pedal at all."

Father Ricardo took his foot off the pedal and turned the key. The engine cranked, and after several seconds of sputtering, it roared to life. Tim closed the hood and hopped into the van, sitting next to Father Ricardo in the passenger seat. He slammed the door with a thud.

"Let's get the hell out of here!" Tim said.

The priest put the van into reverse and backed up several feet. Jamming the shift lever into drive, he sped away from the bloody ritual, leaving a cloud of dust in his wake.

CHAPTER THIRTY-FOUR

The Shuar Blood Dance triggered a panic within Hope, one she could no longer contain. Her heart pounded hard in her chest and she felt feverish; she felt herself hyperventilating and neither Peter nor Mary was there to calm her.

Images flashed into her head—a fire ball, a raging inferno. An aura of tension surrounded her. There was something wrong! Something horrible! A burning cross, a burning skull, the images kept coming. Hope's fever grew hotter; it felt as though a fire burned all around her. Heat blisters erupted on her face and neck, and painful welts rose on her arms and hands. Her legs felt like they were on fire.

"Stop the van! There's something wrong! Stop the van!" Hope shouted.

"What's wrong?" Tim asked.

"I don't know, but I'm burning up, something isn't right. I can't explain it, but something's terribly wrong!"

"Hang in there, we'll be in Macas in less than a half-hour and we'll take you, Jason, and Brenda right to the hospital."

Upon hearing Hope's words, the priest accelerated and the van raced through the thick forest. The twilight cast long shadows across the road. The passengers jostled back and forth as the van bounced hard along the dirt road. Father Ricardo drove as fast as the road would allow. Streaks of red and orange faded in the western sky and the road grew darker.

"No! Stop the van!" Hope shouted, her words ignored once again, she no longer had the strength to protest.

The dirt road curved up ahead and Father Ricardo slowed the van just enough to negotiate the turn.

As the van entered the blind spot of the curve, a dark figure stood in the middle of the road; a large wooden cross rested across his shoulder. Father Ricardo, having no time to react, spun the wheel to his left. The van catapulted off the road and into a ditch, slamming head on into a large tree. A geyser of steam erupted from the smashed radiator.

Everyone was thrown forward; Hope slammed into the seat in front of her; Jason tumbled to the floor; Ryan screamed about an injured shoulder. Tim, who wasn't wearing his seat belt, fared the worst. Blood trickled from a gash on his forehead and he appeared dazed; his head had slammed into the windshield, spider-webbing the safety glass.

Father Ricardo, Matthew, Luke, and Dr. Drake all appeared to be uninjured. Luke had fastened Brenda's seatbelt and she appeared to be at least physically okay.

Matthew was the first to speak. "What the fuck was that?"

Hope spun around to look; the figure holding the cross still stood up on the road, taking slow, methodical steps toward them. The cross looked identical to the one missing from outside the open-air church.

The figure appeared to be a man covered in dirt, silhouetted against the twilit sky, but it wasn't a man. Hope could only describe the thing as *It*. And *It* carried the cross in a Christ-like fashion, almost as if *It* were mocking Him.

It got closer still; it now stood less than ten yards away and Hope began to make out its facial features. She gasped. *It* looked like Moxo, but it wasn't Moxo.

Moxo's dead, Hope told herself, but this thing also looked dead. Dirt covered the entire body; loose grains fell from its hair. Maggots and worms squirmed in the open wounds, feeding on dirty strands of tissue around shreds of stomach and neck.

Hope screamed, "This isn't real! This isn't real!"

"It's coming for us! We have to get the hell out of here!" Ryan said.

"Just shut up and stay in the van; it can't get us in here," Bill said.

All eyes turned to Tim who responded with a loud moan.

It now stood less than five feet away. Hope stared into its dark, dead eyes. When their eyes met, the thing smirked at her; it was the same smirk that appeared on Brenda's face less than an hour before. Hope now knew what she was dealing with. No, this wasn't Moxo; it was an entity taking the form of Moxo as he lay two weeks dead in the ground. She'd been a fool. Did she really think that the *Iwanci* would just let them drive away?

The smirk disappeared from the thing's face. Showing great strength, it swung the cross like a sledgehammer, slamming the crossbeam into the roof. The deafening sound that followed reverberated inside the van. It struck with such force; the roof indented three inches inward above Hope's head. Another disturbing sound followed—the unmistakable sound of cracking wood. Following this, Hope turned to her left in time to see a dead tree, its trunk as thick as a redwood, snapping off at its base. It first leaned, and then fell forward, looking like it would fall right on top of her.

"Tree!" Hope yelled, leaning backward. The tree gained momentum as it fell, slamming with great force into the roof of the van, crushing it like a soda can. The tree took out the seat in front of her, pinning Bill Drake between the roof and the floor, which were now only inches apart.

Bill's head and shoulders laid on one side of the twisted steel, while his legs and torso laid on the other. Bill stared up at Hope. Unable to speak, he mouthed the words, "Help me!"

But Hope couldn't help him; there wasn't anything she could do. The tree had missed her, but the razor sharp metal biting into Bill's chest would rip him to shreds, should she make any attempt to pull him out. The rear door provided her only means of escape; she could make a run for it, trek back to the village and get help. She tried to open the latch, but the frame had twisted and despite throwing her weight against the door, it refused to budge.

The steady hiss of ruptured propane tanks blended with the screams and commotion coming from the front of the van. The smell of noxious fumes filled the air around Hope, and she began to gag and cough on the gas. Bringing her shirt to her mouth, she breathed through the cotton, using it as a filter, but it did little good. She tried her window but only succeeded in opening it a crack. Pressing her face against the crack, she breathed in what little air she could.

The van listed to the left. The thing had climbed on top of the fallen tree. Still carrying the heavy cross like Jesus, it took slow, deliberate steps along the trunk until it stood on top of the van. Hope heard footsteps on the roof, followed by silence. No longer did she dare go near the window. Knowing it might strike at anytime, her heart felt like it might explode in her chest and her hands began to shake. It lay in wait for them somewhere on the roof, but where?

The force of the tree striking the van slowly brought Tim back to his senses. Looking behind him, he saw the angled roof sloping down to the jagged metal trapping Bill Drake. The serrated edge cut deeply into his chest, as a pool of blood formed on the steel floor around him.

Hope sat trapped behind Bill; Tim prayed she was still alive.

"Hope, are you all right?" Tim asked.

"I'm not hurt, but I'm trapped and there's gas everywhere; it's hard to breathe!"

"What about Dr. Drake?"

"He's alive, but badly hurt."

"Sit tight, I'll come around and get you out. Maybe I can pry him out with a crowbar."

"Don't! That thing is somewhere on the roof!" Hope said.

"It's directly over me, I can hear it," Matthew said with his face pressed against the window, his eyes looking upward.

"No, it's above me; I can hear it creeping forward," Luke said.

"What the fuck are we going to do?" Ryan asked.

"Matt, shut him up and stay away from the window; move toward the center of the van," Tim said.

Father Ricardo folded his hands in prayer. "Our Father in Heaven, deliver us from evil..."

"Father, God helps those who help themselves; now move away from that damn window!" Tim said.

Hearing footsteps above him, Tim gazed up through the sunroof. It stared down at him and snarled. The Thing, still holding the cross, extended its arms and flexed its body, looking like a man about to swing a sledgehammer.

"Duck!" Tim shouted, but it was too late—the windshield exploded. The short beam of the cross smashed through the safety glass, causing crinkled shards to fly everywhere, cutting into Tim's face and arms. The pendulum-like cross missed Tim's head by inches.

Unseen hands lifted the cross out of the van; Tim braced himself for another assault—but none came. Looking up through the sunroof, he saw nothing but darkness descending on the treetops. His heart pounded, causing him to bleed faster through his many cuts. Tim checked on Father Ricardo; he too looked dazed, and his face was also bleeding.

Where is it? Where the fuck is it? Tim thought. A minute passed—then two—then three, still nothing. Everyone remained silent staring up at the thin, metal roof. Tim strained his ears, trying to detect even the slightest sound from above, but only heard the beating of his own heart. His eyes darted back and forth, looking through the sunroof, then the outside perimeter, searching everywhere at once, but he saw nothing.

Was it gone? Had it somehow jumped off the roof undetected? I can't wait forever; I've got to get Hope and Bill out through the back door. But where is it? It's got to be out there somewhere!

Tim took a deep breath and reached for the door handle and as he did so the bottom of the cross smashed into the sunroof; shattered Plexiglas rained down upon his head. The wooden beam again came down hard, this time slamming through the sunroof like a pile driver. Only Tim's fast reflexes prevented his skull from exploding like a smashed melon. The cross, driven down to the floor, now stood erect inside the van. Its crossbeam lay flush against the roof, obstructing Tim's view. Another long silence followed; the wait became maddening. If only he knew where it was, maybe they could make a run for it, but maybe that's exactly what it wanted them to do. It lay in wait like a coiled cobra, waiting for the frightened turtles to poke their heads out from their protective shell. No, they couldn't leave the van, not without knowing where it was.

A dirty, decomposing arm reached down from the roof, making several quick grabs at Tim's face and throat through the opening that used to be the windshield. Exposed tendons and muscles flexed withered fingers; the dead hand felt cold and clammy as it glanced off Tim's face. The stench of rotting flesh mixed with propane filled the van. Tim ducked several times as the hand reached for him again and again, hunting for his elusive throat. The hand cornered Tim against the door, locking onto his jugular in a firm death grip.

Acting on instinct, Tim grabbed hold of the gelatin-like arm and pulled on it. Using all his strength, he yanked the thing off the roof. It slammed against the tree and tumbled to the ground. Within seconds, it found its footing and lunged at Tim through the broken windshield.

"Run!" Tim yelled as he flung open his door and jumped from the van. He slid open the passenger door with one quick motion. Luke backed out of the van, clutching Brenda's wrists, and struggled to drag her from the vehicle. Matthew and Ryan grabbed Jason by the ankles as they passed and pulled him off the floor and out the door; dragging him along the ground more than a dozen yards away from the van. Father Ricardo, after bolting from his door, vaulted over the fallen tree and reunited with the three boys behind the vehicle.

The Moxo-like thing crept across the dashboard and tumbled onto the floor. Tim slammed both doors shut in an effort to contain the creature. He saw Luke struggling and helped him drag Brenda back to where the others were standing.

It had only taken seconds to evacuate the vehicle, with the exception of Hope and Dr. Drake, who were still trapped inside.

Tim raced to the rear of the battered van and pulled frantically on the handle, but the mechanism didn't work. Father Ricardo also yanked on it again and again, but the doors didn't budge; it didn't take them long to figure out why.

The force from the impact had twisted the frame, knocking the doors out of alignment, rendering the handle and mechanism useless.

Think! What should I do! Tim thought. Hope's pounding on the rear window broke his concentration.

"Help! I can't—breathe! The gas—I'm suffocating!!"

Hope pounded hard on the window, and shouted over the hiss of the ruptured tanks. Propane quickly replaced the remaining oxygen in her small compartment. The fumes overwhelmed her and she awaited death, but her inner voice told her to fight on. Vertigo made her head spin and speckled flecks danced through her field of vision.

Needing air desperately, she pressed her face against the cracked window, fearful of an attack. Sucking on the gap, she breathed in a lung full of air, relieved that it would buy her a little more time.'

A sudden familiar stench blended with the propane. She'd first smelled it while she sat with Kuja outside Moxo's hut, and then again during his funeral procession. The stench assaulted her senses a third time when it rose from the footprint stamped on the white linen, the same cloth formerly draped over the cross. The van now reeked of the same sick odor, the smell of rotting corpses, the smell of death. And the odor kept getting stronger, blending with the gaseous fumes.

Hope looked down at Bill Drake, his breathing became labored. With her face pressed against the window, she drew in another breath. Leaning over Bill, she pinched his nostrils together and breathed into his mouth, filling his lungs the best she could.

As she pulled back from Bill, he released a shrill scream and his body moved from side to side—something was pulling on his legs. The sharp metal dug farther into his chest as his body slid forward. His screams were deafening; jagged metal tore through his flesh, as if pulled through a meat grinder. Bill screamed as his body slipped farther through the serrated gap, and his neck reached the razor sharp metal. Hope grabbed his arms to try and prevent him from being pulled forward any further, but *It* was far too strong. Despite Hope's best efforts, the shards of metal ripped through his neck; his eyes bulged as warm blood spurted from his throat onto her arms and legs; still she hung on, but her attempts to save him proved futile.

A sudden yank threw Hope off balance, causing her to lose her grip. Bill gurgled, and then fell silent. The constant upward pressure against the sharp metal severed Bill's head from his neck. His facial muscles twitched several times before all movements ceased. Blood gushed onto the floor like maroon paint. The detached head slammed into Hope's ankle and rolled to the listed side of the van.

Bill's headless corpse disappeared from the gap, yanked through to the other side. Hope threw up the contents of her stomach; still gagging, she rushed to the window for another whiff of air. She'd just sucked in her third breath when something grabbed her blood slick ankle from under the gap of jagged metal. Hope turned her head and screamed; bony fingers sprouting from a decrepit hand yanked hard on her ankle; a rotting arm pulled her toward the meat grinder. She kicked her foot several times, but still it hung on.

Hope nearly fainted from lack of oxygen and the pungent stench. Gripping the top of her seat, she kicked and screamed for life. With one last kick, she broke free from the cold, dead hand. Screaming for help, she pounded frantically on the rear windows with both fists. Tim and Father Ricardo violently yanked on the door handles, both men red in the face, but the doors didn't budge.

Hope pressed her mouth against the cracked window and stole another breath. The creature crept forward on its stomach, forcing its maggot-infested head through the gap. Its dead, cloudy eyes stared up at Hope as it grabbed at her feet. She kicked at the thing repeatedly to keep it off her.

Shards of metal ripped through its decomposing arms and shoulders, releasing a putrid brown liquid that dripped onto the floor, mixing with Bill's blood, fouling the already pungent air. Despite the new gashes, the creature kept coming, forcing more of its body through the gap.

Hope pounded on the window, bloodying her knuckles, "Get me out, it's almost here!"

Through the window, she watched Tim and the priest searching for something on the ground, as if somebody had lost a ring or a watch! *WHAT THE HELL ARE THEY DOING?!*

Tim bent down and picked up a shot-put-sized rock.

A loud creaking noise filled the chamber; it was the sound of bending metal. Its head and neck were through the opening. Hunching its back, the Thing pressed upward, crunching the metal, lifting the tree—widening the gap.

Hope felt helpless, trapped like a cornered animal. In another moment it would be on her. Kicking at its head, she delivered several sharp blows with her heel, but only succeeded in knocking loose a shit load of maggots; each one bounced off the floor, wavered and disappeared, because they too were creations of the *Iwanci*.

Hope inched backward on her hands, climbing on top of the seat, kicking and screaming all the while. The Thing's torso had forced its way through the gap, creeping forward on its hands and knees, grabbing at her kicking feet; its strong hands latched onto an ankle, holding it for a long second before she again kicked free. The Moxo-faced creature's hand reached for the seat cushion. The second hand followed, pulling itself up from the floor, moving steadily toward her. Sliding back farther, she crawled on top of the duffle bags, pressing her back flat against the steel doors. She could go no farther; pulling her knees to her chest, she breathed in deep, sucking in the propane, coughing and choking; wanting to take her last breath before that thing devoured her. Endorphins shot through her, creating a euphoric state as her body prepared for death. She prayed that the end would come quick. She began to lose consciousness.

Its hands were again upon her, grabbing her foot, her ankle, her calf. A pounding resonated inside her head, followed by the sound of breaking glass. A sudden rush of air enveloped her head and she felt angels pulling her backward across the duffle bags; her hand touched something smooth and metallic. The cold steel felt balanced and heavy in her hand—like a gun.

Twisting and kicking, she broke free again. The fresh air half revived her; she felt hands under her armpits pulling her backward. The creature lunged at her as Tim pulled her through the smashed rear window. Those dead, cloudy eyes stared back at her; the awful smirk creased its lips.

Her legs cleared the window, and Hope, still holding the gun, leveled it at the image of dead Moxo and pulled the trigger. The flare, shot from just a few yards away, slammed into Moxo's face.

The propane-filled van exploded in a huge fireball. The eruption blew Hope and Tim backward more than a dozen feet, igniting their clothes, searing their arms, legs and hair.

Matthew, Ryan, and Luke ran to their aid, throwing handfuls of dirt over their rolling bodies to extinguish the flames. Hope, despite her pain, stared back at the van, now a burning inferno. The creature stood deep within the fire as flames consumed everything around it. The image of Moxo began to waver, transforming into something else. The feathered face of a child appeared in the flames. With piercing eyes, it stared back at Hope, its mouth locked in a silent scream. The image wavered in the fire for a brief moment, and with a whooshing sound it imploded into itself, creating a back draft that shot through the van, igniting the cross. Flames shot up the post, devouring the crossbeam. The raging furnace consumed the fallen tree; the dead wood further fueled the fire.

The fire burned into the night until the cross turned to ash and the smoldering van became nothing more than a blackened shell.

EPILOGUE

Nine days had elapsed since the death of Dr. Drake and the injuries sustained by Hope and Tim in the van explosion. They spent three of those days recovering in the burn unit at the local hospital in Macas. They had both suffered from second degree burns that covered much of their arms and legs. Doctors determined early that skin grafts wouldn't be necessary.

Brenda and Jason received medical treatments at the same hospital. Brenda received an antidepressant in the psych ward, where they placed her under careful observation, but it didn't seem to do much good. Doctors added a dozen stitches to Jason's stump, disinfected the wound, and prescribed a strong antibiotic. He began to perk up after taking the second dose.

While in the hospital, Hope and Jason gave statements to the local authorities about the deaths of Peter and Mary. The police questioned Luke, Matthew, and Ryan separately at the dorms next to the Cathedral.

A joint effort conducted between local authorities and a team of U.S. Army personnel provided little results. Despite searching the rainforest for three consecutive days, they weren't able to find any trace of Peter or Mary. They found nothing, no evidence of head-hunters, no field of shrunken heads and after exploring over a half-dozen caves, they called off the expedition. They simply didn't have the manpower and resources to search through the hundreds of large hills and small mountains nestled in the foothills of the Andes; most of these rock formations concealed a labyrinth of caves. It would take months, maybe even years to explore them all.

The Invisible People, true to their legend, had vanished without a trace, taking all evidence of their existence with them.

On the morning of the ninth day, doctors discharged Hope, Tim, and Jason from the hospital. After reuniting with Luke, Matt and Ryan, they all boarded a puddle jumper back to Quito and then an airbus back to the states.

Brenda, discharged the day before under a doctor's supervision, was booked onto a special medical flight back to Philadelphia. Father Ricardo accompanied her and the nurse to the airport, pushing her wheelchair up to the gate. The priest hugged Brenda and blessed her as they parted, but she remained unresponsive. The nurse wheeled her away, following the flight attendant onto the tarmac and up a special ramp leading into the plane.

Over the next few days Hope, Tim, and Jason continued receiving treatments as out-patients at University Hospital in Philadelphia. Doctors admitted Brenda to the psychiatric ward at the same hospital after she showed no visible signs of recovery.

In between doctor's visits, the Burlington police department badgered Hope constantly, always having *just one more question.*

Hope also started seeing a psychologist, Dr. Bell, a mousy woman in her late forties. During the second session she told Hope to "dwell on the past no longer."

She would tell her story just one more time, as the doctor put it, to "Face it and erase it," in an attempt to purge herself of the tragedy.

Despite her mother's concerns, Hope prepared to tell the story in church at a special funeral service held for the friends and family of Mary, Dr. Drake, and Peter.

⇥✢⇤

Hope sat in the third row with her mother; family members of the deceased sat in the first two rows. Mary's grandparents wept openly as they sat together in the front row. Peter's mother, Sandy Miller, sat beside them, a constant flow of tears running down her cheeks.

Tom Miller, Sandy's now estranged husband, stood near the rear doors along with some other men, his back leaning against the wall. Hope had said hello to him when she first walked through the vestibule. He flashed a sad smile and his voice slurred as he offered his hello. His breath reeked of cheap vodka, but she tried not to judge him, knowing that everyone deals with grief in their own way.

Father Carlson, dressed in his white robe, sat in a plain wooden chair against the left wall at the very front of the church; two altar boys, also dressed in white, sat in chairs beside him.

A large, gold cross stood mounted high on the wall behind the altar. Near the ceiling, a series of stained glass clerestory windows graced the upper walls, depicting Christ in various scenes from the New Testament.

The house of worship was almost full and Father Carlson waited for a couple of stragglers to find their seats, and then gave a nod to the organist. She sat perched on a raised platform to his left, near the front of the church. Striking the first key, she began the prelude, filling the large chamber with rich organ music. The melodic sounds cued the altar boys, who rose from their seats and walked toward two white candles that stood in large cast iron holders on each side of the altar. Each boy ceremoniously lit one candle and returned to his seat.

Without remains, there wouldn't be a formal burial, but in lieu of caskets, three large easels stood evenly spaced on the floor in the area in front of the altar. Each easel held a collage of pictures of the deceased. Mary's collage contained the most photos; many of them were from her Sweet Sixteen party.

With the pews now filled, the priest approached the pulpit and motioned for the congregation to rise. More than four hundred parishioners rose to their feet and when they did so, the organ music stopped.

Father Carlson looked at the family members seated in the front row and cleared his throat. "My name is Father Paul Carlson. We are here today to honor, respect, and pay tribute to the lives of three of our own..."

Hope's thoughts floated back to the rainforest, back to Peter and Mary.

"Bill Drake gave of himself his time and his resources in service to God and this congregation. As Church Council President he served..."

She tried hard to focus on Father Carlson's eulogy, but it became impossible. The image of Dr. Drake's body pulled through jaws of jagged metal flashed through her head.

"I will always remember Mary Drake's smile and her love of life. The contributions she made to our congregation were many. At this very lectern she inspired us with her readings..."

Gazing at the floor, Hope saw Mary lying in that pit impaled on spikes, blood gushing from her stomach, gasping her last breath. She flinched and her mother squeezed her arm. *Why am I seeing this!*

"Peter never hesitated to roll up his sleeves to lend a hand, always more than willing to pitch in with any project, whether it be the carwash, directing the Christmas Play, or helping in the soup kitchen. He selflessly gave of himself in his ministry to others."

Jolting images of the blade slicing through Peter's neck replaced Father Carlson on the altar. She began to tremble.

Anna Rose steadied her, "Are you okay? What's the matter?"

"I'm fine, Mom." *Stay in control. Not now, take deep breaths.*

"Hope Holloway has offered to share her thoughts and prayers with us here today." Father Carlson extended his hand, "Hope, will you please come up to the pulpit?"

Tears swelled in Anna Rose's eyes, "Don't go up there if you're not feeling up to it."

"I said I'm fine." *God let me get through this.*

Her mother handed her a handkerchief. She palmed the white hanky and rose from her seat. Walking slowly, she bit her bottom lip and made her way to the lectern. The congregation fell silent as she stared into their solemn faces.

Luke sat with his family in the third pew. In the fourth row Matthew and Ryan looked uncomfortable in their suits and neckties. Jason sat in the fifth pew next to his parents; the right sleeve of his suit lay flat and empty, his stump still too raw to be fitted with a prosthetic.

Tim Kirby paid his respects from the rear of the church, fending off icy glares from several members of the congregation. He stood against the back wall next to Tom Miller.

Brenda wasn't in attendance, as many more months of diagnosis and treatment still lay ahead of her at University Hospital.

After taking another deep breath, Hope began to tell her story to the congregation. Her voice cracked several times as she spoke over the collage of photos, her saddened words filling the church.

"...Peter and Mary were brave and they never gave up their will to fight. Peter's valor and quick action saved us all, and Mary, in her time of dying, only thought of the wellbeing of others. No, they did not die in vain; they saved five of *us* who wouldn't be here today had they not bestowed upon us their gift of life."

Hope now wept openly and said, "Excuse me, I need a minute." Sniffling, she took a step back from the pulpit and unwrinkled the cloth she held in her hand. After dabbing her eyes several times, she blew her nose and took another deep breath. After another sniffle, she returned to the lectern and continued.

"One day we will become mothers and fathers. Many years from now our children will give us grandchildren and none of these lives would've ever existed, had it not been for Peter and Mary. It's true that Peter will never become a father and Mary will never know the joy of motherhood—but I'm proud to call Peter my boyfriend and Mary my best friend.

"I love them both and they are always in my thoughts and prayers. I keep Peter's knife in my pocket and wear Mary's locket as a symbol of her love."

She held the locket away from her chest for all to see before allowing it to come to rest against her bosom.

"Today we mourn their deaths, but as long as I live, Peter and Mary will always be in my heart. May they both forever rest in peace."

Hope gripped the podium with both hands and fell silent.

Mary's grandmother buried her face in her hands and her grandfather used a tissue to wipe tears from his eyes. Hope prayed that her words had brought them a sense of peace and comfort. Sandy Miller's swollen eyes gleamed with pride; she raised her head, seemingly proud that Peter had been her son, proud of his bravery.

Hope looked into the sea of faces. In row after row people wept, men and women, young and old, it didn't matter. They all came together as one, sharing a great sorrow.

One by one she came upon the faces of Matthew, Ryan, Jason, and Luke, and they too were crying. She wondered what lay ahead for all of them. A new sadness overwhelmed her. The waning moments of the service marked the end of their time together. Individually, they'd try to glue back together their shattered lives, but she knew this would be the last time they'd ever meet as a group.

Father Carlson swung the censer of burning incense back and forth as he walked up and down the aisles before circling the photo collages. The constant pendulum-like motion and the wisps of smoke dissipating into the stale church air mesmerized her. With a final swing of the censer, Hope's mind drifted away...

━━◦◦━━

A cloud of red smoke rose from the fire as Kalku threw a handful of powder into the hearth carved in stone next to the great statue of Chon-Chon.

With his eyes closed and his head bowed, Kalku placed his palms on the blue quartz sculpture. Praying to the great feathered deity, he fell into an altered state. Inhaling deeply, he took long, steady breaths. Remaining motionless, he allowed himself to fall into a deeper level of meditation, purging his mind of all thoughts. A slight vibration emanated from within the quartz. His fingertips acted as receptors to the faint pulsation. His mind began to decipher a message as only he, the great shaman Kalku, could. And the message was clear, clearer than the etchings scrolled across the white ones' stomachs.

The white devils have escaped into the outside world and were now beyond Chon-Chon's reach. Only he possessed the mystical knowledge needed to avenge the feathered one, and avenge her he would. Removing his hands from the quartz, he came out of his altered state. His eyes flickered and then opened, gleaming with wicked anticipation.

The shaman began to chant, telling the story of the five white ones who escaped with their souls. Five figurines rested on a stone slab before the fire. Four of the figurines resembled males. The fifth appeared to be female, all identical to the ones used in the previous ceremony.

Somewhere below, a lone tribesman beat an animal skin drum and as he did so, the shaman began the dance of the Seven Year Curse. Clutching the leafy female doll, he swayed his body back and forth in time to the rhythmic beat. Extending his arms, he moved the figure up and down, snaking it from side to side.

The drumbeat stopped and Kalku approached the altar. Chanting words of death, he snatched a handful of fine red grains and sprinkled them over the figurine. He placed the female figure down next to the fire and repeated the process with the four male dolls.

One by one, he tossed the male figurines into the fire. After each toss, a red plume of smoke rose from the blaze. Only the female doll remained. Shaking the leafy figure, he demanded the return of her soul. Tossing the last doll into the fire, he watched it burn, incinerating into a final plume of red smoke, sealing the fate of the five white ones.

The curse has been cast; the seeds of death now sown, gestating within each of his white victims like an embryo in the womb. He'd accept nothing less than their total destruction. Seven rainy seasons would pass before Kalku exacted his revenge, reaping his deadly harvest.

ABOUT THE AUTHOR

As a kid, Rick always had a passion for books. He remembers taking on Jules Verne's *Twenty Thousand Leagues Under the Sea* as a fourth grader, consuming all 360 pages of the sci-fi classic. The book transported him deep under the sea, riding side-by-side with Captain Nemo in his fantastic submarine. That fervor for fiction ignited a fire within him that remains today.

A natural storyteller, Rick would frequently entertain his friends and classmates with short tales of adventure. After high school he entered Rider University on a basketball scholarship and enrolled in his first writing class. These classes provided the foundation that he would build on later in life.

After graduation, he put his writing on hold for a number of years. Financial advising became his occupation of choice. Today he runs a successful wealth management business, but he never gave up his passion for storytelling.

With his wife Janet settled into her own career, (managing editor of a trade magazine,) and his son Rich and daughter Jessica beyond the threshold of adulthood, he once again returned to writing. Soon thereafter, Rick had his first story published in *Boston Literary Magazine.* The following year, he had another short story published in the literary journal *The Foliate Oak.*

The editorial staff of *The Foliate Oak* also selected his story for their, *Best of Foliate Oak Anthology.*

The author lives in central New Jersey with his very understanding wife Janet who supports him in all of his endeavors; and his daughter Jessica. His son Rich has left the nest and now lives and works in Philadelphia.

If you'd like to share your thoughts about *Blood Dance*, please contact Rick at rickpoveromo@gmail.com, he'd love to hear from you. He hopes that you've enjoyed reading his debut novel *Blood Dance* as much as he's enjoyed writing it. He is currently working on the sequel.

www.ingramcontent.com/pod-product-compliance
Lightning Source LLC
Chambersburg PA
CBHW062012170626
46813CB00001B/120

9 780099 164100